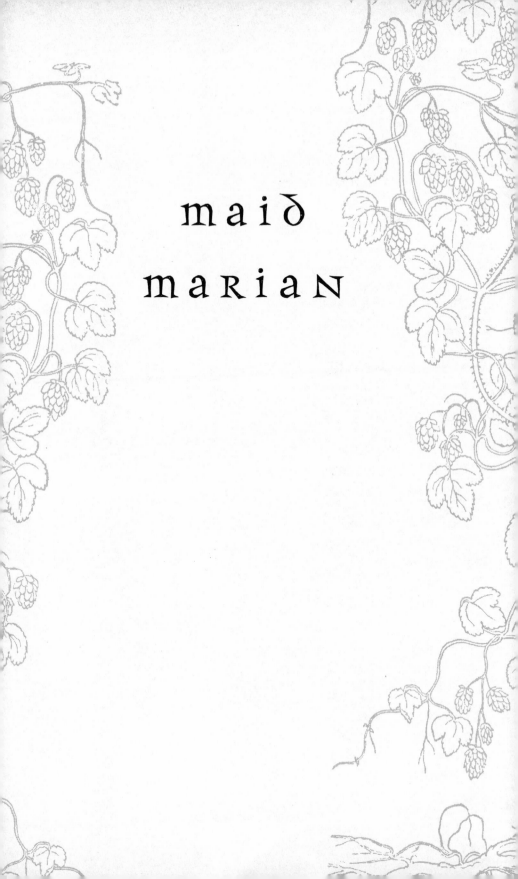

maid
MARiaN

maid MARIAN

a novel

ELSA WATSON

CROWN PUBLISHERS

NEW YORK

Copyright © 2004 by Elsa Watson

Published by Crown Publishers, New York, New York.
Member of the Crown Publishing Group, a division of Random House Inc.
www.crownpublishing.com

CROWN is a trademark and the Crown colophon is a registered trademark of Random House, Inc.

Printed in the United States of America

Design by Lauren Dong

Library of Congress Cataloging-in-Publication Data
Watson, Elsa.
    Maid Marian / Elsa Watson.—1st ed.
    1. Maid Marian (Legendary character)—Fiction. 2. Great Britain—History—
Richard I, 1189–1199—Fiction. 3. Robin Hood (Legendary character)—Fiction.
4. Sherwood Forest (England)—Fiction. 5. Women outlaws—Fiction.
6. Outlaws—Fiction. I. Title.
    PS3623.A8697M35 2004
    813'.6—dc22   2003014671

ISBN 1-4000-5041-3

10 9 8 7 6 5 4 3 2 1

First Edition

For Kol, my polestar:

*"Our chief want in life is someone
who will make us do what we can."*

—RALPH WALDO EMERSON

part one

"A bonny fine maid of noble degree"

Chapter One

I DREAMT THAT NIGHT of Atalanta, the fleet-footed maiden of my schoolroom lessons, who raced every man who dared to challenge her. Atalanta, dark hair flying, flashed through my dreams like a blackbird in flight. She danced everywhere, in the wind, in the sun, across a field of ripening wheat, but when a hand gripped my shoulder she danced away, a spark disappearing into blackness.

The hand belonged to the queen of England, who herself contained all the power a king's widow deserved. When I opened my eyes, I saw her there, heard her raspy breathing in the windless night, saw the age spots on her hands. She sat by my side, stroked my hair, and spoke without preamble.

"Your husband is dead, Lady Marian."

"Dead?" I stared at her a moment, stunned more by the words and the notion than by the loss of a husband I neither loved nor trusted.

"Dead? How? How has he died?"

"A long sickness brought on by riding a tournament too early in the season. He had the best physicians, even the king's own man, but bloodletting, no matter how well done, cannot save one who is already far gone. These things happen, you know, tragic though it may be. I would not trouble yourself, my dear child, if I were you."

I believe I gasped, for to find my prospects so instantly altered stole away all of my breath. The queen had bid me not to trouble myself, but the more I considered, the more discomfited I became. In the strange ways of the mind, my thoughts became twisted, raveled together, so that Atalanta seemed almost to have brought death to Hugh's young heart. I thought of his face, of his blood pooling in the catch basin, and a deep shudder skidded down my spine.

The queen saw me start, saw me fall befuddled, and took the chance to gather her skirts and slip through the door before I found my tongue. I caught a look from her as she exited, a penetrating glance such as one uses when peering through smoke. 'Twas the look of the wary, of one who guards a secret—I had not expected it to fall from the face of my queen.

There I remained, all perplexed and alone. Annie, my tender nurse of childhood, was away on an errand of her own—I had no one to comfort me, no one to help me discern my way. For what course was I to take from here? What future lay spread for me now that Hugh was no more? Too, I was struck by the irregular honor of finding the queen in my own chamber. Surely this was no coveted task, to tell a young bride of her bridegroom's death. What, then, made her come to me herself?

This question kept me from my sleep near half the night. When I dozed at last, the queen's cold eyes played in my dreams, mingling together with glimpses I'd caught of her years before, when I was a child—dressed in her crimson cape or bending from her carriage window. I knew her little, and she knew even less of me. What could have prompted her attention? The strangeness of it caught in my throat, like bread swallowed down with no wine to follow.

The next morning, when I ventured forth, I asked after Hugh

wherever I could. At first the reports of his death seemed mild, but news traveled slowly from across the channel, and I had to let the rumors mellow before the wilder tales surfaced. Then I heard riddles enough to confound Aristotle. The knights told me that Hugh had been stricken by God for having got drunk on the feast of the Assumption last August. The monks said he'd been thrown from his horse and trampled to death beneath its hooves. And his own page thought he had choked on a bowl of eels, prepared for him specially by the king's cooks.

These confused, dissimilar reports frightened me and made me wonder what veil of secrecy had been pulled around Hugh's death. My fear reminded me of a resolve I made four years before, at age thirteen, to never trust any living person in this world. It seemed my young husband might have survived his life better had he learned this lesson as well as I.

MY EARLIEST MEMORY is of Nurse feeding me gruel with a horn spoon and me thrusting the spoon aside, just to see what would happen. My wedding was sometime later, when I passed my fifth birthday. I recall very little beyond the stiffness of the clothes I was made to wear and the weight of some jewels tugging at my headdress. I was taken by Nurse to kneel in the chapel, to smell the incense which even today can make me feel reverent. I saw Hugh beside me, looking miserable in his velvet tunic, his blond curls falling like tufts of wool against his brow. We had been raised as obedient children, so we knelt in our places and repeated the words we were told to say until finally it all finished, and we could run and skip again.

I recall Nurse telling me afterward that Hugh and I were married. She showed me a ring in a leather box, which she said was a symbol of it. I thought perhaps marriage meant that Hugh and I were brother and sister, for I knew other children who had siblings and longed to be like them. Nurse said yes, it was something like that. And from that day forward, I noticed that when I pushed my spoon rudely away, she stowed her reprimand and merely offered the spoon once more with a coaxing smile.

My childhood, as any childhood should be, was made up of small habits and smaller routines. Recitations to the tutor were followed by meals, followed by naps, followed by playtime. But like any child—or any adult looking back upon childhood—it is the odd changes that break out in memory, glowing among the dim grays of youth.

Christmas and Easter burn bright in hindsight. If King Henry and his lady, Queen Eleanor, were in England, they were sure to call every noble person to Westminster Castle for a grand court, so all might recollect the king's majesty and vigor. We lived far to the north of London, and while travel during the winter months is always bitter, our long journeys through snow and mud seemed scarcely survivable.

The empty scent of winter still brings those journeys to mind—the soreness of being jostled all day on an ill-fitting saddle, the outer wraps that froze stiff from the damp mist of breath. Worst of all were the hours spent waiting while the men pried vainly at a wagon wheel, stuck fast in the mud. I liked to watch the men at their work, to learn what I could about horses and wagons and while away the next hour imagining how I might loosen a stuck wheel, were I master of the cart.

Days would pass, the air would grow warmer, and we would arrive at London town and then Westminster, both of which have grown similarly crowded and muddy in memory. There, in a wink, the relentless cold was changed over for heat and noise and the merriment of Christmastime. The great stone walls were always stuffed thick with men and ladies decked in velvet, trimmed with fur, hung all about with their best brooches, mirrors, and tassels. Fires leapt up the chimney towers with flames higher than my

Nꓱ Ꭵ Ꭰ Ꮇ Ꭺ Ꭱ Ꭵ Ꭺ Ꮑ • 7

head, and dogs, excited by excitement itself, ran barking through the halls. Within the castle all was good food, spiced wine, treats made of sugar, colored yellow with saffron. Everyone was loud and joyous, and my eyes couldn't move quickly enough to take it all in.

At these great courts I was generally called to pay my respects to Hugh's mother, Lady Pernelle of Sencaster. This lady, I've heard, once was lovely, but years of worry had tightened her face until she resembled a walnut shell, hard and fixed in its dents and wrinkles. She was effusive in her love for Hugh and, as my mother-in-law, regularly stared at me with what I called her gaze of "measuring up." It was plain that I would never approach whatever height I ought to reach and this left me feeling compressed in her presence. As a result I avoided her, taking up instead with Hugh, or climbing onto Nurse's knee instead of Lady Pernelle's. I suppose I alienated her by behaving thus, but children will act on instinct and rarely consider consequences.

Hugh moved in and out of my early life with the evenness of the tide. I was never surprised to see him; he was never surprised to see me. We simply picked up our play wherever we had left off the time before. In wintertime we threw balls of snow and slipped about on frozen lakes, and in summer we pranced on hobby horses or wove ourselves daisy chains. We were great friends. Once, at a meeting of some important people at Leicester town, we ran off and hid in the dovecote, pretending to be wild pigeons. I believe we had just perfected the art of cooing deep in our throats when it became dark and we, being young, fell asleep. Nurse found us there, well past midnight, surrounded by birds sleeping on their perches, with feathers matted in our hair.

I remember that night vividly, for when Nurse carried me away from the dovecote to my own place in our bed, the night air was freezing cold. I remember wanting to bury my face in her warm neck, but just then I looked up and saw the sky filled with more stars than I'd ever seen before. My thoughts of the cold vanished, and I gasped in silence at that great vision, so like a sheet of watery diamonds, glinting on rolling waves of the sky.

THE ONE GREAT MYSTERY of my young life revolved around the existence of my parents. Through play and chatter with other young nobles I learned that it was customary for children to live in the same home with their parents, which I did not. Nurse and I lived in one chamber of Warwick Castle, a place filled with several great people of importance, but none, I knew, was a parent of mine. The more I questioned, the more I found my position to be irregular. Even Hugh, it was revealed, lived with his mother in their own lands during the times when I didn't see him. Perhaps Nurse was my parent, I proposed to my playmates. Oh no, they laughed, thinking this quite droll. For they all had nurses and knew the difference between a caregiver and a mother.

This perplexed me, and when I put the question to Nurse, I could see that it perplexed her also. She seemed not to know what to say regarding my parentage and simply clasped me tightly to her. I interpreted this to mean that I had somehow been born without parents, and she was too ashamed to tell me.

But not long after, Nurse brought a strange man to our chamber. He was very tall with bright scarlet hose and a red face to match, causing me instantly to christen him Apple Man after the sweetest of autumn fruits. Apple Man also had a very round stomach, which, when I noticed it, made me bite my hand to keep from giggling, for then he appeared more appley than before.

"She's askin' about her family folks," Nurse said, gesturing to me but speaking to Apple Man.

"Is she now," he said in a smooth way that reminded me of cream with honey. "And what is it you wish to know, Lady Marian?"

He crouched down so we could see each other better, though it was difficult for him on account of the stomach. I appreciated the effort and did my best not to laugh again.

"Have I got any parents?" I asked promptly.

Apple Man looked as confounded as Nurse had and stammered out a few noises that I didn't recognize as words. Then he flushed even redder and said, "Yes, my dear, of course you have parents."

"Oh!" This was reassuring news. "Where are they? May I see them?"

"Um, no." His face was nearing purple. "They live rather far away, in Denby-upon-Trent. Do you know where that is?"

"No," I replied. "My tutor says he hasn't good enough maps to teach me geography."

"Ah. Well," Apple Man said with an odd glance at Nurse, "we shall have to remedy that. Lady Marian, your parents cannot see you because they are not very well. Can you understand that?"

Of course I could. As Nurse had explained to me several times, every person had to keep watch of themselves in wintertime—not sit upon stones or let their feet grow damp—or they might become too ill to see visitors. It had happened to me once and kept me from going out into the best snowfall of the year.

"Yes. Will they get better?"

"I . . . I don't know."

So this was how my parentage was explained. I had parents, apparently, but they could neither be seen nor found, since I had no knowledge of the place in which they lived. I asked Nurse afterward if she knew where this Denby was, and she said she had been there once, to bring me away to this castle. Had she seen my parents there? I wanted to know. Nay, she told me, she had not. It had been Apple Man who'd hired her, who'd given me to her and left her instructions to make our residence in Warwick.

She knew Denby to be my native land, she said, land that would probably belong to me one day if no brothers and sisters stepped forward. This brought my questions out thick and fast, for I was desperate for a brother or sister, but the laws of inheritance and lineage were too much for Nurse, and she begged me not to ask anything more. Nurse was in her element discussing games, animals of all kinds, or the relative merits of barley beer to milk with fruit. She had reached the limit of her understanding, and I could not learn what she did not know.

But my confusion remained—truly it intensified—for now I knew that I had parents and therefore had something to fixate upon. I conjured up visions of them, phantom-like, to see how I liked them, but they often resembled some person I knew and that left me more dissatisfied. Many of the girls of my acquaintance spent particular time with their mothers, so I too kept my eyes alert for the woman who might turn out to be mine. And, true to my tendency to think myself unduly important, I chose for my matriarch the woman of greatest prominence in the land, Queen Eleanor.

I saw Queen Eleanor rarely, for, though I did not know it at the time, she had been locked away in Salisbury Tower by her husband, King Henry. Eleanor, it seemed, had once roused their sons to band together against the king, and for this he had her sealed away. As I say, I knew very little of this, for I saw them together at every court Henry held on English shores. He let her out for public events, knowing how the people like to view their queen, then caged her up again to await the next holy day.

To my young mind it seemed quite different, for when I went to Westminster the queen was nearly always there, and when I left her at the end I assumed she stayed on, perhaps continuing the merriment and feasting until I was called back again. She seemed to be a lady like any other, although she was raised quite far above that position by the adoration of Nurse, who thought her the greatest lady she had ever seen. Long before I first saw the queen, I knew of her, knew that she loved songs and poems and was also ruler of Aquitane, a vast stretch of land in France.

I thought she was perfection itself and, as such, was worthy of

being my absent mother. So during one court in Westminster, I
waited in the host of other ladies as she moved through us, nodding and greeting. When she reached me I put out my hand and
cried, in the soft voice a kitten uses, "Mother."

She stopped abruptly and looked at me, reaching her fingers
under my chin to tip my face into the light. I remember little other
than two blue eyes, bright as enamel and cool as the sea.

"Who is this girl?" No one answered. "Are you Marian Fitzwater
of Denby?"

I nodded. Her voice was stern and unforgiving, the way I
thought a dragon might speak.

"And Lady Marian, did you just address me as mother?"

I began to feel the earth falling away beneath me, and I believe
a tear quivered in my eye.

"Yes."

"Dear child, I have children, by the dozens, it seems, but I am
quite certain you are not among them. Do you not know that your
mother is buried at Lincoln?"

Buried. I knew that word, and I knew it to mean that my mother
was dead. I heard a rushing sound in my ears, but I turned, half
blind, to face this woman who had given me my first answers.

"My father?"

"I do not know where he is buried, but wherever it is he has been
there these many years. For goodness sake, don't cry, child. It's not
as if you ever knew them, is it?"

She strode on and left me there, a numb mass of flesh and
bones. Here was the truth I had so longed for. I had no parents,
would never see them, could never live in the same home with
them. The glowing phantoms I'd so carefully built by piling my
hopes and dreams together disappeared in a breath of wind, turned
to dust, and vanished completely.

It was then that I learned to mistrust my elders, to look for the
meaning behind their words, to feel suspect of their smiles and

caresses. For if one man might lie to me, as Apple Man so soundly had, why shouldn't the others? If he could placate me with falsehoods, how could I trust the words of his fellows?

And so, though I was little aware of it at the time, the first chills of disillusionment stole across my heart that day, leaving a child mixed with one part shrewdness and three parts youthful ignorance.

Chapter Two

W HEN I WAS A CHILD, all the world seemed at my fingertips. The sky was vast, and I felt myself equally vast
beneath it, taking into my heart every tree, stone, and
stream within my eyesight. But as I grew my vision dimmed, and
with it the expanse of the world closed in upon me. The sky fell
lower, the trees stood taller, and rivers carried their flood away to
greater seas I would never know.

But even as the natural world closed in, the world that humans
had constructed, of politics and nobility, stretched before me as an
ever expanding field upon which I might learn to play. In my thir-
teenth year I began to see the myriad loops and twists that attach
people to one another, and I was fascinated by them. My tutor
could not tell me enough of kings and court and battles for land
and fealty. This was my world, the world of my fathers, and I was
just beginning to awaken to it.

That year I was called to a Christmas court in London town,
and I was delighted to see that Hugh had come there also. I had
not seen him for several years, since he had been living across the
channel in Anjou, the king's native land, learning the arts of war
and conquest. He had grown a great deal in this time, and the boy

who had been just my height before soared above me by a head. Now his curls were blond no longer, but the very shade of chestnut bark, precisely arranged by a careful hand.

He stood surrounded by a gang of young men and seemed absorbed in their jokes and jostling, so I took my place with the young ladies and did my best to enjoy their company. I had several longtime friends among them, girls who had told me things about life and love that Nurse seemed not to know. Red-haired Lady Cicely was my favorite, but I noticed that the other girls shunned her somewhat, so I also avoided her. I was a shy child in groups and gaggles and had no stomach to forge a friendship that might cause me to stand alone and be looked at. Much better to blend in quietly to the heart of the group and be an audience for the bolder ones.

Lady Clarice was a great talker and told us many stories of her sisters' romances, for she was the youngest of five girls and knew more than we of courtship and marriage contracts. Lady Betony resided in London town and as such was self-appointed mistress of style. She pointed out the most fashionable of the grown-up ladies and explained the importance of the handkerchief and powder box. She liked to praise the brightest and fairest, but she also had a sour tongue and was ruthless to those dressed in the handed-down elegance of their mother's gowns.

This kind of talk entertained us well until the sun broke one afternoon, and we dropped all talk for a romp in the snow fields. We stood on the edge of adulthood then, but we were still attracted to the pleasures of youth and were quick to forgo our attempts at sobriety. We slipped and skated and patted the snow and soon were joined by a group of boys.

These boys played rough, and in one frenzied moment a handful of snow went down my neck. I turned to see who my attacker was but only caught sight of fleeing dark hose and a green tunic. Filling my mittens with a great wad of snow, I dashed after him as fast as I could, chasing his tunic around bends and hills. I was faster than most of the girls, but I had a hard race to catch this rascal, for he seemed intent on getting away.

Finally he dropped over a snow-topped hill, and I dropped too, catching him clean on the neck with my snowball as I fell. I laughed aloud at my revenge, but when he stood I ceased all laughter. My attacker was Hugh, and when he rose, breathing hard, his face contorted to a shade and look I had never seen on a person before. His features seemed twisted with some great emotion, dark and hideous, almost as if he might cry, though I did not think he would.

In another second he bent over me and slapped my face with the back of his hand.

"Hugh!" I cried, clasping the stung cheek. "Why . . . ?"

"You should know better, wife." He said the last word with vicious scorn and kicked a pile of snow on my skirt. "You are to obey me, don't you know that? I am your husband, and I can do with you what I please."

With that he dragged me to my feet and pulled me, slipping and sliding, around a second bend to where a group of tall boys were building a wall out of snow.

"Look what I found," he cried, casting me down at their feet. I bit my lip and felt the rusty taste of blood.

"A girl! What do you want with her, Hugh?"

"Who is she, Hugh?"

"She's my wife," he said, proudly this time. "She's got to obey me. Isn't that right, Marian?" He kicked me hard, and I muffled a cry. "See? She's been disobedient this afternoon, and I propose we show her what happens to girls who spite their masters. What do you say to that, lads?"

They all cheered at this, and I began to cry. I had no idea what boys of this age might want to do with me, but I was quite certain I would not like it. More than anything I wished for one of my comrades to come, to save me, but they would never venture this far from the castle. I thought perhaps my life was ending.

Hugh yanked me up by my hair and ordered me to hoist my skirts so his scruffy friends might see a lady's legs for themselves. I wore thick hose and so was not afraid for the cold, but the very fact that they wanted to see made me frightened to show. Had we been but four years younger I might have taken off all my clothes, but suddenly this smaller act had a depth of meaning I did not care for. Perhaps it was the sneer on Hugh's face or the way the boys looked at me, so silent and so desperate.

My hands shook as I reached for my skirt, for I saw I had little choice, but at that moment I was saved. Two of the castle servants came near us, dragging a toboggan loaded with wood, and their voices disrupted the group of boys. They fled, falling over one another in their rush to escape, leaving me alone, wet and senseless. I wiped off my tears and went after the servants to travel with them and perhaps get a ride on the back of their sled.

AFTER THIS I TOOK PAINS to keep a distance between Hugh and me. Nurse spied the bruises on my face and arms and questioned me, but when I explained they had come from Hugh, she could only hold me and shake her head. This, it seemed, was the way things could be between husband and wife, and I learned at that moment that it was a vast deal different from the gentle bonds of brother and sister.

Nurse did her best to comfort me, suggesting that he might grow to be more even-tempered. Perhaps, she thought, by the time we went to live together, he might know more of life and ladies and would have learned some respect for me. But I saw a dark look in her eye and knew that she did not believe it would happen.

That Christmas court was very strange, for after this incident I stayed in my room a day or two until the bruising on my face had gone. And when I stirred without again I found that every lady my age was brimming with news of Queen Eleanor. The queen, it seemed, wished to interview each young lady who was not yet wed, for it was her responsibility to make marriage recommendations to the king.

As Lady Clarice explained it to me, if a landed vassal of the king bore no sons, the king could take his eldest daughter to give in marriage to whomever he chose. As she spoke I understood at last how it was that I lived where I did. My parents had died, as I now knew, and I was left as their only child. Since my father's lands by rights came to me, the king had the power to use me and my lands to make alliances with others of his nobles. This was how I came to wed Hugh and so young. The king desired to make Hugh's parents pleased with him, so he gave them me and all of my lands to be part of their family from that day forward.

The queen flourished in these sorts of decisions, and it was for that reason she chose to come among the young ladies to see which of us added beauty or wit to the value of our hills and furlongs. I felt certain she would not visit me and so did not worry myself, for ever since our last encounter I was quite in dread of Queen Eleanor. But I was already wed to Hugh, I told myself, so did not warrant her attention.

NURSE AND I WERE SITTING alone the next afternoon when the door flew open to admit the queen. We both were flustered, but Nurse caught the whip end of the queen's eye, for she scurried about in a noisy way that bothered Lady Eleanor. At last Nurse left, waving at me bravely as she went, then closed the door behind her.

"Well, Lady Marian. I trust you know me by now as the queen, not as your mother?"

I blushed deeply and clenched my fists, wishing with my whole being that she had not chosen to mention that.

"Yes, my lady." I glanced at her face, saw the disdain in her brilliant blue eyes, and felt my heart curdle between my ribs. But then I looked to her pale brows, to the place on her temples where gray met gold, and thought I saw the shadow of long-faded beauty which gave me heart.

"Very well then. And do you know why I am come to see you today?"

"No, my lady."

"I am conducting discussions with every young lady, surely you have heard that?"

Her tone of condescension was so great that I struggled to defend myself.

"Yes, my lady, but I understood that you were speaking only with marriageable young ladies. I am already married and so did not expect to . . . have the honor of speaking with you."

She smiled here for the first time. "Well spoken, child. To tell the truth, I came to see what you've become. It is always worthwhile for me to know my ladies a little better."

I thought of her years in Salisbury, closed off from the rest of the world, and wondered how I could rightly be called "her" lady. But I said nothing.

She carried on as she had before and began to quiz me about my studies, to ask what I read and if I enjoyed it, to see what I knew of the world. As she questioned me I began for the first time to see gaps in my education and was ashamed to feel as backward as I did. She had just asked me how I got on with the nobles in my home castle, and I was replying that I did not go among them much, when Nurse bobbed in, searching for her best stitching needle.

"My apologies, my lady," she gasped, falling over herself in a curtsy, "but I've misplaced me needle." As she spoke she seemed to realize the error she'd made in entering and looked at me with desperation. I leapt to my feet and snatched my own needle from out of my stitchery, pressing it gently into her hand. She bobbed again

and rushed for the door, somehow managing to create more noise
from five steps than a herd of twice as many sheep.

The queen made an exasperated noise and turned back to me.

"Has she been with you long?"

"All my life, my queen."

"Well." She peered at me a moment. "You are quite fair, Lady
Marian. I suppose you know that?"

I did not, but was unsure what response to give. I wished to be
truthful, but I had already had to admit such a lack of knowledge
that I was beginning to feel deplorably ignorant. I believe I opened
my mouth but never managed to make a sound.

"Now, child, there is no shame in a woman admitting her own
beauty. When you have been told of it more often, you will not feel
so shy. Does Hugh of Sencaster not compliment you?"

This I could answer. "No, he does not."

"Well, that is something he may learn in time. Come, Lady
Marian," she said, creaking slowly to her feet. "There is an issue
that must be rectified this moment. That Saxon nurse of yours is
clearly no more than a common cottager. You deserve a companion
with greater éclat."

I rose and followed her, noticing as we went that she had aged
greatly since the day I called her mother. I knew her to be more
than ten years older than King Henry, and as we walked I deduced
that she had lived sixty years and some beyond. I was amazed. She
still commanded such power, was so sure of her own mind. I did
not like her much, that was true, but I admired her greatly.

She led me to Lady Cicely's room, she of the flame-colored hair,
and we entered without knocking. Nurse was there, as I thought
she might be, stitching and chatting with Lady Cicely and her
nurse. Nurse's stitchery fell to the floor as she rose to curtsy, but
the other two ladies had the presence of mind to set theirs aside
before rising, and I felt the weight of Nurse's blunders land
squarely upon my own shoulders.

"Lady Cicely," the queen declared, her eyes like blue larkspur, "you shall hereby change nurses with Lady Marian. You"—she nodded to Nurse—"shall attend Lady Cicely from this day forward. And you"—she spoke more softly in the direction of Cicely's nurse—"shall attend Lady Marian. I trust this arrangement will be suitable to you all."

As abruptly as she had come, she now turned and left the room, not pausing to close the door behind her. Aghast, I ran after her, for the shock of change had made me bold.

"My queen," I gasped, "please! What can it matter who is my nurse?"

She spun about with a look of frustration, as she was not accustomed to having her orders questioned. "She is nothing more than a coarse Saxon, Lady Marian. Cicely's nurse was born in Normandy and has once attended her lady in Paris. She has everything of refinement, breeding, and manners which your common nurse lacks. I have done this on your behalf, Lady Marian, that you might be better bred in these next five years than you have been in the last. I expect your gratitude."

Without waiting for me to express it, she walked on, her robe billowing out behind her like the sail of a retreating ship, one that bore away all sense of security.

STUNNED, I WANDERED to my own room. The loss of the one person who had always loved me was a sorrow I had never considered. The worth of Nurse, which an hour ago had been next to nothing, suddenly pressed upon me so heavily that tears ran from my eyes. I had no mother, I had no father. I had most recently lost Hugh's friendship and had begun to doubt the other ladies of the court. But Nurse I had never doubted. Nurse, always cheerful, always warm, I never wondered at until this moment.

To hear her called a Saxon meant little to me, for at that time I knew nothing of this distinction which reft England in two. But *common, cottager, lacking in refinement*—these were words I understood. And as they echoed through my mind, I saw Nurse as I had never seen her before. Where in my youth I had never looked behind her care and her warm ways, I now saw the farm girl with her awkward movements, I heard the errors in her poor French, I recalled the inconsistencies in her judgment. Nurse, I saw, was everything the queen described her, and yet I found I loved her still.

All that night and half the next I paced my room, scarcely heedful of Cicely's nurse who now took residence within my chamber. She was a dark and sallow thing, and I hated her perfect French near as much as I despised her dainty embroidery. I wept alone and longed for the comfort she could not give, the comfort I could only find in my own nurse.

But my nurse was gone, not only in fact but also in memory. Queen Eleanor's words had done their work; the nurse of my youth—perfect, brave, exquisitely idealized—no longer existed. A dark, lonely curtain of comprehension had lowered before my eyes, one that would never rise again. It was a painful awakening and it left me with an aching heart. I struggled and bore it as I could.

Young as I was, that night I faced a grim reality, but I was determined to learn from my lessons and make myself more powerful from them. And so I declared that I would never again trust another living person beyond myself. For who could I know, truly, but me? Who could I trust not to change, as Nurse seemed to have changed before my very eyes, or to be kind, as Hugh had shown he could not be? How could I trust a queen who did not care whom she injured? Or Apple Man with his pockmarked lies? No, I could rely on no one. And so I took the weight of my future on my own slim shoulders, and I rose in the morning ready to carry it.

MY FIRST ACT was to rouse Lady Cicely's nurse from her slumber and drive her down the hall before me to Cicely's tapestry-hung chamber. As we entered, my own nurse cried out and ran to me, folding me in her strong arms as though she might be able to keep me by force. I embraced her, feeling my heart crack open anew, jostled by the comfort of being held like a child. But I stuck firm to my new resolve, for I saw that from this day forward, Nurse and I would change positions, and where I had been the child before, she would now place her trust in me. She might hold and comfort me, but in our future dealings with the world I must be the thoughtful one, the one who speaks, the one who governs.

"Lady Cicely," I said, breaking free of Nurse at last, "I beg you, do not be nervous but listen to me a moment. You and I, it seems, are in the same bind. Neither of us can like what the queen has done with our serving women."

"No, indeed," she agreed, twisting a strand of orange hair about her finger. "My mother went to such great trouble to find Nurse Matilde for me, you've no idea! She will be so upset to hear I've lost her. And your lands are far to the north, are they not? Surely, we shall never see one another again. Oh, Mama, how you shall scold me!" Here her round face crumpled from the weight of her fear, for she stood in great awe of her noble mother. This, then, would be my angle of approach.

"I propose, Lady Cicely, that we change back." I paused a breath to let my words dance round her ears and then continued. "My nurse belongs to the land of Denby, to me, and to my regent. She is not the queen's to do with as she pleases. In the same vein, your nurse was contracted by your mother and so, by rights, must go where your mother has sent her—that is to say, she must go with you. The queen has no province over these women. True, she has authority over you and me, as vassals of the king, but we are not permitted to do what we wish with our servants. We are hardly of an age to question agreements made by our seniors and betters. It is not right that we should even consider the act."

I began to see that the more I spoke, the more she warmed to my words, for she was terrified to face her mother with a Saxon nurse in place of a French one.

"I'm certain the king would comprehend this if he knew. And the queen need never know if we exchange nurses again. Tomorrow we all leave this place. How could the queen see what attendant we ride away with? Hasn't she, surely, more important things to attend to? And once this holiday has passed, she will take her place in Salisbury Tower. It is a simple matter to bring a new attendant to the next plenary court, and it could easily be a full year before we are called to court again."

I glanced at Nurse from the side of my eye and saw her, seated, clasping a hand to her broad bosom. Perhaps she was seeing a new side of me, as I had been awakened to a new side in her.

"Let us do it, Lady Cicely. No, this is better. You do nothing, I shall do all." I motioned to Nurse to rise and follow me. "We shall retire to my chamber and Nurse Matilde shall remain with you here. Tomorrow, leave together as you always would and say nothing to your mother. We shall all forget this, just as, I'm sure, the queen has already forgotten it." I nodded slightly to Cicely and she, in her nervousness, bowed to me. Nurse and I hurried away and fairly flew back to our room.

"Oh, m'lady!" she exclaimed the moment the door was closed behind us. "How you have saved us! I couldn't think what I was to do, me placed over there with that new lady. We should have traveled so far west tomorrow! Oh, dear Lady Marian, how can I ever thank you, ever find words of thanks sufficient?"

It hurt me slightly to hear her express her gratitude thus, as if I were merely her employer—nay, her benefactress. But, in truth, I was, and it was a reality I had to embrace.

"Nurse, you need not thank me, truly. For you know that I have acted as much on my own behalf as on yours. Please, let us speak no more about it." She nodded her head, and we fell onto stools, shaking more now than we had before.

"Nurse," I said, when I'd caught my breath, "I have never asked you before . . . but what is your Christian name?"

" 'Tis Anne," she said shyly, "but in my youth I was always called Annie."

"May I call you Annie then, rather than Nurse?" I believe my voice wavered as I asked, for it seemed a momentous question to me. She, however, answered easily.

"But of course, m'lady, you may call me what you like. It shall be good to hear my own proper name spoken aloud once again."

And so it was settled. From that day onward every last nuance was changed between us, and, for the most part, it was to the increased pleasure of both. At times I still longed for the earlier days when I blindly trusted my nurse to care for me, to chase away all of my fears and keep me protected and warm. But I also knew that was no longer possible; that time had flown its way forever.

Chapter Three

WHEN WE RETURNED HOME I embarked on a new course of thought, of habit, and of vision. I was determined to learn as much as I could of the world, for my encounter with Hugh left me frightened of what might become of me when I was full grown. I knew of no way to prevent the day when I must join him in Sencaster, but I felt certain that a store of knowledge and understanding could only serve me well in the future, whatever might lie along my path.

I began my new course by asking Annie about her youth, for the queen's words had left me curious about Saxons, of whom I knew next to nothing. She told me proudly that she was Saxon indeed and came from the village Wodesley in north Leicestershire, where she had been born. The village was small and inconsequential, but its inhabitants worked hard for their daily bread and were honest folk, or so she told me. Annie had been the unfortunate second of two daughters, and since the dowry money was slated for the marriage of her elder sister, she was sent forth to work at the manor house for wages. From there she had advanced, inch by inch, to her present position at Warwick. This, she said, she was quite thankful for, for the meals were good and the rooms were warm, and she had only me to tend, who had never caused her any grief.

"And your family, Annie? When did you see them last?"

"Oh, not these many years, I'm afraid," she replied. "And they've fallen to hard times too. My sister Polly's man, Edgar, was killed in King Henry's wars, and Polly's moved home since, together with her four babes."

"Do you not miss them?"

"Law! Ever so much, Lady Marian, more than I can tell you. But I've my duty to do by you, and I won't be running off to Wodesley when I've you to care for. I do what I can and send my wages, but Saint Alfred knows I'd give a month's silver to see them once more."

She worked with her spindle as she spoke, and as she pulled at a thick lump of wool, my eye caught the shape and form of her hands. I'd not noticed before the way her blue veins surfaced from the backs, nor the yellow curving of her nails. Annie, I realized then with a start, had aged herself just as I had, growing older each year with the turn of the wheel until she was a maid no longer.

"Annie, you've known me all my life. I'm fourteen now, what age does that give you?"

"I've lived nine-and-twenty summers, m'lady, many of those here beside you."

"And have you never longed for a family? To marry and tend to a house of your own?"

She looked at me sharply, but lowered her eyes to her work as she answered. "There's not a woman alive doesn't think of love and family matters, to my way of thinking. But a body's got to go where it's needed, and as I've never struck a man's fancy, I suppose I'm needed here more than elsewhere. I've not your lovely face and manner, Lady Marian. We'd be hard put to keep the lads at bay if it weren't for your being long since wed."

This enflamed my mind for some hours, for I was just at an age when I'd started to notice the tallest and comeliest of the stable boys. To think of myself as a beauty was strange enough. But to loosen my mind to thoughts of men who might have stopped to pledge troth to me threw me to such a distracted state that I scarce could concentrate on my stitches.

MY INTERROGATION OF ANNIE continued until I knew more of Wodesley village than I did of the castle in which I lived. And not long after, I was startled to learn one thing more, that a complete Saxon language existed—a true surprise, since I had heard only French or Latin spoken about me. I asked her to speak it, and as she chattered I thought its tones did sound familiar, as if I had heard the rhythms before and had discounted them as murmurs or nonsense, mere background sounds that had no meaning.

The more I questioned, the more it seemed that a hidden world lay beneath my own. All of England, I found, was filled with villages of farmers and smiths who spoke nothing but Saxon. They considered themselves almost as a separate race from the French-speaking Normans, though we were most of us born on the same green-treed island.

This piqued my interest, and soon I proposed that Annie teach me some of this mysterious tongue. We got on slowly, for Annie had not a teacher's acumen, and I found the language to be more complex than I had expected. Indeed, it was as unusual to my mouth and mind as Latin ever had been, and in some ways proved far stranger since it shared so little with the southern tongues. But I struggled forward as Annie giggled at my mistakes, and after a time I began to improve.

During these days I harassed my tutor with constant questions, for I felt a deep desire to understand what teeth and gears caused the world to turn. I knew that I was powerless, as a wife and a woman. But if I could not have independence, at least, I determined, I would have knowledge. My tutor was stubbornly addicted to his poems and philosophical treatises, or so it seemed to me, but at last I gleaned from him this one truth. What I owned of value was my land.

Land brought rents, raised up crops, and maintained workers. Without it one had little power, for one had always rent to pay. But with it, all those rules reversed; the landowner sat on the seesaw's high end. My lands, it was true, were already joined with Hugh's, but even so they were my property, and I was determined to hold them tight.

I pressed my tutor on this further, for I was curious to know who governed my patch of dirt and trees, since I had no parents to watch it for me. In answer, I was surprised to learn that Apple Man had sole control of it. He, it seemed, had been appointed regent by Hugh's mother, Lady Pernelle, and had managed the land since my marriage. I had known that I must have a regent, for every landed child has one to manage her estate until she is full grown, but to hear that it was Apple Man threw me into fits of laughter. I had scarcely thought of him seriously since our meeting so long ago, but now I found that I had to consider him a great deal and more carefully.

Apple Man's name, it happened, was Sir Thomas Lanois—a rather disappointing name, I thought, for such a comical creature. But each time I laughed I reminded myself that he must be very clever or he would not have gained his position. And so I forced myself to think of him as Sir Thomas and was able to keep my composure better.

I drafted a letter to Sir Thomas, for I had developed such a hunger to see the lands of my birth that I could hardly think of anything else. In my letter I asked that he allow me to come, to tour Denby-upon-Trent and acquaint myself with its hills and valleys. I did not add that I wished to measure what sort of man he was, but that was no small part of my plan.

In due time I received a reply heartily encouraging me to visit at my earliest convenience. This letter I showed to Lord William, head of Warwick, that he might allow me to travel out beyond his walls. He saw no reason for any delay, and within a week Annie and I had packed our things and were traveling to the north and east, loaded with small gifts for my regent.

We rode a full two days and a half before approaching the region that held such interest for me. One of our guards was locally born, and he kindly informed me the day and hour we entered Denby.

"This here's the River Trent, m'lady," he called, nudging his horse in my direction. "It marks the border between Denby and Sherwood Forest, where Robin Hood keeps his merry men."

This was the first I'd heard of Robin Hood, and the name caught my ear as a bird does a worm, making my heart beat doubly fast.

"Who do you say? There, in those woods?" I glanced at the crowns of oak and elm, like unshorn sheep grazing in the distance, and felt an odd thrill pass through my veins.

"Robin Hood, aye, the greatest outlaw of these parts."

"Outlaw!"

"Indeed, m'lady. He and his fellows live deep in the wood, shooting the king's deer for their suppers and making some mischief for the poor sheriff. There's songs by the fork-load sung about him here—should you like to hear a stretch?"

There was little I wished for more. Soon Annie joined us, and we three passed many miles together, listening to the songs of this local bandit who was so beloved by the people of Nottingham. The tale was in Saxon, and our guard's accent differed somewhat from Annie's, so I was hard pressed to follow it all and still turn my eye to the beauty around me. But these few verses I heard rightly and kept safe in my memory.

> Robin Hood he would and to fair Nottingham,
> With the general for to dine;
> There was he ware of fifteen forresters,
> And a drinking beer, ale, and wine.

"What news? What news?" said bold Robin Hood;
"What news, fain woudest thou know?
Our king hath provided a shooting match,
And I'm ready with my bow."

The tale wound on in riveting fashion to describe this outlaw, all clad in green, and his uncanny skill with the yew bow. He seemed to relish donning disguise, for it was dressed as a bellows mender that he won this match, taking away a pipe of fine wine as his prize.

I was entranced, for I'd never before heard a bandit hailed as a hero, and the very thought of the outlaw life, of fleeing and hiding and lying concealed, made me long for adventure of my own. Annie asked if Robin Hood were not a very handsome fellow, and our guard replied that he had heard it said. I needed no more to light my fancy, for in those days I relished nothing better than the thought of clandestine romance with any man other than Hugh.

These thoughts were like sweet blackberry wine, thick and intoxicating. But when at last the tale had ended, I forced myself to once more take an interest in what passed to my right and left, for these were the lands I had traveled to see. And I was glad when I looked upon the soft landscape of Denby-upon-Trent. It was a beautiful place, full of clear, fast-running streams and everywhere decked with primrose and snowdrops. I was enchanted.

To my eye its lush fields, winding hedgerows, bold maples and hawthorns were the very idea of rural perfection, and I thrilled to see farmers laboring over the earth that I knew, at root, belonged to me. I did not question the notion that a girl of my age should own the rocks and dirt, for all of my peers owned their own acreage and thought no more of it than one would think of owning a purse or a book of poems.

The River Trent itself was visible from much of the country-side, and as we rode I began to feel akin to it, for I knew its smooth and glassy surface camouflaged a robust current. This was a trick I struggled to learn for myself, to keep my thoughts deep beneath my smile. I watched the river often, hoping to learn what I could of its art.

So occupied was I with this delightful prospect that I scarcely noticed the plow, the oxen, the farmers, and seed bags. It was the space that held my eye, the manor house that stood so tall in every town, the mills and churches that dotted the landscape. And when at last we reached Denby Manor, the great keep of Sir Thomas, I was in raptures over its strength and beauty. Such grandeur I had not expected, and I believe Sir Thomas found me in a more admiring mood than I was generally wont to enjoy.

I was taken to see him in the keep's great hall, where he sat with his clerks going through accounts. He was positioned at the end in a tall oak chair, spread round with cloaks of velvet and silk. Our first encounter was truly awkward, for although I curtsied and he bowed, neither of us was sure how much reverence was due the other, and neither was willing to give more than the proper share. I was surprised by the elegance of his attire, since, lovely as the area was, it was still a rural zone and far from the fashionable courts. And yet Sir Thomas wore gold and jewels such as I have rarely seen beyond a duke.

His jerkin and hose, disappointingly blue rather than apple red, were woven through with golden threads, and his pointed-toe shoes were also stitched with gold embroidery. Ermine lined his collar and cuffs, rung his velvet cap, and skirted the bottom edge of his tunic. A heavy gold chain hung round his neck and various gems were sprinkled like dewdrops across the cap. I was surprised, as I say, and slightly ashamed to see this, my regent, dressed more richly than I—though I too wore my brightest ornaments. He seemed, therefore, not only more luxurious than he had on our first meeting, but also somehow taller and larger, due, I supposed, to his high seat and the fact that he had grown even more rotund in these past few years.

At last we both were seated, and I began a frank discussion.

"Sir Thomas, how good it was of you to allow my visit. I have seen a great deal of Denby already and am quite delighted with its landscape."

"Indeed, Lady Marian, it is a beautiful spot. Any person with an eye attuned to beauty and art, as yours must be, cannot help but be transfixed by it." His face was round like a flattened plum, bland and pale as egg on toast.

"Yes, truly, that is the case. Can you tell me, Sir Thomas, what sort of people inhabit the land?"

"Oh, the usual common sort. Farmers, laborers, smiths, and tinkers. We have some excellent clergymen and some traveling friars. And, of course, the bad element runs loose sometimes in the woods and dales. You must be careful in your travels, Lady Marian."

"Yes, of course. But what number of inhabitants are there? Are there no other nobles beyond yourself?"

"Indeed, there are a great many commoners and a few other nobles, but, I assure you, there are no young ladies to rival your beauty, fair lady."

This was not going as I had hoped, and I sought to alter my course.

"Sir Thomas, I understand you must be quite dear to my husband, Hugh of Sencaster, and his family."

"Yes, 'tis true. You may perhaps know that I am cousin to his mother, Lady Pernelle of Sencaster."

"Ah, but of course." I sighed inwardly. His every answer seemed designed to hide as much information as he pretended to share. Again, a different tack was needed.

"What a marvelous household you keep here, Sir Thomas! After our long travels I quite expected something more rustic, but this house shines like a true oasis in the wilderness." He laughed, and I laughed, pleased to see that my compliments had been well received.

"I think you will find that we are not so remote here as we may seem. Why, King Henry himself traveled this way not one full year ago and slept within these very walls. He, I trust, found everything to be quite adequate and of the greatest comfort."

"Indeed! The king himself. Well that is an honor, truly." On I prattled, praising first one thing and then another, throwing honey upon every item of richness I had spied since arriving. At last the lord seemed to mellow and settle back into his chair, pleased to hear the young girl before him shower him with platitudes. That, I felt, was my golden moment.

"One more thing, if I may, Sir Thomas. Could you please tell me who employs my nurse, Anne Bailey, and my tutor? And who funds my lodging at Warwick Castle?"

"Well, I do, but of course, Lady Marian. It is one of my duties as your regent to ensure your well-being. I trust everything has been handled satisfactorily?"

"Oh yes, quite perfectly, thank you. I have had no complaints, I promise you. I simply wondered if perhaps, rather than continuing to bother you with the tedious details of my management—now that I am full fourteen and can arrange these things for myself—I thought perhaps I could be given the allowance you set aside for my care and be permitted to arrange these things by my own hand."

Sir Thomas looked a little pale at this question, but he recovered himself quickly enough. "You wish to receive monies from me rather than your nurse and tutor?"

"I simply thought these must be annoying details for you to manage, you who have such a vast tract of land to govern. I am quite certain that I can take over any contracts without causing you trouble. And I do not wish to be a burden to you, Sir Thomas. Perhaps"—I smiled winningly here—"your clerk could draw something up, explaining how much I am to expect, and how often?"

Here I rushed on, standing and bowing before he could respond, for I wished to trap him into acquiescence. "Thank you so much for seeing me, Sir Thomas. I know how fully occupied you must be with hearing disputes and the like, and I do appreciate your willingness to sit and speak with me. It is such a pleasure to be in the land in which one was born. I quite feel it in the air. Good day, and thank you, Sir Thomas!"

I dashed away, completely unconscious of his gracious mumbles echoing behind me. I had little faith in the success of the interview, but to my great surprise a clerk came to my chamber that very evening, bearing a piece of parchment which outlined the arrangement. I was to have so many marks of silver each year, to be paid, as is customary, on Lady Day, and was to have full control over my employees. The clerk also brought the year's contracts for both Annie and my tutor, and these I happily placed in my purse along with the original parchment.

When Annie and I rode forth from the manor the following morning, I felt a great sense of accomplishment. I had sat with my regent in a most adult way and convinced him to give me the control over my own situation, which I so desperately craved. True I was not mistress of my own fate, since Hugh was still my lord and master, but for the next few years at least I, and I alone, would be in charge of myself.

As I say, I was quite pleased with myself and rode home the next day with a full heart and new appreciation of my own powers. The one thing I failed to realize was that Sir Thomas had won a victory too. He now knew what I was about. I had shown him my wit, my frank style of speech, my desire to have, to own, to control. I had told him exactly what it was I wanted, and, since it caused no grief to him, he had happily supplied it. I considered this a conquest, but what I did not see was that Sir Thomas made off more the winner, for he had gained knowledge while I had gained nothing more than a simple contract.

Chapter Four

YEARS FLEW BY on golden wings, and as they passed I grew ever more anxious over Hugh. I had reached seventeen years, the age at which most unmarried women were exchanging rings, and yet I remained mercifully alone. This, I knew, would not last. One day soon I knew he would arrive to take me and establish me in Sencaster, and there I would stay for the rest of my life.

But for the moment, Hugh seemed content to live a life of independent extravagance in the court of Anjou. While his mother governed his lands in Sencaster, Hugh entered teams in tournaments of sport and lost many horses betting on them. At times, desperate for adventure, he rode forth himself to fight on horseback and was often "captured" by the opposing side and held until his friends raised ransom money with which to free him. His debts increased, but he stayed away, and I was contented.

At last, my tutor began to include more of politics in my studies, and so I was not surprised to hear that Prince Richard Coeur de Lion, now the oldest of King Henry's sons, had formed an alliance against his father. As a boy Richard had been gifted Aquitane, Queen Eleanor's native lands, that broad French expanse that produced such quantities of wine and wheat. Living and ruling beneath the southern sun, Richard had grown into a bold warrior, fierce and cunning. Long spite matches with his father had made him ruthless, and he had at last made a pact with Louis, the king of France, to join in war against King Henry.

Lest King Henry should receive more sympathy in this case than he deserves, it should be remembered that he had attempted numerous times to cut Richard from his inheritance and leave the full swath, from Scotland to Gascony, to the youngest boy, John. John was Henry's pride and joy, the boy he had raised alone and unaided while Eleanor lived abroad in Aquitane or paced her fine cell in Salisbury. As a boy John had been granted no dukedoms, unlike his elder brothers, and so had earned the name John Lackland. But now, if Henry had his way, John would have it all in the final throw.

This, Richard could not abide. He saw that if he joined forces with Louis, they two together could defeat Henry and seize his lands. And so war raged in Normandy, the advantage first leaning toward one party and then the other. At last Richard began to gain; Henry fell ill and was forced to succumb. Meeting with his enemies to surrender, Henry asked to see the list of all his allies who had betrayed him. Disloyal John's name was first on the list. Exhausted and heartbroken, Henry died soon afterward.

The very day of Henry's death, Queen Eleanor released herself from her tower prison and made her way to London to govern the country while it awaited the arrival of its new king, Richard Coeur de Lion. This news brought tremors to every noble heart, for there is little more dangerous to those with titles than a shift of power at the highest seat. Would Richard keep them as they were? If they had been loyal to Henry, would Richard see them as his enemies or value their allegiance to the throne? A time of great change had come upon us, but few could do more than gossip and worry and wait to see what would come to pass.

They had not long to wait, for Queen Eleanor was a woman of action. Working on behalf of her royal son, she called every noble in the country to London to hear their oath of loyalty to the new king. I packed my things and prepared to go, reassured that the queen would be too busy to do more than receive my oath as vassal.

Annie could not accompany me, for we would not risk her being caught in my presence, so I gave her leave to take a horse and visit her family in Wodesley village. I sent her off with a special commission—to learn more tales of Robin Hood, that outlaw of the northern woods. She and I were still in raptures over the song of the shooting match, for we repeated what portions we recalled at least once per sennight. Lately I'd asked her to mix with the castle staff and not return until she had a new tale, for as Robin Hood was a Saxon hero, the best reports of his wily deeds came from Saxon mouths and minds.

I traveled alone, or so it seemed, for though I was surrounded by guards and ladies, I had no friend to share in my thoughts, no Annie to sing me the song of Aelbert, great hero of Wodesley, or to relate the deeds of the Saxon saints. And so the road seemed longer than ever. The only novelty was the joy of traveling, for once, in the warm winds of early autumn.

Queen Eleanor had seized the disorder of the London court with the chill and strength of a firm north wind. Prisoners lying untried and moldy in Henry's dungeons were heard and released to spread the news of Richard's clemency. Offices that had gone unfilled were sold off to the highest bidder to gain funds for Richard's treasury. And lady vassals who sat unwed, hiding in their darkened corners like frightened spiders fleeing the broom, were gathered together to be married off as suited the queen.

Despite these changes, Westminster Castle received me as always, and I was soon wrapped in the plush voices of the same ladies I had always known. They were now grown, same as I, and seemed to feel a change in their fortunes in the very air of the place. And they were correct. King Henry had spent several years abroad before his death and in that time these ladies had been left unwed, spinning and weaving in their natal homes. Queen Eleanor, who knew how to make swift friends of the powerful men of the realm, prepared herself to deal them out like a pack of so many cards.

Her hand was decisive, and she lost no time. Lady Betony went to Yorkshire, to wed an earl nearly six-and-thirty years her senior who could scarcely speak for his constant coughing of blood and phlegm. Lady Clarice was wed to Sir Guillaume, the second son of the lord of Rouen, who had gambled away all of his fortune and was certain to begin on hers before the wedding breakfast. Dear, simple Lady Cicely was perhaps luckiest of all, for she was wed to a boy of six whom she could surely bully for the next ten years or more.

"By then," she said, half choking on tears, "I expect I shall be past childbirthing and so will never know that pain. Although perhaps then he'll have me annulled or locked in a tower like Queen Eleanor. And who can say, in ten years I may have died and will have lived my whole life without knowing a man in my marriage bed. 'Tis almost as if I marry no one at all!"

I patted her hand and wished her well, for after all I could not see that her situation was any worse than mine. But she was frightened and could not hear my words of condolence.

The other ladies ignored her as always, and by now I had learned their reason. For what was belied by Cicely's red hair and broad freckled cheeks was her Saxon heritage; her forefathers had risen from the Saxon lot, advancing themselves from reeve to bailiff, to steward, then lord. 'Twas for that reason her mother had sought out so French a nurse for her only daughter. For though this island held nearly two hundred Saxons for every Norman, the Normans held the more advantageous position by far, and Cicely would do well to imitate them.

Some of the ladies in our group were pleased with this court and looked toward their future wedded lives with hope and brilliant expectations. But in the main it was a sad affair. As I'd expected, I was not noticed, and so it was all the more surprising to wake in the night and see Queen Eleanor bending over my face in the dark, come to tell me that Hugh had died.

I did not grieve overmuch for Hugh as I had known him when last we met. But like a mother bird who can bring to memory nothing more than the fledgling's face, my heart recalled my dovecote friend and wept for him as though the world would end. My childhood days had sent me so few close companions that I felt a great kinship to Hugh—to the tow-haired boy he once had been. Acknowledging the loss of that child was like cutting loose one of my own limbs and casting off my youth in the bargain. I'd not tasted sorrow like this before, and I despaired that Annie was not present beside me to weep and wipe away my tears. She too would be sad when she heard the news, though her hatred of the man Hugh had become may have tainted even her memory of the child.

Soon after I heard this news of Hugh's death, I was called to Lady Pernelle. I supposed I was meant to exhibit a share in our common grief, a thought that made my stomach seize hard with fright. My gowns had all been dyed black for mourning and after I said my early prayers for God to have mercy on Hugh's soul, as all widows must do, I stepped into the hall enfolded in my new-sprung raven's feathers. Servants and nobles dispersed before my black-cloaked figure as I passed, for no one had words for a lady in mourning.

Standing before Lady Pernelle's chamber door, I composed my face as best I could to convey a sorrow I did not feel, to demonstrate an appropriate show of horror at my widowhood. I entered softly and found her seated near the casement window, gazing out. When she saw me she spread her arms, and I went to her, obediently entering her prickly embrace.

"My daughter," she sighed, stroking my hair with stiff fingers. "How shall we bear the sorrows of this life?"

I lowered my head and said nothing, and she went on.

"Our darling boy, dead and gone. Oh, what is to become of us?" Here she dropped her face into her hands and sobbed. I too made an attempt at weeping, but I have never excelled at public displays, and I believe all I managed to draw from my throat was the softest sounds of choking.

"Ah, Marian," she cried when her weeping had ceased. "This is a difficult time. We must both observe long mourning for Hugh, of course we must. It shall be no hardship for me, an old lady, but for you, my child, it will be a burden. To be widowed so young!"

I nodded slowly and lowered my head as if to hide tears that did not fall. And when Lady Pernelle turned her head to gaze through her window, I looked up and eyed her carefully. True, she wept and grieved aloud—Hugh had been her firstborn son. But despite all this talk of mourning, I noticed she had found the desire to hang pearl rings from her ears and cover her head in a wimple woven in the most current pattern, newly arrived in London town. Another glance told me that her eyes were dry as a summer desert for all the sorrow she professed.

At that second she shifted her gaze, and my own eyes jumped quickly away. A guilty feeling then crept in my belly. For why should I wonder at her dry eyes? Had I never drained the reservoir of my own tears but still felt sorrow enough to weep?

I covered my mouth with a quivering hand, then lowered it to my lap. "Dear Lady Pernelle, such a mother you have been to me. I cannot think what my life will be, now that Hugh has gone from us."

This seemed to provide an opening she had been waiting for. "It need be no different than it is now, sweet Marian. I decry any who should cause you to change, but for the necessary alteration of mourning. Nay, let us go on in every other respect just as we have always been, as mother and daughter."

I bowed my head, but in my heart I wondered at her words. How could she say we might go on when all had changed? How could she remain my mother when every thread of our alliance must necessarily be snapped?

"I should be grateful for such a continuance, Lady Pernelle," I replied. "For the moment I shall content myself with gentle prayers to speed his way to the kingdom of eternal peace."

BUT, OF COURSE, I was not content. All that night her words would sound within my brain, clanging and biting at my nerves. I could not grasp what she was about, for in no way could we two remain as we had been, especially in her own case, for she had been long employed as regent to Hugh, and that office no longer existed. Perhaps she might remain in situ as regent for Stephen, Hugh's young brother, but her lands would diminish as my tracts were returned to me, and our relationship must wither as well.

I was bewildered, but mostly over my own future. Nine months or a year of seclusion spread before me as my contribution to the current mode of mourning. But I foresaw that not long after I shed my weeds, I would become one of Queen Eleanor's marriage prizes. She, I knew, would waste no time in selling me away to the highest bidder, using my increased lands and youth and meager beauty to gain some earl's favor for Richard. I had gained a shrouded reprieve, but by its end I must be ready for what was to come.

These reflections brought no soothing relief, but only increased my agitation. Why had Lady Pernelle spoken only of continuance and said nothing of what must materially change? Was she too bereaved to mention the dower payment she now owed me? And what had brought the queen herself to give me the news? What part could she have in this affair, what cause to bother with one such as I? These thoughts brought me long hours of disquiet, hours in which I paced my chamber from casement to door and back again. At last I hit upon a resolve. The following morning I would wait on the queen in her vast hall. I would speak with her in that public place and see that my interests were well in hand.

WHEN I SOUGHT ADMITTANCE to the queen's court, the crowd parted before me as a retiring tide makes way for the shore. They filled the hall with whispered murmurs, for though death and mourning were as common a part of life at court as the life of the fields, to see a young woman so recently draped was cause for exclamation. The queen, disturbed by this ruffling of the crowd, called me forward with alacrity.

"Come, my child, come here before me. Lady Marian, why have you sought us here? Ought you not go into seclusion?"

I curtsied so low my hands brushed the rushes that covered the floor. "Yes, my queen, I shall do so presently. But before I do, I wished to ask you what may become of my dower. Am I not owed some portion of the Sencaster lands, as is customary on the death of a husband?"

Another wave of noise came from the crowd, for this was a sharply pointed question for a woman to ask. The queen looked uneasy and frowned at me, making her seem even more than eight-and-sixty years, if that were possible. She cleared her throat once, then again, and looked to my left at some being who stood there. I kept my eyes fixed on her feet, though I was desperate to know whose approval she sought.

"It has been decided by our most holy bishop of Canterbury that your marriage with Hugh of Sencaster was unlawful on grounds on consanguinity. Your marriage is to be annulled."

"Annulled!" I raised my eyes without thinking, then forced them down again. "Excuse me, my queen, but is it not highly unusual to annul a marriage after one of the parties has perished? And, may I ask, how it has been determined that consanguinity was a factor? For I do not believe Hugh and I were in the least related."

"What you believe and what I know are two differing things, Lady Marian. You will hear my judgment and obey it without question."

Oh, how I struggled! I looked down to where my own two fists gripped my blackened skirts and again was able to find my voice.

"My queen, I shall obey your judgment in this as in all things. I understand that this marriage of twelve years is to be annulled, and I will act upon that knowledge. And as this marriage has been annulled, I shall cast off my clothes of mourning and defer seclusion. I thank you, Your Majesty."

"No!" came a cry from my right-hand side, and I glanced that way at last. It came, as I had suspected, from the gaping mouth of Lady Pernelle. She, I saw in an instant, was the source of this annulment. Who else could have bargained with the queen to keep me from my rightful dower? What she could have given Eleanor in exchange for this favor I could scarcely guess, but the effects of their collusion were apparent.

"Lady Pernelle, do you wish to speak?"

The crowd moved reluctantly and made a space for Lady Pernelle to come forward and curtsy low before Eleanor.

"My queen, Lady Marian must do honor to my dead child, for how else will his soul find its way to Saint Peter and the gates of heaven? She is his widow, she must mourn for him!"

"Your Majesty," I said, "if the marriage is to be annulled, I must believe, as the bishop declares, that my bond with Hugh has never existed, unholy as it has been proven to be. Surely the crown would not ask me to mourn as a widow for a man to whom I was never truly wed."

"But she must, my queen! Think of my child!"

Through all this the queen said nothing, and in the silence that followed I determined to make my final attempt. I had only one last straw to grasp at, and so I stretched forth my hand.

"Your Majesty, I trust that my lands of Denby-upon-Trent,

those that I brought to the marriage as my dowry, will be returned into my own holding, as is customary upon an annulment? If you agree that it will be the case, I will do such homage to Hugh of Sencaster as would be fitting in his widow."

The queen was silent for a moment, then she coughed and nodded to the richly clad clerk who sat at her right hand. "It shall be so. Lady Marian of Denby shall upon her annulment of marriage to Hugh of Sencaster be in receipt of her original lands, namely Denby-upon-Trent, Denby Manor, and its surrounds. In return she shall go into a widow's seclusion until Lady Day of the approaching year."

These words were final; she was done with me. I curtsied low a second time, ignoring the beating of my heart, and rose to go. The room and faces floated before me in a blur, but I cared not. I had lost, for at the death of Hugh I should have been the gainer of a substantial piece of his property. Hugh's mother had dealt me a vicious blow. But I was no poorer than I used to be and at least had salvaged my original holdings. And to my mind eight months of seclusion would be no hardship, for I had gained a taste for independence and wished to savor it as long as I could.

And so I found myself, at the age of seventeen, a widow. Everything in my life seemed to have progressed completely counter to what was normal, like a river flowing into high land. I was raised far from my parents, but surrounded by adults of consequence. I was taught nothing of Saxon, the language of the land to which I'd been born, but was thoroughly educated in the tongues of Paris and of Rome. Before puberty I had married, by seventeen I was widowed, and as token to my backward life, I fully expected to die a virgin.

Chapter Five

BEFORE I LEFT Westminster Castle, a group of newly betrothed ladies, those who had been my maidenly friends, came to visit me in my chamber. They looked sadly at my black skirts and twisted their handkerchiefs in their own bright laps.

"We would have come to you before, Lady Marian," Lady Clarice began, voicing, as usual, the attitude of the flock, "but we had such fears as to your state. How wretched for you!"

They nodded in unison and gripped their hands, each thinking of her new fiancé and weighing, I supposed, the amount of sorrow she would feel at his death.

"Please, my dear gentle ladies, do not trouble yourselves," I said with a smile. "As you well know, I had not seen my husband these three years, and though we were good friends as children, we had grown distant in older age. I expect my heart will heal in time."

This brought a happier murmur to their lips and laid a foundation for easier topics.

"How horrid, Lady Marian, to have to dye your gowns all black!" one of them whispered amid titters of agreement. "I should have been made so ill to do it."

"As should I," said another. "Lady Pernelle was not so quick to cast her violet gown into the vat."

"Nay, she wore it just yesterday, did she not? And, Lady Marian, to think of there being no dower for you!" Five heads nodded in amazement and five pairs of eyes looked at me for my response.

" 'Twas a shock, I admit it, but upon reflection I understand better. Since Hugh and I never lived together as husband and wife, an annulment does seem warranted. Although it is strange to annul a marriage so quickly after the husband's death." They nodded at this but did not observe, as I thought they would not, that this was not the reason given for the annulment. These were not ladies of great penetration.

"Indeed!" was all they had to add and soon talk turned back to fashions and trifles.

"Shan't you be very lonesome in your retirement, Lady Marian? I don't know how I should manage to go four months together without visitors and traveling, and you shall have far longer to manage!"

"Aye," I agreed. "I expect I shall have to read and study a great deal and content myself with quiet pursuits."

"Could you fathom a full year spent on stitchery alone?" groaned Lady Clarice. "No, indeed, Marian, you must do something for your own enjoyment. Hire a legend singer, that's what I say. Lady Claudine had one come to her when Lord Phillipe died, and she said the time fairly flew by. And I too have often lost myself in a troubadour's song of romance. It shall be a distraction to you at a time when distractions must be welcomed."

"Oh, a bard, yes, that's the very thing," echoed another. "And the moment you are released you must endeavor to get a gown of this Vexin silk. The colors are so splendid, it will be just the item to raise your spirits. I think a ruby shade would suit her best, do not you ladies agree?"

SO ENDED MY TIME in the public eye. Our party moved in somber silence on the journey home, and I was allowed many long hours in which to consider what had passed. I had come to town a married woman and now I left a maid again, and yet a maid who had agreed to do a widow's work in mourning. This was odd, but as I've said, I am no stranger to the unusual twists my life seems wont to weave for itself.

Lady Pernelle's actions at court caused me grief for some long time, for as I reflected upon my own behavior in her presence, I saw that I had failed to grasp the extent of her duplicity. I did not trust her—I, at least, had been true to my own oath in that manner. But I had not seen her true motive, and it had cost me. Had I understood it all, I might have acted, might have given Queen Eleanor some offer of my own in exchange for what was legally mine.

Lady Clarice's final advice also rang in my head and while thinking back over her words made me smile at my pretty friends, I saw some wisdom in her charge. A bard, perhaps, was not necessary, for Annie had a good ear for tales and retold them with theatrical grace. But a hiring I must make, indeed, if I wished to keep abreast of what passed in the London court. I would be wed again, this was certain, but I would be powerless in the contract if I had no foreknowledge of the event.

Consequently, not long after my return I charged Annie to go forth and seek from her peers an unusual man. The man I sought would be like no other, crafty and independent, clever in the ways of the world but sharp enough to be able to hide away his own comprehension. It took her time and many a bribe of an apple tart laced with barley sugar, but when the west wind blew the scent of October ale, he came at last.

His name was Clym o' the Tower, in reference, I supposed, to time he had spent imprisoned for crimes against the crown. I questioned him closely in hesitant Saxon and found his misdeeds to have been of the sort that could not hurt me—poaching the king's deer and a score of fresh trout from out of a Needwood forest glen.

Clym was a dark man of ordinary looks, but some quirks of his manner made me smile. He wore a cap of red felt, and this he twisted in his hands as Aladdin might have rubbed his lamp, wishing for his magic genie. Clym had eyes that danced with light, and he took pains to make Annie laugh with his ribald humor and silly jests. He seemed uncertain what to make of me, a young widow employing him to spy at court, but he understood the value of steady pay and did not question my motives.

"What I want in particular to know, Master Clym," I said, offering him a place near the fire, "is anything which relates to me, Marian Fitzwater of Denby, or to my lands. In addition, if you hear any mention of Lady Pernelle of Sencaster, Stephen of Sencaster, or Sir Thomas Lanois, please bring it forward." Now that my suspicions of Lady Pernelle had grown, her close connection to my regent had not been lost upon me. Sir Thomas, I was certain, would do what he could to retain his position as regent of Denby, and he needed watching with a careful eye. I'd not forgotten his boldfaced lies, and while a light falsehood could be forgiven in myself, in my regent it was a damning flaw.

Clym repeated these names back to me as proof of his steady memory; then he spoke. "Ye needn't worry about me skills in this topic, m'lady. Ole Clym has many a trick in his pocket for just such a case, I assure ye. If I canna find placement in the kitchens or stables, I'll make friends of the jester or the clerk. There's many a man in the Westminster court who likes a drink of sack or Malmsey, and 'tis no hardship to find them out. I myself am a decorated prize winner at the holding of me own liquor, so ye needn't fear lest I'll forget what I hear. An' ifn I see that any one of them suspects me, I can change me getup and garb so fast they'll think ole Clym had died in his sleep and only new George popped up in his place."

"Are you, then, a master of disguise like the outlaw Robin Hood?"

"Nay, not like him, not even I. Robin Hood's the greatest of men, and I only one of the least. But I have the knack, as he does too, of makin' meself appear other than I be. 'Tis not so hard for one such as I, of normal height and average hair, with no distinctive marks about me."

"That skill must have served you well when you too were outlawed and hunted by the king's guard."

"Aye, it served me for a time, it did. But I was turned in by one of me own kind, I was, sad to say. The cruel outlaw of Needwood is no great man like Robin Hood. Guy of Gisborne is a wretched creature who'd slice his own mother for a gold coin. He rules our woods and not much kindly, for ifn he takes a dislike of you, he'll whisper it loud to the king's guards and off you go to London Tower."

"But how may this Guy of Gisborne alert the guards when he himself is an outlaw?"

"Aw, he does 'em favors such as this and they let him be for his service. 'Tis a wretched way for a man to live." Here Clym shook his head, clutching his red cap to his breast. "But as I say, I've been released by Queen Eleanor, and I've naught to fear now from the king's guards."

"And, Clym, will you promise me that while you're under my employment you will commit no crimes to reawaken their interest? 'Twould be no favor to me if you were caught up for stealing or poaching or shouting too loud after a round of drinking."

"Nay, sweet lady, I shan't shame ye. Ole Clym knows what way his money is comin' from and he won't forget it. I'll stay in the court and listen for ye, and when I hear a word of interest, I'll fetch a page and send him to ye, so you may know what I know."

I was pleased with this funny man, and I sent him forth to do his best. I did not know how it might go, for I knew little of the art of spying and less of disguise and life in costume. But I paid him handsomely so that he might not want or let his hand wander and land himself in some great trouble.

WITH CLYM DISPATCHED, Annie and I settled ourselves for a long winter of quiet companionship. This year there would be no Christmas court, no minstrel's music nor ginger candies. During these days more than ever I valued Annie's affection for me, which proved to be as constant as the seasons. She entertained me with songs of battles, impossible riddles, and tales of Saint Mildred, Saint Aelfgith, and their overwhelming devotion to God. But our favorite were the tales of Robin Hood and his merry men, the outlaws of Sherwood Forest, for these were the most daring men of our time.

Over and over she told me the tale of Robin Hood's battle with Little John upon a log bridge over a stream, and how they fought with blackthorn cudgels until Little John knocked Robin flat and doused him in the chilly water. Then she told how good-natured Robin praised Little John and brought him for feasting to the outlaws' camp, where he invited his victor to join the band. From that day forward Little John became his only right-hand man, beloved and honored by Will Stutley, David of Doncaster, Adam Bell, and all the other men of Sherwood.

Robin Hood, the rumors told, earned his coin by seizing gently upon rich friars, bishops, and nobles who passed through the Sherwood roads. If he deemed their purses full beyond what he meted to be right, he forced them to his forest lair to feast with him and his merry band. After the meal, the drink, the talk, the outlaws performed deeds of arms for the entertainment of the guests. And when that finished, Robin came forth to claim the excesses of their purse, leaving a third with his guest, taking a third for his own coffers, and setting one third aside for the poor.

These poor he sprinkled with coins and pennies, relieving their hunger and bringing fuel to their hearths. If the funds came from the bishop of Retford, he spread that money in Retford's towns, easing the burden of the bishop's taxation. The folks of the shire worshiped this outlaw as if he were a true Saxon saint, and the village ladies remembered his name in their daily prayers. By the men of the shire he was also remembered, for even if they had no cause to love him for his generosity, they knew him for his feats of arms, for none was more accurate with a yew longbow than Robin Hood.

Annie and I were caught by the romance of these tales, for to those in seclusion with nothing more than embroidery and spinning to employ them, the notion of one who does as he pleases is enchanting. Robin Hood had no master and feared no man. Even the sheriff of Nottingham, whose charge it was to catch this poacher, was impotent against him and had himself been forced into the wood for a night of feasting and purse-lightening.

In this way the winter passed, slowly, as all trying things do, but steadily. Time, I thought, could be a great ally when something dreaded loomed ahead, for it played no favorites but marched forward with its measured steps, neither stalling nor hastening out of its rhythm. And so Lady Day came and went. I shed my black gowns and went again with my head uncovered, a maid once more.

Not long after the day had passed, a rider came from London town bearing word from our good Clym. He said a letter had arrived from the queen to be sent to the north to Lady Pernelle. The queen herself was across the channel, assisting Richard with matters of his realm, but the chancellor had received the letter and sought to pass it to its recipient. The delivery instructions had been taken down by a court clerk with a taste for thick wine whom Clym had wooed and entertained until he heard all there was to know. We had little time, Clym reported, for the letter was due to be taken forth with other correspondence for Yorkshire at the end of the week.

What this letter could contain, I was not certain, but given the timing, coming so quickly upon the heels of Lady Day, I thought it might pertain to me and to my impending marriage. Perhaps the queen sought Lady Pernelle's approval for the match, in accordance with the bargain they had struck. Or perhaps Lady Pernelle stood to gain in some way from the new alliance the queen had planned—she surely had relations of whom I knew nothing. I guessed and wondered but could not determine it, and so I ceased my speculations almost as soon as they had begun. I could not discern the words of the letter unless I had a sight of it, and this, I decided, I must have.

A host of plans came to mind, but I plucked out the brightest one and laid it down, unpolished but gleaming, before Annie. She exclaimed at my boldness and gasped at my daring, but when I pressed her she agreed she could find no fault in my plan, for if it failed I should be no worse off than I was now, that much was certain.

And so I went forward to see Lord William to ask his leave to travel forth from Warwick, for I was determined to ride to Sherwood and seek help from Robin Hood.

Chapter Six

LORD WILLIAM AGREED to what I asked, which was not leave to ride to Sherwood, but permission to travel to Denby to visit an old servant I knew to be ill and possibly dying. No such servant in fact existed, but Lord William was oblivious to my affairs and thought me only a considerate mistress with a gentle, if not overly generous, heart. Permission obtained, I chose my guards and bade the groom prepare our horses, for Annie and I would take to the road at first daybreak.

Sherwood Forest was a two day's ride from Warwick Castle, but instead of bearing to the north where we ought, we rode farther east toward Denby, so none might catch at our true purpose. My host of guards was a difficulty, for they trod at our heels like a pack of hounds we would have to shake. No group of outlaws was so foolish as to take on a host of armed men, and therefore I would have to shrug them off. Moreover, 'twas crucial that they believe we rode for Denby-upon-Trent, or all our hypocrisy would be exposed.

I rode all day in my usual silence, anxious about our future steps, although, as is often the case, I ought to have saved that nervous energy for it gained me nothing. We stopped that night at an inn of my choosing, a half-timbered house all thatched with straw, which boasted its wares in its very name, the Keg and Spoon. The innkeeper's wife was coarse but merry, eager to make all the pennies she could by tending well to a great lady. I asked her to feed and sup the men at their own table in her bright hall, close to the flames of her roaring fire. In addition, I made this bargain, that she should receive an extra penny for each hour my guards stayed awake below, and I promised too that I would pay for every tankard and skin of ale that was consumed. This last I bid her tell the men, that they might feel free to make merry with revels while the moon was high.

Annie and I supped and slept, me wrapped in my cloak to keep some distance from the grimy sheets that dressed the bed. In the early hours Annie heard the cock's crow, shook me awake, and we made ready. I paid the innkeeper's lady six pennies and one more extra for her good cheer, and Annie and I slipped to the stables, two women escaping their own escort.

We startled the groom's boy, asleep in the straw, but he wiped his eyes and saddled our horses without much noise or objection. I bade him tell my late-waking guards that my serving lady and I had grown restless from waiting and had chosen to ride forward without their company. They would be sure to catch us, I added, on the way to Denby Manor, and we should be happy to meet with them then. The boy took the message and lay back in the hollow he'd formed in the straw, pulling wisps of it over him for a blanket.

All that day we rode to the west, through the open fields of Leicestershire. We had agreed that we ought not stay that night in an inn, for if our guards sought us in this region they could find easy news from an innkeeper or servant. Instead we rode for Annie's village and her family home, a bit out of our way to the west, but where we could find a safe place to sleep where no Warwick men would think of searching.

In the late afternoon we neared her village, and as we grew closer the men on the roads began to hail Annie by name, welcoming her home. She flushed and grew cheerful, excited to encounter her native space of friendly faces and warm hearts. The village contained little more than one great house, a rugged chapel, and perhaps ten cottages along the road. Annie led us confidently to a cottage in good repair, somewhat on the edge of town, and there we stopped our horses.

This cottage peeped cautiously at the world from under its heavy weight of thatch, in truth not much more than a stable in size. The mud-work walls had once been whitewashed, but the rains of winter had rinsed it away so that patches, like tear streaks, showed brown through the white. The yard was neat, though of plain bare dirt, clean swept by wind and the housewife's broom.

We had come at an odd hour, Annie explained, when most of the townsfolk had just retired from the fields and animals stood at the stable door, anxious for milking and a clean bed of hay. But even so I had scarcely time to take in the browns of the house and yard before a group of Annie's kin surrounded us, embracing their daughter with laughter and tears.

" 'Tis so good to see you, Ma and Da, and Polly, ye too. Here, let me present to you my mistress, Lady Marian Fitzwater, of which you've heard me speak a thousand times if I did a one. We are in need of a place to sleep for this night only and thought we might rest ourselves here."

She spoke in Saxon and, for all my practice, went so fast that I scarcely understood nine words out of ten. Her family turned as she spoke and regarded me in heavy silence, wondering, I supposed, why a noble lady would wish to sleep a night in their cottage. I stared back at them with a nervous heart, feeling a lost lamb in the midst of a goose gaggle. At last I did as I always did in a host of strangers I meant to please, I began to smile. I smiled first at the children's faces, for at times it is easier to show warmth of heart to a child than to an adult, but then, emboldened, I smiled too at the man and two women who stood before me.

Some smiled back, some looked amazed, and this gave me courage to open my mouth.

"I'm very happy to meet you all," I said, conscious of my Norman accent. "Annie has told me so much of you."

"Ah, Miss Marian," the old lady exclaimed, clasping my hands with her two strong ones, caressing my soft palms with her calloused fingers. "You're right welcome to our home, of course ye are. 'Tain't much, this house, but you're free to sleep in it, this night or any other."

As if her action determined theirs, the others quickly followed suit, repeating her words and shaking my hands. The children reached out to stroke my silk skirts and exclaim to each other over my shoes, my hair, my strange way of speaking.

They were seven in total: Annie's father and good-natured mother, her widowed sister Polly, and Polly's four children. I knew their names as well as my own, for I'd heard Annie speak of this brood more continually than anything else. But even so, I made a show of repeating each one, for that seemed something I could do to cover my feeling of strangeness. The eldest was Riccon, a tall boy who already helped his grandfather in the fields, then Bess, then Nat, then baby Jackie. Riccon and Nat soon tired of Bess's game of eyeing my clothes, and moved on to our horses which stood as we'd left them, resting in their reins. Annie's father saw the boys go and leapt up to tend to the beasts as if his heart allowed him no rest while animals stood uncared for. He led them away, saying nothing to the two boys who trailed behind, to find a stable and some oaten meal.

I worried over her father's silence, for he had said scarcely three words to us since our arrival, but Annie whispered that he was just quiet and slow with strangers, so I tried to relax. I too was quiet with new people and by this time wished with all my heart that we had chosen to sleep in an inn. But we were here and all was settled, and this was where we should remain.

I expected that we would retire inside, for the light was growing faint and a chill would soon be in the wind. But the women of the family remained without, talking rapidly of this or of that neighbor, who was now reeve and who now hayward and whose daughter was to be married to the miller in the next village over. I stood by, quiet and dumb, looking from time to time at young Bess, who would giggle and hide when she caught my eye.

The women settled on rounds of wood, and Polly found for me the cleanest among them. Bess had no seat, so she hung behind her mother or aunt, smiling at me with a toothy grin or wiping a dirty hand across her cheek.

While the women spoke, I observed them, noting the strong thrust of their chins and the way they all had of clucking their tongues. Polly and Annie resembled one another in look and gesture and tone of voice. Both shared a height far beyond what either of their parents possessed and auburn hair that could be traced neither to their mother's gray locks nor their father's dark ones. They were both buxom women, broad and fair, with rosy cheeks, strong hands, and quick tongues.

But, unlike Annie, Polly and her mother shared the rough reddish skin that comes from life in the open wind, their clothes were of homespun, and their hands were gnarled from heavy work. Beyond those distinctions of environment and habit, they three were no more different than ducklings born from the same clutch of eggs. I wondered, seeing them, if my own mother had been so like me.

From time to time Polly or her mother looked at me shyly with a crooked smile, but they had no words to share with me, and I knew even less what to say to them. At one point Polly asked if the journey from Warwick had been a pleasant one, and I said that it had, yes, thank you very much. That said, we lapsed again into silence while Annie lambasted Eadom Tanner, an unfortunate villager who came late to the haymaking and had been fined and beaten by the steward.

When the father of the house returned, Annie's mother went in to fetch the supper. I was glad to see her go, for our noon meal had been taken early, and I felt a rattling within my belly. In time she returned with two wooden bowls and wooden spoons, and these she handed to Annie and me. Annie set to and began to eat, but I hesitated. Would the others not be eating? Their eyes were on me, and I sat frozen. At last Annie looked up from her bowl and whispered to me in French, which was now become our secret language.

"Go ahead, m'lady, and eat. They haven't bowls to go around, so we must dine in shifts, ye see."

"Annie," I said, hoping my voice did not convey the terror I felt, "what is it?"

She chuckled softly and moved a bit closer. " 'Tis meal porridge of oats and rye. They've no bread here till the harvest comes due, and this is the best they can manage. Look here, m'lady, they've placed some bits of meat in specially for ye."

I looked at the meat, twisted and unrecognizable, and lifted my spoon. I was loathe to offend such gracious hosts as these people were, but as I raised a piece to my mouth I felt my stomach heave with fright. With a powerful bite I got it down and much of the porridge and then determined that I could protest I hadn't hunger enough to finish.

The remains of my supper were promptly given to Riccon and Nat, who ate it down in four quick bites. I sat still on my log while the rest of the family consumed their meals, scraping the porridge from the bowl as if it were a rich cream pudding. Still we remained seated outside, but I did not question. I felt I had acted poorly about the supper and was ashamed—of that, of my accent, my manner, my clothes. There was no end to my current shame, and as apology or perhaps as penance, I sat in silence.

When the night grew darker I calmed somewhat, sensing some safety in not being seen. After a time I noticed Bess at my elbow, clutching tightly to a crude wooden poppet, no more than a stick with two knobs for arms. I coaxed her in silence to let me see it, and when she did I brought forth my handkerchief, resolving to give it up for this girl.

In those days I carried my needle and thread always about me for embroidering, and these I fished out together with my small eating knife. Working in silence, since I feared, for some reason, to let the others know what I did, I cut the linen and fashioned a gown. The sleeves and skirt I stitched tight with thread and with quick stitches I gave the shift a silken girdle, blue on white.

All the while I was working, Bess stood close by, watching my hands in awe and silence. At last it was done, and I handed the poppet back to her mistress, pleased with this project as I had not been pleased with any in years. Bess clasped it to her with shining eyes and did not stray from my side again all that night or the following morning.

AT LAST ANNIE SAID it was time to retire, and I rose, grateful, for I was chilled to the bone. Her mother went in and lighted a lamp, and Annie bid me follow as well. When I passed through the door, I saw for myself why we had stayed outside as long as we could, for within the house was cramped and dark, filled with smoke from the fire, fumes from the tallow lamp, and the scent of dampness.

As near as I could discern in the dim light, the house had one room, heated by a fire on the floor which was overhung by a cauldron, dangling on a metal hook. No chimney carried the smoke away, so what did not find its way out through the door or the one bare window, remained within. The far end of the room held a bed, and it was to this that Annie led me. It was in truth less of a bed than a great straw mattress, molded from use into hills and dales and lumps of straw.

Annie conferred with her mother a moment, and I was shown to a spot on the mattress where the roof above was known to have no leaks, and here I laid myself all alone, wrapped in my gown and cloak, to sleep. Annie lay on the inside, beside me, and young Bess was placed on my other, where she snuggled in close like a puppy. Soon the rest of the family entered and laid themselves along the mattress. Then someone blew out the tallow lamp, and we went to sleep.

In truth, I should say, we were meant to sleep, but I could not relax myself. No sooner had the eight beings around me calmed their breathing and finished their coughs, but a scuttling sound began to emerge, sounding, I was certain, as if it came from directly above my own head. I lay still and listened, reassuring myself that my companions seemed to feel no fear, and yet I could not be composed. The noise continued, then another joined, and soon it sounded as though races were being run by some strange creatures within the thatch.

I lay stiff as a shield, keeping quite still, but in another moment things grew worse. A shrieking sound, as if some animal were attacked or bitten, pealed above me. Another squeal followed, and I let forth an involuntary sound, something like "ah!" Annie rolled her head to face me and whispered softly, " 'Tis rats a-fighting in the rooftops, m'lady. Do not fear. They fall through the thatch but rarely, and if one does Da will get him with his boot."

I exhaled a shaky breath as I thought through her reassurances. Rats in the roof that might fall through—I believed I would not survive this night. Long I waited and listened hard, hearing them run and sometimes squeal, but after an hour or so had passed and none had in fact fallen through, I was determined to go to sleep. 'Twas the only way, I told myself, to make this wretched night go by, and so I rolled onto my side and shut my eyes, praying that when I opened them next it would be morning.

But I was not so very lucky. I awoke in the dark, feeling that need that often comes to me in the night, of relieving myself. But what to do? I could not rise without waking Bess and Annie both, and once I did, where should I go? Again I lay in fitful silence, hoping to fall asleep again, but it would not do, I had to go. With a sigh I rolled to face Annie and grasped her shoulder to shake her awake.

"Hmm . . . ?" she murmured, and I shook again.

"Annie," I whispered, as soft as I could, "I need to get up. I need to use the closet." In Warwick Castle one did, in fact, relieve one-self in a closet of sorts that hung out over a vast trench, and this was the word she and I had long used for that particular place of business. Annie was tired and wanted to sleep, but she had been a nurse too long to not respond with automatic speed to a charge who needed a trip to the closet. She slipped from the bed as slow as she could, and I followed. In the dark she searched about, then found a bucket at the foot of the bed that was used by the family as a chamber pot. Pointing it out carefully so I should not kick it, she said, "You may go there, m'lady. 'Tis our form of a closet."

I was mortified. To relieve myself within the hearing of all these people? I could not. "Nay, Annie, please, they shall hear me! Is there no other way?"

Even in the dark I knew what expression her face was forming, for I'd seen it before. It was a look she had when she felt I was being unreasonable, but I did not care. We went to the door and pushed it open, waking, no doubt, every last sleeping person, and I stepped out into clean, cool air.

The moon was high and for that I was grateful, for it gave me the light to be unafraid and to find a spot near a buckthorn bush that was to my liking. Soon enough I returned to Annie, and we made our way back to the mattress, careful to avoid the bucket as we went.

THIS TIME I SLEPT a sleep of relief, deep and dreamless, beside my companions. Far earlier than is reasonable, we were all startled awake by the sound of a horn crying through the village streets, then a brazen cock had the gall to crow just below the open window. No more was needed—we were all awake and climbing from bed. I slipped outside as quickly as I could, desperate enough for open air to leave the smoky warmth of the house. The light was still dim and the morning misty, but even so I could make out a man, hooded and cloaked, blowing his horn up and down the road.

" 'Tis the hayward," said Annie, shivering beside me. "He's wakin' the folks to call them to the fields. There's sure to be more haying today. Da and Riccon will go together and perhaps Polly too today."

I said nothing, only watched the family disperse to their chores while these three made ready for their day in the fields. It occurred to me then that I had been present for the whole of their time away from their work, from yesterday evening to this early morn. How it must have sped by for them! Today they would pass another full day beneath the hot sun, then another night on the lumpy mattress, and another, and another. Thus stretched the regular order of their futures. 'Twas no wonder Annie preferred our slow life of embroidery and spinning before a great fire, capped by a night of easy slumber. I scratched at my arm without glancing down and heard Annie exclaim, "Law! What a bite you have! Ma, you'll have to air the straw out soon. It seems to have got some fleas in't."

Chapter Seven

ANNIE AND I RODE AWAY from Wodesley with opposing hearts, for she bid the place good-bye with a tear, while I could not urge my mare to a quick enough step. This very day we hoped to meet with Robin Hood and seek his help. I must admit that I felt a great nervousness at the thought, for if this scheme did not succeed, I didn't know what I should do. So much seemed to depend upon chance that it made me shake to think of it. But I resolved to push it from my mind and content myself with riding, step by step, closer to Sherwood, where things would surely work themselves out.

As our horses advanced, the day grew soft as a day in June can sometimes be, warm and mellow and laced with birdsong. Fairy bells, daisies, and early roses peeked up from every grassy byland, and green leaves danced for joy at the sunlight. Ash and hawthorn, white birch and elm, lined our way, leading us into clusters of limes, thick with flaxen flower buds. It was a pleasant ride so long as I could keep my mind steady, though as we neared the famous forest I found that task to be increasingly difficult.

We had agreed between ourselves that when we were stopped by the outlaws, as we hoped—nay, required—that we would be, I should be the one to speak. Annie agreed to it even more now, for as we progressed through the silent wood, we both became anxious. What would we do if the outlaws proved to be more vicious than they were in the tales? It was all very well to have crafted this plan from the safety of our fireside, but now that we had come on purpose to be abducted, we both began to feel that we had been foolish.

But now there was little choice left other than to continue forward. Foolish as this scheme might be, 'twould be far more folly to turn back when we were so close. So on we went through the deep canopy, seeing less and less of our beloved sunlight as the forest closed above our heads.

The longer we rode without seeing a soul, the more alert I became for movement. But for all my attention, it was Annie who spied them when at last the men appeared, standing still by the roadside. Four men stood silent, clad in green, one of them the size of a lesser giant, taller by far than any man I had laid eyes on before, and broader too. In spite of her knowledge of who they were and that we rode forth on purpose to seek them, Annie shrieked a little in fright. The giant stepped out before our horses and pulled them easily to a stop, his hands on the leather bridles.

"Heigh-ho, fair ladies!" he said with a grin in smooth Saxon, proving himself to be a cheerful giant. "How comes it that two such beings as fine as ye should ride through our wood alone and unguarded? Know ye not that this wood is alive with thieves and miscreants?"

"Is that what you and your companions are?" I asked, my voice wavering more than I could control.

"Perhaps we may be, perhaps we may not," he responded. He had a nice smile above a dark beard. "But I may certainly tell you that we fellows are not untouched by the beauty of a maiden face. Give us each a kiss, my lovelies, and we shall give you leave to ride along your road."

Annie, I saw, began to smile, so I spoke quickly. "Enough of that, you saucy beggar. Do you think we came riding hence to press our kisses on your lousy pate? Unhand the horses and let us pass."

The giant raised up all the taller at my harsh words and looked offended. My mare stamped lightly on the ground, anxious to be down the trail since she saw no stable near. The giant stood firm.

"Nay, ladies, if you'll part with no kisses for me and my mates, I'll have to commend ye to my master."

This, at last, was what I sought. "Very well," I said in haste, "take us thither, and we shall see what your master makes of your behavior to ladies in the wood."

He laughed aloud at this, a bold, round laugh edged with only a hint of malice, and I saw that his fellows had a chuckle also. Perhaps, I thought, we should find Robin Hood to be no less of a brigand than these men of his, but that was a risk I felt forced to accept. Taking our horses by the reins, these green-clad men said nothing more but led us into the ferny bracken to the very heart of Sherwood Forest.

We rode so long that Annie and I became exhausted in our saddles, wearied by the scratches and slaps of twigs that bit our arms as we passed. Somewhere in the deep forest, they led us into a flowing streambed and walked our horses through the water for perhaps half a mile. Ancient oaks were more common here, together with poplars and gleaming holly. At last the darkness cleared before us, the trees thinned, and we arrived at the very place.

A large clearing eased from side to side, flanked by a soft-running stream, and in its midst stood the broadest oak I had ever seen. The oak was aged enough to show a host of roots above the ground, and upon these sat a score or more of men dressed to match our captors. For a second I thought they were fairy folk, twisting cobwebs into dreams, but a further glance showed the mendacity of their work. Scattered across the meadow were more men, some tending fires, some cutting at meat, and I wondered how many more were hidden in the trees and underwood that bordered this field.

As we were led in, our giant gave a lusty cry, and a dozen men came running forth, some on purpose to help us down, others to take our horses off apace where they were turned loose to dine on rye and field grass. I looked at them all, at every face, wondering how I would make out the leader, until one approached with such a countenance that I knew him to be Robin Hood.

His eyes shone blue and bright with knowing, and a ready smile hung upon his lips. He was not tall, though taller than I, and his face was lean and rich with shadows. He stood apart from his comrades by virtue of a curious morphing power of expression that made him seem about to laugh, about to weep, about to reckon very hard at something—all in the space of an instant. This puzzled me, perhaps frightened me, and so I contented myself with noting that he looked far younger at six-and-twenty than I expected and left my observations at that.

"Greetings, fair ladies," he said as his eyes darted from my face to Annie's and back. "Who have we the honor of welcoming to our Greenwood tree?"

"I am Lady Marian Fitzwater of Denby-upon-Trent, and this is Anne Bailey of Wodesley village." My voice quavered like a dying flame.

"Bonny Annie," he said, kissing her hand with all the gallantry of a landed knight. "And Lady Marian." He turned his eyes on me, and I felt my heart begin to bolt. "I am Robin Hood, leader of this band of revelers and forest yeomen, at your service." Annie giggled and received a smile, but I stood frozen. "You need not be so pale, dear lady," he said, raising my hand softly to his lips. A vicious blush rose in my cheeks. "We all do honor to woman here, as each of these lads has had a mother."

I blushed again and said nothing, unsure as I was of what to say.

"Come," he said, taking us each by the hand and leading us to a patch of the field where the grass was short and great squares of wool were laid about. "For though we are but a band of thieves, we will not treat you roughly—unless rough treatment is what you're after." He winked, and my throat ran dry, compelling me to a short fit of coughing. "Are you well, Lady Marian? Would you care for some wine? My men and I would invite you to stay with us for our evening meal and enjoy our entertainment as honored guests."

He placed us each on our own patch of cloth and jogged off, eager to see to some aspect of the feast or to speak with some grouping of his men. My eyes clung to his back as he went. This, then, was the famed Robin Hood. More handsome, more youthful, more quick in his motions than I had expected, but what amazed me most was the ease of his tongue and the honor he did the Saxon language. For from his mouth the words seemed rhythmic, steady, and—even to my ear—as gentle as the smoothest French.

A glance at Annie reassured me that she was no longer afraid for herself but had begun to enjoy these lads and their teasing ways. Indeed, every man who passed us by had a smile for her, for she was just the sort of maid to catch a yeoman's eye. She smiled back and laughed and giggled and soon had a ring of ready admirers, the likes of which no lady would shun. I, it seemed, was more of a riddle, a cipher that they would not trouble themselves to unravel, and so I sat alone and unpestered.

After a time, Robin Hood, no doubt playing the role of good host, placed himself at my side and bade me enjoy the feats of arms his men performed at the far end of the field. I faintly saw some men with bows and others with cudgels, but all was too distant for me to make out, so I turned instead to my silent companion. This moment I took as my grand opportunity, and I spoke to him in an earnest tone.

"Good Robin Hood, might I speak with you regarding something of a most serious nature?"

"What?" he responded, laughing. "Lady Marian, how can you be serious when such magnificent sport is being played before you?"

"I have never been a great viewer of sport, I must admit."

"Nay, indeed? If that is so then you ought to watch close, for this is some of the best in England. If you are ever to be made to enjoy feats of arms, I boast it will be here in our green field."

"I daresay I won't, not from want of respect for the players or the difficulty of the challenge, for I am sure I could do little with such a branch as they bear there. But my excuse is one of poor eyesight, for I cannot see clearly beyond twenty paces."

"Indeed?" he said, turning to dart his quick eyes at my face. "Is it the truth that such clear eyes as yours are in fact so cloudy?"

" 'Tis the truth," I said, wondering if it were a compliment to be said to have clear eyes.

"Well, there you have a disadvantage, but I declare, 'tis not your fault. You have been cursed with Norman eyes."

I stiffened, my chin rose, and in an instant I became angry. "And what makes you state that Norman eyes should fail more often than Saxon ones?"

He shrugged with indifference, but I thought I saw a smile play on his lips, and this made me all the more irate. " 'Tis the simple truth. In sharpness of sight, straightness of tooth, and length of limb a Saxon has yet to meet his equal. And, in honesty, the Norman is so far below his equal in these cases, he scarcely enters upon the same field."

I did not completely comprehend his illusion, being unused to sporting terms, but as to his meaning I could have no doubt. My anger grew, and I spoke without thinking.

"Is that so? Indeed, I had heard it said by cowherds and groomsmen, but I must have forgotten this 'simple truth' you speak of. Normans are inferior to Saxons in every way, are they not? 'Tis no simple matter of clarity of eye or the sturdy limb, Normans are also dull in the brain, is that not so? Laggard and slow with weak intellect, poor creatures that we are. That, I suppose, must somehow explain why a handful of Normans rule all of England and the Saxons in it!"

I saw Robin Hood's jaw stiffen, but I did not care. I had heard enough in my travels of the weaknesses of Norman blood and our malformed faces and twisted bodies. I had not meant to offend this host, this man from whom I had hoped for aid, but I could not let his cutting remarks go without defense. 'Twas the wretched griping of the conquered that he expressed with these words and while there might be truth in his views, I knew there was also strong truth in mine.

In another moment he rose from his seat and strode away without so much as a word or glance in my direction. I sighed and gazed at the forest floor, still angry, still tempered, but now confused by the shame at having given offense. Perhaps I had been wrong to speak so to a host. 'Twas the end of my plan of asking his help, that much I clearly saw.

At the far end of the field the meat was roasting, and as I smelled its charring odor my stomach gave a hopeful jolt. Breakfast this morning had been warmed-over porridge from last night's supper, and my stomach had not been hardened enough to accept a bowl of it when offered. Our day had been long, and I now felt a hunger as keen as I had ever known. But it came into my head that as punishment for my angry words Robin Hood might see fit to keep supper from me, and this thought brought childish tears to my eyes. This was hard, I ought not to have come. I wished I had never heard of this man and his band of outlaws, dressed in green.

BUT I WAS PROVEN WRONG. Before another half hour had passed, Robin Hood returned to my place bearing a wooden bowl of roast pork and venison. He sat down beside me and, not knowing what hunger I felt in my belly, lowered the bowl and sought instead to speak.

"Lady Marian, I was impertinent, and we have quarreled. I am sorry. I would not wish to make ill words with any guest."

I, for a moment, forgot the bowl.

"And I am sorry for what I said, for I can see it caused you pain. What you said was true, my eyes are bad, and it is a failing of my race. The Saxons, indeed, are noble at heart, which the Normans may not prove to be."

"Nay, you need not apologize for speaking in defense of your own clan. You ought to do it. But I say in all honesty that my words regarding the strength of your eyesight were meant in jest only. They are fair eyes, whatever their flaws."

Fair eyes!

"I have a fault of being too serious," I said, plucking at the grass. "Another time, if I may be allowed another time, I will be less quick to anger, I promise you."

"And I, as tribute, will give homage to one of your Norman saints. Saint Lucy, I believe, may be one of your favorites?"

I gave a start, my brow frowned, but then I saw his jest and laughed, for he had caught me in my promise far faster than I had ever expected. Saint Lucy, indeed! As patron saint of eyes and eyesight, Saint Lucy was a bold choice.

AT LAST WE SHARED a bowl of supper, and I daresay this woodland meal was one of the best I had ever eaten. Perhaps my hunger made all food taste like nectar, or perhaps the king's deer are more tender than most. Whatever the cause, I was well pleased and sampled everything with my highest compliments.

When we had finished, and men had brought round fat skins of ale and Gascon wine, Robin Hood turned his face to me, though 'twas now so dark I could scarcely see it.

"Lady Marian, you wished before to speak with me in a serious way, and I turned things into jesting. If you will agree to tell me now, I will promise to hold my tongue and listen through."

I smiled in the dark, for angry though he was able to make me, he also had a winning way, and I was hard pressed not to be pleased with him.

"I have a difficulty, Robin Hood, and I had hoped that you might help me. A letter shall pass along your roads from Queen Eleanor to Lady Pernelle of Sencaster. I wish to see the contents of it, for I believe it holds information relating to my own future fate."

"Surely you are not in trouble, Lady Marian? Not destined for the rack or dungeon? 'Twould be a shame when I've men here who would gladly die for a night in your bed."

I flushed again, pink as a rosebud. Some unbidden voice taunted that, should Robin Hood die for such a price, the world would be much the loser. But then I drew myself together and looked at him imploringly, for I longed to make him serious, if only for one instant.

"Nay, no trouble, if that's the sort you mean. But I believe I shall soon be wed, for as a vassal of King Richard, the queen may marry me to any man she deems worthy. I would fain have knowledge of it before the fact, if I can manage to do so."

"Marry! This is the sort of trouble which plagues young ladies? I had thought you all wished to marry."

I struggled to speak with a calmness of heart. "I might perhaps desire to marry if I loved the man or even thought him worthy, but the queen shall sell me to one with money or one with influence, regardless of character. I, you see, have been once wed and am already widowed, and from the marriage contract of a widow the king shall gain a payment of silver in addition to the gratitude from the husband."

"Now come, you think so highly of yourself as that? To believe your husband would love the king for having gained you for his wife?"

I fought against exasperation. " 'Tis not I that will make him grateful, but I come with lands, left me by my parents. The man who weds me will gain those lands and with it taxes and revenue, and for this he would be grateful. The queen sees all this and will choose a man with wealth enough to pay the king in silver. But she will also choose a man whose loyalty is somewhat lagging, for a marriage gift can boost allegiance one-hundred-fold."

"Ahh," he said, his voice soft at last, "this is the state you find yourself in. I had not known how it was for ladies to be sold off so." He was quiet for a moment, then spoke again. "But is there no chance you shall love this fellow? Perhaps all might be well in the end."

"Nay," I said firmly. "I will not love him. I believe I shall never give my heart to any man, for once it is given, I lose all dominion over it. 'Tis better to be a slave by circumstance than to serve blindly through a cloud of love."

"Is that so?" he asked, plainly surprised, for his eyes snapped like an April sky. "It pains me to hear that no man will tempt you, for we've pretty faces enough in our band to please the most particular lasses. But if wedded life seems a bondslavery to you, I would scarce push you to it. We've a number of liberated bondsmen here, one that sold for fifty marks at Dublin Bay, and I hear from them that the serving life is not one to relish."

The instant I heard his reply, I regretted my words, for life in Sencaster, no matter how grim, could hold no comparison with true slavery. And yet the brisk air of this Greenwood tree made me feel that to take up my former fate with a peaceful heart, to foster the whims of parents-in-law and a willful husband, would be impossible.

"And so you wish me," Robin continued, "to send my men to intercept the queen's letter? With the intent that you may see which man she sends you off to marry? How, may I ask, will that alter your fate, Lady Marian? For it seems to me you cannot avoid the wedding day, whether you know the bridegroom's name or not."

"Yes, you may be right. But I feel that I must attempt something, and nothing can be thought of until I know what the queen has decided. It is, perhaps, a fool's errand, but I must try whatever I may, and so I beg for help."

He was silent again, and I supposed he must be thinking of the risk to his men in attempting such a thing. I spoke hastily.

"I understand you may not feel this small campaign worth the risk to yourself and to your men, and for that reason I have brought with me one hundred marks in silver as payment. Perhaps this may make the letter more worth the taking."

Here he was again silent, and I remained silent also. I had told him all, given every incentive I had, and could do no more than wait. When at last he spoke a strange emotion played upon his face.

"Are you telling me, Lady Marian, that you and your mistress Annie came into this wood on purpose to seek me? That my men did not catch a noble lady unawares on the Nottingham path, but that you meant all the while to be caught? This is pretty! What a joke on my men who thought they had snared themselves a fancy bird!"

" 'Twas deceitful and wrong to do it, I suppose, but it is true."

"Oh, nay, say naught of deceit and wrong. We are bandits here, remember? Nay, indeed, say no more of that. 'Tis charming to think that you sought me out, and in exchange I will fetch your letter. Know you what day it passes through Sherwood?"

"The post was to leave London town yesterday, on Friday. I know it stops in other shires, but I had heard it would pass to Sencaster on Sunday or on Monday, if all went well."

"And if all has gone well, my men and I shall cause such a nuisance that these letters will not arrive as scheduled. The poor men of the post. I do pity them at times."

"Indeed? I would have thought an outlaw's heart would be hardened against pity by necessity."

"Perhaps I am not the wisest of outlaws. But no more of that."

He grinned and looked to me, then away. "It sounds to me, Lady Marian, as though you have but recently acquired the fine Saxon tongue. How has that been your plight? Most of the nobles in this shire speak Saxon better than their Norman French."

This was a blow. I had so hoped that my speech did not sound odd to him, so proud to be carrying my own side of our conversation. But of course his ear would hear my accent just as any sheep would recognize the wolf dressed in sheep's clothing.

"I was raised in Warwick Castle where the only language spoken was French. I did not even know a Saxon tongue existed until I was thirteen. Annie has taught me all I know."

"You have known each other long?"

"She was my nurse from infancy, the only parent and one true friend I have ever had."

Again we two fell silent, then Robin Hood called for Allan a Dale and his harp, for he wished us all to hear a song. In another moment the young man came forth, accompanied by a pretty maiden and, placing himself near the fire, began to strum a tune. His melody was long with many verses, and I became restless during it, but I saw that it was the custom of the place to remain silent during a song, and so I stayed quiet also. Had this been the court in London, all conversation would have continued. But harps and songs were common there and perhaps less valued because of it.

At the end of the song most of the men left their places to look for sleep, and Robin Hood became again the dutiful host.

"For a night's sleep we can offer two choices. The Blue Boar is a splendid inn not two miles off, and a group of my men would lead you there if you wished a roof and fire and bed. But if you feel less particular, Allan a Dale and his bride, Ellen, will give you a place in their bower, just there on the edge of the field."

I felt unsure, for I did not wish to travel two miles before finding a bed for the night, but neither did I wish to intrude on the bower of a newly wed couple. But as I pondered, Ellen came forward to bid us stay in such warm tones that I accepted. 'Twould be no intrusion, she promised me, for a curtain was hung across half the room, and so Annie and I should have a space to ourselves.

I collected Annie, and we traipsed behind Ellen, making our way carefully in the dark. In her tiny house of rough timbers and twigs, a reed wick was burning in a pot of oil, providing just light enough for bedtime. Ellen found deerskins to cover the floor and thick woolen pallets to soften the bed, before slipping away to leave us alone. We both lay down, still cloaked and clothed, and I, exhausted from my trials, felt nothing more than warmth and comfort until the first rays of dawn crept in through the chinking.

Chapter Eight

I ROSE IN THE CLEAR AIR without waking Annie and slipped out to the robber camp, stretching my limbs as I went. There I was surprised to see that most of the band had already risen and sat breakfasting on brown loaves and water. The number of men astounded me, for here I saw three times as many as I had counted the night before. Where did they sleep? How did they manage a band of such size, all outlawed, all wanted, in the midst of the king's forest? Robin Hood, I thought, had time to do much more than jest, for it was he who made an easy life for all these men. I looked at them, at their scarred faces, and thought how much they must love him for it.

Well might I have dwelt on these fellows, for as I walked beneath the Greenwood tree, every eye seemed locked upon me, tracing my form, my figure, my face. Their attention made my movements stiff, and I was grateful when Robin Hood sought me out with a plate of bread, for he looked unperturbed by my presence, as if to have a fine lady in the midst of his camp were as commonplace as bees and honey.

"Your men give me an awkward feeling, good Robin Hood," I said to him. "They eye me like a cow at market or a pretty bauble they'd like to snatch."

"Aye," he answered with a grin, for he seemed to find my complaint amusing. " 'Tis the way of menfolk apart from their women. Any one of them would give two marks just for a look beneath your skirts."

This startled me, and I believe I gasped. My upbringing had been an odd one, sheltered and solitary, and it had not prepared me for such a fellow as Robin Hood. I blushed to my collar, so startled was I by his striking eye and ready smile. But what discomfited me even more was his willingness to give me individual attention, despite the mass of fellows about us. A more reticent man might have turned from me to join his men, but there was nothing reserved in my host; he was all brazen recklessness, as pert and salacious as Eros himself.

"Tell me, Mistress Lucy," he said with a smirk, as if no mention of my skirts had been made, "did your night in the forest pass away smoothly? Were you not frightened awake by strange sounds in the dark, by the hoot of an owl or the wind in the trees?"

I could see by now that he took pleasure in barbing. Mistress Lucy, indeed. I too, I thought, could play at that game.

"Nay, Sir Robin, no sounds troubled my sleep. But I did have a dream that stays with me still—of a lawman, tired and hungry in the wood, who followed the scent of cooked venison here. Have you no fear of being found out by the king's men? For if they cannot find you with their eyes, their stomachs would surely lead them here."

He laughed loud enough for the fish in the river to hear. "Now you're at it, Lady Lucy. This is the way to behave in Sherwood. Nay, I say, I fear not the hunger of the king's guard, for they never travel without bread and cheese. They know little of wanting food. But I am glad you were not troubled as you slept—'tis not many a woman who relishes a woodland sleep."

"When it is a matter of being tired, any bed will seem the softest in the world."

"Well said." He began to rise from where we sat. "Today my men and I will attempt to take your mysterious letter. You and Miss Annie may stay here with Ellen and pass the time however you like. Only, I pray you, shoot no arrows at any target while you are here. I would not have any of my men injured by a sharp lead point to the eye."

I made a pretense of laughing at this, though I laughed far less at his joke than he.

"You have my word on it, Robin Hood. I will not touch a single yew bow while I am here in your wooded camp. But I have been thinking," I said, lowering my tone. "Regarding this taking of the queen's letter, do you not think it would be best if the page had no notion which letter it was that your men wanted? What I mean to say is, could your men not seize them all and leave it to me to sort through and find the one meant for Lady Pernelle?"

"Certainly, if that is what you wish."

"And could the page be kept somewhere, a little far off but quite comfortable, so that once the letter is read through it and its fellows may be returned to him and he sent on his merry way? If we could keep Lady Pernelle from knowing that anyone bore an interest in her letter, it would be far better for me."

I saw him stiffen at my interference, but I cared little. These were important matters and the handling of this venture was not something to be left to chance.

"I had thought, Miss Lucy," he replied in a huff, "that we would make a pretense of taking up the page's purse so that he might suspect nothing more than a standard highway robbery. I trust this meets with your approval?"

"Very much so, I thank you, Robin Hood."

"Then I leave you here to enjoy the day. Ellen will take you under her wing if you wish to employ yourself in some way."

He nodded his head in a curt fashion and turned to go, thinking, I'm sure, that this was the first time an arrogant lady had told him his business as an outlaw.

ELLEN PROVED TO HAVE a sweet and open temper to match her shining face, and she took Annie and me on as her companions with all the generosity with which she had welcomed us to her bower at night. She was to spend the day picking early berries and fruits from the meadows downstream, and we were pleased to join her. The day was bright, the sun was warm, and Ellen's mirthful chatter filled our ears and made our walk seem but a trifle.

We soon found that the topic she loved to speak of best was her own recent marriage to Allan a Dale, the quiet minstrel. She told the tale in a piecemeal way that left us both confused at first, listening, as we were, with one ear only.

"Can you imagine how thrilling 'twas to enter the church there with my father and see him standing, awaiting me? My father was not pleased at all—oh no, he was furious!—but I was happy. Nay, my father turned quite red, purple even, for he wished me to marry *him*, you see." Here she mumbled something we could not hear. "But I just couldn't, for he was so old! More than sixty if he was a day and walked with a stick all the time. I cared little for his fine horses, I tell you, since having those would mean living a life with that old man and his thumping stick."

I was well occupied with enjoying the day, the sun on my back and our pleasant walk, and really did not care if I heard Ellen's story or not. But as she spoke I began to feel compelled to make some sense of her words even against my own inclination. And so, with a sigh, I sought to clarify.

"What old man was that?"

"Oh, Sir Simon of Trent, to be sure."

I ventured a guess.

"And he is the man your father wished you to wed?"

"Aye, he had fairly set his heart upon it, upon me being wed to a lord and all and made into a true lady. But so old, he was! And frail! And there at the church—I had my best gown on, you know, and an early rose twisted in my hair ever so nicely. And there at the church stood Allan and Robin Hood and Friar Tuck and every-one—and the old priest, he was there as well. And Robin Hood, ever bold as he is, he started jesting with the bishop till his face went all white, quite a sight beside my father and his red cheeks."

Here Ellen broke off into giggles, and again I felt compelled to stop her.

"A bishop was there as well?"

"Aye, the lord bishop of Heresford and with him came the prior of Emmet, his own self. They both of them came to observe the wedding, since Sir Simon was a lord and all with, oh, ever so many lands and estates." Again she mumbled something we could not discern. "And he said to me, 'Maid Ellen, do you wish to marry this old Sir Simon of Trent or your own Allan a Dale?' And of course I said Allan, for who would not?"

"Your father asked this question of you?"

"Nay!" she fairly squealed. "Robin Hood said it! He was trick-ing them all, you see, and Sir Simon fairly skipped away, hobbling on his stick as fast as he could go."

I looked at Annie and saw that we both felt this would not do. Here was a new tale of Robin Hood, being told us firsthand, and we could not comprehend two stalks out of the whole sheaf. I reached for Ellen and caught her hand.

"Sweet Ellen, pray tell, what was the state of things before you reached the church?"

"Well, I was in my best gown, a blue woolen one with a little rib-bon, and a new rose tucked into—"

"Yes, I'm sure you were a rose yourself. But what of your father and Sir Simon? Were you to marry the old lord?"

"Aye, that was what my father wished, for he wanted to see me made a lady with proper—"

"Yes, and you came to the church with the lord, your father, the bishop, and the prior?"

"Aye, and the bishop was so splendidly dressed! And his

horses—though they were a little slow, the one was a nice white milky color—but they were so lovely with bells and ribbons and all."

"And at the church, you met with Robin Hood and a band of his men?"

"So we did, so we did! Such a surprise. I gasped aloud, I know I did. There they were, Friar Tuck all dressed for church, and Little John with his sword pulled out. 'A shame on you, Sir Simon,' so said Robin, 'for wedding a girl against her will. How can ye do it, knowing full well that she loves another?' 'Twas a great shock to Sir Simon, yes indeed. He looked at the sword and at Little John and could not hobble off fast enough, nay, not fast enough, stick and all."

It took half the morning to draw the tale cleanly from her, and much of her gown and the rose in her hair had to be endured before we could understand it. But at last the scene in the church came clear, how Ellen arrived with her father's party of smug nobles to find Robin Hood placed in opposition with his green-clad Saxon force. Robin Hood scared the old groom away and placed the young couple together, to have one wedding in place of the other.

Little John had called out the banns there in the church, Robin paid Ellen's father one hundred marks in return for his blessing on the union, and the youths were wed. Ellen's happiness, as she told it, knew no bounds, though they might have reached the heights of ecstasy when Robin Hood convinced the bishop to give her his chain of beaten gold as a wedding present.

Convinced seemed a word often used in connection with Robin Hood, and I wondered with what level of force he bent the world to his own desires. But straight upon the heels of that thought, I imagined him away in pursuit of my letter and realized that I cared not how much force he used, just so he gained that one bit of parchment. Such hypocrisy shamed me, and I resolved not to question Robin Hood and his methods so long as I stood to gain from them.

THAT NIGHT THE BAND returned empty-handed, for, as Robin Hood supposed, the page had his orders not to ride on a Sunday and had kept himself in some cozy inn. Again fresh meat was roasted over open fires near the Greenwood tree, and again Robin Hood found a place beside me, pausing in his continual motion. For he, I noticed, was rarely still. He checked the fires, he checked the meat. He jested briefly with Friar Tuck, examined the fishnets in the river, paused to advise David of Doncaster on the proper waxing of his bowstring. As I watched the crowd, his green hood appeared first here, then there, tracing its way through the groups of men as if they were nothing more than saplings that he could bend apart to pass by.

At last he stopped and sat beside me, and for a strange moment we both sat in silence, unsure what topic to introduce. I recalled my day and Ellen's story and thought a compliment might make some amends for my offense of the morning.

"Ellen told us today how you managed to wed her to Allan a Dale. It seems she's indebted to you for her every happiness."

He laughed. "I trust Allan will take full responsibility for keeping her happy. I did it to please him, if you wish to know how it truly was, but I am glad to hear that she is well pleased in the bargain."

"I was surprised to hear that you found such ways to help the poor beyond a simple donation of pennies."

"If you think the donation of pennies so simple—"

"Nay, good sir, you mistake my meaning." I softened my tone. "I only meant that you had done good in an unusual way, and I was curious to hear of it."

" 'Twould be far better to have funds to give. The sheriff of Nottingham and the bishop of Heresford seem bent in competi-

tion to see which of them can squeeze the most out of the laborers here. 'Tis a sad affair, I tell you truly, to see the bishop's man
taking off a wife's last chicken or sack of grain."

"Indeed, taxation is a vicious thing. But if you had seen King
Richard's army as he left on crusade and known what funds it took
to raise it! The taxation must be hard to witness family by family,
but it is, I think, a necessity if we wish to have our land defended
and well ordered."

The instant the words had fled my mouth, I regretted them.
Surely the perplexed look on Robin Hood's face meant he had no
wish to enter into this conversation, for he looked as if he struggled to reconcile something at odds within himself.

"Forgive me," I said. "You must think it bold for a woman to
speak of such matters."

"If I did, Lady Marian, I would think that boldness a virtue
rather than a fault. Nay, in the common turn I do not discuss such
things with any person, man or woman. I find I need time to form
my thoughts. This much, though, I've thought out plainly. I've
naught to say against King Richard, for if he deems the holy lands
to be in peril of falling to infidels, then I say too that he is right.
But the taxation you may witness here has little to do with armies
and order. The housewife's hens are sold at market to buy another
jewel for the sheriff's cap and do little to keep her safe at night."

"But, even so, the king must allow his barons some benefit from
the odious task of collecting the tax. Much as I know he receives
from his lords, he cannot take all or his own barons would surely
rebel against his crown. Indeed, perhaps the fault may lie not with
the percentage of the tax he takes, but with his desire to raise so
much. Surely, he need not have traveled off on crusade before he
had lived one full year with the crown on his brow, although I do
think that if he were going, he needs must have taken the fullest
army he could muster. And that required a drastic increase in the
amount of the tax."

He turned to face me and spoke low, but I had the sense that this control of voice took great restraint, for he certainly felt for the subject with passion.

"This increase in tax has broken men's backs. I have seen families in winter without clothes to wear, banded twenty in a home to share wood for heat. Know ye, Lady Marian, that in this time of year most laboring people eat but one meal a day, and that of vegetable pottage only, as their grain is all gone? This time of great work, with plowing and sowing, is done by those almost too weak to stand, but too hungry to do otherwise. How can you say that this must happen for the king's crusade, when in Nottingham town sits a fat sheriff in silk and velvet, drinking Gascon wine and dining on pasties stuffed with suet and raisins? Who takes the last pennies from a villager's store to buy red-dyed linen trappings for his horse? I say to you that the king's war may be well or may be not, but the freedom he allows his barons and lords is not well at all. Were he here, no doubt, he would rein them in and cut their gluttonous behavior back."

I found this surprising, for I had no such notion that King Richard would restrict his barons were he nearer. If they were happy and gave him no grief, I was persuaded that he would be pleased and might be inclined to give them more freedom in the control of their lands rather than less.

"And so, as he is not here to do so, you undertake this task for him?"

"Someone must," he grumbled, and soon he rose again and disappeared into the dimming light of evening.

I FOUND MYSELF, on the following day, thinking often of Robin Hood, tracing back through our debates to follow a path not taken, an argument missed in the flash of the moment. I wished more than anything for a second chance to argue things out with him, for I had very few worthy opponents, and I loved a debate as nothing else. I feared, however, that he took our disagreements more personally than he ought, for after each he seemed compelled to pace a while about the camp, as if he needed time in which to compose himself enough to return.

Annie and I spent this day helping Ellen collect small twigs and branches for kindling fires, and this time, since we knew the tale, her prattling did not bother our ears. She was, indeed, a cheerful soul who loved nothing better than to recant every particular of her wedding day, and we were willing to nod and smile through a second day's telling of her blue gown and the early rose. Without giving her tale a whit of attention, we murmured at all the proper places, though, in truth, she did not even need that slight encouragement.

That night Robin Hood's band returned early, for they had intercepted the page and seized the contents of his prized satchel. Annie and I went running to meet them along with the men remaining in camp, our mouths full of praises for their brave deeds. Robin Hood, smiling broadly at his success, thrust a sack brimming with letters in my direction.

"Your mail, Lady Marian, has arrived."

I smiled and thanked him and was desperate to ask what had become of the page, but I dared not risk offending him while the precious letter lay in my hands. I held my tongue and contented myself with pawing through the leather bag until I found a piece of parchment addressed to Lady Pernelle of Sencaster, sealed with the royal mark of three stacked lions, swimming in wax.

Taking the letter near the fire to warm the seal, I gently pried the wax oval back and unfolded the stiff sheet. I let my eye pass over the start, filled with salutations and courtly niceties, but when I saw the letter's purpose, read its message once and twice, I sat back, hardly noticing that the letter had fallen to my lap. In another moment Robin Hood came close to peer at me, for I suppose my face had gone so white he may have feared for my life or wits.

"What is it, Lady Marian? Does it bear bad news?"

I said nothing, only held the letter out to him, but he would not take it. His eyes moved quickly from letter to ground, and he said with a harsh voice, "I cannot read it, so do not give it to me."

I blushed at my mistake and fumbled with the sheet before me, sorry to have given him pain. "It says," I said, lowering my face under pretense of reading again, "it says the queen grants her permission for me to marry Sir Stephen of Sencaster, Lady Pernelle's only living son."

He sat beside me and fiddled a moment with a tear in his legging.

"Forgive my ignorance, Lady Marian, but does this truly come as a surprise? You told me yourself you were sure the queen meant to marry you to some noble man. Is this Sir Stephen so very bad?"

"Nay, you misunderstand my reaction. 'Tis not Stephen—he is but a boy, no more than twelve or fourteen at most." My hand fluttered above the sheet in an effort to make him understand. "I told you I was wed before. But I did not tell you that it was to Hugh of Sencaster that I was married, Lady Pernelle's older son. Hugh died in the court of Anjou and on his death Lady Pernelle sought to have that marriage annulled, meaning that I lost my dower, my right as a widow to part of Hugh's property. The queen agreed and sided against me, and I was left without. I barely regained my own lands."

"So it seems to you as if Lady Pernelle wants your lands attached to hers at all costs?"

"I do not know, it seems so strange. After she was so cruel to me at court when Hugh died, I am stunned to hear she should want me back. Perhaps there are no marriageable ladies available now? But they cannot be in a rush to marry Stephen away, so young as he is. I do not know what to think."

"Has she no other reason to want your lands in particular? Are they adjoining hers or of some special value?"

"They are near hers but do not touch. And I do not believe they are of any significant value beyond the grain they grow and the lambs they support."

Again Robin Hood's face looked queer. "Do you manage these lands yourself, Lady Marian?"

"Nay, since I was a child they have been governed by my regent, a Sir Thomas Lanois. 'Tis strange, but I know little of him. He is cousin to Lady Pernelle. I believe she appointed him when I was still married with Hugh."

"Perhaps all she wishes is to let this Sir Thomas remain where he is. If you were wedded to another man, he would give Sir Thomas the boot, would he not?"

"Yes, I suppose you are right. But Stephen is her only remaining son. Would she waste his one chance at marriage to keep her cousin in his place? Perhaps, perhaps she would. I honestly cannot venture to guess what Lady Pernelle has in mind. She is an enigma to me."

I fell into a deep reverie, lost in my own thoughts of Lady Pernelle and her odd behavior, for truly, with all the guesses I'd had of the contents of this letter, its actual information was some I had never imagined. Robin Hood wandered off, seeing, I supposed, that he could not assist me, and I was left alone to ponder. But my thoughts were old; they stayed to their path and cycled round, never providing anything fresh, never reaching a finishing point.

At last I grew frustrated and shook myself, forcibly occupying the paths of my mind with the task of resealing the letter and placing it back within its bag. This I took to Robin Hood and thanked him again for having brought it to me.

"Pray, do not thank me more, Lady Marian. My rugged ears cannot take such soft words." The sack was given to Will Stutley with orders to lead the page to his road and send him lightly on his way. "Perhaps a bit of sport will suit you this evening," Robin Hood said, turning back to grin at me. "I will take care to place you close to the action, so your weak Norman eyes may make it all out."

For once a distraction did seem welcome, and I smiled and thanked him for it. And so, while the venison cooked and the pullets turned helplessly on their spits, garlands were hung on far-off trees as targets for the archers. Closer to us, men warmed up their wooden cudgels by knocking them in practice against their neighbors'. Soon regular matches began, and Robin Hood, scarcely able to keep his seat, shouted out encouragement and advice.

"There y'are now, Little John! Excellent parry, Gilbert! Watch your crown as you go, we want no broken pates this evening. Keep the feet moving, Little John, or he'll knock you o'er, you bet he will. Go on, Gilbert! More force into that crack and you'd have had your man down flat already."

I watched their sticks flying and knocking, one against the other, and sat amazed. So fast they moved and with such surety! Rap, rap, rap—each knock with the cudgel was strong enough to break a bone or stun a man, if the placement were good.

When they had finished, and Little John had succeeded at last in tripping Gilbert to the ground, Robin Hood glanced at me and grinned.

"If I knew no better, I would say you were enjoying yourself, Lady Marian. But I thought you did not like viewing sport?"

"Well, perhaps you were right," I said, laughing, "when you said there was no better in all of England than in your grove. I do not believe I have ever witnessed sticks flying so fast."

"And you may never again, that is the truth. But now we shall have some shooting, and that'll be less pleasing to you, as the target must be a good twenty yards off. But you may trust that when I shoot, I'll hit the mark, and you can envision it in your mind's eye and cheer for me all the same." He grinned wickedly and strode off, flexing his bow as he went, preparing it for the confining string.

In honesty, I did not know what to make of Robin Hood. He seemed so foreign to what I knew, and yet I found myself fascinated by his manner, charmed by his odd ways. I knew that tomorrow Annie and I must be gone, riding home to live as we had before. Robin Hood would recede then to memory and to legend, and I would be a solitary bird once more.

He shot his arrows like a cocky fellow, looking at me with a saucy smile before loosening his bowstring. Every arrow found its mark—this I knew from the cheers around me—and Robin Hood shot as long as they cheered, until no more arrows remained in his quiver. When the men brought forth Robin's targets, all stuck with goose quills, I saw in amazement that he had not used the garlands of ivy the others shot at, but a peeled stick no thicker than my thumb, which was bound to the trunk of a far-off tree.

When he had finished, Robin Hood strode back to where I sat and threw himself down on the grass. He grinned like a hound who has just retrieved its first bird, touching upon the ecstatic joy it finds in being such a hound. Robin Hood shone with pleasure, with pride, with shooting as well as he knew he could—with, in that sense, the pure wonder at being a man.

He reclined on his elbows and stretched his legs out before him, but he would not be still. He rolled on one arm to look at me, then back to see what his men were doing, then away toward his quill-stuck target. A less discerning observer might have called him impatient, but I thought I knew better. He was happy, or better, he was delighted. It must have some continuance, some expression in his very posture.

"Indeed, Robin Hood," I said, thinking I might humor him, "you are as good a shot as the legends say. How did you come by such a skill?"

"Oh," he said, smiling brightly, his cheeks warmed from his sport, "I have practiced with bows since I was a lad. 'Tis a simple game when there is no wind, is that not so, my merry friends?"

The men nearby him cheered and laughed, clearly pleased to see their leader outshoot them all. I wondered then at this strange dynamic of three score men living in the forest, dependent on one for their plans and survival. Robin Hood kept them safe from the law, and in return they did his bidding and seemed quite happy to do so. I wondered how it would be to be outlawed, to never perhaps visit home again, to never go forth without disguise. It seemed to me that the revels in this camp were made all the brighter by the bleakness of an outlaw's situation. To be wanted by the king could mean an end to life, but these few had found a respite, a reprieve, and they enjoyed these hours of freedom with every smile and laugh they could muster.

In another moment Robin Hood leapt to his feet to check on the meal and fetch some water, and I watched him make his way through the crowd, greeting his men and passing jests to any who left themselves open to teasing. Little John, I had noticed, often took the brunt of his wit, but he bore the words with a shy smile and did not seem offended by his friend.

When the meat was finished, Robin Hood returned, calmer and in a more restful mood. We dined together, and as we ate he pressed me on my future plans, making me ashamed to admit that I had few plans to share.

"Do you think you will wed this Sir Stephen, as the queen decrees?"

"I do not see that I have much choice, unless some catastrophe should strike and save me at the final hour."

"You could run, or better yet, now that you are away you could simply not return."

I had thought on that and was sorely tempted, but my fear of the king's troops was too great. "I would be caught, I fear, if I were to hide here as you do. The arts of disguise, I think, are not among my skills."

"And so you shall marry him?"

"I do not know. I can see few other options before me. If I wed Stephen I lose my freedom and my lands; if I hide away I lose only freedom. Perhaps I may flee if I have the nerve."

"But why return at all if you think you may decide later to flee?"

"If I do not return to Warwick, Lord William will send his men to hunt me. If I remain here, I hate to think what could become of you and your men when I am found out. And too, I cannot help but believe I may devise some plan yet that will make the queen forget about me, now and forever. Some scheme may still save me, and until I have had the time to think all these factors out, I will not go into hiding and make myself the queen's enemy. If she thinks I am obedient, I have better odds of deceiving her later."

"Aye, that is certainly true. Once you are marked as the king's enemy or the queen's, many a door is closed to you. 'Tis a pity, though."

"Why is that, pray?"

"Your Norman men know little of how to please a lady, this I've observed in my day. And a Norman boy!" He shook his head, but I saw that he glanced sidelong at me. "You deserve a hale fellow, Lady Marian, one who will tame your vixen ways."

"Tame me!"

"Nay, nay, I've misspoken. 'Twould be a shame to lessen your fire by one degree. Nay, you've need of a robust fellow, a right hearty lad who will take you firmly onto his knee and keep you there till you sing with delight. You've need of a Saxon, mark my words. You'll find no match among your own sort."

I opened my mouth to retort, to claim that my father had been a Norman or perhaps to express my shy admiration of Lord William. But a second's thought made me fall silent, for in truth I could think of no Norman man who'd caught my fancy the way this woodland rogue had done. This perplexed me beyond all measure, and I could not speak for some minutes, so stunned was I by his brash manner.

We sat in silence after that, each mired deep in private thoughts. A sack of new ale came round, and we both drank. Then, as a habit, I loosened a few drops onto the ground. Robin Hood saw me do it.

" 'Tis a strange Saxon custom for you to observe, Mistress Lucy."

"What is? Oh, the little libation. Annie has taught me well, don't you think?" I smiled and reddened, though I knew not why. "I suppose you might say 'tis my gift to the mother or to Diana—whatever name she goes by here."

"We called her Dame Hilda in my youth, but you may use your Latin names if you prefer. There is no shame in the old religions."

"Well, I do not think our rector would agree with you. He speaks at length against paganism and the evils of pantheistic thought."

"And yet you spill your drops regardless?"

I laughed. "Aye, that I do. I do not like to be told by others what is right and what is wrong."

"Perhaps I have been mistaken, Lady Marian, in thinking you are such a Norman. You seem quite Saxon underneath."

"Or perhaps," I said, in retort, "I am just as much of a Norman as ever, and 'tis the Normans themselves you have underestimated."

Chapter Nine

I HAD BEEN ASHAMED to tell Robin Hood that I had no plan for saving myself, for what fool returns to the lion's cage without ropes and pry bars for her escape? But I had one idea. In all my thinking, my mind had hit upon one truth time and again. It came from the tale of Pyramus, who, thinking his lady Thisbe dead, took his own life for sorrow. 'Twas a bloody veil and rent cloths that made him consider the false to be true—this delusion held me fixated, for it seemed to contain the whole of my salvation. If I could somehow weave the illusion of my own death I might free myself not only from the threat of this marriage, but from all future weddings the queen might plan. The idea was drastic, and my heart recoiled from the very thought, but it was the only way I had discovered to regain my sad life to my own control.

Through less extreme measures I might, surely, escape from this marriage, but what would that gain me? If I did not marry Stephen, I would be sent next to wed William or Jack or Miles. I could see there would be no end to it, for the king must have his funds and must use me to increase his influence in this country. I should speak, rather, of the desires of the queen, for while Richard crusaded under the holy white cross in Palestine, she ruled his lands in his stead.

Given this reality, how could I not consider the most radical plan? It meant the sure loss of Denby-upon-Trent, for a woman widely supposed to be dead could not attempt any claim on property. But somehow my lands, which once seemed the only thing I owned of value, had become worthless when I placed them alongside a life of tedium in Sencaster. My journey to Sherwood had made it plain that I was suited to a life of action, of fresh air and novelty, not the stilted warmth of Lady Pernelle's fire. Now that I had faced her treachery, how could I, in faith, condemn myself to do her bidding all of my days, as an honorable daughter must rightly do?

Nay, I could not, and if this stance meant the loss of my lands, that was a fate I would have to endure. For what use were lands if I could not live in them and manage them for myself? I now saw that, dear as it was, Denby and its delights were shackles as well, making me a pawn in the queen's great game. Without it I was freed from playing.

But the problem remained of staging this theatrical death, and for that I held a whispered conference with Annie late at night as we lay on our skins in the woodland bower.

"Annie," I hissed at her dozing face. "Annie, wake up! I must speak with you."

She yawned and nodded with the sluggishness of a human body long deserted by its dreaming mind. "Speak as ye will, Lady Marian, and"—she paused a moment to yawn audibly—"I will listen."

"Do you recall telling me, when I was young, of old Dame Selga who lived in the great wood near Wodesley village? The woman who brewed potions of love for your friend Mildred and helped Dick the Smith place a charm on his fields so earth that had been sterile and barren began to produce?"

"Sure, I know of Dame Selga. You know how I told you I once saw her house when I went with Polly, fetching wood from the forest."

"Good, yes, I remember. Annie, I wish you to take me to her when we leave this wood tomorrow. Will you do it?"

With a jerk and twitch Annie was fully awake, propped on one elbow, giving me a sharp look.

"Why should ye wish to see Dame Selga? What would ye want with an old woman such as her?"

"I would speak with her, if I may. 'Tis important, Annie."

"Has this to do with the letter you read today of the queen? Has it to do with your being sent to marry young Sir Stephen?"

"Yes, it does, of course it does. She may be able to help me, may give some good advice. And I think, Annie, you had best help me too, for have you thought on what will happen if that marriage comes off?"

"Nay—what do you mean?"

"Only this: that once wed, I will be taken to Sencaster, not left in Warwick Castle as I was before. You know this, for I am of age now and should be living in my husband's court. And if I go, do you think Lady Pernelle will allow you to go there with me? She might at first, as a kind of gift to her new daughter, but you know she would not keep you long. She keeps no servants from outside her own estates, you know that, 'tis a point of pride she never fails to express. And if that happens, what will you do, Annie? I'll be in no power to help you, not as bride to young Stephen."

I heard her gasp throughout this speech, and though it pained me to paint this picture of sorrow to her, I felt it necessary. She could not go blindly home, attend me happily in this marriage, not knowing it would alter her life as much as mine. As painful as it was to open her eyes to the harsh light of day, I felt obliged to do it.

"I had not considered it," she said at last, laying her head back down. "Oh, Lady Marian, at times this seems a wretched life."

"Indeed it does, Annie, indeed it does."

We were both quiet, each spinning her skein's worth of thoughts in the dark, until she spoke at last.

"I will take ye to Dame Selga, if that is where ye wish to go."

"Thank you, my friend," I said, reaching out to press her hand. "Thank you."

A HOST OF FELLOWS came to bid Annie good-bye the next morning, standing about to hold her horse's bridle or tie bundles behind her saddle. Robin Hood came to wish me well, catching my hand in his in something between a handshake and a squeeze. In this morning light, with a cool breeze brushing against my cheeks, my heart soared and opened, felt larger than its mortal cage. I would miss him, I thought, watching his blue eyes as they watched mine. Something in his laughing way awakened a depth in me, an awe, and I had to turn my face away to cover emotions I did not understand.

"As your kin might say, adieu, Lady Marian."

I turned and caught his smile and felt my own face lift in response. I thought of his "Miss Lucy" and the pleased look on his face when he had shot well the night before, and I grinned with all the joy in my heart. I clucked to my mare and we started forward, walking away from the most generous outlaw I ever expected to meet.

Annie and I rode slowly through the forest, scarcely noticing the birds and their love songs, so lost were we in our own cloudy thoughts. The day seemed to echo our disposition, for thin sheets of fog swirled about our skirts, making the road bright and damp with mud. But at every turn Annie faithfully steered us to the southwest, toward Dame Selga and her forest cottage.

I had already determined that we could safely stop at an inn that night, though I do not know what part my memories of the Wodesley ceiling rats played in my rational weighing of consequences. I am sure it was great. But even, I argued to myself, were we to be caught at an inn near Sherwood, miles from Denby, it would not be such a crime. We had clearly left our guards behind, flying forth in search of adventure—that was to be our explanation when we returned to the world of rules and dependence. So I had planned that we had time to visit Dame Selga, then ride to Warwickshire to sleep the night in the Dog and Partridge, an inn we had spotted on our way.

The morning passed smoothly into day, as it often does in June, and we grew close to the wise woman's cottage, a dwelling half-buried by a thick ring of forest. The wood in which her cottage lay was crossed by two paths that ran at cross purposes to one another. Dame Selga, as one might expect, lived at the meeting place of these two paths.

Annie grew nervous as we approached, reverting to her girlhood fears of fairies and goblins and man-eating beasts. I too had been raised on tales of Dame Selga and her mysterious dark powers. But I struggled to calm my heart and keep my wits sharp about me by commanding them to observe carefully all that passed in the wood around us.

I noticed, through this attentive state, a change in the forest as we neared, for dark though the canopy made the land, plants and flowers twined together here with an unexpected burst of verdure. Exotic vines climbed English oaks and twisted together with ivy and mistletoe. Blooms in brilliant red and gold shared earth with flags and forget-me-nots. Strange birdcalls floated to my ears, and though it was neither cold nor dark, I shivered deep inside my cloak.

Presently we entered a clearing, and in it stood Dame Selga's cottage, small and neat. Wisps of smoke curled from the lone window, hinting that someone was at home, so I turned to Annie and whispered loud, "Call to her, won't you?"

Annie looked pale as linen, but she raised her voice to call out "Dame Selga! Dame Selga!" a time or two. Her calls were answered by a leggy hound who dashed out to inspect our horses and smell our boots. We passed his test, it seemed, for he proved friendly, knocking his head beneath Annie's hand for a pat or two. While she obliged him and we dismounted, I saw an old woman in a wool smock and black apron come forth from the house, making her way with slow easy steps in our direction.

Leading my horse, I approached her also, for it seemed to me that most of her visitors must shy away, and she might be pleased by a change in attitude. When she reached hearing distance I called to her.

"We are sorry to trouble you, Dame Selga, but I come in hope of your advice."

She said nothing but hobbled on, never pausing until she stood a young tree's breadth away from me. She was small, shrunken even, for her head did not rise above my shoulders, but her face was pleasantly soft and wide, and I relaxed upon meeting her eyes. We had nothing to fear from her, of this I was instantly certain.

She grasped my hand, but instead of shaking it, she rolled it over and spread it flat, brushing the palm with three of her fingers. I held quite still, feeling almost that she was a bird I wished to observe and would not frighten away with breathing if I could help it.

At last she spoke, and I realized then that it was her voice that had terrorized the children of Annie's village and brought them to nightmares in the dark. Her tone somehow ranged between a shrill cry and gravelly coarseness, possibly the result of smoking the pipe I saw peeking forth from her apron pocket.

"Welcome, daughters, welcome." She walked to Annie, who nearly twitched from fear, and, brushing her palm as she had mine, Dame Selga said, "Ye come not both of ye for my advice, is it right or is it wrong?"

Annie began to stammer silently, but I spoke as clearly as I could. "It is right, grandmother. Only I wish to hear your advice today."

"Then enter with me, child, and we shall see what there is to see. Ye can wait out here," she said with a gesture to Annie, who looked, in truth, as though she might faint. I tried my best to catch her eye as I followed the old woman, but she had sunk down onto a log and was patting the dog with all her heart.

Dame Selga's cottage was dark and smoky as Annie's family's had been, but this time I was prepared. She led me in with quiet ceremony and showed me to a three-legged stool, close to the fire. When I was seated she grasped my chin with her gnarled hand, tipping it up so she could look close, though, indeed, the light in the cottage was quite dim. At last she dropped my chin.

"I do not know ye," she said heavily, seating herself on a wooden chest. "Tell me yer name."

"I am Marian Fitzwater of Denby-upon-Trent."

She nodded, mulling this over. "I have never been to Denby."

"Nay," I said, "it is many miles from here."

She thought another moment, then turned to me, quick as a wink, her eyes sharp with intensity.

"How do ye know of me and my living here? Tell me, lass, how do ye know it?"

"The one waiting outside, Annie Bailey, was raised in Wodesley and told me of you. She brought me here when she heard of my need, as a friend only. Truly, Dame Selga, we have never spoken of you to another soul."

This seemed to calm her, and she returned to her original posture of tranquil contemplation.

"And what do ye wish of me, Maiden Marian?"

Here we were at the difficult part. I hesitated to ask it straight, for perhaps what I sought could not be made.

"I do not know the value of what I seek, or even if it is possible—"

"Ask it, Marian, do not jabber on."

Chastised, I took a breath and did my best to come to the point.

"I wish to appear to have died without in fact having done so. I wish to seem as if I am dead, but for a short time only."

This caught her attention and again she turned her sharp eye on me. " 'Tis a strange request, Mistress Marian. Are ye not a noble lady? How can ye have such a need to deceive as this?"

I let out a sigh of exasperation without meaning to do so. "Everyone assumes that noblewomen have no problems, just because they do not want for bread. 'Tis far the reverse, if I may say so. My need for deception is very great indeed, greater perhaps than a dairy maid's might ever be."

She nodded and said nothing, but brought a small bowl of twigs and forest duff and placed it in my hands.

"Cast three pinches into the fire and let me see what there is to see."

I did as she asked and with each throw the fire leapt up in a cloud of sparks, frightening me, for Dame Selga had leaned so close I feared she might have her nose singed. But when I had finished she sat back in silence, looking no more sooty than she had before.

"I have a powder that ought to be what you seek." She stood slowly and began to rummage within her chest, examining bottles and vials by the low firelight. "Ye have a wish to remain as Diana, do ye not? Maiden still though ye be of age to be wed?"

Her reference to my favorite character of Ovid's tales surprised me, but then I supposed she was well versed in every array of god and magic.

"I do not wish to marry one I have not chosen. Surely you see many a maid with that same complaint?"

"Ah, yes, who to marry, who not to marry, 'tis all the young ones seem to think of."

"Do you not, then, think it so important?"

She paused a moment, tipping her faded face to one side. "Aye, 'tis important, I suppose. But I had never seen a noblewoman with such a complaint before."

This seemed to catch her fancy, so I tried to explain as I had to Robin Hood that while a farmer's daughter might decline to marry the man her father chose for her, a noblewoman had no such voice. I spoke at length and told her too of my childhood marriage to Hugh, and by the time I had finished she was seated beside me, clasping a glass bottle between her fingers.

"This is for you to use as ye will," said her gravelly voice as she pressed the bottle into my hand. "Mix this with water and drink it down, and you will appear cold and breathless for a full night's passing. But after that time ye will awaken, so plot your work most carefully."

In all my talking I had somehow forgotten what it was I had come for, and to have it now, in my very hand, filled me with wonder and gratitude.

"Thank you, grandmother," I whispered to her. "What can I give in exchange for this?"

"Oh, silver, if ye have it," she laughed, grinning hollowly, for she had very few teeth remaining. "Even an old woman must eat."

"And smoke a full pipe," I said with a smile, placing a sack of ten silver pieces onto her lap. "I will keep your secret, grandmother, and tell nary a soul where to find you."

"Good day, child. Keep your wits sharp about ye." She turned her face back to her fire, and I left her smoky cottage, a glass bottle now heavy in my purse where my silver marks had been before.

ANNIE SEEMED CALMER when I reached her, and we mounted our horses in silence. But after we had ridden barely a mile, she turned to me, her face still pale.

"Just tell me this, Lady Marian. Are ye or are ye not going to kill him?"

"Kill who? Stephen? Oh, Annie, no, no, I shall not."

"Then . . . ?"

"If I am brave enough to use what Dame Selga has given me, I promise to warn you of it well in advance. And do calm yourself. No one will die from her powder. Its affects are temporary, she assures me.".

My words calmed Annie, but I must admit they did little to settle my nervous heart. I liked Dame Selga and trusted her well, but I was not sure my trust ran deep enough to warrant drinking down her powder. I thought of myself, lying cold and breathless, while lords and ladies gathered round to mourn, and a cold spot opened within my belly which refused to be made warm again. Each time the bottle swung against my side, the cold place deepened, and I wondered if I would have the nerve to drink when the moment came.

But I had gained the powder, I assured myself, and that had been my only goal. The decision that lay before me could be made at any point. I had the powder, but if I chose, I need not drink it, now or ever.

WE PASSED THAT NIGHT at the Dog and Partridge, sleeping sound in wide beds, dining on wheat bread and wine. The following day we left for home, preparing to face our angry guards. My lips were already laced with the tale I would tell of having slipped northward on a whim to see Denby's fields in summer, burdened with their golden bounty.

Riding homeward that day I realized, through the preoccupied state of my mind, that I felt a tremendous relief in the notion of returning to my comfortable room. This journey had been filled with newness at every turn, and while I had tried be at ease in each situation, I had in truth been waddling with the awkward gate of a seafowl placed on land. At last my steps were turned to my own safe inlet, and I welcomed it with a quivery lip and a thirsting heart.

But on my arrival I found, sadly, that home had changed in my

absence, or perhaps it was my own eyes that swung now from a different angle, allowed in more color and less light. The chamber I
had known from childhood—nay, from babyhood—had become
skewed. The bed seemed brighter, the walls more firm and con-
strained in dimension. My shoes on the floor beat out a new sound,
and even Annie, steady Annie, looked suddenly foreign in this place
where she had reigned in my eyesight for all of my life.

"How odd these old walls look!" I breathed, knowing my words
did little justice to the tumult that I felt.

"Aye, there's naught like a journey to put a fresh tinge on
things," she said cheerfully, setting to her work with the wisp of a
song.

What she said was true, but it did not touch the center of what
lay so heavy in my heart. I thought of our beds on the journey, the
straw mattress of Wodesley village and the skins and wool of Sherwood Forest. Between those and my box bed seemed a chasm so
great I could not see across. Here I lived in my own room with a
constant fire and every comfort. What luxury I had always known!
How I should hate to exchange this bed for a narrow place on the
Bailey straw ticking!

I thought of Annie and the many times she had come from village to castle, leapt across that chasm as if it were but a trifling
ditch. And now it seemed that the journey across and back had
affected even this place. By traveling in those foreign lands I had
hardened the comforts of this world and given their richness a bitter taste, like metal and sulfur, sticking on the tip of my tongue.

part two

"To walk in the wood"

Chapter Ten

THIS STRANGE SENSE of dullness, of having tarnished what had been glowing, continued for weeks. I moved through my world like a fish in a pot, not recognizing a single face or feeling that I knew what my hands were doing. With silent eyes and a gaping mouth I marveled over the richness of the very eating knives at mealtime, the opulence with which Lord William cast off meats that were displeasing. I saw with new vision the woven tapestries in the great hall, the masterpiece of scarlet dye that Lord William's wife had commissioned from across the channel. In my youth it was the first scarlet fabric I had ever seen, and while red-dyed cloth was more common now, it was scarcely less dear. A hanging of that vast dimension would surely trade for a foursome of horses or several cottages of the sort Annie's family shared.

But what amazed me most in the weeks that followed our return from the wood was the ease with which I took up my old life again, the comfort with which my hand grasped the spoon and lifted the gem-studded goblet to my lips. I knew this world and it was easy; I had encountered another that was far more difficult. Why, then, did I not rejoice to be returned to comfort and ease? Why did I not allow myself to fall back to my earlier ways, as ought to have been simple to do?

At nights I lay in my downy bed and could not banish thoughts of Bess or of fair Ellen and how well they would love to change places with me. By day I saw a youth sporting with his hounds and thought of Riccon; I saw a fine lute and wondered how pleased Allan a Dale would be to own it. Then at last one night as I lay awake I saw that I was feeling guilt for my soft place. For I now knew those who bore a far harder lot, and this tainted the pleasure I was able to feel.

Too, my odd sensation may have had something to do with the uncertainty of my future, an uncertainty that kept me full of dread and allowed no peace. Day and night I forced my weary mind to consider every alternative, search for each hidden option, anything, anything that might keep me from swearing vows with Stephen. I had, for once, leisure to think, but the more I pondered, the more it seemed that I had no choices beyond a wedding or Dame Selga's white powder.

I could not flee, not on my own, for I had no notion of where I might go or how I might live beyond Warwick's walls. My every choice seemed to include a loss of Denby, and so, sad at heart as it made me, I began to think of it less as mine and more as some distant fairy land, desired by all but owned by none.

BEFORE THE LEONINE WINDS of July had floated to my chamber window, pages from Sencaster and London town brought me notice of my upcoming marriage to Sir Stephen, and a date was set for the wedding service. I was, I found, to have three weeks in which to conjure up some solution, though two weeks passed in the blink of an eye while I did nothing more than sit in my chamber, cradling the glass bottle in my palm. I felt at once paralyzed and fluid, for while I could not summon new thought or move myself to decide on some action, I also floated on the tide of time, lapping ever closer to my wedding day.

But lest you should assume that my lack of options caused me to become less observant, I ought to report that in this time I could not fail to make one comparison, which gave me much food for later thought. Watching Lord William interact with his under-barons, knights, and nobles, I was struck by the arrogance of their manners, the contempt with which they seemed to address their own overlord. This was not the way of the Sherwood yeomanry. Nay, those men trusted Robin Hood to be their better and gave him their loyalty because he proved himself so. Lord William had proven nothing beyond how well he was loved by the present king, and considering the twists of royal politics, I counted this as no great accomplishment.

Lord William's place was tenuously held; Robin Hood's was held through love and earned respect. The distinction was paramount and its repercussions now flooded my eyes and ears to such an extent that I chastised myself for not having noticed it before. Rumors of Lord William's weakness were everywhere present in his court. It mattered not if he overtaxed or undertaxed, if he coddled one noble or another, the result was always the very same. In his best moments he was thought a simpleton, in which case his lessers were well occupied with plotting to overthrow him; in his worst he was a tyrant, hated for clutching his power too tightly and mistrusted at every turn.

Why was this? I asked myself. Was it the result of a ruling class that allows its king to select its leaders, rather than a more democratic approach? Perhaps it was, but I could not free myself from the thought that war was the true enemy that forced the circumstance, for without the nobles, a nation at war would have no barons to summon, no standing armies to call to its aid. A locally elected noble might hesitate to raise an army from among his peers. But then I thought on the Sherwood men and doubted my own reasoning, for surely they had the makings there of as fine an army as one could wish for, and I scarcely thought that Robin Hood would pause in sending his men to battle simply because they were his fellows.

These thoughts of Robin Hood piled a second sphere of confusion onto my already taxed mind, so I pushed him as far from my waking thoughts as I could manage. My dreams he might, and did, invade, but I kept him barred from my calculations. This was a feat of which I was quite proud. But in hindsight it may have been this very act of turning away that kept me from determining for myself what my fate ought to be.

WHEN NEARLY ALL of my three weeks had passed, a group from Sencaster arrived in great splendor, showing their colors to the best advantage. Lady Pernelle rode at the fore, followed close by her remaining son and his host of squires. I saw all this from my chamber window, for I had been placed there to cleanse and prepare myself for the new life I should undertake beneath the eyes of God and the absent king.

My feelings toward Lady Pernelle were as clouded as ever, and they were not made less so by an interview we had the night before my slated marriage. She came to my chamber, speaking in soft tones and petting my hair.

"Dear Marian, how good it is to see you again. And how lovely you look, my own daughter. I declare you appear to have aged somewhat since I last saw you. I hope your time of mourning offered ample moments of prayer and introspection?"

"Indeed, Lady Pernelle, I also feel that I have aged greatly since we met in London." I kindly said nothing of how she had aged, for I was on my best behavior.

"It pleases me greatly to welcome you a second time into our family. I trust that, with the conclusion of this marriage, you will remove from Warwick to Sencaster Manor, to reside there with Stephen and myself?"

"I shall do as you wish, Lady Pernelle, in this as in all things."

This brought a smile to her lips and made me hope she had forgotten our skirmish over my dower.

"Very well, that is what I wish. We shall all be one family, as we were before. Stephen is quite ecstatic to see you."

"And I him."

She prattled on about how Stephen had grown, about how he was loved by other boys his age, and his delight in his hounds and hawks. As she spoke, a constriction grew within my ribs, and I had to command my lungs to move, to heave my chest up and down so the air could flow. Robin Hood had asked me why I did not simply marry Stephen, as I would have to marry some man, and at the time I had not known the answer myself. But now I saw it, in blazing letters. Lady Pernelle had become my enemy, she made herself such in the London court, and this was now a battle between us. I might marry—truly, it appeared I would have to—but I stubbornly refused to wed as Lady Pernelle wished it, not if I could discover an exit.

That night I sat with my bottle of powder until tears trickled down my cheeks, for hot though my hatred for Lady Pernelle burned, my fear of this powder was proving stronger. The cold place that formed after seeing Dame Selga had refused to vanish. It had, in fact, grown in depth and quality each time my reckless imagination saw a vision of myself lying dead, or nearly so, and nothing I could do would warm the place. I thought of myself mixing the potion, drinking it down in a fit of haste, but the vision made me shiver so violently the bottle slipped from my hand and nearly smashed against the grate.

This was the hour, but I could not do it. My fear of the powder, of its possible failing, was greater, far greater, than my hatred for Lady Pernelle. Sobbing aloud, I pulled my wrap close about me, desperate for some feeling of warmth, but none came. I would not drink the potion down, I would not feign my own death, and yet the cold place still remained. For in the place of my fear of the white powder lay a dread of marriage to my dead husband's brother and a life of servitude to his mother.

I thought on Sherwood and the freedoms of the forest and felt my heart grow tight with sorrow. I should never see that place again nor, most likely, my own lands. Robin Hood's words came to me once more, asking why I did not flee, but even as the thought passed through me, I slipped from my stool onto the floor, exhausted by fear and my sense of impotence. I buried my face in the floor-piled rushes and wept until Annie came and put me to bed.

DURING THE NIGHT a summer storm slipped overhead, lancing the sky with bolts of fire from Jove's great chest of arms. I awoke to rain, dressed to rain, said my morning prayers to rain, and could not help but think the sky had heard the tears falling in my heart and painted them on its larger canvas. I was as broken of spirit as any wild mule made to haul a cart, and I stood, compliant, drooping in my unbreakable harness.

I was sent to make my final confession, for every bride must sweep the cobwebs from her soul before taking her marriage vows. Lady Pernelle, escorting me below to the chapel's confessional, told me herself that she had arranged for me to pass a full hour's breadth with the rector. Perhaps she saw into my guilty heart and knew how much time would be required to purify my devious mind.

Scarcely hearing or seeing the world, I entered the confessional and knelt in silence, forgetting now to heed the tears that flowed down my cheeks as I crossed myself and dumbly spoke the ritual words. The grille slid open, and a kind voice spoke softly to me, in tones of comfort.

"Dear Lady Marian, do not cry. You need not think your life as black as that."

Suddenly my eyes grew sharp, my ears more focused, and I could feel my heart shudder in its fragile cage. I looked up with a gasp and saw his face, those jesting blue eyes and smiling mouth, and had to clap a hand to my mouth to keep from laughing clear out loud. Robin Hood, the very man, sat in the place of our holy rector, one finger lain against his lips.

"How," I whispered, soft as I could, "how are you come here? Surely, you will be caught at this game?"

" 'Tis no game, I assure you. I am here as your final hope."

I nearly laughed again at his arrogance, so well placed as I thought it was. My final hope he was indeed, my golden cord from this maze of terror, and at last I felt prepared to grasp it.

"Very well," I said, half choking, "what do you propose, o dove of hope?"

He grinned at me and in that instant I breathed again, full and easy.

"That you flee with me back to Sherwood Forest. I swear you will find safety there."

This, at last, was what I required. A guide, a sanctuary, an escape route had been placed before me, and I clutched at them with desperate hands. Yes, I would go. The frozen mind that before had failed me melted in the light of his smile and sent cold water to fill my eyes. "I will go with you, Robin Hood, if you think we can escape this place cleanly."

He merely nodded. "This booth has a passage to the rector's chamber, just beyond this curtain. Stand back a moment, and I'll pass you through."

So quickly did we spring to action! My decision was made, and I scarcely had time to draw a fresh breath through my new attitude before it was time to move my feet, use my hands to make the thought material. I stood back as best I could while Robin Hood seized the partition that had divided us as confessor and holy man.

With a huff and a grunt he spun the wall so that a narrow space
swung open, and I squeezed through like a rabbit from the warren.
He pointed my way through the curtain and, as I passed, replaced
the partition as it had been.

In another moment he joined me in the empty rector's cell, he
still laughing and I half speechless. Two habits of the famed black
friars lay on the bed, and these were pulled quickly over our
clothes. I took care to hike up my skirts underneath, lest they trail
behind and give me away, and to pull the hood down low on my
brow. Then I turned and followed the outlaw from the chamber to
the empty passageway.

As we walked, my mind began to move again, to swing its arms
and legs about, and by the time we descended the circling stairs I
had passed ahead of Robin Hood. I knew this castle with a child's
knowledge, complete and indiscriminate. Down these stairs, up this
corridor, a few quick turns to the right and left, and I brought us to
the servants' hall where no one would question a pair of friars.

As luck would have it, my wedding feast had caused a great bustle in the kitchen and yard, making it simple for us to ease into the
throng of workers and make our way through the great gatehouse.
Once through we were safe in our ignominy, for no soldier of Warwick Castle was brave enough to question a holy man on the road
and risk hearing his sermon as an answer.

The rain fell heavy on my woolen habit, but I scarcely noticed.
Here I was, who not a hundred heartbeats before had wept in sorrow at my marriage confession, now walking the roads in a monk's
habit, free to go wherever I pleased. A bubble raised within my
throat, and I began to laugh, to giggle, giddy with joy over my own
luck. What last night had seemed impossible had just been accom-
plished in no more space than the blink of an eye—I had to laugh
at it.

Robin Hood attempted to silence me, reminding me that we
were in disguise and that female laughter from a monk's hood

would draw attention. But the roads were vacant on account of the rain, and I watched for strangers even as I laughed. And what joy I felt! What relief, what delight! The narrowness of my escape was not wasted on me. I felt all the shock that I should feel and a great deal more of the happiness.

When I had given the bubble release, I calmed myself, eager as I was to keep my disguise, and Robin Hood and I walked in the silence befitting a pair of holy brothers. But before we had gone a full furlong beyond the gatehouse, my bubble of joy escaped and flew on, high into the towering sky, and the mundane worries of earthly life crept unbidden into my mind. I began to recall the difficulties that had kept me before from planning escape.

I had fled the castle, sure, that was true, but I had no money, no change of clothes, no cloak, no horse, no silver. And worst of all I had not warned Annie, and my heart grieved to think how she would feel when the others found that I had gone. Lady Pernelle did not frighten me now, for I was sure I could evade her guards with Robin Hood's help, but the thought of Annie's fright over me made me grow sober at last.

"How much time do you think we have until they notice you gone?" Robin Hood asked in an empty stretch of road.

"I was to have an hour in the confessional, so they should notice nothing for three more quarters at the least. And the rain may slow them."

"Aye, a bit. But I fear your costume will slow us more. We shall have to find you a change, Lady Marian, and that quite soon."

I looked down at my own garb and saw that he was right. 'Twas not just that I made a fairly short friar, but my soft cloth shoes looked fully feminine, and my voice, if I should ever be questioned, would give me away in a wink and a blink. So, setting my steps to a firmer pace, I resolved to be like the ship at sea, which wastes no time in fretting the waves or the damp of its keel in the blue ocean, but rather trims its sails to catch the wind.

Chapter Eleven

WE WALKED ON in silence, I pushing hard to keep pace with his longer strides, for I felt, as he did, that every step made away from Warwick was one more step toward my own safety. After perhaps a half mile, Robin Hood turned abruptly to the right, following a footpath over the fields. I followed without questioning, hiking my skirts high to keep from tripping on the clod-laced earth.

Ten full minutes we walked this way until we reached the end of the path at which stood a small cluster of buildings, cottages, and a two-story inn. He set his steps toward the inn's stable and led me directly to the door. There he pressed his finger against his lips and heaved the door open, just enough to allow us both to slip inside.

After the rain and mud of the fallow field, this stable seemed quiet as an empty chapel. But even as I began to breathe easier, glad to be out of the cold rainfall, a stable boy popped up beside us, causing my heart to leap and start, since I now saw danger in every corner. The boy asked us whence we came.

"From Nottinghamshire, my jolly lad," Robin Hood answered in a steady voice. "My brother and I come in seek of a meal and a dry place to rest. Perhaps your master can accommodate?"

The boy nodded yes and jogged off, heaving for himself the heavy door and splashing away toward the great house. In a flash Robin Hood turned to me, lowering his cowl to make his words clear.

"Now, Lady Marian, this is your chance. In the kitchen will be plain working women. If you can get one of their sets of clothing, we might be able to travel the roads in greater safety."

"But how shall I . . . ?"

"Take yourself hence and the idea will come to you," he said, pulling me to the stable door. "I'll stay here to be led off when the boy returns. You must meet me in the inn—just find me out there, wherever I'm seated."

I stammered, stunned at the very idea, but in the next second a plan cracked its seed in my frightened mind and sent down a frail root. I seized on it, certain that my very life was now in question. Wasting no time on modesty, I cast off the habit and my wedding gown so that I stood bare in my linen shift, mindless somehow of the cold. I left my shoes with Robin Hood but took in my hand my wedding veil. He held the stable door ajar and watched as I ran, leaping the puddles, through the pouring rain for the side of the inn.

I chose a spot from which smoke was wafting, thinking that most likely the kitchen, and burst rudely through the only door. As I went, the thought lit through my mind that I was now as much outside the law as Robin Hood, and the lies I was about to tell would surely lock my fate forever.

'Twas the kitchen, right enough, for this room was warm with fires and cooking. When I burst in, a host of ladies turned to gape at me, some in the midst of plucking chickens, others rolling out grain for pasties, white to their elbows with fine wheat flour.

"Forgive me, aunties," I said, gasping, in what I hoped was my most natural Saxon. "But I'm in need of a moment to breathe, safe from the rain and cold outside."

"What is it, child?" asked the largest one, dropping her spoon to come toward me. "What brings ye so in yer simple shift, through a rainstorm such as this is?"

"Oh, auntie, if you only knew!" And here I threw my face in my hands and shuddered as if to hide my sobbing.

"Now, there now, little chick, ye needn't carry on so. None can chase you here, 'tis certain."

The other women had now gathered close, and I slowly lowered my hands from my face, grateful that the rain had left my cheeks wet and shining. " 'Tis my sister, that wretched Alice!" I cried, muffling my own words with sniffs and sobs. "She's stolen from me my very best gown and uses it—oh!"

I made as if to cry again, and they nudged me onto a low stool near the fire. The warm sounds of female sympathy filled my ears and made me brave enough to go on again.

"That Alice! She wants to get my beau, my Ralph, over for herself, and so she stole off my best gown and left me with nothing more to wear!"

Shocked inhalations followed these words, and I felt myself turning the tide of their kindness, until the one who plucked the chickens spoke up.

"But what brings ye here, to this village, child? Ye do not sound as if you were raised in these parts?"

A jab of panic shot through my heart, but in another moment my mouth was open and more tales of fancy shot out, unplanned. "Nay, auntie, 'tis true. I was raised in Dover, far to the south, in that town which meets ships from across the channel." I prayed that would explain the wisps of French that slithered into my every word. "My sister and I had gone forth into service of noble ladies and both came here, to Warwick Castle. Our lady, Lady Margery, had ridden out on a voyage of pleasure with both of us as her attendants. But when I awoke at the campsite this morning, Alice and my lady had gone and with Alice went my gown! And she had the

meanness to take her own gown with her also, so I was left alone
in my shift! Oh, aunties, I do not know what I should have done
had I not spied the smoke from your fires."

Here I fell into sobs again, and this time their sympathy seemed
complete. Feeling ever braver, I lifted before them my pearl-
studded veil.

"This veil was given me as a gift from my lady. Thanks be to
Saint Dunstan, I had hidden it away, or Alice would have had it
too! And now 'tis all I'm left in the world with, for I cannot return
to my lady at the castle dressed in naught but a shift, now can I?"

"Nay, nay" was spoken all around, and in another moment I
heard them whispering among themselves. My veil of pearls would
make a fair trade, this I knew, for a full suit of homespun, and as
my women were no fools, I trusted them to see that clearly. Sure
enough, in another moment the pasty roller laid a heavy hand on
my shoulder.

"Now dry your eyes, child, for here's a solution. My daughter
Emma is about your size, and she's a spare suit of clothes and
shoes. If you will but trade her for your veil, you'll have a warm
woolen gown to wear back to the castle."

I hesitated—or, I should say, pretended to hesitate—thinking
of the value of the veil. But at last I relented and with happiness,
for truly I was growing cold in my shift and longed for some covering for my feet. The women were such as wasted no time, and
before long Emma's gown was fetched, and I dressed myself in a
good suit of homespun and clean white kerchief, full of relief.

I embraced them all before slipping out, charmed to hear them
wishing me well. Into the rain I fled once more, but this time I simply circled the building and stepped in the door on the entry side,
changing my role in a single breath from downtrodden servant to
inn clientele.

THE INN WAS A WARM AND MERRY PLACE, filled with the scent of damp wool-clad travelers seeking a rest from the rain. By the light of the fire I scanned the room, searching in vain for Robin Hood, for I did not see his form anywhere. At last I heard his voice calling, "Here, Lucy," from a table near the wall, and I walked straight to him, feeling more than buoyant over my success.

He too had taken a moment to change, for now he was dressed not as a friar, rector, or Lincoln-green forester, but as a simple tradesman, complete with a sack of carpenter's tools. He smiled when he saw me coming, relieved, no doubt, that I hadn't been caught, for if I were, he would be too. As I sat down on a stool beside him, he motioned to a bundle in his sack, and I saw that my wedding dress was there, wrapped up tight in the friar's wool cloak.

I longed now to speak with him, to tell every detail of my adventures in the kitchen, for I wanted him to be proud of my lies and to think that I had managed well. And more than that, I wished to thank him for helping me escape from Warwick, but there was no time. Before I was able to open my mouth, the innkeeper shuffled to our table to see what we wanted and to check the value of our money.

"Who might ye be and what can I get ye?" he asked, spitting as he spoke, the result, perhaps, of having no front teeth.

"Brian of Staffordshire, come forth to work at the great castle, and this here's my wife, Dame Lucy," said Robin Hood. "Have ye no more of the pullets I saw roasting on your fire?" He placed a few pennies on our table. "We'll take some meat and two tankards of ale, that'll do that trick."

The innkeeper eyed the pennies close and then thanked Robin Hood, spitting even farther and striking the outlaw nearly dead in the eye. I checked my laughter and reached out instead to play my wifely part, wiping his forehead clean with my apron.

"Brian," I said, determined to play my new role well, "I have wanted to thank you for bringing me with you on this journey.

'Twas not necessary, but you know how I have longed to see more of the world, and I do wish to thank you. I would have said as much before, but I could not find the words for it."

He gave me then his Robin Hood smile, full of jests he did not give words to.

"Ah, 'tis nothing, Lucy, 'tis nothing. I'd long had a sense that you wished to come, though you would not say so."

"Aye, that is true, I would not. Do you—" I hesitated, wishing to frame my words with care. "Do you think the roads will be crowded tonight with the traffic from the wedding at the castle?"

"I expect they will be too crowded for us. What say you to passing the night in this inn and venturing farther on our way tomorrow?"

" 'Tis a smooth plan, Brian, and a good one." I sat for a moment, feeling easier than I had all day. But as I sat my mind returned to the morning's events the way a child recalls a forbidden toy, and I couldn't resist questioning my friend a little more. "So tell me, Brian, know you what became of that holy rector who was to have given me my confession earlier, much earlier in the day?"

He laughed and said nothing as our ale was brought, then took a long drink before speaking again. "Ah, that rector was a right holy man, but he had a slight weakness for a night of long drinking. I know not precisely what became of him, but I did hear tell that he encountered a certain knave at a drinking hole. The rumors say the knave bought up a round of stiff Flemish waters and perhaps a second round felled the rector, but I couldn't say for certain. I cannot blame him for missing confession, for I have heard those waters pack an especial kick for the holy man. I suspect he was asleep in the alehouse when you came to give your confession this morning."

"Indeed," I said, laughing, realizing for the first time what forethought had gone into our quick escape. I said nothing while our pullet came but set to happily, more pleased to be eating this simple meal than all the cakes of a wedding feast. I thought for a moment on young Stephen and what wrath he would take from his mother, and breathed a sigh of such relief that I thought I might never have air again.

When our meal was finished, Robin Hood ordered a room, and I leaned forward to question him again.

"Dear Brian, have you no idea when I might again see my sister, Annie? I was quite pained to depart from her and thought you might have a notion of how I could send her word of our safe arrival."

Here he made a bit of a face, then took a long drink from his tankard. " 'Twill not be simple, I am afraid. For your sister Annie lives in the castle, and I know of no messenger we may send who will not be questioned closely—too closely. Have you no kindred who could pass her word from the kitchen or stables?"

I thought a moment and for a time I feared no one would ever come to mind, for we'd formed few alliances with the staff of Warwick Castle. But at last a face bobbed into my thoughts, that of Clym o' the Tower, and I saw my own answer. A message to Clym could be carried to Annie, provided I could find a page with the wits to root out Clym in London town.

"Aye, I do know of one who can do it. Perhaps in the morning we could find a page, one willing to ride as far as London town?"

"If that is what you think necessary, that is what we shall do. Now look you, love," he said with a wink, "the innkeeper's wife is beckoning us. I suspect she means to lead us to our room."

I rose and followed him, still feeling giddy—or perhaps it was nervous—from the fun of playing such a strange part. But when we reached her, I pushed my role as housewife further, asking to borrow a needle for the day, saying I had some mending to do on a garment that was torn during our journey. I realized then my narrow luck that I'd not met this dame in the kitchens, for then I would have been lost for certain. But all was well. She brought my needle and took us ignorantly to our room, bidding us a good night and closing the heavy oaken door.

Safe at last in a hidden place, I sank in wonder onto the bed. Robin Hood, I noticed, checked first the windows, then the door, making sure that none could see inside nor enter by any means but brute force.

"There, Lady Marian," he said in a hushed voice. "Now you may feel safe."

"Ah, Robin Hood," I said, "pray, do not call me a lady any longer. For if I did nothing else this morning, I most certainly discarded my nobility and do not expect to ever reclaim it."

His face looked odd for a moment, as if he feared having injured me in spiriting me away from the castle, and so I smiled to reassure him. He smiled too, rapidly, as he did all things, his features changing with the speed of a child's.

"Very well, Maid Marian, I will address you as lady no more. But as a fair exchange, you too must drop the Hood from Robin and call me solely by my Christian name."

"Is it true then, that Robin is your Christian name?" I asked, surprised. "I would have thought you had changed it when you first became an outlawed man."

"Well, 'tis true, I changed it somewhat. My Christian name is Robert, truly, but 'tis not so far from Robin in sound."

"Robin, then, you shall always be."

"Perhaps," he said with a spark in his eye, "now that Robin has Marian to himself and alone, she might allow him to sit beside her, there on the bed?"

"And do what, pray tell?" I laughed, though I did not feel at all steady.

"Ah, she might receive a kiss or two."

I bolted from my seat on the blankets. "As payment for this morning's rescue?" Fire leapt high in my lungs, constricting my throat. "Nay, Robin Hood, I'll not be selling favors at any price, neither now nor ever." My legs were sick with palsy, horrified to think that the happy flight of the morning might have carried me into the vulture's nest. I thought of Hugh, of the sneer on his face as he pushed me down into the snow, and my heart itched with distrust. What had I done, to place myself in this brigand's care? Could I not see that one knave was much like another?

But Robin showed no competing anger. Rather, he lowered his voice as if he spoke to some wild thing, a frightened dog or newborn colt, and moved himself gently away from the bed to a seat near the fire. "Very well, Marian, very well. I'll not thrust my caresses upon you. But one day, I think you may ask me to renew my offers and then, perhaps, you shall be rebuffed."

He knelt before the fireplace to poke distractedly at the burning logs, his mind wrapped deep in his secret thoughts. I stood as I was, shaking badly, for our interaction had touched upon some deep-rooted fear, and I sought to soothe and suppress the feeling. My heart quivered like a dying wren and my legs seemed to sink beneath me. I stepped to the bed and lay myself there, tucked my face in the depths of my wing, and gave way to silent tears of panic. The bed was soft, the room was warm, and before my eyes had grown raw from crying, they'd dropped to closing, and I was asleep.

When I awoke the light was dim, and Robin stood at the window casement, peering out through a chink in the shutter. He heard me move and turned.

"Ah, you're awake then. I wondered how long you might sleep there."

I sat upright and felt for my kerchief, sensing that it had slipped badly askew. "I did not mean to sleep at all. Has it been long?"

He shrugged in answer and came away from the window. I realized then that an afternoon trapped in a confined room must be agony to one as active as he. He seemed, however, to have managed well enough.

"I think a good rest was merited after what passed for you this morning. And as we seem to be quite safe here, 'tis as good a place as any to take it. No one has passed our door in search of you, and when soldiers came into the yard below I heard the innkeeper say he had none but married ladies here."

"And that made them go?"

"Aye," he said. "You'll find, I'm sure, that royal guards do not tend to look beyond the surface of things. They rarely question and never pry, so a good disguise is a safe place to hide."

He said nothing of our previous quarrel, which pleased me, though it did hang in the air like the smell of rot. I'd no wish to raise the dark points of my past when my future seemed so dim and uncertain. Instead I rose and straightened my new skirts, then knelt at the fire to light a taper, for I wished to work with my needle now and required more than fading light.

"Tell me, Robin, now that you have released me, are you fully prepared to take me on as one of your band in Sherwood Forest?" I asked it in the tone of a jest, but I had no jesting feelings at heart. A thought had surfaced like wood in water, scratching at the back of my mind. Perhaps he would want me to make love with him to earn my keep, exchanging favors for livelihood, the very bargain I'd just refused. I felt uneasy, and so I resolved to speak only of forest labors and to say nothing of sharing his bed—perhaps he would not think to make the request.

"I am indeed, for I thought there would be no other choice."

"Nay, you're right, there is no other." I exhaled slowly, letting my worries flow out with my breath. "But I hope I can be of assistance to you and to your band when I am there."

"I've no fears on that account. If you're as handy with a needle as you appear, we shall have no end of work for you."

I looked up and laughed, seeing then that he watched me as I stitched. Emma's homespun gown was warm but it was also a hand too long, and I was raising up the hem with a thread I had pulled from my wedding gown.

"Skill with the needle may truly be the only talent of the noble lady. 'Tis no boast to say I can sew, but I am cheered to hear that it shall be of use."

I stitched my hem while Robin watched, but when I took up the monk's habit with the purpose of making it into a cloak, he began to pace the room. His circuit led him past the door, where he always paused to cock his ear, then to the window where he stopped to peer down into the yard, to see what passed. At last I spoke.

"Pray, stop that, Robin, you make me nervous. Come sit down here and tell me a tale to pass the time while I'm stitching. There's not light enough to see the yard by this time, anyhow."

He did as I asked and sat on a stool a good distance from the fire's warmth, for perhaps his woodland habits had led him to prefer a slight chill over the hearth's flame.

"But I know of no stories worth the telling," he said as he sat, hands on his knees. "Unless you'd like to hear one of Friar Tuck's tales of the thieving he did when he was a boy."

"Nay, not that, I pray you. Tell me how you became an outlaw and began your life in Sherwood Forest."

This made him quiet, and for a moment I feared I had saddened him. But then he spoke.

"I wasn't raised an outlaw, you know. No one is. My parents thought I would live on in Locksley, where I was born, all my life just as they have. My da had scouted out cottage land for me before I was ten years old, so sure he was that I'd farm that land, same as he had. But I suppose I always had a wild streak, always loved to play the scalawag. And even as a young lad I could shoot the bow better than most.

"One year I had permission from our steward to visit the Nottingham fair and try my best at a shooting match they hold each year. So off I went, through the forest, whistling and singing at the fine weather, happy to have a good noonday meal packed in my knapsack."

I watched him speak and tried to imagine the young Robin, boyish and beardless, on what was perhaps his first great journey. The thought made me smile, though I could not have explained why.

"I stopped for my meal by the side of a stream, but before I was done I heard loud voices, shouts in truth, coming from the woods a little way off. I stashed my bread and went to have a look, and in a clearing I saw a scene that gave me a vicious fright. A band of foresters, king's men, had a man roped up, bound tight to a tree, and one of the foresters had his hunting knife drawn bare in his hand. He went up close to the bound man and snipped at his cheeks and ears with the knife, then put the blade to his throat."

"You must have been frightened," I said, not raising my eyes from my work.

"Aye, that I was, but not as frightened as a moment later when I looked closer at the bound man's face. For I knew him. He was Wat o' Locksley, a simple man of Locksley village who was oft in trouble with the steward for poaching in the king's woods. He'd little sharpness of mind, did Wat, but he was a gentle soul and only poached to feed his young daughters. Wat had no land in Locksley and earned his bread with odd jobs and chores, but the year'd been slim, and I knew he'd found little in the way of work.

"Here, then, stood Wat, and soon enough I spied a bloody deer carcass. And so the tale was spread before me. Wat had been poaching on the king's deer and was caught in the act by the king's foresters, and now they meant to punish him for it."

"And what is the penalty for killing one of the king's deer?" I asked, frowning, fretting over a tale that had ended years before. But it troubled me, for as he spoke, my mind, in the way of mental visions, laid the face of Annie's father over that of Wat, and I shuddered to see him in such peril.

"Both eyes put out, finger and thumb cut from both hands, and then the man is left in the forest to bleed to death." Robin's voice was hard and he stared into the flames without seeing. "That's the penalty."

"For killing a deer! A man's life, then, is deemed equal to that of a hart?"

"It is for the king, for those deer are his own pride and joy."

"But the king has hunting grounds all over England!" I

exclaimed, growing indignant. "And surely each one is stocked with more deer than there are men on this island. I have heard it said, in fact, that the king's forests cover one-third of the country."

"Indeed? I know only of Sherwood, Needwood, and Plompton, but those are grand forests and each hold thousands of deer, I'm certain."

I fumed and blustered for a moment more, then recalled that he was telling a tale and begged him continue from where he had stopped.

"Ah, well, so there was Wat, set to lose his eyes and thumbs. I stood not forty feet off, and as all eyes were on this captive, no one had noticed me. I shook, watching them, but when I saw them seize his hand and press it up against the tree to hack away at his fingers, I stopped my shaking and brought out an arrow. I scarcely remember taking aim, but before I could blink an arrow of mine was stuck fast in the back of the man with the knife, and I was running off for my life."

I lowered my needle, sensing in the silence that this one act was far more momentous than any I'd experienced. A cloud of unfathomable weight seemed to grow within the room, filling my lungs with something dank. Fear, I supposed it was, and regret.

"And ever since you've been an outlaw?" I couldn't bear to raise my eyes.

"Aye, since that day that I killed a man in the employ of the king, I've been a wanted man. I hid out that night in the top of a tree, weeping and wailing like a baby when I realized I could never go home to Locksley again. When it was all dark I did slip back to loosen Wat, for the foresters had all run off after me and were scattered throughout the wood. The man I'd killed still lay where he fell, and I had to step over his corpse to untie Wat from the trunk of that oak."

As he stared at his hands I considered what this had meant for him, a young lad, now estranged from his kin, his village, his every idea of himself. Beside his trials, my loss of nobility seemed small and paltry, and I resolved for the moment to give it less weight than I had so far.

I peered at him then through the candlelight, hoping to read in the hollows of his eyes some conclusion, some wisdom to be gained from his tale. But he seemed to have none. The story itself shook him greatly, and I, the observer, was left only with the poignant thought that it must be a burdensome thing to take a man's life, and I should be grateful I had never yet done it.

THAT NIGHT WE LAY DOWN to sleep on a shared bed, each wrapped in our cloaks, carefully placed on our own far sides. In spite of the fact that we did not touch, my breathing was ragged and would not settle, conscious that he slept just beside. 'Twas silly, I knew, for had I not recently passed a night in the same bed as Annie and her entire family, father and boys included? But I still lay there long awake, seeing nothing in the darkness, but holding my eyes open all the same.

One finger of moonlight entered our room through a break in the shutters, and by its light I saw Robin roll onto his back, saw the shape of his profile clearly in the milky light. Each eyelash, each hair was clear to me, and I felt my palms begin to sweat with some strange nervousness.

"Marian?" he whispered softly, unsure if I slept.

"Aye?"

"I—" He paused, licked his lower lip, then turned his face toward mine. "I won't ask you for what you're unwilling to give. There's maids a-plenty in this land, willing maids, enough to keep a man most happy any day of the year. I've no need to force you, so do not be frightened. I could not bear to have you frightened of me."

I made no reply, but as I pushed the breath from my lungs, I thought I released some of the fumes that poisoned my innards. I'd wronged him by recoiling before. His pride was too great to cause me harm, outlaw or no—this I now saw to my immense relief.

I looked at him, watched his eyes close and heard his breathing fall steady and soft. His was the most beautiful face I had ever seen. I pictured my fingers brushing his lips, my mouth feeling the warmth of his skin. Perhaps, I considered, this was why I'd raged so against his former offers of kisses—perhaps I knew I longed for him, and this made me wary to taste the sweetness of the very fruit I so desired. Some strange paradox within my heart warned that if I thought him fine, he would all the sooner be taken from me, for that seemed the spiteful way of the world.

I began to think of my earlier anger with a cringe of remorse. What harm were kisses? I asked myself. Had I no wish to learn more of the world? Did Robin's sweet smile do nothing to tempt me? Indeed, I was a good deal tempted.

These thoughts left me befuddled. I knew from my studies and from songs of court what relations between men and women were. Despite my tutor's best attempts, I'd read Apollo's pursuit of Daphne a dozen times over and had twice acquired poems from the *Ars Amatoria*. But what perplexed me was my own position, for though I'd read of love and conquest, I'd yet to play a part myself. In truth, I'd scarcely known young men enough to discover calf-love and infatuation.

Now I found that parts of my being were growing eager, while others fell reticent, and this made me feel like a handful of chaff, thrown to the mercy of the six directions. My body seemed the furthest advanced, for recently it had formed a will of its own and cared little for my restraints. My mind, so tempered by romance and fantasy, brimmed to spilling with curiosity. But too, it was my mind that resisted, for it did not know how lovers behaved and feared making some grievous mistake. And my heart, I admit, was most puerile of all, half longing for love from any corner, all the while dreading attachment.

So it was no wonder that I lay confused, wishing to know how to weigh my maidenhood against my raging curiosity. But when, in time, my will grew bold, and I thought I might make some daring attempt, I turned to see that Robin had fallen fast asleep. My chance was lost.

I closed my eyes in the dark and sighed with the weariness of the self-confounded. I knew all too well that by dawn I would have lost my nerve and shrunk to a timid maiden once more. So I fell to sleep half dreaming, thinking of a departing kiss, and Robin's retreating into shadows.

My sleep was disturbed by livid visions of Lady Pernelle and Lord William, one brandishing an old horn spoon while the other sliced all my gowns to shreds. But when I awoke Robin was there, bending over me to shake me awake, for the day was just dawning and we ought to travel.

Chapter Twelve

WE STEPPED ONTO THE ROAD just as the sun was rounding over the eastern hills, pale and lonely and far afield. I was grateful, then, for my new cloak, for the air was brisk as it often is after a rainstorm, and I had to bite my teeth together to stop their knocking.

As we walked, the pendular swing of my own boots brought some fresh truths to my mind. I thought on Robin's tale of the previous night and, my face damp with early dew, perceived more common threads between our two cloths than I had before. We both had left stable lives behind for the great unknown, had cast our lots recklessly into the black of night, trusting that some good might come from it.

It grieved me now to think on Warwick, to realize that I would never again see its familiar gates, never dine at long tables in its great hall. Nay, that life was lost forever. For not only had I fled the protection of my ward, Lord William, and broken a marriage contract decreed by the queen, but I had also lost all semblance of ladylike attitude. Ladies, at that time, were required to hold their chastity sacred above all other things, for that was the virtue that determined their value as marriage prizes. I had just spent a night

alone with an unwed man, and in the crisp judgment of the morning air I saw my worth in the eyes of the king fall as quickly as the
temperature the night of a snowstorm.

I could picture for myself the gasp and shock of the royal court
if I were ever hauled back to London and this crime were made
known. The queen would cast me away from my title, seize my
lands, throw me out. And so I came to two conclusions. The first
was that I must never be caught by the king's guards, or I would be
forced to endure this infamy. The second was that I must embrace
this new life fully and not mourn the loss of the noble one. For if
I could, I was determined to be happy in it so I might not live to
regret my choice.

Denby, I knew, was lost to me. I did not know what would happen to it or who would be deemed its lady now, but I knew I must
be counted as good as dead and therefore would lose everything I
owned. This made me think again of Annie, and as panic flooded
my ears anew I begged Robin to help me find a man who would ride
as far as London and bear my message to Clym o' the Tower.

Robin listened to all my requests with darting eyes, scanning
the road and every face so intently that I thought he might miss
what I said. But he heard, comprehended, and before I could finish
apologizing for slowing our progress with this request, he had
crafted a plan. He would be the one to commission the messenger,
for it would look strange for a carpenter's wife to be hiring a page
for London town, especially when a young lady was sought by the
soldiers of Warwick.

Accordingly, we turned in at a tavern, I feeling much like an ill-
shod mule in my new boots. I was thirsty and grateful for the rest,
for Robin's strides were brisk, and I had trouble keeping his pace
even without blisters and rubbing toes. While I drank a pint of
fresh-brewed ale, Robin inspected the tavern faces, looking for the
man he would approach. And while I was flexing my hot toes, he
slipped away for a hushed interview. I, mindful of my part, pre-

tended to watch the tavern wife cooking in her vast iron kettle while I gave my throbbing feet a rest.

In another moment Robin returned, saying that we could make our way, and I followed him through the wood and mud of the tavern yard. Once we were returned to the road, he whispered to me that all was well. The man he had chosen owned a horse and had business of his own in London town. But as he was not expected there yet, he was glad to take Robin's silver in exchange for a quick visit to the royal court.

Robin told me in a whisper how he had explained that Clym might be a hard man to find, but that he would be known by his good head for ale and his Warwick accent. Our message was simple: that Clym should gather his mistress's servant and travel with her to the wooded place, Sherwood, where she and her lady had met with the outlaws. For as Robin noted, Annie and Clym would never find their way to the Greenwood tree, but if they traveled the roads of Sherwood one of the merry men would spot and retrieve them.

This task done, I returned again to my idle reflections, gazing about me as we walked. My mood was cheerful, reflecting, and wise—or at least I meant to be wise—but over time I began to tire, and as I did what had before been a mere suspicion blossomed to terrible conviction. Robin, I now saw, clearly intended to walk on foot the entire distance to Sherwood Forest. In all honesty the idea of walking any distance of length had never before occurred to me, and it left me aghast. 'Twas not the lowness of it that bothered me, but my own nervous fear that my legs, little used as they were to exercise, might not be sturdy enough for the distance. Even now my feet's complaints had infected the morale of my shins and knees, and we had walked two hours at most.

I fretted and frowned, and after a time Robin asked me what the matter was, for I suppose my worry had slowed my step and caused him to glance at my face.

" 'Tis nothing, Brian," I said, careful to use our false names, "only a fear that I may need to rest my legs more often than you care to do. I know we make this journey in haste and that every mile gained is a mile to rejoice over, but I am afraid I may not be up to the task of so long a walk."

Robin said nothing for a moment, then moved close to my elbow so his words could be quiet. "Perhaps when we have gone a little farther we might find a cart that travels our way and pay the driver to take us along."

The very notion brought me great relief, and I nodded and thanked him for thinking of it. On we strode through the early air, and soon my mind ceased its selfish thoughts and began to take interest in what happened around me.

As the sun grew higher, the road filled more thickly with travelers, some on foot, some on horseback. We stayed far to our side of the path, out of the way of hooves and cart wheels, but even so there were scores of faces to catch my eye. Nobles on horseback held little interest, for I had seen enough of their ilk to last until my dying day, but the Saxon faces were a varied lot, as broad a menagerie as had filled the Arc. In truth, these men and women were better novelties to my eye than the African parrot I'd once seen in a Westminster viewing garden.

Some wore clothes of neatly dyed homespun; some wore tunics patched with rags. Some carried great bundles of tools and goods; others carried nothing more than their purses. From time to time we saw a beggar, walking farther off the side of the road to avoid the kicks that might come his way from the decent people who traveled past, and these piqued my interest also. They were glum and soiled, smelling afoul and often walking with a reluctant stride. Their clothes were tattered, and they wore no shoes. I wondered how they managed to survive, living as they did with no home, no land to farm, no means of earning pennies for supper.

Women also passed our way, either on their way to farm the furlongs in the village fields or carrying baskets of goods for market.

Some brought eggs or hens to sell, honey, ale, or vegetables from her cottage garden. Others went forth with an empty basket to purchase things for her family's larder that she could not supply herself. I entertained myself for hours searching their faces for beauty or plainness, comparing their looks to Annie's and her sister's, noting the similar cut of their gowns to my own suit of homespun wool.

In the fields beyond, the bustle of haymaking occupied the hands and feet of each village. Great tracts of hay land were dotted with workers, men and women, some swinging scythes, others coming behind with rakes to sweep up hillocks of mature grass. In other villages we saw wooden carts piled high with cut hay, lumbering behind tired oxen to haylofts and barns in the lord's manor. One field we passed was alive with shouting, and Robin explained that the hay work was done there, and they played at the custom of pitchfork raising.

He said the last day of haying the lord's land habitually ended in a competition. Each man who farmed strips in the village fields could thrust a pitchfork into a haystack and carry off any amount of hay he could keep on the tines without dropping off. 'Twas difficult, Robin explained, for a greedy man might try for too much and lose the whole bundle in the bargain or, worse yet, could snap the handle of the fork and then be laughed at by his neighbors.

Their work seemed merry and I wondered at it, wondered if they thought it so or if it only seemed joyous to me because I had never had a share in it. I knew by now that most common people thought the noble life was all ease and beauty—a notion with which I could not agree. I hated to make the same mistake, to think them happy because they laughed or content because they did not complain. Perhaps we all were in this trap, red with envy over what was different, wearied by the drudgery of our own lives.

Around noontime we stopped to buy bread and cheese, and Robin found a cart heading north in which he was able to purchase two places. That afternoon we made good time, riding easily over wooden wheels, and when we stopped at a roadside inn, Robin declared we should be in Sherwood the day after next if all went well.

ALL WOMEN, I believe, love to think of themselves as flower blossoms—bright, fragrant, tenderly perfect. I, however, am a strange female, for if I had ever imagined my soul encased in plant flesh and matter, it was as some thorny vining thing, striving and stretching for more fertile ground.

But in the days I spent with Robin Hood, traipsing the stones of Watling Street, I noticed a change in my green leaves, for they seemed to turn independent faces toward some sun they alone could see. My age-old wariness drained from my branches as easily as a summer rain, and I found, amazed, that my old terrors began to subside. Where before I might have whimpered over where the next day's sun would shine and what leaves ought to angle where, I felt a new calm, an easy sap, and I dropped my troubles to the ground.

Robin and I traveled in the haze of a gentle camaraderie, both friendly and considerate. On the road we laughed and jested together or heard tales from the other's world, and still we were mindful of each other's burdens. I felt I owed him a great deal of gratitude for having come so far, alone, to rescue me on my wedding day, and so I took care to help where I could. If I spied a hole in his carpenter's garb, I borrowed a needle and mended it. When his bundle of cloaks seemed to grow heavy, I offered to carry it for a time.

He, as well, was courteous to me, lifting me on and off the cart backs, checking each inn's room to ensure our safety, building a great fire if I seemed cold. We each were appreciative of these small gestures, and so it was natural, I suppose, that what passed on the second day might happen between us.

Robin had lifted his parcel of clothing—the cloaks, my wedding dress, and his Lincoln-green suit—over his head to let it hang across his shoulders, and I stepped forth to straighten the straps since some had twisted. Bits of the boldness of the previous night still lingered in my veins, like the memory of heavy perfume. I suppose it was this that compelled me forward, that made me stretch tall when our heads were near, that impelled the impulsive little kiss I dropped upon his cheek. His skin was cool from the air of the day, and I felt a small shiver pass through my bones when I sniffed his scent of woodsmoke and sunlight.

But the moment I'd gifted this little kiss, my mind filled with panic. I leapt away, stepping aside as quick as a jaybird flees a farmer's stone. I bit my lip and turned quite red, but when I caught a look at Robin, I saw that he did not blush or simper. Nay, he smiled like a satisfied cock, smirking at my inexperience. This smile burned against my pride, adding shame to my embarrassment, and I had to stare at fields and roadways a good while before I'd recovered my face.

We walked on and said nothing of it, talking only in bits and starts of the weather or the state of the road, since we had now turned off Watling Street and made our way on lesser paths. For my part, I said nothing because, in truth, I knew not what to say. I felt I had gambled my last penny, and indignation rose in my throat to cover the ulcers of my distress.

The blush this small kiss raised in my cheeks took hours, I think, to subside and clouded my thinking for half the day. In time I wondered why I had done it. Now that I'd seen Robin's smirk I felt no interest in giving him kisses—I wouldn't have kissed him for five marks of silver. I decided at last that it must have been merely an expression of thanks, a kindly gesture to my traveling companion. This soothed my pride somewhat, but then I found, to my horror, that my own reaction may have made me seem foolish, for I'd leapt away so fast that the kiss was left with an ominous weight, far more than such a slight peck deserved. I felt a fool, and in my anger at my own conduct, I worked myself into an irritable mood, the cause, in part, of the quarrel we had later that same afternoon.

Robin was speaking of matters of state, of the rule of the land, and its kingship. Prince John, it seemed, had recently established himself in Nottingham Castle and from its walls raised a hoodlum army of mercenaries from across the channel. Robin's hatred of Prince John I understood, since he lived and reigned frighteningly close to Sherwood's forest edge. But as Robin spoke I heard him consistently disparage John for attempting a throne of which he was not worthy, implying that Richard was the more kingly of the two.

"King Richard is a lion among men," he said, swinging his arms to match his stride. "If more men had his courage and heart, England would be the better for it."

"That may be," I said, laughing a little, "but you must not wish all your countrymen to copy him in his attitude or our shores would be quite empty of men."

"What mean you? Richard has every loyalty to England that he ought to have and more, I daresay."

"Well, I daresay that you are wrong or at least badly mistaken. How long, pray, has Richard been king?" I did not wait for an answer. "A twelvemonth? And how much of that time has he spent on English shores? One month or two?"

"But he is at war, fighting in Palestine. He cannot be expected to waste his time ruling at home when he feels obliged to wage war in the holy land." Robin kicked at a stone on the road.

"Granted, he is at war. But in his youth, when he made his name as the great Richard Coeur de Lion, did your countrymen see him more often than now? I think not—he lived and breathed for Aquitane!"

"But he was duke of Aquitane. 'Tis no slight to say he spent time in his own land." A second kick, delivered with force, spun the same stone into a ditch. Our tempers were rising with our voices.

"Richard speaks no Saxon, you know, only French."

"Nor did you until recently!"

"Know you not that he once said, soon after he had gained his crown, that he would sell off London town itself if he could find a worthy buyer? Believe in this, Robin, King Richard bears no great love for England. His heart, like his body, belong in Normandy and Aquitane, just as his father's did before him."

"Nonsense!" he cried. "You know nothing of it. He sold noble titles and gave out lands to raise funds for his holy war, not from a sense of disloyalty. Richard, I say, is my king, and I will fight for him and against John as long as I have breath in my body."

"Very well, do as you like. But I hope you shan't be too disappointed when Richard returns from his Palestine, only to dismiss England for France."

We turned apart and would not speak, each fuming at the other's pig-headedness. I was certain that I was right, for I had heard whispers about Richard since I was young and knew that his every last nuance of culture belonged not to England but to Aquitane. He was a Norman through and through, not a removed one such as I.

Despite my anger, as time wore on, I did admit that I admired Robin's headstrong loyalty, though I hated Richard for having caused him to place that loyalty so foolishly. Perhaps it was the result of Saxon breeding, I considered, that caused Robin to stubbornly place such value where none existed. Richard was king and, as such, was worth defending. But beyond that he had no virtues that made him a lesser king than his father or a better one than his younger brother.

BY EVENING we had tacitly agreed to say nothing further on the subject, and by the morning of the following day our quarrel seemed long forgotten. This day we would arrive at Sherwood, and the closer we stepped the more buoyant of spirit Robin became.

"Have I told you, Marian," he asked, breathing in the scent of swelling apples, "how my cousin has joined our band?"

I happened, at that moment, to glance his way and catch his eyes resting on the base of my jaw, the place where blood and air met to mingle beneath my skin. A curious feeling, like twisting wool, stole up my legs and down my back. I swallowed hard and looked at the road to cool my head.

"Nay, Robin, you've never told me. How did it pass?"

"I came across him with Little John and David one day, near the edge of Nottingham town. I didn't know him by sight, for I'd not seen him in a dozen years. Too, the man we saw looked such a dandy that I could not pass without challenging him to some sort of match."

I laughed, thinking of how often I had the impression that Robin did nothing more all day than roam the woods in search of sport. Indeed, to hear him tell it, the rich travelers who filled his coffers were mere annoyances, postponing the true purpose of life.

"He was dressed all in scarlet," Robin went on, "and had a rose in his hand that he sniffed at from time to time like some mollycoddly minstrel. I leapt out and jested with him right off and offered to fight him for the flower. Well, no sooner had we settled on cudgels as our sport of choice than he stepped off the path and for his stick yanked a sapling clean up by the roots! I needn't tell you how that made me quiver, how I wondered what foolishness I'd made myself part of, and when we started battling I knew for certain I was in trouble. He was the strongest fellow I'd ever fought, for all his feathers and scarlet hose."

"Did he beat you?" I asked, laughing, for I had long since learned that the merriest tales began with Robin's being soundly beaten.

"Aye, he did. Knocked me up all black and blue, such that I could scarcely walk the next day. I had to ask Allan to lace up my boots, my ribs ached that badly. Anyhow, when I was drubbed so hard I could do naught but lie moaning on the ground, Little John and David popped out of the thicket, barely able to speak for laughing. When those two rats recovered themselves, they asked the minstrel how he did and where he learned to fight so well. And he said his uncle, Robert of Locksley, had taught it all to him when he was a boy, and it was this uncle he was off to seek."

"And that was you, Robert of Locksley?"

"Aye, none other," he said with a grin. "So quick as a wink Little John explained how he'd found his uncle and done one better, for he'd knocked his uncle flat as a puddle. My nephew was flummoxed at first, but then he saw me for who I was and fell into laughing his own self. Then we all sat while I rested myself, and Will explained how it was he sought me.

"Will's the son of my ma's brother, Edward Gammet. Edward's a farmer of Maxfield town with close to a yardland of strips to work in his lord's fields. One day, Will said, when he and his da were toiling at their week work—" Here I looked puzzled and he paused to explain. "Week work is the work a farmer does as a favor to the lord, the one who rents him his farmland. 'Tisn't always a week, sometimes just days, that he gives to rake his master's hay or sow his fields. At any rate, Will and his father were working the lord's fields with the other men of Maxfield town, when all of a sudden the reeve came up and walloped old Edward on the pate with his rod.

" 'What was that for?' young Will asked on his father's behalf. 'Fer stealin' out of the lord's grain, slipped into his own pockets,' the reeve replied. Well, Will was about to have none of that, for he knew his father never stole a thing. Their words turned to arguing, and Will made a fist and hit the man square in the face, a thing he'd never done before in his life."

"And had his father been wrongly accused of stealing grain?"

"Aye, he had, but that scarcely mattered for poor ole Will. For the reeve died from that blow on the head, such a thing as Will never expected, and he was forced to turn outlaw or face a hanging for his crime."

"But he did not mean to kill him!"

"Nay, but how was any there to know what intention lay in his heart? And besides, it matters not, for the law is the law and cares little for circumstances such as Will's. No, he was outlawed from that very hour and fled Maxfield town to find me, as he quickly did—or I found him, I ought to say."

"So he has joined you?"

"That he has! I've changed his name, for the king's soldiers would love to find out old Will Gammet if they knew him to be in the midcountry still. Now he goes by Will Scarlet, on account of that scarlet hose, and no stronger man, I say, can be found in all of Nottinghamshire."

" 'Tis a bonny name," I said. "And was his the worst beating you ever took?"

"It may be," he said, considering. "The drubbing I got from Friar Tuck when we first met was something fierce, but I believe this to have been worse, for it was more than three days before I could move like myself again."

We walked in silence for a while, Robin beaming at the thought of his powerful nephew—or cousin, as he liked to call any of his kinsmen. After a time my own thoughts began to stray, and without thinking I spoke aloud.

"I wish I might learn to fight."

"Do you truly?" he asked, turning, and I blushed, realizing I had expressed an idea that was meant to stay within my mind.

"Well, perhaps . . . I know not, truly. But I wish I might defend myself if I met a thief on the road, say, or found myself alone in the wood."

"You might, you know, learn enough to defend yourself. I could teach you."

"You could?"

"Aye, but not the bow and arrow, mind," he said, laughing loudly, still pleased by his tired joke. "That rule still stands in Sherwood Forest—Maid Marian must not touch a yew bow or, by Saint Withold, we'll have a mess."

I let him laugh till he had done, then drew him back to my proposal. "What would you teach me, then?"

"The cudgel, I suppose. You've little strength to match the likes of Will or Little John, but you are small and should be quick, and that will often turn the tide of a match, especially against a big man."

This idea caught my fancy, and I walked the whole of the morning lifted by the thought of taking up sticks against the strongest of men and knocking them easily to the ground.

Chapter Thirteen

THAT NIGHT WE ARRIVED at Sherwood Forest and cut through brambles and forded streams until we strode for the Greenwood tree. All about us, limes and sweet cherries were weighted with flowers, while red berries dangled like grapes from the hawthorns. A few determined, dusty yarrows waved their heads from the byways, coaxing us past fern and bracken toward the outlaw camp. The men were eating when we came, but they all leapt up to hail Robin, as happy to see him as a band of wolves is at the return of its fiercest hunter.

They stood about and greeted him, and he clapped shoulders and called every man in their midst by name. Listening to the murmurs of the crowd, I realized that they had not known where he went when he left for Warwick, and more than a few seemed taken aback at the sight of me. Perhaps 'twas the first time their master had ventured out to fetch a new band member, or perhaps I was the first woman retrieved, I knew not. But they were mostly kind, if silent and awkward, and I gave them space to welcome their Robin.

Soon Ellen came out from her forest bower, drawn by the noise in the clearing, and she at least was glad to see me. Her attitude pleased me, for I knew I must take up my space in her tiny abode once again and hoped I would not intrude too much. But she smiled as she embraced me, and I allowed myself to be led away toward food and drink and a soft seat.

I spoke no more to Robin that night, for he was absorbed by his own men, but at some point I was introduced to the famed Will Scarlet, a handsome youth who shared his uncle's bright blue eyes and ready smile. Will did not tease as Robin did, so we were able to converse easily without any flashes of my temper. I told him how I had heard his tale from his uncle's lips, and he laughed at the memory, assuring me that he still carried a rose from time to time to remind good Robin of the beating he took.

Will's conversation was pleasant enough, but seated there I felt all the delayed exhaustion of my travels and feared I made a dull companion. I was glad enough when nightfall came and yawning became appropriate, for soon after Ellen rose and led me to bed.

THE NEXT MORNING I ate my bread in a sea of merry men, watching as Robin selected a handful of his favorite friends to join him on the day's adventures. Little John was left in command of the camp, and when I had finished eating, I went to him to see how I could make myself useful.

"Pardon, Little John, but is there no task I could do today that would be of use to you and the men?"

Little John looked me up and down, then said with a bit of a sneer, "Aye, we every last one of us could use a lusty maid in our beds. Will you begin with Dan o' Millpasse or are you set on the captain himself?"

I flushed deeply and felt my nails dig deep in my palms. "Nay, Little John, your lot will take a rutting goat to bed before you'll bear me away. Or has that been your habit already?"

"You ruddy tart of a——!"

I took a step back, then folded my arms as if waiting for him to reach the meat of his insult. "Pray, Little John, what sort of tart is it you make me out to be? A slattern? A minx? A shrew perhaps? Ah, or what's more appropriate—a maid who seeks to employ herself to the good of your band? Such cruelty."

Little John's dark eyes peered at my face, then swung away. Perhaps he feared what Robin would say if he heard of this squabble, or perhaps he was shamed at having been bested. "What, indeed, can you do, Mistress Marian? Can you cook, or hunt, or fish?"

"Well, no. But I'm happy to learn—"

"They aren't things that can be taught in a day," he replied, sniffing a little. "Can you dress a deer, perhaps, or cut steaks from its hide?"

"No, of course I can't."

"Then tell me, kit, what can you do?" His hands were now on his hips in something between a fishwife's stance and a taunt.

"I can fetch and tote, gather things, keep the camp tidy—"

"We haven't much need for that, as you can see," he said, gesturing proudly around the camp, which was, in fact, quite neat.

"I'm handy with a needle," I declared defensively, resorting more quickly than I'd hoped to do to my one true skill.

"How handy?" he challenged, chin raised high.

"Quite," I replied.

"Well then," he said, grumbling a little, "Lawrence Ganniel's in need of a new tunic. You'll find a bolt of Lincoln green in the storehouse. Ellen can show it."

As he finished, he turned away on his heel, leaving me to sigh and search for Ellen. His insolent manner perturbed me, but I recalled my decision to embrace this new life and swallowed deep to calm my bruised heart.

I found Ellen sweeping out her bower with a willow-twig broom, singing as she worked the packed-earth floor. At my request she stopped her work and led me to the house of stone in which all the worldly goods of the band were kept safe under lock and key.

The storehouse was made from a Roman relic, a base of ancient pale stones on which the men had framed a small tower. It was sturdily made and dry within, perfect for keeping the flour and wine safe from the damp of the forest. There I found every tool I needed and several bolts of wool and linen, flaxen thread, and steel needles. Thus equipped I made my way, with Ellen's help, to Lawrence Ganniel and began my role as the outlaws' seamstress.

'Twas well I did, as it turned out, for the merry men's garments were in a sad state. From time to time in the years before, Robin had taken his bolts of cloth to village housewives and paid them silver to stitch up dozens of hose and tunics. But as each woman was accustomed to cutting garments to fit her own husband, most of the clothes had been made too small for this crew of yeomanry. Little John, I had already noticed, wore hose made for a man nearly two feet shorter, and small Allan a Dale had to roll his cuffs to free his hands enough to play at his harp. Robin himself had rent a great gash in his tunic front which he'd attempted to mend himself, but the stitches were always popping out and each time I saw him the hole gaped wider, flapping like a wounded truce flag.

I set to my task with a heart not high, not happy, but resigned, for truly I had sagged quite low after my talk with Little John. But now I had a clear task before me, and that provided a pleasant prospect for me to sit and dwell upon. This work, I soon saw, would be never ending, for Robin had promised each of his men two suits of clothing every year, and I'd be kept busy the whole year round with stitching the new and mending the old.

In this way my days began to melt away into a sea of Lincoln green, for that was all that ever passed under my needle or before my eyes. Sometimes for an evening hour I sat with Robin and laughed with him at his day's events, but just as often he was called to shoot or led away by Little John to hear of some jest that he might like. And when this happened I changed again to that thorny creeper, the anxious vine that worries each dawn over the amount of sunlight to come. I sat at my work or in the bower and felt great chains pulling at my limbs, so distracted was I by the state of my heart.

For what had I to look to now? No chance at Denby, no happy life, only yards and hems of Lincoln green. Despite my resolve, I began to wonder what bargain I had made in coming. For if my complaint of noble life had been its repetitive, solitary nature, the confinement of the needle and wheel, how could I say I had changed my lot? And when I considered my hard-packed bed, the itch of my gown, and my lack of companions, I truly longed for Warwick again.

The outlaw's life was not the thrilling path I had hoped it would be, and at times I wept on my dense pillow, fearing I should never be loved by any of this motley crew, except perhaps for Ellen. And even Ellen, sweet as she was, would never make a true friend for me, for when we spoke she misunderstood near half my words, and I was too lazy to make the effort to follow her convoluted tales. Nay, it was Annie I missed, sweet, steady Annie with her clear-eyed retorts and laughing manner. I longed for Annie just as I longed to feel the confines of French on my tongue, to relax in the ease of my native language. It seemed I'd become a vine transported, rooted into foreign earth.

At times like these I sat alone, or often as not Will Scarlet would come to take pity on me and seat himself at my side. I found his manners kind and gentle, and as he wished to hear my tales of courtly life, we had much to discuss, for I was in a mood to talk of little else. I told him of the regalia of London and he, who had never left the shire, closed his eyes and tried to imagine the crowds and noise of the royal court.

But then one day as I sat with Robin, a strange thing passed. We had been speaking of Prince John and his castle guard, for by now such a force had been brought to Nottinghamshire that it flowed at times over into Sherwood and threatened the peace of our merry band. Robin longed to cause some mischief that would embarrass Prince John before all his men, the sort of prank he often pulled on the sheriff of Nottingham, but I pleaded with him not to do it. While the sheriff might be easily tricked, I doubted that the prince would be. I remembered John a little from his youth and recalled that he was as crafty a soul as I had yet seen, smarter, perhaps, than any of us and certainly more ruthless.

As we spoke I saw that Little John was calling to Robin, beckoning him to hear some tale from Friar Tuck. Little John and I had not yet made amends, and for this I felt an odd sense of guilt and a ridiculous need to please the man. So with a sigh I said to Robin that perhaps he ought to go, for Little John called him thither.

He looked at me strangely, then turned away, his eyes fixed on the rugged ground. "Perhaps you'd like some time alone with your new friend Will, is that it?"

I was puzzled by his manner. "Nay, Robin, 'tis Little John calling for you."

"And you wish that I would go?"

"Not at all, nay, indeed, I do not wish it. Only he is your friend and I—I feel that I have angered him somehow and wish to make things well with him."

"Angered Little John? Nonsense!" His face was averted still, and I knew not what to say next.

"Pray, then, Robin, stay a while longer. I would not trade your company for Will's or Ellen's or any. I simply do not understand."

He sighed heavily and ran his hands through his cropped hair, leaning his elbows on his bent knees. He seemed, I then noticed, as miserable as I had felt since our arrival at the Greenwood tree. I wondered how long he'd been so unhappy.

"Listen, Robin," I said on impulse. "Can't you try to return to camp early tomorrow so we might have that cudgel lesson?"

He brightened a little and turned to me. "You still want to learn?"

"Very much. But, I beg of you, let my first go not be in the camp. I would not wish to have the men nearby to jeer at my mistakes."

"Very well then. I know a clearing where you may practice without anyone near to see you. We'll go tomorrow."

We smiled together, and as we did I felt the chains fall away, my mouth bend to a happy shape, my sap surge and course again. That simple plan seemed to make me well, so well that I was not sad to see him move away to Little John, so well that I found patience to sit with Ellen and hear her tell me yet again of her wedding day and dress of blue.

I STRODE OFF with Robin the following day with a song in my heart, for the sun was high and the grass was green, and for once I felt I needed no more than those simple things to be content. Just outside his clearing, Robin felled a stiff blackthorn limb for me to use as a staff, while I stood in the sun and watched him work. Soon enough he brought it to me, and I took the long limb in my hands, startled at its uneven weight.

"You'll have to adjust your hands to balance it," he said, hoisting his own cudgel into the air. He then explained how every inch of the staff was part of the weapon, excepting the places where my hands gripped the wood. "You can do great damage to a man by knocking his hands where he holds the bar, but take care never to let it happen to you, or you'll soon be done for."

We tried a few beginning knocks, to give me the feel for wood against wood, and as we worked my hopes took flight, then faltered and crashed, dead on the ground. This would not be the easy sport I had envisioned, for every time the cudgels met, my hands recoiled from the sharp sting. Soon my arms ached from holding my staff, and my eyes burned dry from moving too fast. I begged for a rest and stood a moment, breathing hard, then I hoisted my staff a second time and took some more practice knocks.

Before long I had learned the basic blows, and Robin began to add footwork to our exercise. He had me step with a lunge each time I pushed my cudgel in to strike, taking advantage of my slight weight to throw what I had into the blow. This went well, and I was pleased until my skirts wrapped round my legs, and I tripped, stumbled, flailed about. I fell hard, and my own stick fell upon me, causing tears to spring to my eyes.

"Are you well, Marian?" Robin asked, offering his hand. I seized it and stood, but as I did so I wavered and reached to steady myself against his arm. "Stay a moment, you've had a hard knock," he murmured, gripping my arms so I could not sway.

My heart was beating fast and hard, the result, I thought, of my fall. I held my breath and looked to his face, surprised to see it bent near mine. His mouth looked inviting, and I held quite still as he leaned closer, ever closer, until at last his lips brushed mine. For a moment the world grew warm and heady, and a sensation akin to drunkenness flitted about on my palms and neck. I could smell his sweat mixed with the tartness of crushed grass and of buckthorn leaves. Neither of us issued a breath, each frightened, I imagine, of scaring the other off, until a loud splashing in the river nearby startled us both, and we breathed again. Robin turned, releasing me, and I followed his gaze to the stream where Little John dunked and splashed in the clear water.

"Lord! Little John, you son of an ass! A murrain take thee!" Robin shouted, full of anger, then dropped his voice to an irate mumble. "I told him not to come by here, and what has he done? Just that, the bastard."

Robin paced off to curse at his friend, and I took my cudgel and made for camp, glad to slip like a little raven through the trees, far from their anger.

Chapter Fourteen

FROM THAT DAY ON I rejoiced to see that my fog had lifted, though into its place rolled storm clouds wrapped around fine weather, a mess of friendships, emotions, and attitudes. Robin and Little John were up and down, friends today and foes tomorrow. Little John's behavior in the stream had been just the start; soon after comments and vague slights puffed into larger quarrels between them. And the angrier Robin Hood became, the more Little John seemed to hate me, perhaps because I was the newest addition to the band and as such was the one to take the brunt.

Robin and I were never alone, for the men liked to have him near, like a totem—the sight of him seemed to put them at ease. In my heart I blamed Little John, imagining that he roused them to want their leader always close, or incited them to draw him near their sport, into their talk and away from me. It may have been that they drew him off with motives as innocent as lambs in springtime. But from my vantage it seemed mean and jealous.

The days stormed on in this turbulent state, and at times I felt that the only stable things about me were my needle and cloth, for they never changed form except on my command. At times I knew not what to do, nor where to turn, but to my stitching. My cudgel too became a solace, for I took it with me to the clearing each day and practiced my knocks without a partner, sometimes beating against a dead tree to toughen my hands and arms to fighting. I laced two strips of soft leather about my pole to use as grips, and this did something to protect my palms and keep blisters from heeding my progress.

When the mood of the camp became thin as the pasty crust that falls to shreds, such that I thought I might jump from my skin, a wondrous thing passed. David of Doncaster and Lawrence Ganniel, now my good friend on account of the well-tailored tunic he wore, were sent one day toward Nottingham town to watch the southern roads to the forest. They returned early, a sure sign that they had come across something worthwhile, but they cannot have known how wonderful their seizure was to lonely me.

For it was Annie they led and Clym o' the Tower, recently come from Warwick Castle on my request. Oh, how I cried out with joy at her face, and how she exclaimed over me as well! Our words fell out in a rush of French, landing pell-mell, each on the other. Annie told me raggedly how she'd feared, oh so greatly, that I had killed myself when I disappeared on my wedding day, flung myself into some raging river. Indeed, even now she wept over me as though I had truly died, and nothing less than my full explanation would settle her nerves and soothe her sorrow.

So I related how I'd come away, saved by Robin at the final hour, and how we had walked in disguise to Sherwood. She thought the story was a jolly one and laughed throughout, especially as she pictured me tripping over mud in the long friar's robes.

It was such relief to both of us to see each other again that we did nothing but talk for hours, each telling and retelling her own tale in greater detail, expressing her fright in superlative fashion. Annie told me with fluttering hands of the chaos that had enveloped the castle when it was known that I was gone. Lady Pernelle, she said, had screamed and been taken to her room in a fit of frenzy. Young Sir Stephen had not taken things ill, but had ridden out that very day on a hunt, not the least bothered by the absence of his bride. Guards and soldiers had been sent forth, but when they returned without news or word, Lord William had declared what Annie feared, that I must have taken my own life and therefore would be sought no more.

Word had been sent at once to the queen, and just as Clym arrived at Warwick, so too did parchment with Eleanor's seal. She declared me undeserving of the gifts of this life, too wicked and worthless to merit such a husband and mother-in-law as she had ordained for me. I was wasted in God's eyes, she had written, so reckless was I in my zeal to die.

This, of course, was the gravest of crimes, for to welcome death before taking sacraments was a solid crime against God. Annie said she had wept for days thinking of my soul writhing in hell, and nothing more than Clym's honest report of my safety could shake her from the gruesome thought. She told me Clym had been forced to tell the self-same tale three times over before she could even comprehend, and here Clym came forward to agree, laughing at what a state she'd been in.

Annie was welcomed by one and all, for the men remembered her winning ways, and Robin was glad for my sake to see her, knowing what anguish I'd felt over her. I put her at night in my corner bed, hidden within Ellen's bower, and we spent the dark hours reviewing our fates and discussing our new life among the outlaws.

WHAT A DIFFERENCE my friend's presence made to life in the camp! Now my days of sewing flew by, made light by our constant French prattle. Annie, accustomed as she was to farmwork, proved able to handle any task Little John proposed to her. Soon she taught me to tend the fire, a bit of cooking, and preserving meat. She even proposed brewing up soap from ashes and lard, seeing the camp had none about, and began her work with capable hands. Oh, thanks be to Annie, soon soap would be had!

But more important than her practical help was the outlet she allowed for my thoughts, for I could tell her anything and she would hear it, used as she was to my odd turns of mind. I told her of my distress at having no path to follow through the mist of life, and she nodded her head and pleaded patience. Then I spoke of how I longed for Warwick in the dark of night, and she smiled and said I must take my lot without a grumble. But most of all I spoke to her of the personalities of the outlaw band—a thing I could not discuss with Robin—for several of them had puzzled me, Little John far above the rest.

I caught her one day as she sat by the river gutting the trout that lay caught in the trap. She wished to teach me how to do it, and we set to with knives and fingers. As I watched the scales fly off the fish back onto my arms and into my hair, I introduced a topic that might take my mind from what I did.

"Have you not noticed, Annie, an odd thing among some of the men here? 'Tisn't true of the main of them, not of Lawrence or Adam or even Robin, but some have a strange way of fixing their eyes upon my bodice when they ought to meet my face."

Annie chuckled and flicked a fish scale in my direction. "Oh, aye, we had the sort in Wodesley too. To them you're naught but a drink of sweet cream—no head, no limbs, just a pair of teats ripe for the milking." She gave me a broad wink. "You wouldn't know, for your life's been so small in Warwick Castle, but men are a confounding lot. They place a vast weight on kisses and trifles, and think not at all on great troubling things."

"You seem to understand them well enough," I said.

" 'Tis the blessing of experience," she said with a nod. "I've had a da and two brothers—may their souls be resting on the streets of heaven. And I had fair friends among the Wodesley lads."

"Then can you tell me, Annie," I said, wrinkling my nose to avoid the fish scent, "why Little John dislikes me so?"

Annie looked startled. "Does he now?"

"Indeed, he does! He never has a kind word for me and always seeks to draw Robin off when we two are talking together."

"And you've no thoughts of why it might be so?"

"I've no idea! I've tried my best to be kind to him, but he seems set against me. Some of his words have been downright vile."

Annie bit her lip a moment. "I daresay, Marian, for all your sharp wits, sometimes you do miss the very porridge that's been set right before you. Are you telling me you do not know why he should behave this way?"

"No! Truly, Annie, if you've got him parsed, I beg of you, tell me what you know."

"Oh, I know nothing, but I can suppose well enough to see the truth. Marian, tell me, what do you think this camp was like before you came? What do you think they did of an evening?"

"Sat and talked, I suppose. Heard Allan a Dale sing and held mock fights and such—as they do now."

"And who do you suppose sat with Robin Hood and heard his stories as you do?"

"I don't know. Little John, perhaps, or Will Scarlet."

"And who do you think he jested with and told his troubles to?"

I shrugged. "Little John? He is his right-hand man."

Annie placed her hands on her hips and gave me one of the looks that told me I was being obtuse. "So you stand here now and tell me all this, but still have to ask why he dislikes you?"

I gasped a little. "Annie, are you saying he's jealous?"

"Of the time you spend with Robin, I do suspect he is."

"Nay, but that cannot be. Those two are together all day long, and they often sit near each other at supper."

"But you are there too in the evening time, are you not? And who's to say, perhaps Robin talks of things with you that he would not mention to Little John. Lord knows it's a rare bird that likes to speak of laws and politicking as eagerly as you take to it. Perhaps Robin enjoys this talk of kings and tax monies, as he finds with you, and perhaps his men are ill suited to it." She paused here to give me a hard look. "I know you may not believe me now, but trust it, my girl, I am right."

We locked eyes for a silent moment. Then, with a sigh, I gave in.

"But Annie, if what you say is true, then what am I to do about it? Is there no cure?"

"None that you can manage, dear," she said, kindlier now that she'd won her way. "This is for Robin Hood to handle—your interference would only make a mess of things."

"But what if Robin doesn't know?"

"Don't you worry, love," she said, patting my hands. "I've been meaning to have a talk with that one since I arrived here, and I'll make sure he's straightened out. For once you just leave things to your Annie, there's a dear. I'll make it right, just you see."

My faith in Annie was firm in this matter, for she knew more of men than I. And so, my burden lifted away, I began to relax and worry less about the band. 'Twas an exciting time for me, for with Annie's arrival and her willingness to teach me things, my daily tasks were becoming more varied. Soon I spent mornings walking the woods in search of beehives or special flowers or in brewing ale over a fire.

Annie's warm ways also helped me come to know the men, for she was always bold and outgoing and led me to speak where I would not have done so myself. With gentle attention, she set me to waxing bowstrings alongside Adam Bell or constructing bower tops with Martin Loverd. With her steady hand behind me, I made friends with the men and they with me, especially the quieter ones among them, who welcomed my retiring ways.

Clym o' the Tower also found a change in life under the Greenwood tree, for he was dubbed one of Robin's band and a prouder Clym I had never seen. If I had thought his old felt hat took a wringing when he spoke to me in Warwick Castle, it was nothing to the gripping and tearing it bore during his first interview with

Robin Hood. Robin, working from reports of mine, praised him as
a man of disguises, and Clym reddened about the ears to hear himself spoken of this way. But in exchange, Clym swore to serve
Robin as faithfully as any of his men could do and was made welcome.

My talks with Robin increased in number after Annie's arrival,
for if she and I were not sitting together, she would invariably
gather a group of the men about her, and she always saw to it that
the number included Little John. With jests and barbs she kept
them laughing while Robin and I discussed the news from Nottingham, which grew more serious by the day.

"He amasses so many men," Robin said, speaking of Prince
John, "that I shudder to think what he might try. With Richard
away, what do you think? Might he try for the whole kingdom?"

We sat a little apart from the group, both conscious that we
were never in private, for the men thought it their solemn duty in
this time of trouble to attend him like bulldogs. It was an infuri-
ating attachment which I resented to the depths of my bones. I
glanced at his hands and bit my lip, wishing they might reach out
for me and brush my body like some new bow, as yet unbent. My
thoughts often ran thus when we sat together, for this was part of
the game I played. I spoke of the world, of kings and armies, while
concealing the warmest of intimate thoughts.

"I know not," I said, "but I'll tell you this. Queen Eleanor is not
one to suffer John and his army for long. She knows his motives
and designs too well. Trust it, she will see that no harm comes to
Richard's throne."

"Aye, I agree with you," he said, nodding, for he had heard all
my tales of Eleanor and knew her to be a crafty old bear. "But she
is away in Rouen, is she not? What if she hears nothing of John?"
His eyes darkened, and a strange sensation curled inside me, like a
snake coiling upon itself.

"I've heard that William, bishop of Ely, has spoken abroad of

John's behavior," I said, my voice sounding rough even to my own ears, "and will not rest until she knows of it. His hope had been to rouse the English nobles against the prince, but I believe his own bad manners at court have put his peers permanently against him."

"Bishop of Ely—what is he, against a prince with mercenaries?"

On we talked in this vein, and as we did I grew more serious and strove to convince Robin that he ought to lie low. Perhaps when John was more distracted with matters of state, the outlaws might venture forth freely again, but for now I feared for the life of any who went as far as Nottingham town. The place was swarming with purchased guards who caused trouble for every man, whether he were an honest tradesman or an outlaw in disguise.

Robin was always reluctant to curb their mode of life, but he also hated to send his men into certain danger. I believe I had just succeeded in persuading him to live out the coming winter in quiet, but the next morning we got bad word proving that our caution had come too late.

Dick Akeland came running, near dead from exhaustion, to tell us all that Will Stutley had been betrayed in the town and was now captured by Prince John's men. He lay inside the sheriff's prison in Nottingham town, awaiting the hour of his hanging. I had never seen Robin's face go so all white as it did at that news, and I too felt sick, for Will Stutley was an old friend and a loyal member of the band.

Without hesitating, Robin and a dozen men threw on disguises and left for town, each toting broad swords and a leather quiver stuffed with arrows. Annie and I discussed the matter with nervous voices, then slipped through the trees behind them, following the band to Nottingham so we might witness what passed for ourselves.

The town was crowded when we arrived, though whether it was more filled than usual in honor of Will's scheduled hanging, we did not know. Annie suggested we follow the crowd, thinking that it would lead us to the gallows tree in its time, and she was quite right. The main of men passed through the market, then on to the edge of a wooded clearing near the southern walls of town.

A poor broad oak, conscribed executioner, was already strung with a hempen rope. As we neared we saw Will, dejected and weak, surrounded by the sheriff's men. He looked quite ill and a little dazed, and my heart ached to see him thus, even as I considered that this could be the destined end of every man of the Greenwood tree if care weren't taken to keep them safe.

Before long the sheriff stepped close to the tree to proclaim Will's crime to the crowd, that of a hunted outlaw who stole his meat from the king's forest. I saw that Prince John was nowhere near, though his hand had certainly arranged the lot, for left on his own the sheriff had never caught a single outlaw from the forest.

I was straining my eyes over heads and hat tops to catch a glimpse of the sheriff's finery, for I had heard much about it from the men of Robin's camp, and so did not see when the excitement started. From my elbow I heard Annie exclaim, "Lawks-a-mercy, 'tis Little John!" Then all around me the crowd burst into disordered murmurs and even shouts.

"What is it, Annie? Tell me, what passes?"

She gripped my arm tightly and raised up on her toes.

"Why, just then, as the sheriff spoke, Little John leapt out from behind that bush, there, near Will Stutley, and sliced free his hands from their bonds. He had a spare sword, and now he and Will stand back to back, fighting against the sheriff's men."

Indeed, by now I could see for myself that everything beneath the hanging tree had turned to bedlam, for swords were flashing in the sunlight, and the sheriff ran from here to there, shouting to his men and standing in their way. Just then I heard the whistle of arrows and saw that several men were struck, not in the chest or lanky limb but by the tunic, pinned neatly to the trunk of the tree. The sheriff himself had his velvet hat whisked off his head by a goose-quilled arrow, and when he noticed it he sank straight down as if his blood had turned to lead, no longer hindering his men in their work.

Will and Little John made steady progress, and when they were covered by a second storm of arrows, they leapt lightly onto the sheriff's horse and thundered out of the city gate, free across the open field.

The entire battle might have lasted a full minute or perhaps two, and when it was over Annie and I clung to each other, both weak in the knees. I thought of Will and his frightened face and thanked the heavens that he had such a master as Robin Hood, who would never leave one of his men to swing on the gallows. But at the same time I saw that this would be Robin's fate if he were too bold, and I turned my feet toward Sherwood Forest, refreshing my vow to make him keep quiet—at least until the end of winter.

Chapter Fifteen

B Y THE TIME WILL STUTLEY recovered his nerve, the cold winds of winter swelled in force, sweeping down from the north and whistling through the trees of Sherwood. Robin set his men to work building bowers and gathering wood so the band might have supplies enough to last the winter through. Two score or more of the men moved into a broad-mouthed cave that stood near the river, but this was considered too chilly by Annie, who required that we have a wood-built house.

Just as she wished, a bower was built of our very own, and this we swept with happy hearts, squeezing green moss into the cracks and lining the floors with dry grass and deer pelts. We had space enough for our own fire and a propped-up door that could be removed to let out the smoke. We thought ourselves quite lucky indeed. The roof was so cunningly covered with boughs that not a drop of rain fell in, and we were left dry in our little house.

'Twas lucky indeed that we two shared a long experience with dull winter days, for Robin spent most of this time away, staying disguised at this inn or that, gathering news about Prince John. The keepers of the Blue Boar Inn were great friends of his, and I heard that he passed near all of January in their warm barn, exchanging tales as one does in winter when the snow-storms fly.

At times that winter my heart complained, weeping over the lost comforts of Warwick and bemoaning the darkness of our hut. But when these thoughts grew strong enough, I summoned an image of Lady Pernelle and her clawing hands and made myself believe I was happy. And, in fact, 'twas a great help to have Annie near, for she kept my memory honest and recalled the dullness of winters at Warwick with such dreary detail as made me smile.

Perhaps I was growing accustomed to harshness, or perhaps my critical mind was weak, but as it was I firmly believed I'd passed harder winters than that one. Our lives were not so terribly dull, for we had our stitching and friends about. Most days too we had need to call in one of the men to test if his tunic were too long, too short, or nearly perfect. Robin did pass our way sometimes, and when he did he always stopped to sit by our fire and tell us the news and hear how we were passing the time.

I missed his company in a thousand ways, and at first I begged him to return to the camp, that we might resume our talks of the world. Whenever I asked he would tarry longer, passing a night in the cave with his men and bringing his smile to our bower at the morrow. He brought us news and London wine and herbs to burn in our small fire, but then he would always be off again, his eyes expressing his sorrow at parting while his two feet itched to be away. I thought he was bothered by the close crowds of winter, for with us all huddled around the fire, there was hardly room for private talk. Perhaps he reckoned as I did, that if he couldn't have the sun to himself, he would just as soon not see it at all.

Winter was hard on his restless soul, for he had a constant need for doing, and the snow and cold kept him sadly still. I think he looked with envy sometimes at our work with the iron needles, for he could not find quiet tasks enough to employ himself for half the day, and this made him irritable. He knew it did and this, I believe, was what caused him to stay apart. It was his habit of many long years, and sad as it was to be without him, I did not question it.

MARCH FOLLOWED FEBRUARY in the usual way and with it came heavy rains and winds, the sort that flood small river towns and leaves them caked with mud. But late in the month the sun began to shine with some strength, and I felt the blood that had been thickened by cold begin to run swiftly in my veins. Each day I stretched my limbs a bit more, first with long walks and then with forays into the clearing to work with my cudgel. I was determined to show Robin that I'd lost no skill over the winter months, so I practiced steadily, thinking of how my progress would please him.

Soon he returned to join our band, merry as ever but sobered somewhat by news that Prince John was attempting to gain the chancellorship of England, a position that would give him near full control over the country until the king's return. I tried to assure him that Queen Eleanor would never allow such a thing to pass, but I fear Robin was beginning to doubt the queen's interest in our island.

But on the small scale of our daily lives, spring breezes seemed to awaken us all and breathe new life into our souls. Allan's songs were heard with new joy, piping tunes were to be danced to, and sport of all kind was undertaken at the least suggestion. My tensions with Little John still remained, although Annie did much to relieve them by gracing him with her own attention. She smiled and winked and kept him entranced while Robin and I sat together, deep in the grasses at the edge of the meadow. He liked to tickle my nose with a grass blade, teasing until he made me laugh, while I plucked flowers to tuck in my hair. But we both felt restless near the Greenwood tree and longed for a chance to slip away.

HE AND I HAD fast become the best of friends, and I found myself thinking of him at all hours, preparing tales he might enjoy, practicing smiles meant just for him. I dreamt of him so often—and in such warm dreams—that I believe his image was worn in grooves upon the insides of my eyelids. His vision, his words, his breath in my ear followed me day and night, thrilling my bones down to the marrow. All these things seemed natural to me, and I thought very little of them until one day in early May when I found myself walking a path with Ellen and heard myself ask this question of her: "Ellen, tell me, how did you know when you were in love?"

"In love with Allan? Why, I had known him near all my life, and I can't think of a time when I did not love him."

"But as more than a friend, I mean, or a brother."

"Oh, I don't know. Could have been when he first sang me the "May Ellen" song, for it's as romantic as any I know. Or when my father—oh, and that man—told me, you know, who I was to marry. I could not tell you, honestly, Marian, only that I knew when it was time to know."

I frowned this off, for it did not help me, nor did I understand why I had asked it of her to begin with. Ellen was no one to ask serious questions of, but did I seriously wish to ask it? And why might I? These questions left my mind disturbed, and I passed several sleepless nights, but still I felt no nearer the answer until a misty night in June when I had an hour of true revealing.

ANNIE AND I WERE in the camp filling pots with oil and rags to use as lanterns the rest of the year, and so we knew nothing of the danger until it was nearly done with. Robin and Little John had left early that day heading west, while most of the men were sent south and east. Now that Prince John vied for the chancellorship, we all assumed he was sufficiently distracted to allow our men free reign of the forest—a false assumption we would soon regret.

Together Annie and I did our work, talking and singing as we often did, chatting with the other men left behind to tend the fires and prepare meat enough for the evening meal. The sun grew heavy, low and languid, and the men returned from the south and east, but Robin and Little John were not among them. As a group we waited, quiet but unafraid, until the sky began to darken, and then I felt my first pang of fear. For the sun sets late in the month of June, and I had never known Robin to stay out so long before.

We worried and waited, and some made jokes to hide their fright while others sat with drawn faces, unsure what to think or do. At last we ate, biting our meat with tortured mouths, and retired to bed though we were not sleepy, mechanically grinding the rhythms of the day.

I passed, that night, through a sea of anguish and delirium, fearing the worst and seeing my dread mix itself in with terrible dreams. Somewhat toward dawn I dreamt again of Atalanta and heard in my sleep the lines of the poem I had read so often in my Ovid text but had misplaced from my conscious mind.

For Atalanta was green in love, untutored—she did not know what she was doing, and loved, and did not know it.

I woke with a shock, gasping and starting, eyes flung open to meet my fate. The words still rang in my head, echoed against my beating heart, and I had to think to form a breath, force my lungs to accept the air. Truth became black and white to me, and I opened my eyes wide in the darkness and saw what I could not see before.

I loved Robin Hood.

The night, the earth, the cosmic design—all were clear to me in that instant. A realization of vast proportion had dawned in my mind, and I greeted it with the open acceptance a sudden knowledge is worthy of. I had loved him long and earnestly, perhaps since the day we met, perhaps less time, I did not know. But did it matter? This was love, I knew it at last, and for a moment a golden light entered my breast and let me shine.

But not a full heartbeat later, I opened my eyes again in the dark and had to fight back the pain of tears. For what did it matter whom I loved, if Robin would never return to me? A whole night he'd been gone, a full score of hours. I bit my hand to stop my cries and thought instead that I should have hope, for would Robin not hope were he in my place?

Knowing that my night had ended and no more sleep would come to me, I rose and dressed and slipped to the camp to kindle the fires against the cold. For when they returned, I told myself, they might be chilled from their night abroad and would wish for a fire to warm themselves by. When this was done I found other tasks to occupy my trembling hands, mending and fixing in the demilight of a newborn day.

I had just sat down to shudder and gasp a second time, to admit the fear that had crept in stealthily past my resolve, when a snap in the forest caught my ears and brought me running to meet my love.

Robin and Little John stepped into our clearing looking as if they had never seen a more generous sight. One was supported by the other, and when I grew closer I saw that it was Little John who was injured, leaning his giant's weight on his friend. They called out when they saw me, and I exclaimed too, rushing to help them make their way to the fireside and seats of rest.

When we neared the fire I saw that Robin's face was dark, his eyes fixed as the wolf's eyes are when he is backed off by men with clubs. I sat near him by the fire, my heart still shaking with the truths of the morning. Neither of us had the strength to speak, but for one instant he extended a hand to touch my hair, and the world seemed to stop in its place. A moment later he was master again of his band of men, calling them out of their sleeping places to tend to Little John in his distress.

Soon the camp was alive with noise, every man crying out with joy and triumph at seeing his friends safely returned. Broth was heated for Little John and hunks of bread passed all around. Then, at last, the men were seated and quiet enough to hear the tale of what had kept their master from them all the day and through the night.

Robin began, speaking slowly and with calm tones, almost as if he hoped to keep from frightening us by holding his voice firm as a bowstring.

"The tale begins yesterday morning, when we all stepped out for the day's work. Little John and I went west as we often do of a Tuesday. We hadn't been gone two hours when we spied a fellow by Rudd's creek—the spot with all the blackberry brambles. Neither of us knew his face, and he was dressed like a mad fool, in a horse-hide—"

Here Little John interrupted. "He looked a fright, I tell you plainly. The hide of a horse upon his back, a horse's head-skin on his own pate, and even the tale stitched on his arse!"

"Aye, he was, dressed all up in horse hide, and I agree 'twas a hideous costume. Any road, Little John was game to meet with him, but I thought I'd better do it, and so I sent him on toward Mansfield while I went up to the stranger."

" 'Twould have been better had I gone, Robin, I'll say it again."

"Aye, perhaps, Little John," Robin agreed, looking toward his friend with such a gaze that I knew he felt pain for what Little John suffered. "But we went our ways, whatever the merits, and I made for the man in horsehide. 'Good morrow, fellow,' I said to him, and he replied the same to me. But then he went on, as if he'd a yen for conversation. 'You seem a good archer, judging by the bow you bear on your shoulder,' he said. 'Tell me, if you know these woods, can you point me in my way? For I must be lost and I've a need to make good haste this morning.' So right quick I offered to be his guide, for if he wished to leave the forest, I was ready to help him do it.

" 'But no,' he said, 'I seek an outlaw named Robin Hood, and

I'd rather meet with him than with forty pounds of gold, I would.' That gave me a cold feeling, I can tell you. But I kept a calm front and replied that I thought 'twould be best for him to avoid the fellow, for a fight with Robin Hood might mean his end, so I said. So after a bit more chat we agreed to have a quick shooting match to enjoy the day, and we broke off to set up the targets."

Here the men interrupted his tale with their knowing laughter, for they were aware how this match would end. Robin smiled faintly at their confidence and continued.

"We shot a bit, and he proved good, but not as good a shot as I. He struck right into the garland ring more than once, but when we gathered up the marks, he saw that I'd hit the pole, and then he felt ashamed enough to sneer and spit in my direction. 'Tell me thy name, good fellow,' said he. But I replied that I should not until I'd the pleasure of hearing his. 'I'm Guy of Gisborne,' he said, 'outlaw of the Needwood Forest.'"

"Guy of Gisborne!" cried Clym at this, leaping to his feet in fear and looking, despite himself, around the dark edge of the clearing.

"Indeed, 'twas he, and I've time now to thank you, Clym, for telling me of him, for once I heard his name spoken I knew this man was not to be trusted. So then I told him who I was, and we drew swords, for he told me right off that Prince John had offered him a knight's fiefdom for my head.

"We went to it with the swords and were pretty well matched. Once I nearly lost it all from tripping over a root in the path, and I thought I was worm meal as sure as Saint Dunstan. But as Guy came to strike me down, I caught him with a backhanded stroke and sliced his head clean from his neck, like taking the cap off an egg. And 'twas the end of Guy of Gisborne."

At this the men let out a cheer, but I saw that Robin was far from rejoicing. This, then, made the second man he'd had the misfortune to kill in his day, and this second death seemed no easier for him to bear than the first had been.

"Now, I think, we ought to turn to Little John, to hear his tale, for I followed after him toward Mansfield to see how he made out with things."

"Sure now, Robin, and don't forget to tell them how you put on Guy of Gisborne's horse suit and wore it into town yourself!"

"Ah, aye, I did do that." Here Robin turned a bit to me, as if embarrassed by the deed. "I meant to act the part of Guy, to make Prince John believe me—Robin Hood—dead. Otherwise I feared he'd fill the forest with his soldiers, all in search of Guy."

The men nodded at his quick thinking and turned their faces to Little John, eager to hear what became of him.

"So," Little John began, propping his hurt leg upon a wood round, "I went to Mansfield to see what passed there, and no sooner had I entered the village than a host of the prince's mercenaries surrounded me. One struck me hard in the leg with his cudgel, and I went down fast like a hamstringed horse, straight into the mud. They took me off to an open field and tied me soundly to a post, and I tell you now, I thought that would be the last of my days, I thought so truly. For the prince's men were fierce indeed, not soft and foolish like the sheriff's clods, and I thought I might die in that spot and never see this clearing again.

"But I stood and stood on my hurt leg, and soon the sky began to spin before me, for I was injured enough for it to affect my brain, I think. At any rate, for a time it all went black, but when I woke I felt more whole than I had all that day. The shadows were long by that time and looking out I saw that horsehided man approach, blowing his bugle for all he was worth, and then the tears streamed from my eyes, for I thought that stranger had killed our Robin.

"I saw him talk with the sheriff a while, for the prince himself was nowhere near, and at last the horsehided man approached me, his knife drawn, as if he wished to slit my throat. I cried out, I'm sure I did, but as he came he spoke to me and—what surprise!—I heard dear Robin's own voice come from beneath that wretched horse-hair pate. Robin drew near and cut my bonds, then put the stranger's bow in my hands and bid me shoot if I found a mark, and off we ran for the forest edge.

"We lit off fast, but the sheriff's men were right behind, for they'd never been far off, and once they saw me light away they notched their arrows and went to work. I stumbled as I made my way, my leg not up to the weight of running, and as I fell I saw the sheriff, the man himself, leading the charge with swords a-flashing, for he was truly angered at me.

"I set my arrow against the string and let it fly, and as I watched it struck the sheriff straight in the neck and felled him, clean as a tree falls in the wood." Here Little John laughed nervously and looked quite green about the face. "Then Robin came back and helped me up, and we made off to the woods together."

A silence followed their frightening story, as each of us thought over what had passed. Robin, our leader, had nearly been slain by a hired assassin, the worst in the land, and Little John, the right-hand man, had killed the sheriff, the appointed ruler of Nottinghamshire. My hands, I fear, began to shake at the mere remembrance of the tale, and I looked at their faces for reassurance but found nothing there but sorrow and fright.

"And the night," Clym asked quietly, seeking a full report of their time. "Where did you pass the night?"

"High in a broad oak," Little John chortled. "We slept on a branch nearly ten feet up, with me tied on so I wouldn't fall off in my sleep, for you know how I like to toss and turn."

Again the crowd tittered nervously.

"I think," said Robin, standing stiffly, "we ought to move about our work and think no more on yesterday. Guy of Gisborne can harm none now, so we've nothing more to fear of him. And as for the sheriff, well, he is no more and too should frighten us no longer. Once Little John's leg has mended, he will be off for Barnesdale Forest in the north to hide away till the sheriff's men cease searching for him. The rest of us will keep a quiet life here for a month or two and venture into no towns or villages."

The men nodded at his suggestions, but still they sat for several moments before any rose to start his work, for this was a blow to their security. Each was reminded in the fear of the moment of his first flight to the forest and all the worries that accompanied it—'twas a sobering atmosphere that hung beneath the Greenwood tree.

When they at last began to disperse, I rose with shaking limbs and scurried off to the edge of camp, too unnerved to tend to my work. My nightmare visions of Robin's fate had been horrific, but somehow I was more badly frightened by the truth than I had been by my dreams. They both lived, I told myself, speaking sternly; Robin lives and is well, so do not fret. But I did fret, and in my distress of heart I ran for the clearing to be alone.

No sooner had I reached the grove and taken my cudgel up in my hands than my fear dissolved away into anger. Fury roared like wind in my heart, enflamed by awareness that while I loved, I too might lose; while I remained warm and safe, I still might fall to grave peril. For had Robin died in the northern wood, what would have become of me? I'd have lost my heart, cracked my soul until it bled. And worse perhaps, I also would have lost my home, my comfort, and security. Without Robin there was no life at the Greenwood tree, and had I lost him I would surely have lost that as well.

These thoughts worked me into a frenzied rage, so incensed was I at having allowed my heart to be caught and stolen away. I bashed my staff against the practice pole until it made my palms sting and shudder; then on I went, cursing the weakness of my heart and the imperfection of my memory. I thought I worked quite alone, but as I paused to dash away tears of self-reproach and disgust, I saw with a start that Robin approached and came to sit on the sward beside me.

"Marian," he said, his voice ragged, "what troubles you?"

"I am in no state for talking, Robin," I cried, ignoring a fresh pain in my shoulder.

He sat in silence for a moment, then raised his face to me again. "Come, Marian. Speak with me."

"Nay, Robin, I beg you, nay. Unless you wish to hear words of spite, do not stay here. Make your way back to camp."

I saw him frown, for I'm certain my actions held no logic for him. But he could not see the regret in my heart, the way my desires split in two, each as powerful as the other. I had neglected the one, my own safekeeping, in favor of the other, and none should pay the penalty but me.

But as he stood and strode away, a new panic rose on par with my anger. For what if I lost my chance at love through being overzealous for preservation? Confused as I was, both heart and mind, I could not bear to see Robin go, to see his eyes leave my face, to watch his shoulders vanish in the wood. Despite my mind's most ardent warnings, my body formed its own design. I ran after him, fast as a hare, until I stood panting in his way, my cudgel still heavy in my hands.

"Wait, Robin, wait," I gasped. "I'm in a sour temper, but you're not to blame. I'm only cross with myself, for I'd not seen till now what a snare I'd worked my way into."

"What snare is that?" he asked, his eyes strong upon me.

"Of caring more than I'd intended," I blurted. "I cannot stop myself from thinking what danger you were in just now and how very close you came to . . . dying. What would I have done without you, Robin? How should I ever have mended my heart?"

He took the cudgel from me and tossed it away, light as a twig, then pulled me close until our bodies met, one warm against the other.

"Shouldn't you rather have a heart besmudged by tears and scratches than a perfect one ignorant of life? Come, Marian, lose your fear for a moment. Embrace this hour and none other, and grant yourself a touch of happiness."

His words rushed like water between my ears, bathing my over-heated soul. I longed for nothing but Robin then, and I raised my face to greet his, as trusting as a summer's rose. We kissed a time, as the sounds in my head changed to ocean tides, to trickling currents, and rabid streams. This was the life I'd so longed for—this was my place of true serenity.

I cannot say how much time passed, there on the green sward of our grove. It might have been hours or half a year. But when I noticed the sun again, and the bluebells thick on the woodland floor, I also knew that Robin was entwined in my fate as surely as Orpheus to Eurydice. My internal fury had not yet subsided—my fear was still quaking, raw in the light—but too I had Robin to charm and delight me, and this rose like cream to the frothy top.

I was steeping these thoughts as I traced Robin's face with my two fingers, smoothing the worry away from his temples and brushing back danger with his ruddy locks. He too had expressions to make with his hands, but after a time he lay back with a sigh and caught my fingers tightly in his.

"It was, I admit, a close escape. First Guy of Gisborne, then Little John." He shook his head. "I fear our time here is fading away. Dangers grow strong on every side—our Greenwood tree is not what it once was. But I promise you, Marian, it will not always be thus with me." He rolled onto his side so I might see the solemnity in his eyes. "Somehow, in some way, I swear I will make my life legitimate. This is no way for us to be, always fearful of the law." His eyes matched hue with the sky above us, cloudless and pure. "Marian, you are more dear to me than . . . than perhaps the sun in the sky. And if you will be my own true love, I swear I will stay clear from danger until I leave this outlaw's life for one that we both can bear to live."

"Oh, Robin!" I cried, wrapping my arms about his neck. "Aye, please, let's do! Live with me always, will you, Robin? I will do whatever I can, only promise to always be my friend."

"As much as I can and more, my love. I swear it, we will find a way."

Chapter Sixteen

FROM THAT DAY FORWARD we were in love, and no happiness of mind, no tinkling of bells or twitter of skylarks, could compare with my delight. For me the month was silver and gold, each day floating on gossamer wings, high above the dark fields of doubt. Robin met me each morning with a kiss and a smile, and I left him each night by caressing his face and promising nothing but sweet dreams for us both. We were as close as a pair of stock doves, cooing and loving from dawn to dusk.

Robin proved to have a romantic soul, for he never went anywhere throughout the wood without bringing me back a posy or a small wreath of honeysuckle. More often, in those months, we walked out together, turning our toes toward an old apple tree or gleaning nuts from the ancient hedgerows. For now that we'd reached our sublime understanding, Robin would permit no guard to follow him, no well-meaning man to watch his back. He was mine and mine alone to tease and caress, or mock-wrestle on the woodland slopes till we ended in kisses as soft as goose down. All was merry and joyous and gay—truly I had never known such a time.

In the slow evenings he might take me upon his knee and sing to me songs about our band, made-up tunes that resembled Allan's about as much as a bear does a rabbit, but joking ones to make me laugh. He would sing of Annie or David of Doncaster, perhaps a song of how they would wrestle, and Annie would seize the title from David, long considered the best wrestler in the shire. Or he might sing about Friar Tuck and his solemn piety, the very piety that led him to drink and fight to excess and seek out all of the prettiest girls whenever he went to a market day.

We were happy, but a shroud of sadness was all around us. Little John had gone on his way, and he was sorrowfully missed, I knew, by not only Robin but by the whole band. Robin, at times, foresaw that the parting of Little John might signal the end of the outlaws of Sherwood, although he would never have said such a thing to any other but me. The rest of the men were muddling on, hunting and fishing as they ever had and ignoring the sense we all shared that something great had been lost forever.

Beyond that feeling of darkness and dread, the practical truths were equally grim. Our band was running low on silver. Robin had always retained one-third of the coin in any noble's purse to keep his band in flour and wool, but his savings were shrinking, and we were too shy to find new donors. These summer months used to be our best, when careless travelers would take to the forest with the Lady Day taxes or the Easter hen money. But now we were hiding, doing no more than living, and each day our pennies grew fewer and fewer.

The politics of the realm reflected the turbulence of Sherwood, for John had achieved his long-sought chancellorship and now increased his band of soldiers at a frightening pace. Rumors had spread that he meant to sail for Paris to join forces with Philip Augustus, king of France, against his brother Richard. Robin and I discussed these matters every day, sharing our fears over what might happen.

"I've heard Queen Eleanor returns to London," he said one day after sending Clym, unknown in Nottingham, to bring us the news. "They say she means to gather the nobles and convince them to restrain Prince John. Clym reports that she will offer a silver piece for each one of John's mercenaries who is delivered, bound, to her guard. There's a moneymaking scheme for us!"

He said this jokingly, but I saw nothing in his words to laugh at. "Are you mad, Robin? No deal with Queen Eleanor will end well for anyone but the queen herself, I promise you that. She'll deal behind any ally's back, make more promises than she can keep. The man who agrees to arrest John's men will find himself swinging from London Tower."

"I know how you feel about Eleanor, Marian, but it is an offer of sound money."

"Please," I said, covering my ears, "I cannot hear you speak such words. She's a shrewd cat and if she returns to London it is to pursue her own interests, not yours or mine or even England's. She wants John down—very well and good—but let her do the work herself. She's soldiers enough of her own to do it."

Robin sighed, nodding his head, for we often came to this same impasse. "In that case we're back to our old stunts, and we'll need to begin them soon. Perhaps when the queen's soldiers come to Nottingham, they'll bring a lightly guarded load of silver. What think you to that?"

"I think they won't, and you're better off with your old friend the bishop or the prior of Emmet."

"Ah, true, but those friends seem at last to have learned our tricks. They never travel through the forest now without a host of guards about them. And I think more often they extend the trip and ride through Lincoln where the outlaws of Sherwood can never catch them. Nay, we must take a bold strike if we wish to fill our strongbox again. To trade with the queen, 'tis boldness itself."

I was incredulous to hear him speak a second time of approaching the queen. "Have you gone daft, Robin, even to think of it?

'Twould be reckless and mad to deal with any noble now. You're often called bold, Robin, but don't you see that the opposite face of that same coin is foolhardiness?"

"And can you not see that for all your caution, your coin too has a second side?" His face was growing flushed with anger. "You paralyze yourself with fear, Marian. Life is to be lived, not shied from."

I felt the sting of this well enough, but I would not hold my tongue. "There's more than your own hide at stake in this matter. When I seek to protect myself I do no harm to others and nothing but good to myself—you cannot deride my caution, Robin. Can you not recall the peril I shall face if the queen guesses that I still live? Know you not how far the fame of Robin Hood spreads and how keen every reeve would be to take you, to collect his prize from the queen's own hand?"

"Aye, peril waits on every side," he cried, leaping to his feet. "But we must take some action—I won't leave my men here to waste and starve."

"Then think, dear Robin, sit and ponder until you've found a better way. For if once the queen is involved in our trials, a plague will creep across us all until nothing but barren bones remain." I watched him turn his eyes away and thought a sickness had touched us already. "Do you not recall, my love, how you swore to me that you would find an honest life and take no risks until 'twas done? If you knew but one tenth of how I suffered when I feared you were lost to Guy of Gisborne's sword, you would not speak of placing yourself in the way of danger. My heart cannot bear it, Robin, I swear."

He came forward then and held me close, stroking my hair in his soft manner, touching my cheek with the flesh of his thumb.

So our conversations always turned. The prospects for our band were bleak, and between us we found no way to brighten them. But Robin, I found, did not tell me everything he had in his mind. No, indeed, he made plans I knew nothing about.

TOWARD THE END OF JULY, Robin left us to take a trip abroad for more than a week. He would not tell me where he went, but as he and I had often discussed the notion of relocating the band, I thought he went to examine other forests for suitability. 'Twas Robin's opinion that Prince John's seizure of Nottingham Castle ruined things for an outlaw band living as close as we did, for the occupation of the castle drew in so many soldiers, the odds of escaping from every tight fix grew perilously slim.

Therefore, I did not question him about his trip. I did remember, however, that the last time he left for a long journey, he returned with me, so I joked with him that he went to free himself a new woman from her marriage bonds and bring her back to live among us.

"Tell me, what will you do with your bonny Alice or pretty Sue when I'm nearby?"

"Perhaps I'll send you off each day to fetch me honey and apple tarts."

"And when I return? At least you must promise to dismiss Alice as often as you send me off."

Here he pulled me onto his knee and tickled my face with his chin whiskers until I laughed and had to bury my nose in his shoulder to escape.

"Ah, Marian, 'twill be but a week or a little more, but I shall miss you. Promise you'll keep yourself safe till my return? No trips to Retford while I'm away?"

"Of course I promise," I said, still laughing. "I've no wish to be caught and hung without you there to see it."

He did not laugh at my grim joke but held me close and spoke no more.

TIME PASSED SLOWLY while he was away, and I'm ashamed to say I fell to moping about the camp. Annie was my one solace, and as she allowed me to speak of Robin as often as I chose, I entertained myself that way for most of my lonely days.

But when he had gone and I'd no Robin to make me laugh away my worry, I began to fear anew. I felt like a trapped wild thing, hissing and spitting, for here I was caught, wedged between Prince John's mercenaries and Robin's absence. I could go nowhere until his return. And so I began to stew and fret.

My childhood terrors reclaimed their prominent space in my thoughts, hounding me night by night until I had questioned my every last motive, wondered at my own decisions. Why did I stay here, my fears demanded, caught in the web of Robin's love? If I feared for our lives, why did I not flee, make my way to greener fields where none but I could make decisions? Myself I could trust, the little voice echoed, but none other.

Images of escape, of fleeing the forest, swarmed my thoughts. I longed for Robin, ached for his soothing presence. But too I felt a hatred for him, for had I not loved, I would not have hesitated in this forest one day beyond Prince John's arrival. I should have made myself scarce as a woodcock, sleeping tight in a bed of leaves. Raw anguish seemed to consume my soul, but I could do nothing other than wait for either Robin to arrive or the dreaded troops to come and string us up on the hangman's noose.

I questioned Annie in those days, asking what would become of her if the band did move or break apart, for I feared for her safety as much as for my own. I heard her say what I'd always suspected, that if she were in any danger she would flee to Wodesley village and tell the steward that she'd been dismissed by her employer and wished to become a farm woman once more.

Robin was away two weeks in the end, but he sent Clym back with a message, bidding us to be patient. I did my best, but waiting has never been my strength. I grew more restless by the day, more agitated, more apprehensive. Then one night as I lay wrestling with my dread, I was visited by a dream. I call it a dream, for it must have been such, but its shapes and hues were so vivid, it seemed clearer than waking day.

I saw myself, bound and disheveled, standing in a dusty hall. To my right stood my favorites among the merry men, David of Doncaster, Lawrence Ganniel, Will Scarlet, and gentle Allan, and they too were bound and appeared as miserable as bull calves being led to the ax. Some were bleeding from running wounds; some vomited on the stone floor. But I turned my eyes away from them, for near a chaise decked with violet damask sat Queen Eleanor.

She'd altered little since I'd last seen her. Her brows were now fully brushed with gray and she'd lost a tooth or two, but the face and eyes remained the same. The eyes were fast upon me now, bluer than frost on a frozen lake, so chilling I shuddered where I stood.

"So you see, Lady Marian," she declared, "you cannot defeat me. I shall always triumph, for I am the queen, and you are no more than a female vassal. You attempted to fool me once before, to trick me into believing you dead, but I was not fooled—I have never been fooled. And now you shall pay for having sought to deceive me, wicked girl." She waved her arm and from the shadows that ranged behind her stepped Robin. He too was bound and had clearly been beaten, for his right eye was so swollen it oozed black tears, and his left hand could not form a fist.

"Robin!" I screamed. "What do you want of him?"

"The same that I want from you and your companions—to fulfill your fates. But I'd waste little sympathy on this brigand, Marian. He has ignored your advice and the oath he swore. Just like a Saxon," she hissed, "crude and vulgar. I doubt such a man will find his way to the gates of heaven—I suspect you won't see this one again."

"But I don't care!" I cried, straining against the ropes that held me. "I don't care if he won't hear my counsel or if he is crude at times. I wish to love and to live, not cower in fear!"

The queen turned her chilling eyes upon me, so beautiful, firm, like polished silver. "Listen to me, Lady Marian. If you wish to survive you will heed my words. Cut loose this thieving mongrel. His ignorant ways will make an end for you, an ugly end of pain and heartbreak. Turn him off and get you hence before his deception carries you past saving."

With that I woke, gulping air and grasping the blankets. I feared waking Annie, feared telling her anything of my dream, for while she knew enough of Queen Eleanor to dislike her greatly, she was unaware of my personal hatred. So out I slipped, stumbling badly as I left the bower so that I fell against a stump and cracked my knee on its woody face. I sank to the ground there, deep in dirt, and grasped at my knee like a child, not a full-grown woman of nineteen years.

I WORKED THAT MORNING to distract myself, but I could not shake the cloak of dread the dream had tossed upon my shoulders. It lay too heavy to ignore, a great dead weight, the compilation of my darkest thoughts and hopeless visions. But one thing, I thought, could cheer me, and that was to see my Robin's face, earnest and smiling and full of comfort.

He arrived before the sun had risen past the tops of the dogwood trees. I sighed to see him, certain that my time of worry had ended and that laughter and merriment lay before me. But when he stooped to greet and kiss me, a chill grew in my arms and shoulders. Something was altered in his manner, something changed, for he gave the smile I so longed for, but it lacked conviction. A germ of falsehood had touched his face, and it made my eyes recoil from him.

"I must be off again, my love," he whispered. "I've something brewing that could be grand." He was animated, even more than usual, with his cheeks in high color and his eyes bright and roving.

"What is it, Robin?" I hissed at his ear, for 'twas clear he wished the others to know nothing of our conversation. "What has happened?"

"Not now, sweet. Let me be off—I'll tell you all when I return."

"But Robin," I breathed, standing to better grasp at his tunic, "I fear something grave has happened. You seem so strange!"

"Something has happened, but I dare to hope it will not be grave in the least. It may be the making of us, Marian. The bold step I spoke of before."

"Or it may be our death!" I cried, clutching his tunic front with both hands. Edmund Gray, a boy of twelve who sat nearby, turned in alarm to watch us. Robin saw him and reached to pluck my hands away.

"I cannot discuss this now, Marian. I must away!"

"Hold, Robin! Do not expect me to wait here for word that you've been caught and captured. You do not know the torture of it! I die a dozen deaths at once each time I envision you set to hang. Have mercy, Robin, and pray, do nothing foolish! Silver is nothing—think of your safety!"

"I've little care for that, Marian," he said with a hollow, soulless laugh. And I knew then for the first time that he valued his life as dearly as I. He too was frightened, and seeing this made my panic rise higher than before. It seemed the forest was ablaze around us, and I stood impotent. I could not quench the flames myself; I could not persuade Robin to do it. My only recourse was to flee.

He left me there with my hands clenched tightly in effort to warm them, feeling as if I might be ill. 'Twas then that I spied his traveling companions, for he had not returned to the forest alone. They stood in a mass, well clad in stiff boots and leather doublet, but when I moved closer to get a clear view, a tight pain jabbed against my lungs. These were no outlaws, no yeomen of Needwood or Plompton Forest, but the very captain of the king's guard and Queen Eleanor's personal page. Her page I recognized by his face, the captain by his garments only, but these things combined were enough to convince me of what Robin had done. He had gone to London, to the bear's own cave, and struck a bargain with the queen.

My heart went cold when I thought of it, considered what peril he'd placed himself in—and purposefully too—after all his promises to shy from danger. I knew by the captain's presence here that Robin meant to arrest John's men, the very things we'd discussed and agreed would be foolish! All this risk to raise some silver for the band's coffers—it made me heartsick.

I knew as deep as the soles of my feet that the queen would make no bargains she couldn't get the best of. Robin might produce the mercenaries—at what cost to his own men, I shuddered to think—and Eleanor might pay him his due. But a known outlaw such as he would never be allowed to flee to the woodland. He would be seized, of that I was certain, and if he were seized he would surely hang.

I crept a little closer to the page's horse, for I was determined to know the worst. There I saw a plump bag of coins hanging from his saddle horn, and my stomach went weak with dread. I saw the future spread before my eyes, saw Robin swinging from the gallows, heard my own wailing cries. The queen's voice as I'd heard it in slumber lilted through my memory now. "Cut loose the thieving mongrel," she'd said. His deception would be my ruin. His deception—

In another instant I was stumbling forward, racing for the empty bower. Lies and trickery seemed fast on my heels, woven into Robin's face, dripping from the leaves of the oaks. I thought of the emptiness in his eyes, in the stiff vibrations of his laugh, and nearly choked for tears. In him I forgave many things and overlooked a thousand faults, but I would not stand duplicity, not between our two hearts.

I felt a great sore had erupted on our once bright and polished love. A blackened lesion that stank and oozed and grew with each passing breath. It would envelop his heart and mine, and it would defeat us as no external threat could do. I could not stay to see it pass—I would not. I felt in my bones a need to flee, to take myself from all this madness and find, for once, somewhere safe.

Our Greenwood tree, once noble and lovely, now seemed the stuff of gallows ropes. My sight turned hazy, the earth slipped sideways, and I felt fear as a weight, a burden, an affliction from which I could not escape.

AN ODD BURST OF BIRDSONG far off in the wood altered the spell, and I found I had feet and limbs and hands—all the tools of my salvation. Without further thought I ran to my bower and gathered some things into a sack, scarcely noticing the tears that fell on my hands as they snatched and shoved. When I came across a scrap of parchment, I wrote a hasty note to Annie, telling her simply in words she could read not to worry, that I would be fine, but I could not remain to see my friends taken by Queen Eleanor's hand.

My bag was full, and I turned to go. But as I went my eye fell on the faded tunic and suit of hose I'd been using to size Allan a Dale's new set of clothes. In a flash it was on me, for Allan was small, and my own gown and kerchief were stuffed into my sack.

I eased from the bower with careful steps, but I needn't have worried. The camp was empty. They had all gone to do Robin's folly, even the captain and the queen's page. Annie and Ellen were at Retford market, and for once the cold fires stood unattended. I wiped off a tear as I left the place and turned my feet for the River Trent road.

Chapter Seventeen

As I walked, I seemed to pass through moods as clearly as I went through scenes, first of pine woods, then of fields, then of marsh or fallow land. In the pines came anger, which blinded me so that I saw neither trees nor the path before me. How could he, I cried out, have dealt with the queen when I had told him all I knew of her? How could he have been so foolish, when I had been there to steer him right? What madness was it, I asked myself, that caused a man to ignore his love and believe her powers of thought to be weak and not worth heeding? All the crimes of stupidity and perverseness were there attributed to Robin Hood, and nothing more than a change of view from forest to fields could save him from my mental lashings.

But when fields stretched on either side, expanding for miles up valley and down, my anger cooled. My footsteps slowed to match the tears that slipped so constantly from my eyes. At times I stopped and sobbed in my sleeve, grateful that none passed me on the road, for it would not do for any to see a young boy in green weeping in the dirt. I did my best to remain conscious of my attire and the disguise I wore, but at times my heartache was so great, I could honestly think of nothing else.

At last I paused and sank to the earth at the side of the road, wondering over what I had done. I wept and shuddered and muttered my love's name into the dust, but as I sat I began to think, and the anger that was cooled and steaming rose to the boiling point once more. My fury gave my limbs new life, and I rose once more with resurrected purpose.

The wind was fresh and it calmed my mind enough to consider other matters. I strongly regretted having left Annie, for I knew she would worry over me. But what could I do? I would not turn back now, would not drive myself back to a tangle of falsehoods. I marched past deep grasslands and as I stepped, I considered that, were I in Robin's stead, I would not have played false by him. I would have told him my every thought, would have been transparency itself. And had he, with all the power of conviction, advised me against doing a deed, I should not have done it, even if prodded by knifepoint.

Had he a sworn enemy, a bloodthirsty foe, I would never have taken myself into his camp to barter our lives against sacks of coin. And had I done so, I would have confessed it all to Robin, for thus ran the boundaries of my mind. Falsehoods I might tell by the dozen, but neither to Robin nor to Annie. With these two I strove for honesty always, whatever I might fabricate for the world.

This was the pact, unspoken and silent, that Robin had severed. And so, I thought, he had severed me also, sliced me clean like an unwanted limb, which he could not reclaim even had he wished. These heated thoughts fueled my stride, and I walked on in hopes of exhausting my mind along with my body.

AFTER A MILE or maybe more of steady breathing and dry eyes, I began to look about me, to see the birds settled in the marsh and watch them fish for frogs and dragonflies. I had staggered into unfarmed lands, too wet for the plow and too deep for oxen. This place reminded me of a land I'd heard my tutor describe in my youth, in the east of England. 'Twas called the Fens, a land of salt marsh, and I imagined it smelled as this marsh did, of honey and salt, sulfur and wheatgrass.

Where was I going? At first I took little time to wonder, but as the marsh air cleared my mind, I began to turn my thoughts to it. I approached a crossroads and headed east, deciding on impulse to travel to Denby. I knew not why it appealed to me, for I was better acquainted with Warwick and London, but I had a queer notion that my raw heart would be best mended in my native land. I did not question this fancy of mine, but turned my steps along the River Trent and went to see what my fortunes would bear.

IT TOOK ME THREE DAYS to reach Denby, in part the result of losing my way and in part because I bided my time. At nights I found a patch of wood and curled up in my cloak to sleep, waking at every hoot of an owl, my cudgel gripped and ready to strike. Each morning I woke with a crick in my neck, my body aching from a night spent shivering against the cold.

On the second day what had been anger changed to sadness, for I began to acknowledge what I had done and to realize that I might not see Robin Hood again. This set me low, for I missed him greatly, even after this short space. I had not gone a full day from camp, and yet I felt my heart should wilt if it did not see him soon. And so I wept, for loss and sorrow and for self-pity. But most of all I wept for Robin, for I felt so certain he would hang that my mind drew a crystalline image of it, and I saw his face, blue and swollen, dangling from the hanging rope.

This image haunted me and would not go no matter how I worked to shake it. I had seen hangings in Warwick as a girl, and 'tis a vision that, once seen, is impossible to forget. Even then I had shuddered at the sight and had nightmares after of jerking feet and twitching hands. So clearly did I now see Robin suspended in the sickly air that I came to believe it had happened, and this caused me to wail all the more, grasping at the rocks and dirt and losing my breakfast in the drainage ditch.

My mode of travel served me well, for, as a young man, strangers did not speak to me and rarely gave me a second glance. So long as my hair stayed tight in my hood, I had no worries and strode along unperturbed, but for the tortured state of my heart. I've repeatedly said 'twas my heart that ached, but in truth the pain was somewhat lower than I believe my heart to be. 'Twould be better described as a painful constricting of my ribs, so that every organ housed within whimpered from noon to night in agony. As the days went by I became accustomed to this feeling and also to the tight sensation behind my eyes—the threat of tears—and I began to believe I might live this way.

My pennies held out while I traveled and bought me bread and cheese to eat, though I had little appetite for them. By the time I reached the Denby region I'd grown quite protective of those pennies, for by then I had three shillings, four pennies remaining in my purse, and I knew those would not buy my bread for many more days.

I am proud to say that at no point on my journey did I ever consider returning to Warwick or attempting to reclaim my noble status. It might seem that I would, since I had turned my toes toward my own lands, but my only thought was to live there as a common laborer; I never once thought of Denby Manor or the title that I once held. Nor did I regret my own decision of leaving Sherwood, for the memory of Robin's frightened face remained impressed on my mind, filling me with disgust and scorn. I remembered my vow to watch for myself, and visions of the queen's stern face pushed me forward. She would not triumph while I had wits and strength of spirit. I swore she would not.

UPON REACHING THE DENBY SOIL, my motivation faltered, and I wandered aimlessly. What had I thought I would do here? I asked myself a thousand times. Where would I live and with whom? What work could I do to earn my bread? The panicky feeling began once again to bubble and steep; I felt my throat close and my knees grow weak. Once again the gears of fate turned, and I had no plan to save myself from them—I who so prided myself on planning! I had run blindly, knowing far too little of the ways of the world, and now I found myself frightened and lost.

This feeling of terror lasted till noon, when I spent one of my pennies on a loaf of bread, which brightened my mood and helped me push away my sorrow. I would have to rally my every spirit to gain a roof above my head—all thoughts of Robin would have to wait. So at the first opportunity I dashed to a grove of oaks and changed my clothes, for I was suddenly sure that more pity would be given to a maid alone than to a young boy with a blackthorn cudgel. I left my dear quarterstaff there with a kiss, knowing as I went that I left behind the last thing I bore that Robin had given me.

FROM THAT GROVE I went forth in my shift and homespun, my hair flowing loose, unbound by a kerchief, for I wished to appear as young as I could to rouse more sympathy. Dressed and ready, I summoned all the courage I had in my bones and made my way to the market stalls where the townswomen gathered.

"Good day, auntie," I said to each face that glanced my way. Some returned my greeting, some did not, and to all who gave me a word or two more I made some comment on the weather. If our conversation went further than that, I asked if they knew anyone in need of a helper, for, I said, I went in search of employment. Most said nay, they knew of none, but a few pointed me on to women who might stop to speak with me. And so I passed the main of the day, wandering from table to table in the market, smiling at all but receiving, truly, little encouragement.

'Twas getting late when I met with a woman selling turnips and cabbages. As the market day was over, she was packing her wares in a spacious reed basket. I offered to help her, and she accepted with pleasure, for it seemed she had sold little of what she had brought in the morning.

"Might I help you to carry it home, goodwife? I've time to waste, and your burden seems heavy."

"Indeed, I would be pleased for the help," she said, somewhat gratefully. So I lifted one half of the reed basket, and she took the other, and between us we managed both it and my bundle for a pace down the road.

"I don't believe I know yer face," she said to me, eyeing me sideways, her shoulders hunched over the basket. "Are ye new to Thetbury village?"

"Indeed, I am, auntie," I replied, stalling, for the time had come for me to craft some new falsehood, specially tailored to this woman's long face. "I've come in hopes that I might pay a few pennies for a night indoors, for I have traveled far from my home."

"Have ye now!" she said, surprised, for she, I was sure, had never been beyond the market grounds in her life. "Yer looks seem a mite familiar to me, now that I check a second time. Are ye sure you've never been this way?"

"I may have passed through here," I agreed, looking about me to see if the path might have been familiar from horseback. "But not for many years." Then I gave myself a shake, for this was no time to be sprinkling hints from my true life—I had a tale to construct, and I'd best begin it at once.

"I come from Lott's End, just down the road," I said, hoping proximity would boost her trust. "But I've not lived there in a good long while, for my mother died when I was a girl and my father wished to go abroad. He's from the west country and had a longing to return there."

"The west country, you say?" she replied with interest, for I suppose it sounded most exotic to her.

"Aye, and off we went—that was six months back now. I was pleased enough to go, for I'd heard Saint Edith had passed that way and I'd great hopes of seeing her chapel at Stafford. D'ye know Stafford?"

"Oh, nay. Not me, lass."

"Well. 'Tis a rough town, I'll say that for it. My father took to gambling there, wagering over cocks and dogs, tossing the dice— you know the sort. We weren't ten miles from Stafford when he lost it all in a cockfight. He'd placed all our coin on the taller of the two cocks, but the shorter was a mean cuss, with a taste for blood and ink in his eye. We lost it all, though I knew nothin' of it till the next morn when my da roused me up to hie to Chester, for he'd a sudden yearning to sail across the middle sea for the green isle."

"The green isle!" she gasped, hinting that I'd hit my mark, for no tactic was more secure than playing upon prejudice. "I've heard wretched things of that place, for all they claim to be Christian folk."

"Aye." I nodded sadly, shifting the weight of the basket. "And my da was no better, for that same morn I heard him telling the men he owed how he was going to take me hence to sell me off as bond servant to some rich lord. I'd fetch a fare price, he said, being young and comely and made for work. 'Twas how he intended to settle his debts, by selling me as slave and servant to some foreign jackanape cur."

Here she gasped a second time and dropped the basket to stare at me. I took care to make my face look wan—a sentiment I so truly felt, I scarcely needed to act the part.

"Your own father? To sell you off? Why, you'd have done better to stay put in Lott's End, that's as I say."

"You're quite right, goodwife, I do agree. 'Tis why I slipped off that same day, while Da was busy with his morning tankard. I ran from that place and I ran and ran, not pausing a wink till I reached Denby soil, for 'tis here alone I feel safe in the world."

"As right you should, you poor lamb," she cried. "There's no safer place in all the world. Imagine—your own da!"

This kind woman pulled me to her, and I cried on her shoulder as I had on Annie's when I was a girl and had scraped my knee. My cheek rubbed against her woolen sleeve and my tears caused the scent of wet wool to rise up and sting my nose. I pulled away at last.

"Dear friend," I said, wiping my eyes, "can you not help me? I can work for my keep, and I've a few pennies, but I so desperately need a place to sleep. Might I stay with you?"

She looked wary for a moment, but she peered at my face a second time and perhaps thought again of my piteous tale, for she made a soft tsking sound before she replied. "We shall have to ask my husband, but if he will have ye, you may stay a time with us, girl."

I nearly fell over myself in thanking her, and in my gratitude I believe I carried the whole weight of the basket myself. My friend seemed troubled, afraid, perhaps, of what her husband would say, but I was jubilant. At the very least I had a home for the night, for any man, I was sure, would accept payment for lodging. And if things went well I might even find a place to rest my weary wings longer, taxed as they were from my arduous flight.

My new friend and I passed through Thetbury, a village of no more than thirteen homes, and stopped at a thatched house near the church. 'Twas in good repair, I was pleased to see, and the yard was well swept, but as we grew nearer my friend's brow seemed to lower and darken.

"I shall not tell my husband who ye are," she said, speaking with a note of decision, as if this had troubled her as we walked. "He would not understand yer plight and would want to take ye home to Lott's End—or worse, send word after yer da. Rather, I'll say y'are my niece, for I'm of Belton village and he knows not all of my kin. What shall we call ye?"

"Mary," I said after a moment's thought, for it was like enough to my own name that I knew I should answer readily to it.

"Aye, Mary, 'tis a good name. And I," she said, smiling shyly, "am Meg Tamworth."

"I'm pleased to know you, Meg," I said, smiling back with all the encouragement I could muster. She seemed to buoy a little at my words, and together we hefted her basket home and entered her yard and cavelike house. The air was smoky with supper fires, giving the world a clean, sleepy scent. I felt a pang of genuine hunger at the sight of the hearth, for a great cauldron of meal mush dangled from it, giving off a rich scent that I'd never been attracted to before.

Meg's daughter Janey stoked the fire, and in a moment her son appeared with an armload of wood for the next day's cooking. The boy, Matthew, was perhaps fifteen, tall and sturdy, and I supposed Janey was eleven or twelve. Their great ages, I later learned, were what made it possible for Meg to travel to the market with her vegetables, for Janey could see to the meals herself and freed her mother for other tasks.

Meg was a thin woman, bony even, but with the spreading hips that made her seem well constructed for bearing children. Despite constant attempts to tuck them away, wisps of mousy hair trailed from underneath her kerchief, curling haphazardly about her receding chin. Her husband, in contrast, proved to be a large man, cyclopic, with a great, round, balding head and thick-fingered hands. We had hardly been in the house a full moment before he came, filling the doorway with his chest and shoulders.

"Woman," he cried, "let us see how ye did." He started for the turnip basket, then stopped short when he saw me. Meg stepped forward to explain, trembling like a ripe wheat shaft in a gust of wind.

" 'Tis my niece Mary Cox, come to stay with us, John."

"Yer niece? Come from Belton village?" We both nodded. "And what gives you leave to drop in here and expect our hospitality, young miss?"

My mouth gaped, but as I struggled for a response, Meg leapt in. "Ye know quite well why she's here, John Tamworth—where be yer Christian spirit? Can ye not recall that my dear brother Rupert died not three weeks back? Where do you think the child has to go, with her da lost and all? Sure she cannot live on the kindness of strangers forever—she has come to her kin, just as she ought."

John sat like a stone in the face of this criticism, but it did seem to soften him somewhat. "I don't recall you speakin' of a niece, but if she be so, I s'pose she may stay. I'll have to clear it with the steward when he comes to town."

"Aye, indeed, John," Meg murmured, busying herself with the fire and cauldron.

John continued to look at me coldly, noticing, I was certain, that I bore absolutely no resemblance to his wife. "How did you leave them in Belton, then?"

"Very well," I stammered, "very well, Uncle John."

"You've a queer way of speaking," he said, his eyes narrowing.

"Aye," I agreed, my mind darting for explanations. Meg and I had had no time in which to fabricate our lies. "I used to tend at the great house, when I was younger, with my mother—"

"Before she died," Meg put in quickly, her back still to us.

"Before she died. I expect I picked it up there, 'tis what my father used to think."

That seemed to satisfy, for he grunted and turned again to the turnip basket. I watched him count out the vegetables carefully, and as he did, I saw that Meg grew so nervous that she began to spill bits of meal in the fire as she stirred. The children had slunk into a dark corner, and without wasting time I followed their lead, slipping back against the walls where I was hidden in the shadows.

"You're short the change, woman!" he suddenly hollered, causing me to jump. "I sent you forth with five new pennies and now you've three pennies and a ha' penny, but not more than three turnips and one cabbage sold! How many times have I got to explain it to ye, you daft woman, Meg! Ye know all the prices, but every time the change comes out wrong. Tell me honest now, did ye spend it?" He walked toward her with a stomp and a grunt, somehow looking twice as large as before. Meg cringed near the fire.

"Honest, John, I dinna spend any. 'Tis my own fault—I canna make coins come out as they ought. Bart Dauncey gave me a shilling to break, and I was all a-flustered by it!"

John stopped one pace away and clenched his great hands in the air as if he wished to throttle her neck, but he did not. Instead he turned and walked out the door, perhaps meaning to expend his anger in shouting at the heavens instead of at Meg.

When he had gone the children eased forward to comfort their mother; then we all went outside to escape the smoke and wait for supper. My stomach heaved and tingled with fear, now doubting the wisdom of choosing this house. But I was not about to flee now that my lies had been established. To Thetbury village I was now Mary Cox, and no amount of masculine shouting would convince me to leave that cover behind.

part three

"And I with thee"

Chapter Eighteen

THAT NIGHT WE RETIRED on heaps of straw, for the Tamworths did not own a mattress. John and Meg slept in one corner, and Matthew and Janey shared the other. I was sent to sleep with the children, and I curled up by Janey with a sigh and a whimper, so heavily grateful for a warm place to sleep. I'd not stretched my legs out for three nights running, and they ached on account of it, but now I pointed my toes in luxury, thinking how strange my life had become. Just over a year before I had twitched and tossed in the Bailey's bed, and now I embraced a heap of straw with such tears of joy as I was ashamed to show.

I had taken care to drink no more than a few sips of water with the evening meal and so was saved from any midnight trips to the bushes outside. This was a relief, for I did not think my new uncle John would take kindly to being awoken in the night, and I had no wish to draw his attention.

The cock's crow came far too early, and I rolled from my straw with bitter reluctance. My first day of farmwork stretched before me, and I stuck to Meg like the thorn on a rose branch, afraid I might miss some of her instructions. John and Matthew soon left for the fields, and once they were gone the females perked up, pleased to have the house to themselves for singing and talking while they did their work.

They went out first to feed the stock, and Meg took to her milking stool while Janey showed me how to feed the chickens, the goose, and the ducks. They owned two sheep, she explained to me, but these were watched by the village shepherd and would be in the hills until the end of the summer. Janey proved a talkative girl, not particularly quick or contemplative but amiable enough to be pleasant.

Once the milking was done, Meg set me to churning as this seemed a job that required little skill. She had quickly grasped that I knew very little of the art of farmwork, the result, no doubt, of my having lived so long among foreign ruffians. When I told her I could make soap and rush candles and knew a bit of spinning and ale brewing, she brightened, for these, she said, were items she could sell if she went again to a market day. This brought to my mind the matter of her turnips and cabbages, and though I hesitated to raise it, I could at last bear it no longer. I caught her alone in the lean-to barn.

"Meg, if you would care to, you might send me to the next market day. I've long experience with coins of all types and should be happy to do the selling for you."

She bit her lip for a long moment, and at first I feared I had threatened a task she enjoyed, for perhaps 'twas a treat to leave the house and go among the women of the village. But at last she mumbled something about John, and I understood that he would be reluctant to trust his pennies to a stranger, whether she were kin or no.

"If he will but give me one chance," I said, imploring her, "I promise to return with every last coin." I wished to say that I promised to bring him the proper amount, but I shied from mentioning her own blunder. "And if it worries you, I will leave you with my own store of pennies, that you might make up the difference out of those if I should happen to come home short."

She spent some time chewing over this thought, but by midday she had decided that it seemed a very good plan indeed, and I was scheduled for the next day's market. The rest of the afternoon passed smoothly, oiled by Meg's gentle ways, and I only once had to clench my fists against my flood of memories.

"Y'are a sad girl, Mary," Meg had observed as we swept out the house. "I don't know when I've seen a greater grimstocking."

I laughed aloud, but her words sliced to my very heart, for I'd struggled so to be cheery. I was sad, gray to the core, for if I did not fret over Robin, then I worried for Annie and how she must suffer or over the fates of the merry men. But most of all I grieved for Robin and dwelt on the corners of his smile and the distant edges of his gaze. I tried to temper my sadness with work, for nothing distracted me as labor could do, but even so I fear I made a moping companion for my new friends.

THE NEXT MORNING I left with the basket of cabbages, secure with instructions from Meg on the selling and where I should set out my collection of wares. The market space was crowded already when I arrived, filled with young women laying out their stock. I found my way to the vegetable sellers and marked out the space Meg had said I should have, spreading a cloth upon the ground and setting the best turnips upon it.

I enjoyed the market. The air hummed there and all about me were young people, hawking and bartering. I took pride in my work and did my best to keep my vegetables fresh with regular shakes of cold well water. From time to time I cried out to a passerby, and as the morning passed I grew even bolder, stopping folks with a wave of my hand. By noon I had sold twice what Meg had two days before, and before I packed up I had lightened my load by nine turnips and seven cabbages.

John was so pleased with my work that he almost smiled as he counted my coins, calculating slowly that I had done well and given proper change to each customer. I was told to return there each market day, and I looked forward to those two days as the dim strands of hope in my meager warp. My conscience did pang for a moment or two, while I feared Meg might be offended at having so quickly lost this job, but a look at her calmed my nerves, for she appeared as relieved as I was happy. Had Robin Hood only been near, so I might tell him of my success, I should have been truly pleased.

MY LIFE FELL into a simple rhythm of daily tasks and dreamless nights, but Robin never left my mind for a moment. Each day when I rose I thought of his face, and each night on the straw I saw his smile. In frequent odd moments I conversed with him, making up his arguments while I worked at the churn or hearing his laugh as I walked to market. 'Twas his companionship I found I missed most, for while I liked both Meg and Janey, there were no true companions here.

I say his companionship was valued and missed, but there was more to Robin Hood that made me yearn in the dark of the night. I thirsted after the tangy scent of his skin when he returned from a day of walking the woods. I pined for the roguish look in his eye when he called me to perch upon his knee. And I ached after his calloused hands and the way they could cause my blood to ripple with the lightest touch at the base of my jaw or across the creases of my palm.

Each time a visitor stopped at Meg's door to tell her a bit of gossip, I listened fearfully for his name, for if Robin or any of his band were hanged, I knew the country would shake with the news. But as I heard nothing, I tried not to worry and turned my mind back to my own small work. I had struggled hard to master my jobs, and was just beginning to see some progress in my handling of the carding comb, the kettle, and the milking pail.

One day when I'd been perhaps a week at the Tamworths', Meg made a strange off-hand remark that caught me cold.

"Sir Thomas," she said in the midst of a complaint, "has no love for the folk of Thetbury, not as the Fitzwaters did afore. I can recall a time in autumn when every child had a ripe apple if he came to see the Fitzwaters pass, and all our reeves were honest men."

"The Fitzwaters, you say?" I asked, striving to keep my tone calm. "I'd heard my ma speak highly of 'em, but I know little about them. Did you see the lord and lady yourself?"

"Oh, aye," Meg said, smiling at her spindle, "time and again I spied them. They passed this way each year, he on a spotted mare and she wearing a gold band about her neck." Janey brought her work closer, so she might hear of the frills and finery.

"And what did they look like, Meg?" I asked. My hand trembled so that I had to tuck it beneath my wool for hiding.

"Oh, dark and handsome, both of them were. A touch like you, Mary, but of a greater height. She was a rare beauty for these parts, always wearin' the finest skirts and shawls when they came into the country. My cousin Cedric once had cause to visit the manor in Denby, and he said she was right kind to him, instructing the kitchen folk as to his meals and finding him a warm corner at night. They were what a lord and lady ought to be, to my way of thinking. Not like this Sir Thomas." She shook her head, a motion Janey instantly copied with eerie perfection.

"Nay," said the girl, "nay, indeed, Ma. Recall how he took up our pig for the tax last Lady Day and then your best layer at Eastertide!"

"Aye, Janey, I do recall. In the older times Lady Fitzwater would give out shoes to every laborer who went as far as the manor at Christmastime. Sir Thomas don't care if you walk fifty miles to give him your deepest bow, that's what."

Sir Thomas, I thus discovered, was not highly praised, for taxes had risen substantially since he came to Denby and the gifts had dwindled. I had watched how the Tamworths struggled for funds, and by now I saw how a tax of three pennies might nearly break such a group as they were.

"But was there no child, Meg?" I asked, for I could not resist pressing her further. "I thought my ma spoke of a child of the Fitzwaters."

"Oh, aye, there was. But I understand it died as well when the lord and lady took ill. 'Twas a sad time for Denby, that—I scarce thought we'd ever recover."

This, then, was the way my fate had been reported in Denby. 'Twas strangely chilling to hear myself described as dead—I, who by all accounts, had died several times over! But it did me good to hear of my parents, and I asked Meg questions by the handful. Sadly, she knew little beyond what she'd already related. 'Twas something, though, to hear that my parents had been thought fair and generous and to know they'd been missed by the good folk of Denby.

One night a bit later, John announced that the steward had ridden into town and the next day would hold a manor court. We had heard it already from two passersby, but Meg and I both pretended to be struck by the news and agreed when he declared that he and Matthew would go.

"We shall have to tell him of Mary's coming," John said, his mouth full of Meg's good rye bread.

"Should I perhaps go myself, so he may see who I am?" I asked, in what I hoped was my most sweet-tempered voice.

"Go to the manor court—a woman? Are ye mad, Mary? Tell me 'tis not how things are done in Belton, that they should let a woman present herself to the steward at the manor court?"

"Oh, nay," I cried, attempting to laugh over my mistake. "I only meant it in jest, Uncle John."

"I should hope," he mumbled, turning back to his bread. I felt my cheeks flush hot with annoyance, despite the coolness of the

evening breeze. Women, I was learning, had no place in village politics, which struck me as strange, since we lived in a land that was
ruled by a queen.

The following day they left for the manor court, then went
straight on to the fields. That day I took four eggs and some lumps
of butter with me to market day, for we all had been busy about the
house and had managed to gather some spare things to sell. But
that night I heard some frightening news, for John announced that
'twas time to mow Sir Thomas's home farm, and I would be needed
to rake the cut shafts.

I knew nothing of field work, and the thought alone made me
tremble, especially when I recalled that it meant a whole day spent
with John and the field-men. But Meg told me later that many
women would go, that she had gone herself in the past, and 'twas
not as hard as it might seem. I nodded and acted as though I
believed her, but when we rose the next morning I was filled with
dread, and I followed the men out with a tremulous heart.

The home farm, I learned, was the expanse of fields that Sir
Thomas owned, surrounding the manor house. Thetbury's manor
house was mean in comparison with Denby Manor, but even so it
was the greatest house in the village. We were, I found, to do week
work there, which meant toil donated by the grown workers of
every household in the village.

As this was the first day's work of the week, it came with a wet
boon, or a noon meal with ale and wine, as a gift for every worker.
Since the steward would be present to oversee the wet boon, I
expected to see him also at the fields, for I thought he would want
to survey our work. But when we arrived there was only the reeve
to place us in order. Matthew whispered to me that the reeve was a
bitter man whom I should avoid, for it was his right to beat any
worker he thought guilty of laziness, and for this purpose he carried a stout crabtree staff.

Nearly every face I'd seen in Thetbury since my arrival was present on the fields, both men and women, standing with scythes or long-handled rakes. I joined the rakers and was put in position, and all too soon the work began. We were to follow the cutting men and drag the newly sliced shafts of hay into hillocks. Behind we were followed by boys like Matthew, who pulled our hillocks into greater mounds which the cart could take up at the end of the day. On either side of me glowed merry faces, red with sun and the warmth of work, but happy, for they had time to gossip as they raked.

I, however, found it hard going. I struggled to do my work well, but my rake seemed to catch on every bristly stalk, and great clods of dirt clogged my tines. What I lacked in technique, I hoped to make up by the sweat of my brow and by sheer willingness, and I thought I had begun to improve, for I was never more than a few steps behind the rest of my band. But when the men were given a break, Uncle John took a moment to catch my ear, whispering loud in an angry breath.

"Get a move on there, Mary! Ye do not want to catch the mean end of the reeve's stick, now do ye? Come on, move it faster—ye shall not go shaming the Tamworths today, or I'll make you suffer for it later, I promise ye!"

His words brought a new sense of terror to my heart, and I moved from then on at a double-quick pace. My mind never strayed from my rake and my hay shafts, and I attacked them with a frightened ferocity, desperate to keep abreast my mates. My shoulders ached from yanking and tugging, my skin itched from loose grass and chaff, but I ignored every discomfort. This was field work, and I was coming to learn that it took far more talent and strength of limb than I had ever imagined. At last the reeve sounded his horn and all worked ceased. I followed the girls toward the manor house, jealous of their merry laughter which rose as easily as songs from the pampered, or odes from the lips of the idle.

Matthew caught up with me as we walked, to give me advice on the art of the rake. He told me then, to my despair, that the week work would continue until every one of Sir Thomas's fields was mowed and stacked. I looked about at the vastness before me and then behind, to the paltry amount we had just finished, and felt tears rising high in my eyes.

Matthew hastened to bid me be calm, for he claimed that I'd improved already and that each day's work would come easier than the one before. I nodded and pretended to be pleased, enjoying a moment of chat with Matthew, for he was a kind lad and meant well. Indeed, it was he who first noticed that I was the object of some attention, for he leaned in close and whispered.

"Mary, I do believe that Walter the Miller has his eye on you! Do not look now, but I've seen him starin' a handful of times already this morning. I shouldn't wonder if he'd try to sit with you at the noon meal."

I bided my time, noting Matthew's observation while I held my face as firm as marble. But when a moment of confusion came, I looked where he'd pointed and saw the miller, a middle-aged man with a round red face, peering my way. I nodded grimly and dashed ahead to join the girls, determined to be surrounded by them when it was time to choose seats at the table.

In the manor house we sat at long benches and waited while Sam Dell, a Thetbury cotter, filled up our tankards with fresh ale and old wine. Our group was merry on account of the wet boon, for most had ale only as a treat and drank dingy well water with all their meals. I looked more forward to the meal itself, for we were given chicken and wheat-barley bread rather than rye—a treat indeed.

I noticed the miller's face several more times, always pointed boldly in my direction, but I shied away from every glance and prayed he would not single me out. I had no wish to cause trouble in Thetbury by declining the advances of the miller, and if he persisted I knew I would do it, for what young elm thinks the chestnut attractive when she has known the love of an oak?

When we'd eaten, we all were released for the day, and I went home with a joyous heart while John and Matthew went to their own fields. All afternoon long I indulged myself in complaining to Meg of my morning troubles, and she, as always, listened with grand sympathy, for Meg had a most gentle heart.

THE NEXT MORNING we took to the home farm again, and the next, and the next. On the last day Matthew was called to the fore to join the men with their scything work. He paused on his way to tell me of it, hefting the awkward weight of the scythe as he told me he thought it his father's doing that he was put to work with his elders.

"He says if I go up to work with the men they'll push me to do more with each stroke than I would with the rakers. He says men always respond to a challenge, that they take greater strides in competition than they would have the will to do otherwise."

"Yes, 'tis true," I laughed, waving him off. "Men and dogs, I think, both do it." He ran froward with a nervous smile and took his place ahead of my band, and I was left to think for a moment on what he had said.

There was wisdom there, I reasoned, that stretched beyond the haying field. All that morning I allowed my mind to dance its way through Uncle John's notion, and as I did my thoughts, as always, turned to Robin. I considered how our life had been and how our companionship had pressed us both to strive and advance. In our arguments he'd made me defend my position better by fighting ably for his. He'd pushed me to learn to spar with a cudgel, to speak for my views, to even walk fifteen miles in a day. As I worked with my rake I let my mind spin like a slow millstone over this thought, cracking and rumbling till the stuff of my reason seemed light as dust.

And that very night as I lay on my patch of straw, the dark seemed to open in a tunnel above me, the way the clouds can sometimes do when they part to let the sun beam through. Robin, I saw, had done far more than encourage me to reason and give voice to my thoughts. Nay, indeed, his influence was far greater than that.

Since I'd arrived in Thetbury village, I'd been plagued by the memory of my two great failings, or what I saw as my very worst hours. The first was when I was set to wed Stephen and had failed to settle on a plan of escape, for in the end I'd left myself at the mercy of my own indecisions. My second shame was my flight from Sherwood and the haphazard way I had followed my fate. I am a woman who values more than anything the well-laid scheme, the artful program. And yet, at my own most crucial hours, I had been too immobilized by fear to settle on a course.

I'd always longed to strike at life with great cracks and blows, but when I stood with the staff in my hand I fretted too much over what stroke to take. Robin threw his own life down in a rush, caring little for perfection, but with a bliss I envied deeply. Like a flash in the dark it all came clear—the greatest thing Robin had shown me was how to live free from worry. "You paralyze yourself with fear, Marian," he'd said. "Life is to be lived, not shied from."

Robin was bold and daring and wild—this, I saw, was what he had that I'd never managed to find for myself. With him beside me, I too could be brave and flee Warwick Castle or learn how to fight. I could face the queen's chill blue eyes, or Lady Pernelle's grasping hands. I could even be brave enough to fall in love.

Love. With a stifled moan I opened my eyes to face the darkness and felt ashamed at my own cowardice. For I had fled the nest of love. I had been too afraid to see what would become of Robin and the queen, and I had fled. When life had appeared too chaotic and chancy, I went my own way to save myself. Now I feared I had lost what was best of me as part of the bargain.

'Twas pitiful to look back on it now, to recall how my heart had contracted and tremored in the face of danger—the very same danger I was sure Robin had looked dead in the eye and had a laugh with. I was sunk in regret, for I now saw that whatever Robin had hidden that morning, it did nothing to excuse my flight. I ought to have waited to hear him out, I ought to have had some faith in him. Perhaps I was hard on myself that night; perhaps I was not hard enough. But however it was, I awoke the next day feeling that I had slumbered in a cocoon and now emerged as a new-winged creature.

My first thought was that I should make haste to Sherwood to find my friends and rejoin them at once, but the morning news made me reconsider. The battle between Prince John and the queen had heightened, and Gil the Carpenter said there was fighting now near Nottingham town. He also brought word that King Richard was expected to return by Christmas, to sit once again on the throne of England, and ban his young brother from raising such armies.

I heard this news and thought hard on it, for if it were true that they battled in Nottingham, Robin most surely would have moved his men to a different forest or a remote hill town. And so I decided to remain where I was rather than chase them about the countryside. I tried not to fret and told myself that Robin lived on, believing for once more in hope and good wishes than in my own apprehension.

Chapter Nineteen

THE SUMMER LEAVES changed from green to gold, and still the news did not improve. I resolved again to stay as I was while the world of the nobles settled itself, content for the moment to be Mary Cox of Thetbury village. In the autumn we had more work than before, for after the week work to harvest Sir Thomas's home farm grain, we had our own to sickle and thresh. The whole family went to our fields at harvest, and I bundled sheaves like Ruth in the Bible, struggling to bind off my bundles and feeling my arms ache in much the same way. I nearly wept, truly, when the priest came past to collect his one sheaf out of every ten, as was his due. I had few quarrels with God's church, but I resented losing one of my bundles to feed the bishop, when I knew 'twould be a greater charity to take it home to our own barn.

The threshing was horrid, for the chaff and dust made a cloud in the air and settled in hair, in eyes and noses, and itched beneath our very clothes. At times I felt half blind from dust and was often chastised for clearing my eyes, when I ought to be tossing up shovels of wheat to let the loose chaff fly off in the air.

We wasted no portion of our grain, for even the rye straw was gleaned and bundled for bedding and strewing on the floor in winter. Meg and I brewed barley ale and sold it in skin sacks on market days, and even the chaff was saved up in sacks to feed to the oxen over the winter. As the days grew cooler, John and Matthew went regularly into the woods, taking with them the wood penny as payment to Sir Thomas for collecting dead wood from his forest.

When at last our family threshing was done, Meg and I hauled the newly bare kernels to the mill, bringing with us the precious two shillings eightpence we would pay the miller to grind our wheat. The mill, Meg said, was owned by Sir Thomas, but Walter the Miller rented it from him for twenty shillings a year. 'Twas illegal, she told me, to grind one's own grain, for as part of Sir Thomas's agreement with the miller all Thetbury grain had to pass beneath his stone.

This bitter news and the loss of two shillings eightpence put me in no mood to smile at the miller, no matter how obliging he tried to be, for the family funds had become my own, and I felt in my heart that we were being cheated. Meg laughed when I told her so and said I would weep to witness the spring when our taxes were paid and see what a lot of shillings were owed to Sir Thomas as tallage for our strips of land. And then there were the hens and eggs at Easter and the Lady Day tallage, and tithe to the church if any animals were born in April and May.

"And if you were to wed, Mary, my girl, we would owe another tax to Sir Thomas then, called the marchet."

"Well," I said, "I've no plans to marry, so you may at least keep the marchet money until Janey goes."

"I wouldn't be too hasty," she said, with a coy look, "I've heard many a man in town ask after you, and John tells them freely that you've never been wed."

I blushed for a moment, an appropriate gesture for a maid, though Meg couldn't know why I truly reddened. For not only had I in fact been wed, but my heart belonged fastly to another and

while he lived I could not be made to darken a church door with
any man of Thetbury.

NOT ONE WEEK LATER as I carried a noon meal out to Uncle
John and Matthew, down in a waste field slaughtering hogs, I happened to see a most curious thing. The day before we'd heard news
that Sir Thomas was coming to pass his annual night in Thetbury
Manor, and I'd had my eyes turned sharply for him, for I wished to
spy him before he saw me. So as I walked I kept on the lookout,
and I hadn't very long to wait.

I saw a crowd gathered on the main road and slipped in behind
those in the back so I could peer round without being seen. There
came Sir Thomas, apple round as ever, but with him came a velvet-
decked lady. Without thinking of my own disguise, I threaded my
way through the crowd of villagers to where I could see the dame's
face as she passed. And who do you suppose the lady was? None
but Lady Pernelle of Sencaster.

She and Sir Thomas were waving to the crowd with such exag-
gerated condescension, it made me almost laugh to see it. If they
only could have known that in honesty and manners these villagers
were far more noble than they! For that one moment I understood
Robin's inherent dislike of the Norman tribe, for having played
Mary Cox the Saxon for so long, I'd come to feel like one myself
and fostered a native's rigid hatred for the ruling class.

The irony of this made me chuckle, for I recalled that as a noble
lady, near a lifetime ago, I'd ridden through Thetbury village
myself. But I was not a noble now, and from my low position on
foot I could see the conceit of these two rulers much better than I
ever had while I was seated upon a horse.

Lady Pernelle! I was so astonished, I scarcely knew what to think
at first. Sir Thomas, I recalled, was her cousin, and perhaps they
were close friends as well. But then I turned round what Robin had

said so long ago, before I knew what the kiss of love was, when I was so desperate to avoid being wed. "Perhaps she wants to help her cousin keep his post," he'd said, or something to that effect. But why, I had argued, would she care so much for her simple cousin?

Well, here at last was the answer, riding plainly before me. For as I watched, Lady Pernelle's horse stepped into a puddle and stumbled. Sir Thomas, all concern, reined in until their steeds were shoulder to shoulder and took her hand gallantly in his. These were no simple cousins; this was plain when they turned and smiled at each other's eyes. Nay, indeed, these two were lovers.

THE FIRST FROSTS CAME late in November, and from that day forward our lives were focused on the hearth and on drying wet clothes before we took cold. This, without question, was the most miserable winter I had ever passed, for we all five were crowded about the fire from morning till night, sucking in smoke as if it were ether and propping our shoes up on log rounds to dry.

I had a great deal of leisure in which to sit and think, for we scarcely found words enough to pass the time from waking till breakfast, and after that the little house fell into ponderous silence, ideal for thought. I had a number of things to consider. First and foremost, I began to believe in the days before Christmas that I had committed a great wrong in fleeing Sherwood Forest for Thetbury, a wrong not so much against Robin and the band, but against what was best for my own course. For now I'd transported from forest to village, but to what purpose, I wished to know.

I regularly awoke on my pile of straw wondering what I was about living there—did I wish to remain there the rest of my days? And if I did not, why stay at all? As near as I could tell I was learning little beyond raking and churning, so why was I content to remain in this place? Was it merely because I knew not what else to do? In Sherwood, at least, I had been near Robin and Annie both. Here I felt deathly alone.

If these questions hadn't been enough to occupy me, I still had Lady Pernelle to consider. And the longer I let her face float through my mind, the more certain I became that something sinister had happened to Hugh. I remembered my distress at the mixed reports concerning his death and that the queen herself had deigned visit to tell me of it. This last had been stuck like a thorn in my mind all these years and remained there still, hardened fast. Taken as one, these matters made me crumple my brow and wonder what cause Lady Pernelle might have had to execute her own son and heir.

She had been regent to Hugh, I knew, and ruled Sencaster in his stead while he studied in the king's court in Anjou. Hugh's death made it possible for her to rule on, now as regent to young Stephen, but was that cause enough to warrant a killing? I had heard, of course, of the penchant young nobles often had for begrudging their widowed mothers their dowers; perhaps Lady Pernelle thought Hugh might grow to be one of those sons who shuns his own mother. Given what I knew of Hugh's temperament, it was easy to imagine such a circumstance. But would even that drive a mother to kill her own son? I had seen from Meg what strong love a mother could bear her children, and I would have doubted the possibility, had I not already learned to mistrust Lady Pernelle.

Fortunately for all in Thetbury, the slow pace of winter was pricked with holy days here and there, each one glinting like a half-rainbow in the midst of a hailstorm. Beyond food and drink and meeting with friends, the mass days were thrilling for the news that was spread, giving us items to plumb and mine as we suffered the hours by our hearthside. And the news of this winter held a special interest, for much occurred that altered the face of our world.

King Richard was expected, as I have said, to return in time for a holiday court—but he did not come. Instead the queen held

Christmas court in London, still enforcing, I supposed, her bargain with the English nobles to restrain Prince John from raising an army.

Soon after this came the woeful news that the king had been sailing, indeed, for our land, when he was shipwrecked off Istria, a port town of Italy. From there he had fled over land to Austria, where—horrible but true—he was taken prisoner by Leopold, the duke of that country. This duke handed Richard at once to his liege, Henry Hohenstaufen, emperor of Germany, who imprisoned our king and kept him trapped as bait for a terrific ransom.

The next report held more news of Prince John, for once the prince heard of Richard's capture, he fled to Normandy to declare himself Richard's heir and require oaths of loyalty from the Norman barons. This was a devious thing to try, and so we were not so surprised to hear soon after that he had joined forces with Philip of France and was attacking lands held by his own brother.

The queen, of course, was frantic over Richard and sent English nobles, the bishop of Ely included, to plead his case with the Hohenstaufen without delay. Around me the villagers thought all this incredible and swore in anger at the German ruler, but I looked at their poor faces and felt a great terror on their behalf. I knew the German ransom would be more than dear—it would be the most our land could afford. If these villagers felt their taxes now, they should be nearly killed by a tax for the king's ransom.

THAT DAY I SAT with Meg and Janey while the men trod to the woodpile. We could talk of nothing but Richard's capture, though dwelling so long on the queen made my skin feel sticky as a weld stalk. I listened while Meg spoke to Janey of Queen Eleanor and how she must worry over her son.

"Poor sweet old gran," Meg had murmured, shaking her head.

I thought my ears might bolt from my head when I heard her

words, for to my mind the queen was neither sweet nor poor, though I could not deny that she was in fact old. But for the briefest of moments I wondered how much of my terror of Eleanor was built upon a solid foundation and how much rested on sand towers of my own creation. And in that moment a fresh notion struck me, cold as a splash of river water. I dropped my work to my lap, so overcome was I by my thinking.

"What if," I said aloud, my voice unsteady, " 'twas not from fear of the queen or her guard or even of the gallows that I ran? What if it were from fear of *him?*"

Meg looked at me strangely and reached a hand over to feel the heat of my cheek. But I had never felt less ill. The germ of a great flower was growing within me, and it would be mine if I could but keep ahold of the thought.

"Perhaps I feared allowing a man to have such power over my heart, I who trust so very few." Meg cocked an eyebrow, but said nothing, for at that moment John returned, stamping his feet against the cold. Meg knew of Robin—that is to say, she knew I'd had a love once and that it had ended badly some months prior. So I fretted little over what she would think and delved instead into my own awakening.

Strange as it sounded, the words I spoke felt like truth—it was Robin from whom I'd fled, Robin and the wild ways I feared would land me in the Tower, or worse. For what was more troubling to one such as I, one who denied faith in any person, than to entrust my happiness, safety, and future to another—any other?

It was a thick thought to have birthed, and my lungs ached from the trial. Too, it brought shame, for it pained me to see so deep into my psyche and to glimpse the mud and scum that grew there. For the laws I'd laid down in early life seemed no longer to apply and perhaps had cost me my beloved Robin. The fault was my own and it made me cringe to accept my crime and take my penance.

That day I swore to cultivate faith as steadily as I worked at my spindle, practicing the motions each morning and night. If I could have no faith in my love, I felt I must surely be lost from this life, given up to decades of distress and worry. I must learn to trust Robin as I trusted myself. And perhaps, I thought, should we meet again, I would be ready to take him in close and to walk beside him the rest of my days.

NOT EVEN THOUGHTS of our king rotting in his prison could dampen the thrill we all felt when the last ice thawed and spring danced before us. Even as the rough work of plowing began, the villagers' faces filled with eager light, for the winter had ended and we all still lived. On the hills waddled ewes, heavy with lambs, picking their way from snow to green grass, as pleased for the sun as any of us.

Our cow birthed a calf in the midst of February, and soon we had cream and milk once again. The chickens took to laying with a fresh sense of duty, and the oxen went nobly to do their great work, breaking the sod of last year's fallow land. As the days grew warmer a new whisper spread, for the Shrove Tuesday fair was fast approaching, the greatest of all days in Denby-upon-Trent, and all of Thetbury would be in attendance.

Shrove Tuesday has always been a popular day, for before its moon rises in the night sky every last scrap of eggs, milk, and cheese must be gobbled up in preparation for Lent. In Denby, I found, 'twas a long-held tradition to finish them off in a pancake feast, and we dined that morning as I had never dined before, on sweet fried cakes dripped with butter and mounted with cream. For our noon meal, Meg packed us each a great chunk of cheese to accompany our bread, and our family set off with happy spring hearts to join in the spectacle of a country fair.

I HAD BEEN TO DENBY BEFORE, when I'd visited Sir Thomas as a young girl, but if I'd not known it to be the same town, I would not have recognized it in any way. Every space on the road was filled up this day with broad tents and stands of brightly striped canvas, their cloth flags flying. Stalls and tables were crammed so tightly into the square that one had to walk at a near ant's pace to see it all. Wild sounds and rich colors startled me on every side, grabbing my eyes, ears, and attention.

The air smelled thick with a mélange of scents—roast meat, brewed ale, spices from the East. To my delight I saw cinnamon, ginger, and clove—spices I'd not seen since I left Warwick Castle. On the fields great ribbons marked out sporting zones, and as I gazed on, straining my eyes, Matthew explained that our fair was famed for its football, archery, and wrestling matches. In back alleys were men grouped for cockfights and dice games, a sight that Meg hustled her children past as if the mood to gamble might somehow be catching.

When we arrived, the fair had not yet officially begun, and Janey was glad we had not missed the start. Soon I came to understand why, for when a great crowd had gathered in the square, a herald leapt up on a high wooden table and waved his arms for a moment of silence. Into the quiet he cried, "Hurrah!" and in response the whole crowd cried it back, and then the fair was truthfully started. All around us the trading began, loud at the spice stands, quieter in tone but equally intense at the fabric stalls. Uncle John had brought a pair of shoes for mending and wandered off to haggle a price. Meg and Janey went to see bits of lace from Germany, and Matthew started for the gaming rings.

"Be careful, Mary, or you'll be lost in this crowd. Why don't you come with me to the games? There's plenty to see."

I was so pleased just to look about that I agreed to go with him, for eyeing one crowd is as good as another, and the crush of the stalls frightened me a bit. As we passed through the throng my eye caught a flash. For an instant I thought I glimpsed Robin's face, with his beard and cap, but when I turned, 'twas a different man. I shook myself and kept my eye on Matthew, but as we walked it happened again with the same result. This made me sigh and speak quite sternly to myself, for I knew full well that Robin Hood wouldn't come to Denby, and my eyes were only catching what they wished they could see.

The gaming areas were marked out with pennants and colored streamers, all snapping in the breeze. At each stood a prize on a raised platform, sometimes a barrel of new stout ale, other times an arrow or bugle of gold. Matthew told me that one year the wrestling prize had been a two-year bull, and the way his eyes glowed when he spoke of it made me think he ought to practice his pins so he might claim such a prize one day.

Matthew was keen on the archery match, but as I was far shorter than he, I couldn't see the field from the position he chose. So I tugged at his sleeve and shouted that I would jump up on a barrel that stood at the back. From there I thought I might see better, though I knew full well that at that distance I shouldn't make out more than colored shapes and hazes.

My barrel was one in a line of ale kegs that stood against the Denby tavern, and from my perch I had a better view than I'd expected. The field before me was teeming with archers, or so it seemed, for ten groups of men stood at the field's far end, taking turns firing upon their targets. The targets were so far off indeed that I could scarcely spot them by squinting, but I could tell by the shouts and jeers of the crowd how each archer did, and so made merry by cheering for one man and then another.

"Perhaps this time 'twill be the lad in scarlet," I murmured to myself, catching the thrill of the competition. Before long the winner of each group had been chosen, and ten single men stood to shoot against one another. Each archer had a moment of rest while he waited his turn to pull and aim for the target, and at times some turned to speak with friends in the crowd or take a swig from a sack of ale. One man dressed in gray with a red felt cap seemed to look my way a time or two, but I told myself he must have some comrade in the crowd before me and turned my eye back to the man who was shooting.

So occupied was I with the match before me that I scarcely noticed anyone join me atop my barrels until it was too late. Then, to my horror, I saw Walter the Miller, more red-faced than ever on account of strong wine, teetering on the keg to my left. I tried to move away to the right, but caught my hair in the tavern's roof thatch and, while I struggled to free myself, heard these words come streaming from Walter.

"Oh, Mary," he cried in a blubbering way, "won't you give your old Walter a kiss, now? Ye know I've been eyein' you these long months, and sure you saw how I added some wheat flour to yer sacks at milling time—'twas out of love, ye must know that. Come on, then, Mary, give us a kiss."

He reached for me, and, as at that moment I freed my hair, I turned to face him to ward him off. But in the confusion his hand missed its target and fell on my breast, and before I could think of the error he'd made, I screamed, loud enough to silence the crowd and turn the ten archers in our direction.

Walter froze, but in a second I found that it was not from fear or embarrassment—an arrow, fired in the space of a heartbeat, had pinned his tunic to the tavern wall, and he found himself unable to move. I too stood frozen, one hand in the thatch, my heart beating fast like a tiny blackbird pulled in by a cat.

Soon cries arose of "Who shot that arrow?" and I saw the same man in the red felt cap leap over the ribbons and come quickly through the crowd.

"I did," he said, as he reached my barrel. And then I believe my heart reached a dead stop before it resumed its work at twice speed and filled my cheeks with fresh new blood. For this bold archer was no man other than my Robin Hood.

"Greetings, fair maid," he said, reaching up to me, his voice trembling slightly. His eyes looked cool as a summer lake, and they clung to me like wheat dust. "I apologize if I have intruded."

"Not at all, sir," I gasped, knowing I stammered even more than I stared.

"I am Nicholas Atwood of Lincolnshire, at your service." He smelled of beeswax and a brisk west wind, and looked as fair as Adonis himself.

"Ah, Nicholas, I thank you." We grasped hands, and he helped me leap down from my barrel. I looked at his eyes and saw in their depths a thousand words, a million thoughts, and each one I understood. I pressed his hand tightly and smiled, as if to say that all was well, all was mended—in my heart, at least. "I am Mary Cox of Thetbury village. I . . . I thank you again, sir. Best of luck in your tournament today."

"If I win the prize it shall be yours," he said with a grin, then allowed his voice to drop to a whisper. "And so shall I, if you will have me."

Until this moment the noise of the crowd had been no more than rain lapping dust off a dry road, but just then some man in the throng cried out, "Give him the prize! He's clear the best shot."

This caused a commotion, for Robin was not the group favorite, since he came in the guise of a Lincolnshire man. He pulled away with strong reluctance.

"I must finish this match, dear Mary," he said, "but promise that I may find you after? Mary?"

My added name carried such weight that I could not speak to answer him, but merely nodded, blinking off tears. Here was Robin, here before me! I followed behind him as he trailed through the crush and found a new space near the front of the ribbon, for the men parted ways for me nearly as if I were the queen herself.

From my new place I watched him work, and my heart shot over with pleasure and pride. I censured myself for not having known him by the carefree boldness of his archery stroke, but I did not take my own reproof seriously. My Robin stood there, he loved me still, and my blackbird's heart felt strong again and only waited the moment when it should take flight.

Chapter Twenty

I STOOD WITH MY FEET on solid ground and watched as Robin won the prize, but to this day I cannot recall a whit of that tournament after my rescue from atop the barrel. I was present, I know, but my mind was so wrapped in facing Robin that I could see none of what passed before me and, I am sure, might have been robbed had the Denby folk been so dishonest. Robin won, for I saw his prize afterward, but I did not see him shoot the arrow or hear the cheers that followed his victory.

Nay, I was too intent upon drafting and framing what I should say when we met afterward. But when at last the crowd thinned out and he seized my hand to speak with me, all my forethoughts flew into the wind, and I was left to speak from the heart.

"Marian, my love, how can you forgive me?"

"Forgive you? Nay, Robin, 'tis I who should be asking forgiveness. I was a fool to run off as I did—it shames me even now to think on it. I thought you would be captured, but look, here you are safe and unharmed! I clearly misjudged both the queen and you."

"Ah, but you were right too," he said, sighing, "for I very nearly lost all my men to the scaffold in the end—and I would have, indeed, had it not been for your warnings. Listen now, Lucy, if we are both disposed to love again, let us do it with glad hearts. Then I will tell you everything that has happened since you left Sherwood and how I nearly died of sorrow to find that you had flown away."

I looked into his eyes for a long moment and saw there the pain he'd felt for me and the regret he bore for not having heeded my words. And as I looked, I felt what small grains of anger were left in my heart melt away and disappear, and if I had not forgiven him before, I did so completely then. Whether he did me, I cannot say, but the fact that he was come to Denby seemed reason enough for me to hope, and I fell into his arms with a sigh of relief and felt that I'd found my safe harbor at last.

We stood together in the empty field and kissed as though Eros himself stood by to urge us on. I found I could not control my actions, for my body seemed desperate to gain for itself what it had been so long denied. And so I clung to Robin as if he made up my wine and my bread, pressing my lips hard against his to gather what I could of their sweetness. And he, for his part, twined about me like fresh-sprouted ivy, grasping my flesh where it itched me the most.

Even after we'd paused to rest, panting from the labors of love, I could not separate my skin from his. I clasped his face time after time between my hands in wonder at the beauty I saw there— beauty that had grown dim and inaccurate in my memory. His face glowed more than I had remembered, and the cut of his jaw and finely shaped nose were more definite, more clear, than my mind's eye had drawn. I did not know, in all honesty, how greatly I had missed him until he stood before me. I had to struggle to suppress a year's worth of unwept sobs, for now that my every anguish was ended, they came upon me in a deluge.

At last we found seats on the grass near a tent wall and resigned ourselves to hear every detail. My hand was wrapped up in Robin's large one, feeling the calluses of the fingertips that plucked the bowstrings with such surety.

"I ought to have told you where I went before, I truly ought, but I had an odd notion that you'd like a surprise, and I longed to give it to you—as a gift." He shook his head, and I covered his hand with my other, to give him strength to tell it all. "Well, it was very wrong of me. I'd gone to London to speak with the queen, as you discovered for yourself. But you shouldn't think I went heedless of all your warnings—I did heed them, truly! But a man can grow arrogant in the wood, and I thought, knowing what I did of the queen, that I could forge a bargain with her without causing myself any harm."

We exchanged grim looks, and Robin went on, determined to lay it all before me.

"Clym went with me, as you know, and 'tis thanks to him that anything came off at all, for it was he who found an old friar for us who spoke both French and Saxon. The friar had passed many an evening over tankards with Clym, and he agreed right quick to be my translator. We two went, disguised of course, into Westminster Castle to the queen's own rooms, and there we hid for most of a day, waiting for her to return from court. When she did, we sprang out from our hiding place, my friar declaring that I was Robin Hood, who wished to trade a word with her. She wasn't near as startled as I'd expected—though perhaps she's often waylaid by ruffians in her own rooms."

I sighed at the thought. "More likely she's grown so hard of heart that nothing startles her. I believe her veins may be filled with lead."

"You may be right—she's old enough to have been the very dragon Saint George did battle with. At any rate, this good friar and I stood before her while he told her what I proposed, that my men would take up her challenge to arrest Prince John's men from Nottingham in trade for some items from her hand.

"She sat herself down and sent her ladies off to her bedding chamber to ready some garments, then gave us seats by her fire. We sat there, pretty as you please, and discussed the terms of her challenge, that a mark of silver was to be paid for each man arrested from John's stronghold. I told her I wished to alter the terms, for my men and I would take half that amount plus one simple contract, drawn and signed by her royal hand."

"What contract?" I asked, frowning.

"Hold, love," Robin laughed. "All will come clear, I swear it. The idea of the contract caught her interest, and she asked me at once what it would contain. I smiled then for that was my moment to snatch it all, and oh, how I wished I could tell her myself instead of using the old cassocked friar as translator! But I had no choice, 'tis my own fault for becoming an outlaw instead of studying the tongues of politics." He smiled broadly for a moment, and I could just envision his pleasant mouth, twitching with words he could not express. In a moment, though, his smile vanished, and he looked at me with some great concern.

"Here, dear Marian, I'm shamed to say that I took a great liberty with your life, which I now see I'd no right to do. I cannot tell you how many times I've wished I could have those few days back! For if I had them to live again, I'd tell you all before going to London, and if you withheld your approval, I'd promise you I would not go. But that's all dreams, for I did go and acted alone, and if I have injured you I can only promise to spend all my days mending my wrong."

"Robin, my love, you make me quite nervous with these long speeches. Won't you just tell it to me and have it done?"

"Aye, 'tis best," he agreed, though he still hesitated. "You've a right to know it, so I will tell you. I asked that the contract would state her leave for Lady Marian Fitzwater to wed one lowly Robert of Locksley and that she and King Richard allow the marriage without expectation of monies to the king or any other payment. For, I said, their gift would be the capture of half of Prince John's men, and for the other half she would owe me silver marks.

"Oh, if you could have seen her face, Marian! She went all white and purple, speckled like a great dotted bean, and she nearly choked on her own words when she opened her mouth next to speak. 'Lady Marian is dead,' she said, and I replied, 'Do you think I would bargain with you over the hand of a dead woman?' "

I snickered at this, pleased by this vision of Robin's matching wits with the queen of England. But even as I smiled at his tale, I set a hand against my belly, for knots of worry had twisted there.

"That threw her for a great long while," Robin continued, "and as she coughed and gathered herself, even my friar began to smile, for he hadn't expected such a thrilling translation as I was giving him that night. At last the queen recovered herself enough to ask my full terms, so I explained that I would have your hand for Robert of Locksley, for you see I acted as though he were a friend for whom I'd come to negotiate, and no relation to Robin Hood. And too I said the contract must state that you take control and ownership of your lands of Denby-upon-Trent."

"You did?"

"Aye. And to think you thought me bold before!" He winked at me for reassurance, then went on. "We spoke a long while and in that time she made me see that she would sign this paper, for 'twould be far cheaper for her to gain all of John's men at half the number of silver marks. And as for you and your marriage fees, that was silver she'd reckoned lost, so it cost her nothing to give it up. She was startled, 'tis true, to hear that you lived, and this, I believe, took her longest to grasp. I fancied she had strong memories of you, for she could not speak of you again without shaking her head and saying my friend would have a wily fox upon his hands if he took you to wed."

We both laughed a great while at this, but as I sobered I began to see parts of this tale that frightened me.

"But Robin," I said, "does no one know you as Robert of Locksley?"

"None do," he answered, "for my parents told their steward and bailiff that young Robert ran off to fight for King Henry when he was but a lad and has never yet returned. The king's foresters, those who took old Wat o' Locksley so long ago, never saw my face or knew my name. I've placed all of my other crimes and deceits on Robin Hood's name, poor wretched knave."

"And did you not fear that the queen would send troops to follow you to Sherwood and capture you all?"

"Well that, my love, is where I did heed your warnings, for I made the queen swear that she would not do it, and I arranged that I should take her own captain to hold as our safety. If we were taken, I told her straight, I would kill that man without a pause. So she swore not to make any rash attempts, and she said too that Prince John's men posed a greater threat to the crown than our band in Sherwood ever might.

"Now," he said, raising a hand, "I know what you'll be saying next: that the queen is not to be trusted. And I thought of your words, Marian, and watched my back at every moment. But once I had my contract signed and the silver packed, I went my way back to Sherwood, excited to see your bonny face."

"Then you have this contract?" I said, astonished, for I never thought the queen would comply.

"Indeed, I have," he said, reaching under his tunic and belt. "I've no safer place to keep it than here, but it seems to have suffered no great harm."

Then I looked at this miraculous object, a deed well written, signed, and sealed by Queen Eleanor, granting me leave to wed this dear Robert and regain my sweet fields of Denby-upon-Trent. I raised my eyes from it at last and looked from my love to the tall Denby trees. I felt in that instant that I'd raised my two hands and been given to hold in them the sun and the moon, all I most cared for and all I desired.

"There is one small matter about your title to Denby," he said with a wry peak to his brow. "The queen wrote this out and gave you the land in a legal sense, but she said she would send no troops to help you take it from Sir Thomas. That, she said, we must do ourselves. But if we can manage to oust your regent, she'll not block our future claims to this land of yours."

For a moment I scarcely heard what he said, so quick was my mind in spinning a picture of Robin and me, ruling precious Denby, side by side—for precious it had become to me as I worked its meadows and winnowed its grain. With a squeal of delight I threw my two arms about his neck and kissed his cheek, for this was a dream I had never dared consider.

"Oh, Robin, you bold, bold fellow! The things you will try, honestly! But this is wonderful, this contract, this means everything for us. We may marry, may take Denby, and you may leave the outlaw's life and free yourself from that wretched danger!"

In my glee I was slow to realize that he might not wish to leave the forests of Sherwood, that he might be sorry to leave that free life and the men there who loved him. But when he went on with his tale I learned that his group of brave outlaws was already disbanded and that the life of a forest yeoman had ended for Robin Hood long before this day.

"I'm glad you're pleased with this bit of work, for I feared you'd be angry with me for telling the queen your little secret. I assured her, though, that she'd never find you if she tried to look, and she seemed weary at the very thought, so I don't think you stand in danger. And now that we've this," he said, jerking his thumb at the parchment, " 'tis no matter. Even if she did bear you ill will, she could not force you to wed Stephen now, for this contract tops any other she'd given before. 'Tis there in the writing, you can see it yourself." He looked at me with eager eyes, and for a moment I did not understand that he wished me to confirm that what he said was true. I nodded, for I'd seen the words, and when he looked relieved I recalled that he could not read it for himself and had counted perhaps on the friar's oath that his terms were expressed by the words on the parchment.

"Well, then, once the contract was writ by the queen's clerk, she made some arrangements for our departure. I told her then, in my own Saxon, that if she tried to trick me, by the bright hair of Saint Aelfrida, I'd make her suffer. She said she understood my words, though the friar had not translated them, and she sent one of her ladies, parchment in hand, to order the page and captain to ride with me. The page carried with him the silver and parchment, and the lady found me a horse to ride and a meal for the friar, who was traveling off to some holy place in the south. Clym had long since returned to you, for the journey took far longer than I had expected—'tis a long road on foot.

"When we returned, and I saw you that moment, I knew—ah, Marian—I ought to have stopped then and told you all, but I was so pleased to be at the point of action I could hardly take time to rouse the men. All the long way down Watling Street and Fosse Way, I'd plotted our approach to Nottingham Castle, and I didn't want to waste a minute once I'd come. But I tell you now, I rue my haste, for if I'd had time to speak with you, you might have been there when I returned, and we could have flown the forest together."

I said nothing, merely nodded my head, for 'twas enough that he regretted his actions—I needn't tell him what pain he'd caused. Too, I thought of my fresh revelation, that I'd fled from the weight of Robin's sweet love, and felt too chagrined to tell my part. There would be time enough to lay bare my soul—I needn't begin in the first hour. So on he went to tell me how they'd stormed the castle through guise and stealth, using the king's captain as their foil.

"When we were well outside town, we took five of the prince's guards and stripped their clothes, and these outfits I put on my own body and Will Scarlet's, Adam Bell's, Will Stutley's, and David of Doncaster's. Then I had all the rest of the men go with their hands behind their backs, like this, you see? With their swords well hidden, in groups behind those of us in uniform. The captain I had ride at the fore, with orders to tell the castle guards that we'd taken these outlaws in Sherwood and came to collect the prince's reward. That gained us entry in the castle walls, and once we were in all the men broke loose, pummeling the mercenaries with a demon fire."

His eyes glazed like ice on a pond's edge.

"They each had lengths of stout rawhide with which to tie up the men as they seized them, and after an hour, or perhaps 'twas two, the whole castle fell silent. All I could hear were rude jests from our side and groans from the men we'd taken. And then I had the joy of taking our due from the queen's young page, near my own weight in silver, I swear to it. Our band returned to the Greenwood tree to celebrate and divvy our coin. And then I told them that this was to be our last grand outing, for now that I'd been to speak with the queen, I thought we wouldn't have many days left of merry safety in our wood. The time had come for our group to disband."

"Oh, Robin," I breathed.

"Indeed, my love. 'Twas a sad hour, perhaps sadder for me than for the others. They took it with long faces, as you'd expect, so I explained how I was to leave, but that Will Scarlet and others had determined to make for Needwood Forest. They'd make a new band there and would welcome any who wished to join them. This brought the men to cheers again, and as they hurrahed, I left the group in search of you, for now that I had the contract with me, I wanted to tell you of our great catch."

Here I turned away from his eye, ashamed once again of my own foolhardiness. "But I had gone," I whispered, thinking I would spare him from telling that part.

"You had gone. I was so distraught, Marian, I did not know what to do with myself. Annie was there by that time and had read through your letter, so she calmed me somewhat. And as we spoke the matter over I came to see that 'twas through my own rashness that you'd thought to leave, not knowing what bargains I'd struck.

Oh, I was wretched! But Annie worked at length to soothe me, and in time we talked of where you might have gone, and she told me her thoughts."

"And do you know where Annie is now? Has she returned to Wodesley village?"

"Aye, that she has. I stopped there to see her, seeking news of you, though she had none to give. She seemed a bit restless in her old life, to tell the truth. I suspect she's not taken to the ways of the farmer as easily as she thought she might."

"Ah, dear Annie," I said, feeling a fondness for her that warmed me greatly.

"Hold off, though, Marian, for there's more to my tale. As I was talking with Annie, a great noise came crashing from the wood. Out we went, and there was that dandy, the new sheriff of Nottingham, come with a whole band to seize our men! It pains me to say so, but it seemed the king's captain had told him about us and how to find our Greenwood tree—the bloody scoundrel. I never had liked his looks. So our men set at them with swords and arrows, and I ran about shouting that they should flee, for you know we've our meeting place, where we could regroup.

" 'Twas a nasty moment, for several of our men were killed outright, though bold as they are none was taken alive. But most escaped to the old elm cave, and there we met like a bunch of rats, shivering in the cold and damp. All that night we waited, listening, and when morning came we slipped back to camp to bury the dead and pack our belongings, for we were off to our separate ways. The men split into small traveling groups, most headed for Needwood by roundabout ways. We agreed to meet there in a full month's time. 'Twas wretched, Marian, to leave those men—not so much to leave the life, for I was still determined to find you out and trade that roguish life for a better one with you.

"But I feared for their safety and worried what shelter they'd find for the winter and if they'd have food enough to survive. I knew each man had a good purse of silver from our work at the castle, and a fine suit of clothes thanks to your handiwork, but even so an outlaw's safety is a tenuous thing. Will and I talked about rules to establish, how he should form a river trail that every man must splash through on his way to camp, so no dogs could follow along the scent, and how the men should wear whatever costume the local foresters wore, like we'd done with our Lincoln green. Will's a clever lad, and I know he'll do well, but I still fear for the lot of them and I miss their merry ways."

I gripped his hand a bit tighter here, then rose to standing, for I saw with a start that the sun slanted low, and I ought to discover the Tamworths' location. I pulled Robin up with me and tugged him along toward the Denby town square, explaining as we went, in the shortest words I could find, how things stood for me as Mary Cox and how I resided in Thetbury village. We agreed hastily that Robin should play the part of a suitor come from Belton village, newly arrived to claim my hand. This suited me, for I hoped to keep my own name a secret from Uncle John if I possibly could, thinking the truth would give him more pain than pleasure. To Meg I would tell a fuller tale.

And so we met up with my country family, and I introduced them to Nicholas Atwood, the beau of my youth, whom I'd met with by chance at the archery range. Matthew perked up at Robin's face and told in a rush how Walter the Miller had groped me on the barrels and how I'd been rescued by this archer. Robin then showed them the prize he'd won, a gold-beaten arrow of fine quality, and between that tale and his own charming manner he soon had the family near doting upon him.

When he explained that he wished to wed me, now that he had found me out, he became a favorite with lovely Meg, who had long dreamt of romance for me, and also with John, who wished, perhaps, for one fewer mouth to feed. Robin said he would escort us to Thetbury and would spend the night in the one-room inn, that

he might collect me in the morning and take me off to Belton village. 'Twas his dearest hope, he said with a wink, that we might be
wed without delay.

How quickly my fortunes seem to change when Robin Hood's
wrapped up in them! As we walked homeward I thought it through
and began to feel as the eagle does when she catches a gust of
bright spring wind and soars to the stars without ever needing to
flap her wings. I soared high too in my happiness, and by the time
I reached my straw bed that night I was so far above earth, I could
scarcely close my eyes—the view from above was too enchanting
to miss.

Chapter Twenty-one

THE TAMWORTHS WERE STARTLED by the swiftness of my decision to go, and Janey wept a bit over breakfast, sad to lose her youthful companion. I found a moment to whisper to Meg that Robin was my own true love, come from Lott's End, that he knew my rightful name and my wretched tale. This delighted her better than I had hoped, and she kissed me as if I were kin of her own.

It took me no longer than a minute or two to pack up my things into a bundle, and I left with Meg half the pennies I had brought with me, for living with them I'd never had cause to spend even one. When Robin arrived, Uncle John seemed taken with a fit of protectiveness, repeatedly asking if we oughtn't be wed before I went traveling with a young man. But Robin went on about his family in Belton and how his mother awaited me, as he'd sent her word, and that all would be well after a half-day's journey. Meg, now a convert to our secret romance, aided our cause by claiming to have known the Atwoods in Belton village. She blathered to John of their respectability until he felt compelled to let us depart.

Robin was well versed in the taxes and tallages of village folk, and so he was firm in refusing to go until Uncle John had accepted his payment of the marchet money, for the family would owe this coin when it was known that I had wed. For all his gruff excuses to the contrary, I saw that Uncle John was pleased to take it, and he gripped Robin's hand with something akin to companionship when the money was paid.

I kissed them all with true affection and bid good-bye to that cramped house which had kept me warm through the lifeless winter. For a moment I thought on Annie's home and the disgust I'd felt toward our night there. Now, strangely, I had lived in a matching cottage and thought it the purest place on earth, where hard work brought bread and sleep was peaceful, for each person's body was worn from the labors of day.

Robin and I had formed no design beyond that of walking the road together, as we had once done so long before. And when at last we walked out of Thetbury and began our new journey, I was seized with a giddiness I found hard to explain. There was a vivacity in the air that morning that entered my lungs and filled my whole being, a quickening that came to my blackbird's heart and made me feel joy in every step. And each time I glanced in his direction, Robin was smiling, and I smiled too from my own delight.

"I suppose I must learn to call you Robert," I said, half joking, as we passed the Thetbury fields.

"I've never taken well to that name," he said. "Wouldn't Rob do just as well?"

"Rob will do, I suppose, just as well as Nicholas, Brian, and Robin Hood. How can you have feelings for any name when you've taken up so many?"

"What, this from the mouth of Mary Cox? Do you realize, Marian, with what ease a lie rolls from your tongue these days? When I first met you I don't believe you thought you could take on a tale if you had to, and look at you now, crafting up falsehoods from this side and that!"

"I must admit, 'tis easier than I ever thought it was. Do you remember when we left Warwick Castle and stopped at that inn in the rainstorm? And you made me run to the kitchen women and tell them some tale for a suit of clothes? I thought I would shrivel at the very thought."

"I worried for you more than a little after you'd left, but when you came back in your new dress and boots, I knew I'd found the woman for me. Especially after catching a glance at you in naught but your shift—what a sight!"

I struck at him playfully with the bundle I carried.

"Speaking of love and lovers," he said, "what do you think our Clym is doing but hanging round Wodesley village, speaking sweet words into Annie's ear."

"Clym?" I said, in a harsher tone than I'd expected. "Clym is wooing Annie?"

"What, are you surprised?" he asked. "Did you not see them sitting together in Sherwood? Or have you some bias against a red cap?"

This was meant as a joke, since he now wore a red felt hat much like Clym's, but I was in no humor for laughing. Strange emotions brewed in my heart, and I scarcely knew what words I spoke, so confounded was I in attempting to single one out from the other.

"I never thought her partial to him, that's all. Do you think she returns his affection?"

Robin shrugged and looked at me with a twinkle in his eye that said that while he did not know, aye or nay, he would not have been surprised to hear it. This news disturbed me more than I can say, and I was ashamed to admit that, thinking back, I had no memory of Annie and Clym consorting beneath our Greenwood tree. I, it seemed, had been too occupied with my own budding love to be aware of any other.

My companion had noticed my distress, and since I did not wish to be closely examined on this point, I hastened to introduce a new subject. A sensation deep within my belly hinted that my reaction to his news might not be a fully noble one, and so I sought to hide it away.

"Tell me, Robin, have you heard nothing more of King Richard and how he does in the prisons of Germany?"

"Only that he's written some songs and poems from his cell, describing his lot and charging his subjects to keep brave hearts, for he swears he'll be with us soon. But in my travels these past months I've heard a mix of reports. Some say we'll be charged one hundred gold pieces for his life, and what we cannot raise in funds must be given in noble hostages."

"Hostages! Hmm, that will be a tricky thing. And what of Prince John? Now that you have routed his men, has he changed his tune about joining with Philip Augustus of France?"

"I think not. Those men were, of course, but a part of his force. Knowing John, he has others hidden off somewhere. The last I heard, he was sailing for Normandy to see the queen, to try to win her back to his side, now that Richard lies in prison. It seems a fool's errand to me—she'll only be made more angry by it."

"Well, Prince John has never been quite as clever at playing to his own mother as he seems to be with the rest of the world."

This discussion took us several miles, but as we neared the edges of Denby, I thought to ask Robin where we were headed, for he seemed to angle his feet forward with purpose.

"I have only one thought in my head, Marian, and that is to wed you before you find fault with me a second time and see fit to flee to the ends of the earth. I had thought we might ask Friar Tuck to do it, since he is returned to his former post at Fountain Abbey, a shrine to the Virgin not far from here."

"And after that?"

"After that I have no ideas. What think you, Mistress Lucy?"

I beamed and nodded my head, "Yes, I think I have a plan."

"I thought you might," he said with a chuckle.

"And why is that?" I asked, twisting my face in mock surprise.

"You always have some scheme in your pocket, haven't you? I don't believe I've ever known you to be without a plotted course. I'll never forget, I tell you truly, how you sought me out in Sherwood Forest—wily fox, indeed."

"I have not always had a plan in mind," I admitted shyly. "At times I've felt quite incapable of deciding on what course to take. But you make me feel brave, bold yeoman that you are, and so I have concocted a wild scheme."

"Those, without question, are my very favorite, so please tell it, Lady Marian."

"It has but one flaw that I can see, and that is that we shall be forced to part for a time again. But 'twill be brief and will have an end, and if Clym can be persuaded to pass messages along it need not be such a sorrowful time."

"So long as we may be married first, so I know you shall have no chance of escape, I will agree to whatever you plot for me."

"Well, Robin, if you shall always be so agreeable," I laughed, "I think you will make a most suitable husband. Very well, this is my thought. While I lived in Thetbury I had a chance to observe Sir Thomas pass through the village with a lady companion, which lady was our own Lady Pernelle of Sencaster." I glanced at him to see that he recalled her by name and, seeing that all was blindingly clear, I continued. "She and Sir Thomas seemed most intimate, and I feel certain that they have become far more than cousins, that in fact they are lovers. And if that's the case, then our fight with Sir Thomas for Denby is, at heart, a fight with Lady Pernelle. I'm convinced that she backs him, and that it was for him that Hugh was murdered."

"Murdered! You never mentioned that before."

I explained then how my mind had retossed the details of Hugh's death and had come to a new arrangement of facts and motives.

" 'Twas all too strange at the time to have been a case of simple death. The reports were far too varied for that. Nay, I believe Lady Pernelle was behind it all, and chilling as that notion is, it fits with her later actions. Recall how she struggled to keep Denby from me after Hugh died and how furious she was to lose it? And then that she would maneuver to wed me to Stephen—well, that seems to clinch it all. She thirsts for the exclusive ownership of Sencaster and Denby-upon-Trent."

"But why place all this energy on Denby? You said yourself that it's no special province."

"Nay, but Robin, 'tis not so easy to gain a region! Most are ruled by powerful barons with armies both here and across the channel. Denby is sought because it is not guarded. My youth and ignorance left it open to one such as Thomas Lanois, and now that he's got his toe into it, it shall be far harder for us to draw back."

"So how do you propose we do it?"

I paused a moment and ceased walking, for I wished to be sure we were not overheard. "We must get close to these two plotters, Lady Pernelle and Sir Thomas, to learn all we can about their means and motives. I propose that we go to their courts, I to Sencaster and you to Denby, to work our way into the household and gain what we can of the noble's ear. When we know them better, we'll be able to find the weakness in their hold over Denby and can plan our moment to snatch it back."

Robin was quiet as he considered this, and we walked a full half mile before he spoke again. But when he did, he was amenable.

"Your plan seems to have some merit, but I fear for you in going to Sencaster. Lady Pernelle knows your face, does she not? Won't she recognize you as Marian Fitzwater and catch you up at once?"

I nodded slightly, for I'd also thought of these things. "She may feel that she's seen me somewhere before, but I do not think she'll place me correctly. Lady Pernelle sets a great store on the trappings one wears, on fine gems and velvets. I do not believe it would occur to her to look at the face of one in homespun and match it in memory to one who wore silk. I shall alter my hair somewhat, or go with it beneath a kerchief, and that must muddle her mental picture. And, remember, I shall speak Saxon." I saw that he was not satisfied, so I laid a hand across his arm. "And too, Robin, thanks to you, if I am found out, it shall be no great loss. She won't be able to wed me to Stephen, for you and I shall be already wed, and if she brings me before the queen, well, 'tis no matter. I shall only be released."

This persuaded him a bit more, and the longer we walked, the more pleased he became. I noticed that he seemed unconcerned for his own fate, which amused me, for he would be in far more danger than I. But I supposed he counted on his own knack for living in disguise as well as the fact that none in Denby should know that knave, Robin Hood.

I SHOULD PERHAPS PAUSE here to say that I felt at this time that more stars twinkled above my head than I had ever dreamed possible. Since I was a child, I never had visions of a happy marriage, never fantasized my wedding gown, or foresaw the smiling groom beside me. For I had already paced that aisle and knew, even in my child's heart, that marriage nine times out of ten is little more than a contract made with an unknown man of title and silver.

And yet, for all my scoffs and doubts, here I stood beside a man who meant far more than love to me. He was my friend, my counselor, my encouragement. In a crowd his eye sought me out—me alone!—and he seemed to gravitate to my side. We spoke as equals, laughed as one, and yet were different as night and day. These things, as I pondered them, made me amazed and filled my eyes with silent tears, overcome as I was by my own good fortune.

As we neared the woodland ferns of Fountain Abbey, I prepared my mind to bid adieu to my sweet Atalanta and Diana, my fellow maidens, for it was time for me to leave off girlhood and turn my eyes to a new path. Lady Juno would be my guiding star now, the model to whom I could always look. But this change was slow, for I was sorry to say good-bye to such old friends. So I set myself to work at this task long before we arrived, in hopes that I might make a smooth transition. The trappings of youth can be hard to forsake, and I wondered if I would manage it fully.

Fountain Abbey proved a magical place, alight with dancing narcissus, with shy heart's ease and fields of snowdrops. A brook flowed beside it, mirthful and bright, and I recognized this water as the very place where Robin and Friar Tuck once carried each other on their backs across the stream, time and again, stopping to fight on each far side. But the grass now showed no mark of their tussle, and the water had covered their every last footprint, for those days were far in the past. Robin gave the stream a kindly smile, thinking, I supposed, those very same thoughts, before he turned his face to the abbey door.

Friar Tuck welcomed us with boisterous joy, and when he heard what we were about, he set to calling the banns immediately, that we might be wed the following day. 'Twas strange to hear my own right name mixed in with that of Robert of Locksley, but when I felt odd, I looked to Robin and was reassured that we did as we ought.

I did not know Friar Tuck well, for Annie had always been cautious of him, and I had followed her example. I believe she was a bit offended at such bawdiness in a friar, but once I knew him to be good-hearted, I did not mind his loud joking ways. He and Robin exchanged their tales of where they'd wandered and what they'd seen since their parting at the Greenwood tree, though Friar Tuck had little to add, having come from Sherwood straight to this place. I left them together for a time and walked in the woods to gather my thoughts, for I fully expected every bit of myself to be altered by the next day's events, and I wished to prepare myself in mind and body.

Among the things I bore in my sack were my own wedding gown from Warwick Castle, and for once I was able to look on its soft lace with a happy eye and enjoy its beauty. Friar Tuck had lent me the use of a low green bower, which stood in a grove of young apple trees, and to this I retired to shake out my gown and hang it out fully to air and crispen. That task done, I walked upstream, gazing at the lucid waters until I felt my legs grow weary. Then, in a remote pool, I bathed myself with local herbs and rubbed my hair with lavender flowers that it might be both rich and sweet smelling. And when I was done I spread my hair on a rock to dry in the March sun and felt a peace come over me that I had not known in years—if, indeed, I had ever felt it.

Time passes quickly when the future looms bright, and before I felt ready, I stood in my gown, all silk and silver, and knelt down with Robin in the abbey's lit chapel. A spring rain beat softly about us, pattering on the church's stone steps, and with its rhythms went Friar Tuck's words, easing so gently that I felt no fear. And when all was finished, I went to Robin and was kissed so dearly that I knew, at once, that little had changed between our hearts. We were now only husband and wife, a new set of words to add to our others, and because I now saw that in gaining these two we had lost nothing, I felt I had stumbled on a cask of riches.

That night we retired together to the bower, to sleep among the budding blossoms as the fairies do in their cobweb beds. Robin and I made love by lamplight, adding to its glow the warmth of our feeling, feelings which still today buzz in my head and bring a smile to my face in odd tranquil moments. That night I left Diana behind me and went full willingly to my new role, a transformation I have never regretted.

We remained a fortnight in Fountain Abbey, resting nightly in our bower, for we both were reluctant to part again and wished to enjoy the warm spring days. It occurred to Robin that we might pass all of the summer there, but I was afraid that the lady of Sencaster might be less willing to take on new help in autumn. If I came in October she might think me less honest, guessing that I sought a warm place for winter, than if I appeared in the stillness of May.

I did all I could to prepare Robin for life in Denby, sharing every detail of the land and the town, in hopes that he might sidle into life there with as little trouble as possible. We thought it best that he maintain his identity as Nick Atwood, since some citizens of Denby would remember his feats at the Shrove Tuesday fair. And by the time we neared the moment of parting, we had come to think this a very good thing, for any local laborer who recognized his face would only lend credibility to his guise.

My situation was a bit more difficult, since I knew Lady Pernelle had a bias for hiring natives of Sencaster. I decided to adopt the most remote village I came across in my travels toward the manor house and promote myself as a child of that hamlet who had traveled abroad, working at great houses in shires nearby. I would go, I told Robin, as Kate Thatcher, Kate being a name I had always admired for its resolute sound and clean appearance.

We agreed that when we parted ways, I would head west to Sencaster, and Robin would travel to Wodesley village to tear Clym away from his suit to Annie. Clym would be established as our message bearer and would be trusted to make regular visits to one manor after the next, to keep our discoveries and decisions in harmony. In addition, I now entrusted to Robin every gold band and jewel I had brought from Warwick, part of the haul of my own belongings that he had carried out of Sherwood. These he planned to sell in Leicestershire, that we might have funds aplenty to carry out our daring plan.

At last the time came for me to start off, and as I clung to Robin that morning, I whispered to him that this might be our last adventure. For if all went well we could end this folly by becoming, at last, respectable souls.

"Will it not trouble you," I asked as we lay, legs entangled, "to take on the guise of a Norman noble when once we are settled in Denby Manor?"

"I do not think I shall play that part," he laughed, tickling my cheek with his beard. "I expect to shock all the noble world by maintaining my love of the Saxon ways. You, they may wonder at, for what Norman lady could be so indelicate as to wed a Saxon?"

"Ah, one of those foul, uncivilized creatures? Well, I suppose I fathomed it, didn't I? But truly, Robin, I hope you will feel no pain at becoming the recipient of the very tax you have fought against."

He was quiet for a time, but I could tell when he spoke that he'd considered this long before that morning.

"I've thought, dear Marian, that a Saxon man can do no better than to raise himself to a place where he may affect the tax at its root. We'll take enough tax to live upon, aye, but I scarcely think we will rise to opulence. Rather, let us set an example of ruling grace by taking in taxes what we need only, giving to the king what is his due, and returning the rest to the needy and poor."

"That is excellently planned. I heard in Thetbury that my mother used to give each laborer a new pair of shoes every Christmas Day. 'Tis the sort of tradition I'd very much like to revive in Denby."

"Well thought, my love. Now Marian," he said, turning suddenly serious, "you must promise me that you will think quite hard about your next plan, the one in which we seize back your lands. For I will not accept a dangerous scheme—you must be in safety at every moment, or I won't help you, I swear I won't."

"Won't you now! Very well, then, I promise to plot it as well as I can. But perhaps some of our friends of Needwood might be called upon for the rougher work? For I'm sure there will be rough work to do—there's no suppressing manor guards without it."

We talked like this for a long while, then turned again to our tender good-byes. Robin gave me a ring to wear in remembrance of him, and this I hung by a piece of silk about my neck, for it would not do for a serving girl to go about with rings on her fingers. I found a keepsake for him to wear, a jeweled pin of my castle days, and he bade me kiss it that he might have a caress with him, beneath his tunic, at all times.

Because he had worried so about my traveling the roads alone, I changed back into Allan's old suit and cut a new cudgel to carry with me. Robin was charmed with my new dress, for he said I made the prettiest boy he'd ever laid eyes on. But when at last he kissed me good-bye, he followed with shouts that I should keep my cudgel near me always, for pretty boys sometimes had to fight all the harder.

I shouted back that I would be fine, not to worry, but that he should take care to watch himself. In this way I skirted the path, shouting and walking, until I had gone too far for us to hear any longer, and I found myself alone again. So began a new chapter in my life, for now I faced the world as a prospective servant, disguised as a lad, while within my heart I was, plain as day, a married woman with a task to perform.

Chapter Twenty-two

THE ROAD TO SENCASTER was pitted and muddy, for the recent rains had taken their toll and the spring sun was still too mild to bake the mud into smooth sheets. In the fields about me work continued, and I thought with a pang on my Thetbury family and hoped they had hands enough for their labor. Perhaps, I fancied, Janey might learn to sell goods in the market in place of her mother, and in time maybe Matthew would come to tend strips of his own alongside his father's.

From time to time I passed a family at work on their dirt, still breaking up clods if they were tardy or sowing grain seed from a wooden box. As I watched and—to admit it all—envied them somewhat, I came to realize what greater joy I now took in my life than I had at Warwick so long ago, warm and cushioned though that time was. Tending the land was hard and bitter, and at times the suffering was too great to bear, but I looked at my own limbs, strong now and sturdy, and was pleased for it. It gave me pride to know that I'd felt the stiffness of a full day afield, and I now possessed a sharp appreciation for each morsel of bread I ate, for I knew with certainty what had caused it to grow.

As I neared Sencaster, I turned my thoughts to Lady Pernelle, thinking through everything I knew of her to distill what I could of her character. I recalled how she had petted Hugh and called him always her precious boy, and my belly felt sick for her treachery. I did not know if Robin believed me when I claimed that she'd killed Hugh, but whether or not he acknowledged the truth of it, I was convinced that it was so, and this made me clench my hands in fists. I swore, on that road, to do what I could to avenge Hugh's death, for little though I loved his full-grown form, his childish soul had been precious to me. I would avenge my dovecote friend, this I pledged by the clouds and treetops.

ONE MORNING I PASSED a large market town and, peering about to see which stalls sold herbs from the East, stopped and purchased a small quantity of henna with which I might dye my hair. I hemmed and guffawed with the young merchant, for I've always had trouble lowering my voice to sound sufficiently like a lad, but luckily a heavy rain was falling, and my tone was lost in the sloshing of puddles. With my penny bag of henna tucked tightly in my cloak, I slipped away and made for a wood to wait out the rain in peace and find a small pool in which to wash.

Henna takes some time to set, so I stayed in that wood nearly three full days, coating my locks in loose green powder until they were stained a copperish color, nearly the shade of the robin's breast, though closer to the natural color of hair. Newly altered, I dressed in my old homespun gown, a lass once more, and set my eyes toward Sencaster manor. As I had explained to Robin, I thought Lady Pernelle would be easily fooled by a change of garments and a different tone, but true as I believed it to be, I was not about to chance my future on an error of judgment. I had rather be safe with orange hair than caught in the act with my ebony tresses.

IT HAS LONG BEEN my observation that noble ladies of a certain age fall into two classes: those who surround themselves with plain-faced servants in hopes that they might shine as a beauty among the roughage and those who draw in lovely young girls, praying that the careless noble observer might leave their court with a vague recollection of charm and good looks, extending to the lady what he had observed in the servant girls' faces. One afternoon spent in the manor yard told me that Lady Pernelle was of the latter camp, for every lass I saw come and go had a shapely face and a witching smile.

Based on this knowledge I prepared myself with exacting care the following morning, arranging my hair at its most striking and pinching my cheeks to make them rosy. Thus attired, I plucked up my courage and went to the manor to see Lady Pernelle, announcing myself as Kate Thatcher of Titfield, praying that Kate bore no hints of Marian.

When at last I gained entrance, Sencaster Manor gave me an odd jolt. It put me in mind of when Annie arrived at Sherwood Forest and took up cooking with the fire and kettle as if she'd lived there all her life. "One cook's kitchen is much like another," she'd said at the time, and as I looked about me I began to think the same applied to noble homes.

Just as everything had been done at Warwick, things appeared to be done here. While this house was smaller in size and stature than Warwick Castle, it strove to emulate its betters, like the girl-child who dons her mother's kerchief and gives out orders to the serving folk. Where Lord William had kept cook, butler, and baker, Lady Pernelle did as well. And, as was due the slight difference in economy, where Lord William colored his dishes with saffron, Lady Pernelle tinted hers with blood, not wishing to be outdone in the art of her table. The best ornaments and objects of value were displayed where every visitor would see them, and whether coming or going, all paused to see Lady Pernelle's Frankish powder boxes, marveling over their inlaid jewels.

All this was apparent in my short walk from entry to great hall, and by the time I was called before the lady herself and had bowed so low my copper tresses brushed the floor, I found myself surprisingly at ease. I had to wait, for the lady herself was involved in some discussion over payment of the local priest with her clerk. At last she turned her face to me, and I saw with a start that while her jewels and bright locks remained, her face had grown horribly sour.

"What brings you here, girl?" she asked me rudely, in unpolished Saxon.

"My name is Kate Thatcher, if it pleases, my lady, and I've come in search of employment." I trusted that the lady's own unfamiliarity with the Saxon tongue would keep her from noticing that my accent was not a local one.

"Where are you from, Kate Thatcher? We take no one into this house who is not of Sencaster."

"I was born in Titfield, my lady, to May and Jackson Thatcher of that village. But I've lived most of my life in service in Lincoln and Manchester, at the great houses there."

"Indeed!" she exclaimed, raising her eyebrows, for these were some of the wealthiest castles of our time. She let her eye rest upon me while the hall grew silent as a graveyard. In the quiet, I felt the chill of dread rising and I was certain my own heartbeat would give me away, loud as it was. Perhaps she knew me, knew my face! But I suppose in truth she was gauging my looks, determining how my poppy-red hair would offset her own pale cheeks, for she then said, "Well, Kate Thatcher, I will take you on for a trial. But mind me well—keep your hands off the silver and your eyes on your work, or you will feel the sharp end of my rod. You're lucky I lost a good servant of mine but recently, or there'd be no place for you in this house. Come, Dame Ena will show you to your duties."

The interview was finished far more quickly than I had dared hope, and later that very afternoon I found myself beating out the lady's bedclothes and tossing her floor reeds in the sun to air. My work was not difficult, especially now that I'd been so well trained in Thetbury, for I could churn and bake without effort and thought little of any work in the yard.

I ate my meals in the kitchen with the others and at night was given the privileged place of sleeping within that very same room, with the floor as my mattress, my head on the shoulder of the girl next to me. We all slumbered there, where the fires were warm, and thought little of our discomfort, though truly the Baileys' lump-filled mattress made a better bed.

At first I went about my work unnoticed by any but my fellow servants, and I began to fear for the success of my scheme. Lady Pernelle's sharp eyes did pick out my skill with the needle and put me to work on her finest kerchiefs, her girdles and gloves, and her decorative sleeves. But for all my talent with her delicate fabrics, I still went several weeks with a frustrated air. I wished, above all, to ingratiate myself into this household, to become privy to their intimate chats and evening gossip, but if I continued on as I was, I would know just how well they preferred partridge to pike, but nothing of how I might seize back my lands.

My chance came at last when Lady Pernelle, in a state over an upcoming guest, called all her serving women to the great hall to determine how best to plan the visit.

"Within two weeks' time," she told us, her voice sounding stiff with practiced authority, "we shall all have the honor of entertaining our revered holy father, the bishop of Lincoln town, for he passes this way on his journey to the north and shall grace us with his company. I've already determined his room and bed linens and trust that Dame Ena will remain afterward to hear my instructions." Here Ena bobbed awkwardly, turning quite red in the face about it. "But I wish to discuss with all of you the foodstuffs we shall be serving, for I know the bishop likes his plate, and I expect our table to exceed his expectations. Now," she muttered, more to herself than to us, "what shall we serve the man?"

I knew full well that we'd not been asked, but when the silence of my peers grew heavy, I stepped forward to gain her attention.

"Forgive me, my lady, but it's well known that the bishop loves sweets and fruits of all kinds. Perhaps we could serve him sugared plums, raisin-and-suet pies, and candied citron?" My heart was in my throat as I spoke, but my knowledge was firm, for I knew from Robin that I spoke the truth. Robin had lightened the purse of this very bishop a handful of times and once told me he had often found a sweet lemon slice hidden in among the gold pieces.

"Is that so? Who are you? Kate, is it not? And, tell me Kate, how is it you come by this piece of knowledge?"

"As I'm sure your ladyship recalls, I served for a time in the Lincoln town manor, where we had the honor of"—how had she put it?—"entertaining the bishop on several occasions."

"Ah." Despite the chill in her tone, I fancied my suggestion had met with approval. "Can you purchase for us these things you describe, enough to be plentiful on our table throughout the bishop's visit?"

"Certainly, my lady, I will do as you ask. If you please, how many servings will the table require?"

She looked at me shrewdly, and for a moment I feared she'd had a sudden flash, a qualm of memory, and recalled my face. But no, she merely needed time to consider my question. "Enough for three—nay, make that four, in case of unexpected guests."

AFTER THAT DAY I found myself sliding into the confidences I had longed for. The incident over the candied fruits had raised my worth in Lady Pernelle's eyes from that of a mongrel to a hunting spaniel. Where before I had been a useless cleaner of linens and drapes, I was now a source for consultation, a woman who'd seen the insides of houses much greater than hers and who might advise the lady on the most critical points of style. What tapestry should be hung in the hall? What hairstyles were lately the most in fashion? Should young Stephen wear red hose with his ermine and velvet, or would the green be more becoming? All these questions I answered for her, confident that my knowledge of Warwick's ways had not faded so much as to ruin my good sense.

The bishop's visit was a great success, from the well-laid table to the luxurious furs we placed in the chapel to ease penitent knees, and the greatest portion of the credit for it was owed to me. Lady Pernelle said nothing in thanks, of course, but from that time on I was indispensable—exactly what I had hoped to become.

In the week before I had spent so much time searching markets for citron that I missed Clym's visit and returned one night to find him waiting outside the manor walls, afraid to arouse suspicion by entering. Together we wandered off a pace to hold a hasty conversation, and from him I learned that Robin was safely entrenched in Denby and was nearing Sir Thomas's well-fed heart by rising within the ranks of the kitchen. This made me laugh, for Robin had always been skilled at the fire, and I could too well imagine how he might become the favorite of the manor hearth. He would please them all, I was certain, from the lord to the dairy maids, and in the space of a month I was sure Sir Thomas would be ready to call him his most prized possession.

During these weeks at Sencaster Manor, I'd searched each chamber of my heart to seek out and soothe the ill feeling I bore this purported love between Clym and Annie. And, sadly, in the dark pit nearest my ribs and spine, I discovered the rank air of jealousy. For who had Annie to love but me? Did she not wish to save for me her every attention, her every kind word? I listened close to the peevish voice that asked these questions and resolved that I must hush it completely. Surely I could not allow such a mean spirit to live in my heart. I must embrace—nay, encourage—this romance for the joy it brought and not be overrun by my petty selfishness.

So I cautiously asked Clym how she did and if he'd become acquainted with her family, and I heard in return such a glowing report that it made me blush at my own hard feelings. Everything in his air and manner told me so plainly that he loved her that I shook my head at having been blind to the signs before. And as he told me of Annie's words, of things she had done and what she had said, I begrudgingly saw the chance of love there, on her side too, and forced myself into an air of false joy.

I reported to Clym how my work went, but sadly had little of interest to tell him, for all that seemed to occur in Sencaster was preparation and care of noble guests. But he passed no judgment, merely took my message and bid me adieu, trekking away into the darkness to bear my words to my bold outlaw.

As fortune was kind, June brought me closer still to the household, particularly to young Stephen, who by this time so resembled Hugh as to give me a start nearly each time we met. I doubt I had seen him since he passed nine years old, and he'd changed so by now that I'd scarcely have matched the child's face to the one he now wore. These days he walked proudly, a tall lad of fifteen, young enough still to race in for supper, but old enough to take an interest in the affairs of Sencaster and his mother's decisions.

Stephen had a great love of the hunt, and warm June weather took him often to the hills to chase about with his pack of dogs and return loaded down with limp harts and coneys. His mother encouraged him in this pursuit, but it wasn't until the weather turned poor, during an odd bout of summer storms, that I came to see the reason why.

Lady Pernelle did all she could to keep Stephen from her court in the day, for he was just of an age and temperament that he had begun to question her judgment and add his opinions to cases before her. If a farmer came forward to speak for his land, stating the steward had been cheating him, Stephen was apt to side with the farmer while his mother, invariably, took the steward's cause. If the sheriff presented a criminal slated for the gallows, Stephen would hear the poor man's case while she gripped the arms of her chair with rancor. Stephen's very veins seemed thick with independence and he turned a critical, discerning eye on every problem placed before him. These were matters of temper and spirit which drove his dear mother into fits of rage.

I was brought running from my stitching table, one dreary day, by such howls and shrieks that I thought Lady Pernelle must be dying. But I found her, rather, facing her son, her cheeks all drawn with spite and anger, reaching out to throttle his neck. Stephen was the stronger of the two by far, and as her hands neared his face, he grasped them roughly and pushed them away. So easily did he manage it that he threw his mother to a greater rage, and she shouted out words I'd not heard before, harsh-sounding French words that were new to me but made me blush all the same.

He took it all staunchly with a firm face, saying nothing, but looking at her with a steady gaze that made her fury boil even hotter. This battle went on for several long minutes until at last the lady crumpled, exhausted, like the angry bee who stings and dies. Stephen stomped out to make a nuisance of himself in the stables.

I soon found that this was common behavior whenever Stephen attended court, which he did at the first hint of rain. In fact, the household had learned to react with marvelous swiftness, so that while the lady still stewed internally, the clerks cleared the hall and blocked every door so no stranger could witness the family brawl. Servants and clerks then prepared to jump forward in case they were needed to defend their lady or their young master, for each was an equally valuable possession in the eyes of Sencaster.

Stephen's actions puzzled me somewhat, for he needn't go to the court, of course. He could while away these rainy days in some quiet pursuit that would keep his mother in her right frame of mind and save his neck from strangulation. But he seemed unable to keep away. He was drawn to the court by some unnatural force—this I know, for I watched him one day as he moped in the kennels, vainly seeking entertainment there.

He greeted the hounds and checked their feet, but when the dogs turned to their morning meal, his own paws carried him back to the yard where he stared many minutes at the manor house front. What was he thinking? I could not know, but in a resolute moment of decision, he passed through the door and went for the court where he lasted an hour, or perhaps two, before the wild howls were heard again.

His actions intrigued me, and I longed for a chance to speak with him, for who would know better the ebb and flow of this court but the very son and heir? But serving girls have little reason to speak to the young master, and so I was forced to bide my time and keep my eyes on my embroidery.

At last one day my moment came. I happened to hear him speaking in the halls with his young companion, the bailiff's son, who was being raised at Sencaster Manor. Stephen was talking most vividly of his desire to learn the quarterstaff. It seemed his battle masters considered the staff too common a weapon to teach the young lord, and they tried to content him with new swords and pikes, but Stephen was stubborn. He wished to learn that style of fighting that he had seen at the Nottingham fair, and of this he complained vigorously to his friend. I stole along the hall behind them and when the bailiff's boy had gone, I slipped nearer to where Stephen stood.

"I could teach you the quarterstaff, Master Stephen," I said, looking as serious as I could so he would not think I mocked him.

"You? What, you, a serving girl, can fight with the quarterstaff?"

"I had a superb teacher," I said, with mock humility.

"But girls don't fight. Everyone knows that." His face, sadly, sank for a moment into youthful obstinacy.

"I had not thought, Master Stephen, that you were the sort of young lord who accepted things for what they appeared. Don't you wish to test me, to see if I lie?"

"Yes," he said cautiously, his face brightening a bit. "When can you show me?"

We arranged to meet when Lady Pernelle was at prayers that day, a time when neither of us would be missed. I bade him find time in the morning hours to trim us two stout crab-apple staffs. Then I bounded off to my work at the linens, fearful, always, of being caught.

STEPHEN WAS WAITING in the empty stable when I arrived, a place we'd chosen for its solid roof and privacy, for it was rarely used but for storage. I examined his staffs and, taking up each, wrapped the ends with some lengths of wool I had brought with me. I'd no desire to have my head knocked and, even worse, feared what might become of me if I tapped Stephen's pate too hard. Once finished, I began with patience to teach him as Robin had taught me, beginning slowly with simple strikes, then adding on theories of balance and footwork.

From time to time we stopped to rest, and Stephen, at last, grew talkative, loosened perhaps by the warmth of our fight and the realization that my claim had been true.

"Tell me, Kate, who is this mysterious master of yours? For truly, you are more adept with the cudgel than some of the men I saw fight in Manchester."

"That I cannot reveal, Sir Stephen, for you wouldn't believe it if I told you."

"Try me!" he pestered, smiling and cajoling. "Is he a man of Sencaster? Does he fight in the fairs? Perhaps I've seen him."

"Nay," I laughed, shaking my head, "I won't be telling, and you won't trick me into it by asking all manner of foolish questions. You cannot play me as you play your mother, Master Stephen."

"No one plays my mother," he said grimly, standing so we might parry once more. "She is to be obeyed and not questioned."

"By her servants, perhaps," I said, raising my staff. "But you seem most ready to risk her anger."

Stephen was quiet for a long moment, perhaps to concentrate on my staff, for I did bash his shoulder a time or two. At last I gave him a more routine task, blocking the same strike over again, and he found the breath to express his thoughts.

"Do you know that I had a brother?"

"Nay, I did not," I said, lying as smoothly as I could.

"Aye, Sir Hugh was my older brother. He's dead now."

"That's a pity," I said, looking more sorrowful than I truly felt. "You must miss him."

Stephen shrugged and seemed to put more energy to his blocks than he had before. "I never knew him well," he said. "When he was alive he lived in Anjou, so I only saw him once or twice a year."

I hated to press him on this further, for I'd glimpsed the boy's fragile heart beneath his stern adult facade, and I knew it remained quite close to his surface. But I have never been good at dropping a notion once I thought it had merit, so I steeled my arms for more vicious blows and spoke clearly through the dusty air.

"How did he die?"

My steeled arms were all for naught. Stephen heard my words and stopped, feigning exhaustion so he might sit down.

"I do not know. Mother said he ate a meal meant for someone else and that it had been poisoned. But 'tis odd, that, for Hugh was particular over what he ate and was cautious above all else. He and my mother used to battle as we do, you know," he said contentedly, as if the fact that his brother had done it before him made it less shameful. "At times I thought she might kill him, she'd whip herself into such a frenzy."

"Do you know what they fought about?" I asked with caution, for I feared the moment when Stephen would realize he oughtn't tell family tales to a servant.

"Oh, yes. Hugh had plans for the Sencaster lands that my mother didn't approve. He wanted more fairs—he loved tournaments—and planned all manner of change and upheaval. I remember, the last time I saw him here, he told my mother in a fit of rage that he'd have her locked away in a convent if she continued to stand in his way. He said she could rot there for all he cared and live out her fading years solitary and impotent. I recall laughing at it at the time, for 'twas clear as he said it that he would be the one to find peace and solitude if mother were sent to a convent. But she went into such a temper that she almost died herself of the shakes after she'd gone for Hugh a dozen times. I thought one of them would have been done in for sure."

"And the next word from Hugh was that he had died?"

He nodded, but said nothing. I was relieved to see that I needn't be the one to put the notion of a murdering mother into his head—'twas a thought he'd clearly had already.

Chapter Twenty-three

FROM THAT DAY FORWARD, Stephen and I found time to
work with the quarterstaff each rainy day, and as there were
many that June and July, I learned a good deal from our
chats in the stable. I was surprised to see that Stephen reminded
me more of myself than any person I'd ever met, and I felt some
relief in realizing that had I been forced to wed him that day, I
might have found a friend as a husband. But he still was such a
boy! Even now he struggled always against it, fighting valiantly to
suppress his tears or swallow back any appearance of fright.

In thinking this over I came to see how lucky it was that Robin
and I were such warm companions, while our thoughts and views
were still so different. I was never sure what Robin might be thinking and his words surprised me nine times for ten. Talking with
Stephen was easy and smooth, but his opinions were too often the
very ones I'd considered myself and discarded as unworthy of
expression. He lacked the spark that could amaze me, and this I
prized over all other things.

AT LAST, ONE DAY, the words I'd been praying and longing to hear
trickled blandly from Lady Pernelle's lips. Her noble cousin, Sir

Thomas Lanois, would pay a visit to Sencaster Manor to celebrate Lammas, the loaf mass, at which the first harvest loaves would be blessed. In a thousand ways I attempted to learn if his staff would attend him, but none knew or would tell me, and I was forced to wait and see.

But I needn't have feared. Good Sir Thomas brought with him the best of his household and this included his jolly cook, our own Nick Atwood. The manor was all chaos and turmoil when Sir Thomas arrived, for every servant had fifty new duties and had to go at a run to manage them all. I too had been charged with a host of new tasks, but even so I found time to slip into the kitchen to greet Master Atwood, for had I not done it, I feared my face would crack from smiling and Lady Pernelle would find me out.

"Why, Katie Thatcher!" he cried aloud when I rushed forward to greet him, dodging pheasants and casks of wine. "How pleased I am to see you, my bonny thing. Tell me, have you been good since we parted?"

All of this was mostly said for the benefit of his fellow cooks, but at last we found a quick moment alone, squeezed tight in the pantry with a candle for light. He held me close and kissed me, and I grasped him as though he were the air itself.

"You're looking well, my love," he said after a moment, "though I'm a mite surprised by the change of your hair. Perhaps you've taken too much boiled pork and turnip in your meals? I can amend that for you now, for I'm a cook."

I smiled and dipped my head to show off my locks, newly reddened from a fresh batch of henna, then straightened my mouth to a serious line, for I had information to share. In a hasty second I told him everything, of Lady Pernelle and her struggles with Stephen and how we'd had cudgel practice on rainy days. But even reports of such importance were delayed at times for a kiss or caress, for to have Robin here was such a longed-for thrill that I scarcely believed it for the seeing.

Robin agreed to keep his eye on the weather and to meet young Stephen in our stable if a stormy afternoon passed by, but the days continued on so fair that I began to fear rain would never come. Each day I stole moments to speak with Robin, and at night we crept to the newly filled hayloft and passed the sweet hours in each other's arms.

The hayloft was warm and snug as a den and as such might have made the perfect bed for two sleepy bears such as we were had it not been for the rats. The hungry rodents were everywhere, pawing and squeaking, searching for left-behind seeds and kernels. Their constant presence grated on me and put me in mind of some thoughts I'd had since we'd been apart.

"Rats," I said to Robin one morning as we pulled rough straw from each other's hair. "Rats are the bane of every farm and farmhouse, is it not true? So I propose, Nicholas love, that together with the Christmas boots we also give each village a pair of mousing cats, that they might populate all the homes in town and keep these wretches from eating the grain. Do you know I heard in Thetbury that a babe was once bit by a rat and died two weeks later of no known reason? It isn't right, I tell you, Nicky, to have these creatures so populous that one might bite a sleeping babe."

Robin laughed right hard at this, and I suppose it was a bit funny, though at the time I'd never been more serious.

"I like your idea of giving cats," he said, when he had straightened his face. "A puss and boots for every laborer who comes to the manor on Christmas Day. What can be more Christian than that?"

While Robin and I passed our nights rolling and tumbling in the hayloft, I believe Lady Pernelle entertained a guest of her own, for as the one who cleaned her bedclothes, I can attest that stains were found during Sir Thomas's Lammas visit. This sealed my theory about their love and, added to Stephen's own words of fear over Hugh's strange death, made Robin acknowledge that I had been right.

The pride that this meager success brought lasted me through many long days of cleaning and clearing, but when Lammas mass had been sung and heard, I began to fret about the weather. Fine day followed after fine day in aggravating perfection, and while Sir Thomas showed no signs of departing, I woke each morning sure that he would go before Robin had managed to meet with young Stephen.

For this had become the lintel block in my scheme's foundation. In my whispered nights alone with Robin, I'd done my best to convey to him the urgency of our plight and the need to win young Stephen to us. I was convinced that if we could bring Stephen to understand our place, our rightful claim to the rule of Denby, he might find his way to help us.

Stephen, I knew, bore no great love for Sir Thomas and considered him as unhealthy a wine sack as we two did. I knew too that at age fifteen, Stephen had the right to push his mother from Sencaster Manor and seize control of it for himself. This, I thought, more than anything other, was the cause of their spats in the great hall each day, for Lady Pernelle knew his rights and feared the day when he'd cast her down, just as Hugh had threatened to do.

The case of Hugh, in fact, intrigued me, for at the age of seventeen he could easily have loosened Sencaster from his mother's clinging hands. But Hugh's love of the tournament had kept him in France and kept him dependent, for someone was required to finance his losses. His last threat to his mother made me think, however, that his patience for jousting had reached an end in the months before his death, and he'd turned his eye back to Sencaster.

For a moment these thoughts made me pause to chuckle over Lady Pernelle, for she must now be in a bitter state. The very scene she'd played out with Hugh repeated itself each rainy day with her younger son. What, she must wonder, was to be her remedy? Would she truly be forced to either relinquish her rule or murder both her sons?

This, of course, was what I feared she might try, and it was what gave me such a sense of haste. Months and weeks were not to be wasted, or we might lose our best opportunity, the chance of winning Stephen as ally. Together, I fantasized, we might vanquish the pair of plotters in one blow, placing both Denby and Sencaster into more capable hands. But Robin disliked this plan of mine, which hinged, precariously, I must admit, on convincing Stephen to join with us against his own mother.

What son will turn traitor against the woman who bore him? Robin asked over again. Why should he wish to join with us, solely because he dislikes Sir Thomas? Might he not hold out hope of winning Denby for himself? No, Robin thought it far too early for such a bold move. The risk of it worried him, and he refused to agree to my plan.

I ought to admit that I too was nervous about what reaction Stephen might give, but the gains seemed so great if he sided with us that I was unwilling to discard my scheme. And so, in a state of disagreement, Robin and I sat in the stable one drizzly afternoon and waited for young Stephen to arrive.

"We simply aren't ready—why not wait a month or perhaps two? Where's the harm?"

"I fear," I cried out, "that she will act faster than we do, and in a month or more our young friend might be dead!"

"You're close to her, aren't you? Cannot you make certain that his life remains safe while we win his love in other ways?"

I was weakening, for my stiff resolve had begun to shake, but I tried to hold on to my convictions.

"But what if I cannot manage it? Where will we be if the boy is killed?"

"No worse off than we are now," he said firmly, causing me to sigh. "Our fight today is with Sir Thomas, and if the boy is murdered, 'twill be no different."

At that moment we heard a rustle, and Stephen entered, blinking in the dim stable light and peering at Robin in a cautious way.

"Hello, Master Stephen," I cried out as merrily as I could, considering the vicious words I'd had on my tongue not a breath before. "Pray, come and meet my quarterstaff teacher, Nicholas Atwood."

Robin went forward and bowed to the boy, composing his face to look gracious and kind.

"Good day, Master Atwood," Stephen began, then stopped and started, and spoke with a laugh. "But I know you, indeed I do! You are Sir Thomas's beloved cook, are you not he?"

Robin admitted to being the same, and Stephen enjoyed a laugh over the notion that my mysterious instructor was merely Sir Thomas's cook. Robin then turned and gave me a look that confirmed he had not changed his mind, and with a sigh I opened my hands and allowed my plan to fly away.

"Tell me if you would, Master Atwood," Stephen went on in a cutting voice, "how is it that our manor maid Kate knows what she does of the world? To this day I believe she has advised me on farming, on the levy of taxes, on aid for the poor, and on the proper degree of solemnity one ought to command at church. Does this not seem an odd range of topics for an embroideress born in . . . Titfield, was it?"

I pretended to laugh, though I truly felt bruised by his offhand treatment of my precious advice. To Stephen we had clearly become a comic pair. Robin's face was a witch's brew of thoughts, and I could not tell what he felt the most, but he answered in regal defense of me.

"I am sure you will learn, good Sir Stephen, that there is more to Kate Thatcher than a manor maid, an embroideress, or anything that seems simple to you. That one has lived more lives than a cat, and as she's been a curious kit throughout, she's picked up a few tricks in her way. I've always found her advice worth hearing."

Stephen laughed a bit more at this, and I was just becoming angry with him when a noise in the yard startled me. Like a panicked rabbit I cried out "Robin!" and ducked behind a stall of hay, not one instant before the stable doors both flew open and Sir Thomas entered with three of his men.

Robin, in a flash, tossed Stephen a cudgel so they both might appear to be armed for practice, and that was the way Sir Thomas found them, smelling of wine from twenty feet off.

"Hallo, Stephen. Oh, and Nick Atwood, 'tis strange to find you both out here. I suppose you've had a bit of a skirmish, eh, lads?" Apple Man tottered forward and clapped Stephen heavily on the back, landing, I might add, on the very shoulder that I had bruised two weeks before. "Well, don't let me be in the way of your sport. I came out this way to find young Stephen, but now that I've found him my words can wait."

From my hiding place—from which I had no inclination to move—I could see Robin and Stephen eye each other, unwilling to take up staffs together, strangers as they were. But Stephen looked long at Sir Thomas and, perhaps from dread of an interview, raised his staff and touched it to Robin's, signaling his willingness to start.

As I sat viewing this scene, the first traces of laughter rose in my throat, tickling my eyes and dusting my nose. For here sat Sir Thomas on a firm bale of hay, there stood his men like bored bull-dogs, and here I crouched, rolled tight in a ball behind a great rack of fresh-cut hay. Through a lace mesh of grass blades I could see all the action, and I stifled a laugh at the best part of the scene— my two friends preparing their cudgels. While they'd never fought before, their habits and manners were identical, for what Robin had shown me I'd taught to Stephen, and so they moved in rhythm together despite their discomfort.

Soon enough they began to knock their staffs in earnest, and the cracks flew fast and near the head, near enough to make me glad for the woolen wrappings still on each end. Robin had always the upper hand, but I was pleased to see that Stephen progressed. He had learned well and did not make such a feeble opponent. At last they ended by tiring themselves, for Robin would not strike a hard blow at Stephen, and Stephen could not get his staff end near any of Robin Hood's bones to drub him.

When they stopped to rest, Sir Thomas clapped loudly, perched on his bale like a happy young egg. "Well played, lads, well played. You'll have to work harder, Stephen, my boy, if you want to beat the likes of Nick Atwood, eh, what?" On he continued, baiting the boy, until Stephen's face turned red as a beet, and he tossed down his cudgel in anger.

"Where are you going?" Sir Thomas cried out, working his way awkwardly off his hay bale. "Stephen, I had wished to speak with you! Stephen? I go tomorrow!"

But Stephen was gone, away through the drizzle, and in another moment Sir Thomas went after him, followed by his bulldog trio.

"Robin!" I whispered, sneaking out of my place when they had all gone.

He came back to me and grasped my hands while we laughed away our fright and nerves.

"So much for wooing Stephen to our side," I said wryly.

"The lad just wasn't ready for us," he replied good-naturedly, grinning at me.

"And it sounds as though your lot leaves tomorrow," I whispered, leaning in to be circled by his arms.

"Indeed, it does," he answered. "But look here, Marian, we've come quite a way. I expect we shan't have much longer to wait for Denby. I've found this out—here, this'll cheer you. I've watched Sir Thomas's men at skirmish, and they're no better fighters than you could beat with your old cudgel. If we can but call a few of the old band, I feel sure we can take them and all of the manor."

"And the Denby reserves?"

"They're more fit as farmers than fighters, that bunch. I suspect that when they hear your name, they'll prefer to swear oaths than fight against you."

"I hope you're right," I said, sighing, pushing away the miserable thought that by this time tomorrow I'd be alone once again.

WHEN ROBIN HAD GONE, I renewed my efforts with Lady Pernelle, frantic for something to take up the time I had been devoting to the kitchen and hayloft. I have not, I realize, made much mention till now of how my relationship with that lady progressed, perhaps because I detested the moments we spent together and hated to think on them more than was necessary. But over the summer I became her intimate friend, her privileged confessor, and the maintenance of this role required of me my greatest playacting performance yet.

When I was in a room with Lady Pernelle I changed my mood, swung my temper toward spite and nastiness, and let my mouth fall in a foul expression. This suited the lady perfectly, and in those moments when I was able to reflect her best, her secrets trickled forth to me. At times, of course, she reminded herself of my lowly place and the impropriety of sharing her thoughts with a serving girl, but at these moments she pleased me best, for she would then wander to a window casement and speak her problems aloud in French, thinking I would not understand and that she was safe to converse with herself. I did my best to act unhearing, but of course I never missed a word.

Most of her grievances involved Sir Stephen, for his youthful defection from her style of thinking cut her as deeply as any betrayal. To her mind he embodied every last evil when he questioned her notions or spoke in her court (it was always *her* court and *her* manor; she never once acknowledged his rightful claim to it).

In merrier times she spoke of Sir Thomas, and it piqued my interest to hear her admit that she thought little of him but for one simple function that he performed. He, and he alone, I assumed, was worshiper of her beauty and form. He gushed and raved over her classic face, her well-formed limbs, and her electric mind, and this obsequious attention won him a fixed place in her heart.

I wish I could say that I learned a great deal about the management of such a land as Sencaster from my daily observation of Lady Pernelle, but alas I did not. She spoke very rarely of matters of state, focusing rather on visits to be paid and visitors to come, dwelling, I think, on the social aspects of her rule rather than the theoretical. Her business was done over silver wine cups and pigeon tarts, where I, sadly, could hear nothing of it.

The weather in August drifted from warm to overheated and put me in mind of Ovid's poems of Athens and Rome, the warmest lands my imagination had ever dared tap. By day I thought on downtrodden Ceres, the harvest goddess who holds the shafts swept free by the scythes and sickles of laborers, and by night I contemplated Adonis and thought of my own love, so far away.

It did me good to think of Robin in Denby Manor, for I could envision the very halls and passageways where his feet trod daily. And from there it was but a rabbit's leap to a future vision of Robin as lord of that selfsame manor, hosting his guests in the great hall and tending affairs with his vibrant spirit. I saw myself also in that dream, negotiating with laborers and hearing the cases of the poor and the miserable. In fantasy, I delighted myself with the skill I used to manage our every last concern.

This dream was my constant solace and guided me through my work and my rest. With it in mind I took the jibing from my peers for having run off at nights during Lammas; with it in my bones I ignored Stephen's jokes over my honored teacher, the Denby Manor cook. But most, perhaps, it stayed with me when I froze my own heart to become a companion to Lady Pernelle. It was my promise that my feelings would surely thaw again and return me to my old cheerful ways.

As often as I turned my mind to it, I could find no plan to bring me closer to the realization of that dream, no action I might take now that would carry me to my love and Denby. Robin's words of the weak defenses of the manor guard had cheered me greatly, but these were, truly, my least concern. 'Twas Lady Pernelle who had me frightened, for once we beat Sir Thomas out, she would be on us like a spitting dragon, and we must be prepared to take her.

Chapter Twenty-four

AS SEPTEMBER MOVED IN after August, the weather began to hiss and pout, dropping weeks of rain on Sencaster Manor and flooding the fields for miles around. This put such a strain on our small household that several of the lady's best servants fled the house with shattered nerves, unable to bear the near-constant shouting, for with poor weather, Stephen stayed within.

I knew not why, but since our meeting with Robin and Sir Thomas in the practice stables, Stephen no longer wished to spar and refused to enter that stable again. Perhaps this was from some bitter connection he had made with our place of practice, or perhaps, having fought with my own master Atwood, he saw that I had little more to teach him.

I, of course, thought far more highly of the advice and philosophy I had shared in our meetings than the actual skill I claimed to be teaching, but ever since his dismissive comments to Robin on my odd opinions, I feared raising any matter further with him. And so I said little of our discontinued parries and left him to his own devices. As a result he stayed within, and not an hour seemed to pass without his finding some point of conflict with his mother or of her finding some fault in him.

At times I wondered what drove them to it, what nasty imp sat upon the shoulder of each, promoting such strife and violence. Did Stephen, perhaps, feel this his way of defending Hugh's memory, reliving the battles he had fought? And did Lady Pernelle lunge at Stephen from fear of losing Sencaster forever and being forced into a convent? The more I pondered this, the more I saw that my simplistic reasonings were too far from the mark: these two warred from a deep instinct for preservation that was based on a past I knew nothing about.

Since they were so often thrown together, their habits became oddly entwined. They would drink their spiced wine by the evening fire, content in silence for a quarter of an hour before words began and cursing and slander. This might continue till the moon had risen, then Lady Pernelle's cup would crash to the floor, and she'd fly at Stephen with her talons and claws.

I asked my fellow serving girls what had become of them the winter before, for at this rate it seemed unlikely that either would survive past Christmas. And to my great surprise I heard that while they'd always had spleen-filled words for each other, this summer marked Stephen's first foray into his mother's court. Before I came, I was shocked to learn, Stephen had kept to his own rooms, to his tutor, and his play fellows, and he had left his mother in her own environ.

"What caused this change, do you think?" I asked Dame Ena while we worked at churning the thin autumn cream.

"I can only come to one thing," she told me in a conspiratorial whisper. " 'Twas about the time Sir Thomas first came to stay the night, if you know what I mean, that Stephen started coming round. Something in it got to him and made him turn against her enemy-like—not that they were so lovely-dovey when he was a boy, but back then she had her spats with Sir Hugh, and Stephen was safest kept away."

THIS EXPLAINED A GREAT DEAL to me, but it also put me into a
state, for I saw in a flash that Lady Pernelle was nearing the end of
her own tether. Where before I had thought her accustomed to
these daily spats of venom and bile, I now saw that they were sin-
gular, and I understood why she seemed so tense when Stephen was
near.

Not a full week later I had my own wretched confirmation. I
went to comfort Lady Pernelle after one of her fiercest moments
yet, in which she lunged at Stephen with her dining knife, and he'd
cut his hand in fending her off. How she moaned and shuddered in
her quiet room! Truly, she frightened me, and I had to struggle to
keep my bitter countenance. I could only hold it steady by thinking of sour milk in my mouth, and this left me little time to consider what she was telling me.

"I cannot continue on this way!" she cried, writhing in her bedclothes. "He will kill me one day, I know he will—it cannot be!"

Lady Pernelle had long held delusions that Stephen was
attempting her assassination, a misbelief that might have been
humorous, since she was the one who held the knife, had it not
been extremely pathetic.

"If it is to be him or me, I say now, let it be me!" Her eyes had
grown quite red and wild, and her pale cheeks were sunk to the
bone. In truth, she resembled the very devil. "Tell me, Kate, come
closer and listen. Stephen must be put down—nay, come back and
hear me out! You would not want him to kill your lady, would you,
Kate? Your lady who has housed and clothed you these many
months, who houses all the people of Sencaster? All the people of
Titfield town? You would not turn me out for a boy, a sniveling,
stupid boy, would you?"

I recalled myself and shook my head, looking as evil as I could
manage to fit her mood, for frightened as I was by her, I was loathe
to let any other servant be privy to her devious plans.

"Come, Kate, and listen well. I must have some special potion to do my work—to make things right! For it is only right, 'tis within the law, for I am still ruler of Sencaster Manor, and what I say is the rule of the land. So come, Kate, lean in closer. I must have a potion, do you hear me? And a special one. It must be made of the reedwood tree or of colchium mixed with portion flowers— either one will do the trick. Can you not go and fetch it for me? Please, my Kate?"

I hesitated, and she clutched at my gown all the tighter till I could scarcely breathe. Her breath was sour on my nose, and I squirmed by instinct, but then I managed to control myself, for I suddenly saw my own solution. Reshaping my face in its curdled expression, I turned to the lady and looked her fixedly in the eye.

"My lady," I said, "I may know of a person who can make you this very potion you seek. I daresay, it may not be of the ingredients you specified, but I know a wise woman near Titfield town who lives deep in the woods, far from her neighbors, and is known to concoct all manner of potions. But you must tell me clearly now what result you wish for the potion drinker, and that I'll tell to old Dame Hettie."

I had described, of course, dear Dame Selga with new shifts and braces, but it had the effect I was hoping for.

"He must die," she hissed. "He must die, of an instant—no lingering death." She waved her hands before her face in an effort to express herself. "It must wreck his innards and turn them to dung, his blood to vinegar, his eyes to wax. I wish to never hear his voice again, nipping at me from noon to night—I want it silenced and forever! Go tomorrow, my loyal Kate. Promise me you will go tomorrow and will not return until you have it! Truly, I cannot last alive here one more day, for he will have me if I do not have at him first."

In this way my own greatest fears came to fruition, and I now bore a hand in them. But in truth I admit I was relieved, for glimmering faintly in the depths of this turmoil I saw the light of my own redemption, of Stephen's escape, of Robin's elevation. I grasped at it with both my hands and leapt full after it into the mist.

THE FOLLOWING MORNING I rose up early, yawning and stiff-eyed from my short rest, since I had attended Lady Pernelle until late that night, coaxing her thoughts away from Stephen and toward the land of sleep and slumber. I donned my kerchief and the old monk's cloak that I'd fashioned with Robin our first night in the inn, and started out for Titfield town, a modest village in the south of Sencaster.

In my pocket I already bore what I sought, the very glass bottle of chilling white powder that Dame Selga had sold me in return for my silver. Trusty Annie had brought it away from Warwick Castle in my bundle of things, and I, in my flight from Sherwood Forest, had thrown it into my meager sack, snatching it on impulse with my comb and my pennies. And 'twas lucky I had, for now I found that this very potion I'd been too afraid to use on myself, I was determined to give to Lady Pernelle. Dame Selga's potion seemed to be Stephen's final hope, for if I did not supply his mother with some poison, she would be certain to discover a more lethal variety for herself.

Despite the bottle that weighed in my pocket, I walked the road to Titfield town, in part because I feared Lady Pernelle might have me followed, and in part to allow myself time to think. For suddenly the moment of action was sprung up before me, and I wished for some solitude to plot it all out before I ran too short on time.

One mile or two before Titfield I passed through a large market town, filled with farmers bartering livestock. This suited my purpose, and I paused here to watch the scene until I spied a young man with a ragged tunic who seemed too short of coin to buy the heifer he had his eye upon.

"Good sir," I said, approaching him. "I have a task I would pay for, if you would be willing to take it on."

He nodded a mite gruffly and looked me up and down.

" 'Twill seem to you a bit of a jest," I continued, "but my lady requests to have it done, and she has sent me with pennies to pay for it. I wish to have a man travel the road from here to Denby-upon-Trent, going on horseback, but leading behind him a pig on a rope."

Here the man began to laugh, for such a deed would create a great spectacle, but when he saw that I did not laugh and that I had pennies within my palm, he sobered right quick.

"What should become of the oinker after?"

"You may keep it if you take on the job and if you will find your own horse to ride."

In another minute, all was settled, and the farmer rode off happy as could be, for though he'd not gotten the cow he wanted, he now was richer a pig and five pennies for a day's easy work.

This thing I'd just done may seem odd, but it was truly all to plan. Long ago I'd pressed upon Robin the need for a system for calling Clym to Denby or Sencaster if one of us should have need of him. I'd thought this up, that a man could ride from Sencaster to Denby leading a pig, or from Denby to Sencaster, and that Clym would know which town to visit by considering the direction the man was headed.

The beauty of the scheme lay in the very spectacle it caused, for if Clym did not spot the pig himself, he would be sure to hear of it from his fellow travelers, for this was just the sort of joke they liked to share while walking a road. Robin had liked the idea at once, but it was on his suggestion that we altered it somewhat to make it easier for Clym. If I needed his help, the man should travel leading a pig; if Robin wanted him, an ox should be led.

That done I wandered to the men with carts and hired two of the most swarthy among them to travel this day to Needwood Forest for as many of Will Scarlet's band as they could fit in their cart boxes. These they were instructed to take to Denby directly, to the manor itself, where Robin would greet them.

When I had finished these critical tasks I felt some relief, for small as these steps had been, they served to include my friends in the plot and helped me feel less solitary. And now I was free to walk through the Titfield woods without wasting anxiety on what had been done. I had enough to contrive as it stood, and the green wood soothed me and boosted my mind almost as if the very air there were filled with ambrosia or magical ether. In the heart of this wood I rested myself for a quarter of an hour, time enough to gnaw on my cheese and coarse bread and find myself a creek to drink from. Then, still enwrapped in contemplation, I turned back to Sencaster and the manor house.

LADY PERNELLE HAD BEEN watching for me, and when I returned she hauled me roughly to her own chamber and demanded my potion be delivered at once. I took my time in producing the bottle, but once she had it she cackled and squealed, seeing her son's own premature death in its white crystals. For a moment or two I attempted to calm her, but she began to look at me queerly, and I recalled with a start my playacting character. Grimacing wildly in a reflection of her, I described how she should dilute the potion in some fluid, though I could see that she scarcely heard me, so deep was she in her own plans.

From this moment on my heart began to beat a rigid tattoo of fear, for I felt the same terror of that potion that I always had, and knowing that Stephen would be the one to drink it made my hands shake all the more. Thankfully, he had already retired by the time I returned from Titfield town so no terrible plans might be started that night. But the lady seemed untroubled by this and spent the evening whispering rounds of strange words to herself, twisting a lock of gray hair on her finger.

Sometime in the night Clym arrived. I found him near dawn at the manor gates and persuaded the guard to let him enter by smiling and playing the coquette with him. Inside we huddled in the buttery, pressed between the casks and kegs, and I shared with him the whole of my plan. A short conference explained it all, and I sent him off with a list of tasks and items to gather up for me.

"As you've ever been an outlaw, Clym, this is your moment to show it. Many of these things are under guard, or within the house, and will require every craft you possess to shimmy it out without detection." But Clym just smiled and tipped his cap, and I felt the same reassurance in him that I'd had when I sent him to spy on the queen.

LADY PERNELLE FLOWED through that day with an eerie calm that every member of the household delighted in, not knowing, as I did, from whence it came. And after dining, when Stephen joined her in the antechamber where they took their wine, she hastened all the servants out and bolted the doors firmly behind us.

I wandered the hall outside that chamber for near two hours, but could hear nothing, solid as the oaken door was. I must have fallen asleep on the floor, my head resting on a mound of rushes, for when the lady opened the doors and screamed as though her life had ended, I started awake with such a fright that I think I have still not recovered. I dashed in past her, wild-eyed, and spotted Stephen slumped near the fire in a most unnatural pose, his face as white as chalk.

Too frightened to speak, I crept closer to him, conscious now of the other servants crowding at my back. I reached to touch his pale forehead. My fingers recoiled from his cool brow, but my eyes were drawn gruesomely closer by the twisted expression of his face. His mouth and eyes displayed such pain as made me shudder. 'Twas as if his lips had recoiled away from the very tongue that had met the poison. The skin of his cheek showed the pull of this tension, but beyond those things he bore no mark that could place the blame of his death on poison.

When the servants at last recollected themselves, a group hastened to tend to their lady, who wailed and fainted and cried out at length about the shuddering spasm that had taken her son, so cruelly, from his mother's breast. I squeezed in as close as I could and, taking her birdlike hand in mine, asked in soft tones if she would like me to tend to the body and have it laid in the chapel. She nodded with whimpers, tears lighting her eyes, and I recalled in an instant her grief over Hugh and could no longer doubt that those gestures of mourning had been equally false.

Chapter Twenty-five

I HAD MY OWN REASONS for wishing to have sole control over the body, for I did not know if Stephen would exhibit any symptoms of sleep rather than death, and I couldn't risk allowing anyone beyond myself to be witness to it. So, without wasting a moment, I gathered two guards, stout and sturdy men, and directed them to carry young Stephen to the manor chapel. When they'd lifted him up, I dashed ahead, anxious to prepare a space.

'Twas the custom to lay the body of a deceased noble out for perhaps a day or more, that his family might visit and mourn their loved one before the corpse went into the ground. This, of course, would be the end of us, for Stephen would awaken at dawn and destroy our perilous charade. So I dashed, candle in hand, to the carpenter's shack out in the yard and requested two more guards to carry the rough pine coffin he'd recently finished—for, sadly, deaths were common enough in Sencaster to warrant having a box prepared on any day of the week.

On my way I roused a band of tradesmen from where they slept in a chilly hall and bade them hasten to dig a grave among the family tombstones, telling them that their master had perished of an unknown sickness and 'twas thought best to put him in the ground as soon as we could. The thought of illness hastened them on, and I watched, gratified, as they scurried for spades and snatched up lanterns for their night of work.

I had the pine box placed upside down on the floor of the chapel, before the altar, so that when the men arrived with Stephen, he could be arranged long and still upon it. The guards all hastened away when they could, for the face of their dead master frightened them, and for that I could not blame them. Stephen's features were macabre indeed, and had I not believed in my heart that he would awaken with the sun, I could not have borne to be near him.

I arranged his limbs there as well as I could, closing his eyes with ginger fingers and crossing his arms to keep him in balance upon the base of the narrow box. From a lump of coal I had in my pocket, I smudged his lower lip in one place to mimic the boil and rot of sickness. After a time the manor priest entered, having been alerted to his master's death, and with tears in his eyes the kindly man prepared to recite mass upon mass to speed young Stephen's path to heaven.

When all this was readied and the mass under way, I took a deep breath, for the moment of my final performance had come. With a nervous heart I turned down hall and up passage, tracing my steps to my lady's chamber, and entered there as softly as a serpent. She was not sleeping, she was awake, and as I had suspected, she was eager to see me.

"Ah, Kate, there you are. Come, my dear, and tell me, did you have any trouble?"

I suspected what she really asked was whether I'd seen any signs of poisoning about the body, any mark or darkening that might implicate her in the death. And, in my accustomed way, I had prepared a lie for her.

"I had no trouble with the body," I whispered, kneeling close to her, "but I saw a black mark beginning to show about the lips, which made me worry. I think it might be best for us all if we hasten Stephen into the ground. He ought not be out past the morning."

"Nay, I agree," she whispered in return, oddly calmer now than she'd been at any moment in the months past. "He must be buried this very night. Will you see to it, my loyal Kate?"

I nodded my head, remembering, then, that I ought to be wearing my sour face. But I needn't have worried. Lady Pernelle sat in such a daze, I scarcely believe she saw me at all.

"He is prepared, below in the chapel, if you wish to pay your respects now, my lady," I hissed in her ear.

"Very well," she nodded, humming softly to herself as she gathered her wrap against the chill of the halls. "Was it difficult to lay him out?" she asked, though whether she queried from curiosity or from a wish of making conversation, I could not tell. I feared she was thinking strange morbid thoughts, and this frightened me, but I did as I had planned to do and lowered my head in a sorrowful way.

"Sadly, my lady, 'tis a task I've managed a time or two before, so it was no great issue for me."

She clucked at this and laughed a little, then followed my back to the tiny chapel where the priest was waving his censor of incense, a scent that reminded me, as always, of my wedding with Hugh. Lady Pernelle snapped at the priest as she entered, calling on him to tell how many masses he intended to speak for the boy that night.

"Nine, my lady," he answered, shaking.

"Speak no more than six this night," she declared, her eyes fixed on Stephen's cold form. "You may repeat the final three in the daylight, but we fear my boy died of something strange and think it best to bury him quickly."

The priest nodded dumbly at her instructions and went on with his current mass, only quietly and with far less activity.

"Oh, my son, my Stephen!" came a cry from Lady Pernelle, as

she reached out to touch Stephen's white hand. "What wretched sickness has taken you from me, just as you broached the age of manhood? My darling boy, my cherished one, how can the heavens be so cruel?"

I saw the priest's smooth forehead crinkle at these words, but he said nothing beyond his Latin. Soon enough he turned away, and I alone watched Lady Pernelle perform her act, weeping and wailing over the body, forming each word with more conviction than the one before. I wondered, truly, if she might soon bring herself to believe that an illness had taken Stephen from her, for the more she spoke of it the more fixed it seemed to be in her mind. But as I heard her call him "darling boy," I recalled how she had said the same of Hugh and knew I could let no sympathy for her enter my heart. She had murdered her sons in devious succession and therefore deserved the worst I could do for her.

LADY PERNELLE REMAINED near Stephen's body for the length of two masses, and when at last she turned to go, echoing her final cries to God and the night, I stifled a yawn from the late hour. The lady herself seemed weary as well, and she leaned on me heavily as we ascended the steps to her own chamber.

"Ah, Kate," she said, seeming calm again after all her tears. "I do not know how I shall bear to face the day tomorrow, now that my boy is no longer. What shall I do? Where shall I find my solace now?"

I was too tired to laugh at this, though I found it amusing, but I straightened my face and turned to her.

"My lady, if I might make a small suggestion, would you not feel greater comfort if Sir Thomas came to stay at the manor? He is always such a boost to your spirits, I'm sure he would be quite a help to you now. If you like, my lady, I could send for him, after you retire to your bed, so that he might be expected to arrive as early as tomorrow."

She nodded slowly at my words, for this thought seemed to suit her well. "Yes, Kate, do send for him. I should like to lay my head on his shoulder at a time like this."

At length we reached her chamber door, and I led her forward to her own bed and helped her slip herself within it.

"Kate," she whispered as I tidied the room, "you will see to it that he's buried tonight?"

She looked, for a moment, as weak as a child, and I gazed at her with a puzzled heart. "I shall, my lady, do not fear. All is prepared, I need only wait for the end of the masses to have it done."

"Thank you, my loyal Kate, thank you. Ah, Kate," she murmured, her eyes falling heavily, "you have been like a daughter to me."

I froze at these words, for they forced me back to the night I learned of Hugh's death—she had spoken similar words to me then. I believe she may have felt it too, felt the resonance in her own words and the similarity of our two voices, stretching across the peaks of time, for her eyes fluttered and she glanced at me.

In a flash I performed my sour expression and turned toward her, knowing that to turn away at such a moment would increase her suspicion. She gazed at me long and hard, but at last allowed her eyes to close, and I slipped out with a thundering heart.

BELOW IN THE CHAPEL the night was quiet. Only the priest's lulling voice echoed within the chapel walls, for Stephen, alas, seemed eternally silent. I bade the priest wake me when he had done and lowered myself against the stone wall to catch a brief sleep in the faint candlelight. Before two hours or more had passed, he shook my shoulder, lantern raised, and shuffled off to his own bed, happy enough to have done his duty by his young master and hoisted his soul in the proper direction.

Rousing myself to shake off sleep, I dashed to the pantry to root out Clym, for he was waiting as we'd arranged and followed behind now without a word. We two made our way to the silent chapel and, without speaking, hefted Stephen from his box and propped him, ghoul-like, against the altar.

His box we righted and lined with stones, each wrapped in soft wool to keep them hushed. Clym had chosen these stones with care and reckoned they weighed near what Stephen did, so when we had finished we wasted no time in placing the lid and sealing the tacks with the sturdy mallet Clym had gathered for me. This done, we wrapped Stephen as best we could in a double grain sack, taking care to rent small tears near his mouth so he might breathe air instead of wheat flour. We then lifted Stephen, an awkward load, and towed him as far as the unmanned stable on the dark side of the manor in which Clym had prepared a horse.

While Clym remained there to pack up our steed, I hastened to the yard, stumbling against the wind and the night, drawn like a moth to the grave diggers' lantern. They had finished their hole, and I led them away from its yawning darkness to the softly lit chapel and Stephen's pine box. The men bore it off with anxious hands, for my words about sickness had caused them great fear, but as long as they bore it, I cared not what their attitude was. Once they were gone I blew out the candles one by one until thick darkness filled the chapel. Then I followed with careful steps, leaving this place, perhaps forever.

I WATCHED with the lantern raised high in the night until I was certain that Stephen's coffin was firmly tamped down under yards of earth, then I left the men to finish their work, to smooth the dirt and mark the place for their master's headstone. I had no time to waste with them, for the night stars had spun too far already, and my road lay long before me.

Clym had everything neat and ready in the stable, with poor Stephen's body slung over the steed's back like the sack of meal he truly resembled. Together we put out our candle's flame, eased open the wide stable doors, and slipped our horse out, taking care to replace every gate softly behind us. I led our horse across the open fields where my feet tripped over broken earth and fallow, but I was grateful just to follow a path that was free of guards and steered us away from the brightly lit gatehouse. Our roundabout path cost us precious minutes, but 'twas worth our while to leave no trace, no guard with a memory of our passing by to alert the lady when she rose in the morning.

As soon as we reached the hard-packed road, Clym bid me a hasty adieu and broke into a run, for he was commissioned to reach Denby Manor before any alarm came from Sencaster, to tell Robin that our moment had come and that I was approaching with Stephen in hand. As I'd promised the lady, I'd sent a rider for Denby Manor to draw off Sir Thomas, and I hoped and prayed with my every last fiber that when Clym reached my love, Sir Thomas would be gone, already riding on his way to the north.

Left alone in the dark, I continued on, keeping to the good road as long as I was well protected by the cover of blackness. Stephen's light body shook and jostled on the steed, but I saw that Clym had lashed him on so there was no danger of his slipping off. I cringed at the pain I knew he would feel when he awoke after such a night, but with a sigh I turned my face to the road, telling myself that this was Stephen's contribution to his rescue.

Time and timing had me frightened, so when I could I jogged with the horse, leading it behind me for mile after mile. And when I grew weary I slowed to a walk, keeping my mind from spooking itself by calculating the pace of our travels and checking on Stephen and the tears in his sack. The night was strangely loud on the road, perhaps more so on account of the terrors I'd so recently witnessed. As chilling as the manor had been, whispering with silence, the woods were more alarming still—wild and stormy, alive with strange sounds. They made me feel ghastly alone.

AT LONG, LONG LAST the sky in the east began to grow paler than its fellows on the compass rose, and my own heart began to lift. That night was done, it would exist no more, and this day I might land in Robin's arms if I could make a swift enough pace. I kept my eye firmly on that sky and on the sun as it raised its nose, and when the clouds grew sharp and rosy, I spied what I'd been hoping for. Sherwood Forest loomed ahead, and I bent our steps in that direction, thrilled to take refuge under its cover.

Through Sherwood Forest I would manage a short-cut, following the same path Clym had traipsed during the night. Better still, here I knew we would be safe from prying eyes and Sencaster guards. I had no notion how long it might be before Lady Pernelle noticed me gone, and I feared our odd incident in the night might make her thoughts turn back to me more frequently than I wished. But within these woods I felt secure, and I turned my thoughts to Robin's face and let it lead me, footfall and pace.

The sun was already overhead when at last I heard some sound from Stephen, a low moan and a twitch of the sack that made me halt the horse where it was. I loosened his ties and cut the sack from off his head, surprised to see his face still white, though splotches of pink began to warm his neck and beneath his eyes. As well as I could, since he at fifteen was larger and heavier than I, I grasped his arms and helped him slip down, easing him to his feet and the earth. His legs, of course, proved too weak to hold him, and he landed like a dropped poppet, all wrists and ankles to every side. He fell on top of me, but that was no matter—I was thrilled enough to see that he lived.

Soon enough I had him positioned on the ground with the sack as a pillow, and I watched and waited for his eyes to open and his brain to exhibit some sign of intelligence. His body most clearly was awake, for his fingers flexed and his legs twitched, but I awaited assurance from his face.

In time his eyes began to flicker, a moan escaped his pale lips, and I leapt up and dashed for the water sack to wet his mouth and wipe his face. His battle to resurface to life proved as violent as Orpheus's own journey had been, for he gasped and whimpered as if his whole being were laced in a net of hellfire. Watching, I felt a second time glad that I'd never chosen this potion for myself, for its effects upon the drinker proved brutal indeed. But I reminded myself that in Stephen's case he would otherwise have died, and this helped me watch his shakes and tremors with a more settled and patient heart.

After many minutes of terrible palsies, he awoke enough to take a drink, and then another, and then I saw a faint flush return to his marble cheeks. He blinked at me many long minutes before recalling who I was, but when he did he seemed well pleased, glad to have conquered his own sluggish head.

"Kate," he whispered, his voice strained. "What . . . Can you tell me? What has passed for me this night?"

I nodded slowly and crouched beside him, holding the weight of the water sack while he drank again. I also drained two doses of an herbal liquid into his mouth from vials that Clym had gathered for me, the treasures of Lady Pernelle's own store. These would help to ease his pain and let him breathe in some comfort.

"Indeed, Stephen, I can tell you the tale, but I must warn you, 'tis a strange one." I spoke in French, though for the moment he was too weak to notice the change. "And you must speak out if you feel overworn, for as you can tell your body has been through a dangerous bout."

He nodded weakly and lay his head back, appearing all sagacity and calm.

"You may recall the events of last night, how you and your mother sat in her antechamber and drank your nightly cup of wine."

With a start, at my words, I could see he recalled even more than I, for a yellow look of anger came over him, and he started up upon one elbow.

"Cruel woman!" he cried, still weakly. "I know, Kate, what passed last night. I knew the instant I sipped that wine that there was something unnatural in it. I screamed at her then and told her so, that I knew she'd killed me, wretched, foul woman. She is mother to me no more. But she smiled and tried to smooth my hair, while I felt such pain, such fire in my throat, that I knew I faced my own grave. But how came I here, Kate—am I not dead?"

"You are not," I said, in the firmest of tones. "You live, Stephen, I swear to it."

"Hold, Kate—how do you come to speak French to me? What devilry is this? How does a village maid learn the tongue of kings, and so well?"

"If you listen close, you will understand. All will be clear as I tell my tale, but you must promise to rest and listen." As if in answer, he reclined again and composed his face to make me easy. "You once asked my friend, Nicholas Atwood, how I came to have such bold opinions for a maid servant.

"The answer lies, quite simply, in the truth that I am no born servant. I come not truly from Titfield town, but was born and weaned in Denby Manor. I, dear Stephen, was born Lady Marian Fitzwater of Denby, and I lived my young life in Warwick Castle, awaiting the day when I should again claim the land of my parents."

I saw his eyes light with recognition, for of course my name was not strange to him, but I held up a hand to keep him silent and continued on with my wild story.

"When I was but five years old, as you well know, I was wed to your brother Hugh by instruction of your mother. I assume this was done in harmony with my parents' wishes, for by that time they both were dead and had been long buried.

"Hugh and I were youthful friends, and though we grew distant as we aged, my heart still grieved to hear of his death, and I undertook to mourn for him with a willing heart. But at that same time, your mother tricked me into losing my wedding dower, for she and the queen had the marriage annulled, and I was left with no more for my marriage than my original lands of Denby.

"You may see, now, after hearing this tale, why I was not keen to enter again into the house of Sencaster Manor, for I had once been cruelly misled by your mother and knew a life lived at her side would bring me nothing but misery. And so when I was engaged to wed you, Stephen of Sencaster, I fled from Warwick, thinking that I would give up my title, my noble birth, and my own lands in order that I might gain my freedom."

"But did you escape there on your own? For you disappeared so completely, we all were certain you had died."

"Aye, that was a lucky stroke, for just as I was about to give up all my hope and perform the marriage, the bold outlaw Robin Hood"—here I gave Stephen time to gasp—"arrived to help me slip from the castle. Together we went to Sherwood Forest, where I lived a full year among the outlaws. I've resided in Denby since, till I formed my current plan of coming to Sencaster in disguise to serve your mother."

"But Robin Hood?"

"Robin Hood is the selfsame Nicholas Atwood, formerly cook to Sir Thomas Lanois. We are both of us living false lives in hopes that we might trip up your mother and Sir Thomas and so regain what is rightfully mine, the land of Denby."

It took some moments for Stephen to fully accept the notion that he'd sparred at quarterstaffs with the famed Robin Hood, but when he had recovered at last and thought through my own tale of disguise, he desired to know how he came to be here with me, a part of my plan. I explained then how I'd owned a potion that could perform the magical feat of making a body appear to be dead.

"When Lady Pernelle bade me find her a draft of poison, with which she meant to kill you, Stephen, I substituted my own powder for it. This, sadly, is the one you drank that caused you such pain, but as it also brought you again to consciousness, I trust you will not think meanly of me for having used it. In the night, last night, you were laid out, your masses were said, and your grave dug, but an empty coffin was buried inside, and you passed the night on the back of that horse while you and I fled this far south."

My words stunned him, for I suppose the description of his own grave and masses shook him as deeply as the angel of death himself might have done. But at last he roused himself to the present, to the blue sky flashing above his head and recalled that he was still of the earth.

"And whither do we travel now?"

I smiled to hear these words from him, for they made it clear that he'd traced the full path of the slumbering bear, sleeping through winter, but rising in spring, famished and restless, ready to hunt. I paused in my tale to coax him again to the horse's back, promising a recital of every last word as we made our way through the brilliant forest. The sight of the steed made him rub his ribs, but in time he consented and mounted again, riding this time as a proper man does rather than a parcel of meal.

We spoke at length as we pushed through the brush, and at last I made Stephen see his place in our scheme and the value of his aid. When we neared the far edge of the wood, he paused to thank me, in ringing words, for saving his life from his mother's cold hands. For now that he felt the full weight of it, his voice was quiet with emotion, and I believe I saw the glint of tears.

Chapter Twenty-six

IN TIME we reached the Blue Boar Inn, Robin's old winter haunt, and here I exchanged a stack of silver and our horse for two fresh mares. Newly seated on these, Stephen and I bent our heads to the wind and rode fast as we could, for the hours of daylight remaining were few, and I longed to reach Denby Manor this day.

As we rode, I glanced to the right and left and recalled that sad day when I'd walked this same road on my flight from Sherwood to Thetbury. How different the fields appeared to me now, how changed the fallow marshland seemed! And it was not only the change in season, for where before I had seen them in summer, I now passed a land that seemed thick with slumber, as a man who's taken his fill at table and now has settled for drowse and sleep.

Nay, more thoughts than these filled my mind as we rode, for I pondered the change that my own eyes brought to the view. When I had walked this way before, I'd reached my course's deepest lowland, the dark valley bog where moisture sits and seeps out from the cloying earth. But now I flew on the raven's back, climbing higher with every heartbeat, alert and eager in the clouds' thin air. I nearly laughed to think on it. And when I realized the urge, I did laugh, for it seemed to me that there was no greater show of my change than to laugh now where I could not even bring myself, before, to smile.

STEPHEN AND I RODE swiftly on. As the sun began to set that day, catching stormclouds in its golden net, he said he spied Denby Manor. In a minute more I saw it myself, barely distinguishing its dark mass from the whirling clouds that moved overhead, and I urged my horse to give it her last and take me on to my lover's arms.

Robin had been on the lookout for me, for he came from the gatehouse as we approached. I leapt from my horse and ran to him and was caught up in so full an embrace that I nearly wept from the joy of it. We stood together there a long moment, rejoicing in our own reunion, until we heard Stephen make a cry of pain, for he had tried to dismount alone and had caught his foot in the silver stirrup.

"Now then, Stephen, you've had a hard night. Let me help you, lad," Robin cried, dashing to catch the boy.

Stephen, still startled by the knowledge that the Denby cook was the hero of the midcountry, gaped a bit as he was let down and turned to Robin with a stammering voice.

"Thank you, good Master Atwood. 'Tis pleasing to make your acquaintance again."

His formal words made Robin laugh, and soon enough Stephen's shoulders eased, and he relaxed with a laugh himself. No one, I've noticed, can long depend upon formality when Robin is near, for something in his smile and laugh makes everyone long to be his close friend.

ONCE STEPHEN WAS SAFELY on the ground, Robin became serious, for he had a quantity of news to share. Sir Thomas's guard, he told us both, had been toppled that morning by Will Scarlet's band. A score of Will's men had arrived in the night, and just as the sun was rising Robin had smuggled Will and David of Doncaster inside the manor dressed in cooks' garb. From there the task had been fairly easy, for creeping about the halls in silence, they'd managed to surprise both the captain of the guard and his assistant still in bed, and had bound these men and locked them away.

"When once the masters of the men were gone, 'twas as easy to crush the rest of the lot as to get the juice from a soft apple, for they knew not which way to run. Will waited until the hour of the shift change, when the men are wont to report to their captain, and then sent a signal to his men outside. They attacked from this end," he said with a thumb jerk toward the manor front, "while we trapped and caught men from the other. Soon enough we met between, and the manor was ours, simple as that."

I praised his sharp thinking, for I was truly impressed. As I spoke, I gazed about me and was pleased to see the very faces of the Greenwood tree now poised about the manor gatehouse. Some waved at me and called me "Maid Marian," and I greeted them back as best I could, calling each man by name as I saw him. Inside I met with David of Doncaster and Will Scarlet, happy to see them looking well despite their long year away from Sherwood. Will, indeed, looked much the same, but when I spoke with him at length, I found that he now carried about him a new air, something solid, which came, I supposed, from the weight of managing three score men in an untamed forest.

Together we passed a merry evening, sitting before the great hall fire, toasting one another with sweet Gascon wine. Robin, I saw, was pleased as a schoolboy to be surrounded by these friends again, and he told them tale after tale of his adventures and listened with patience to all of theirs. For his nephew Will he had the strongest praise, both for his skill at leading his men and for his bravery, and it warmed my heart to see Will blush to hear such praise from his uncle.

We were all well pleased, though fear of the morrow hung round our heads like smoke and shadows. Robin feared that one of Sir Thomas's men might escape and ride for London or for Prince John. Will fretted over the number of archers Sir Thomas might bring on us in the morning, and whether we'd have strength to repel them all. But I alone worried over Lady Pernelle. None but me knew how swollen her wrath must be, how eager she'd be to crush the maid who had deceived her. I shared my fears, then tucked them away, determined to stop them from eroding one whit of my joy this night.

Only the call of our shared bed could pull my love from his friends, but that call was strong as drink to Robin and soon enough we let them be. That night, as our guard kept watch through the tempest, I lay abed with my head resting on Robin's shoulder and thought how close our dream now stood. We slept that night in the master's bed, that very same that had been Sir Thomas's and, not so many years before, had no doubt belonged to my parents. I thought of them, lying here in our same places, perhaps thinking of their coming child, and I turned my face closer to Robin and buried it in his warm skin.

WE ROSE EARLY the next day's morning, both more nervous than we chose to admit, for in our deepest hearts we expected to meet Lady Pernelle in all her anger that day. Whether she would come attended by an army or a limited guard we could not guess, but Will's men were all well prepared, and Robin told me again and again how little it mattered how she arrived.

I spent the morning wandering the halls, popping my head into every chamber, hoping to light some memory beyond those I'd formed in my childhood visit. But for all my efforts, nothing came, and with a sigh I admitted aloud that I had been too young to recall either my parents or their home. The servants were instructed to pack up every last article belonging to Sir Thomas, and as I moved from door to door, they paused and called me "Lady Marian," in voices that were nearly reverent. They thought I had died, they confessed to me one by one, killed by the same sickness that had felled my parents. Sir Thomas, it seemed, had encouraged the spread of this lie, for even when I visited as a child, he had addressed me as Lady Marian of Warwick and left no hint of my honest connection to Denby and to this house.

I questioned them all to see if one might have known my mother or tended my father, but most knew the Fitzwaters by name only, and those who had served in their day seemed to know them no better than dear Meg Tamworth. But even so, I was pleased to see that they bore me no grudge for having done away with Sir Thomas so abruptly. Each one said she knew the Fitzwaters were the rightful heirs to Denby-upon-Trent, and they all seemed glad to have things "put right again," as they said.

Pacing these halls raised a nostalgia for my childhood days, and I cursed the fate that had brought me here, but left Annie far off in Wodesley village. I wanted her near now, to talk over old times, to remember the fields and woods of Warwick and the long afternoons we both passed there. I suppose I felt as close then to my own lost mother as I ever have, and feeling this way made me yearn for my surrogate as for nothing else.

In the afternoon I waited with Robin and Stephen in the great hall, each pretending not to twiddle our thumbs as we paced from hearth to door and back. None of us, I knew, could be calm until we had dealt with Lady Pernelle, and Stephen especially seemed to sway in emotion from shaky nerves to a bitter silence. I did not envy Lady Pernelle the look she would face in her son's eyes, but as I knew she deserved it all, I did not waste my sympathy on her.

At last when the sun had slanted its way deep into the western sky, we heard a commotion at the gatehouse and, dashing to every stairway window, we hastened to catch a view of the scene. There, indeed, were Lady Pernelle and Sir Thomas seated on horseback, bickering with our men at the gates, acting as if they bore no heed to the three score arrows aimed at their heads. For Robin had posted men at every lookout and cranny on the manor's facade where a man might crouch, and Denby Manor now resembled some strange sea creature, all bristly with arrows, each one directed at the lord and lady.

At last Lady Pernelle surrendered, calling off the ten guardsmen she had thought sufficient to serve her here. She and Sir Thomas were led inside, and we three hastened to take our places, determined to look at perfect ease when our prisoners were presented to us.

In they came led by Will Scarlet, and I need not describe the shocked expression on Sir Thomas's face when he saw me seated in his high chair. Robin, standing at my side, thanked Will and dismissed him, for we had little fear of our prisoners as one was too aged, the other too fat, to cause a great stir. Indeed, they made a humorous pair, for Sir Thomas was all shock and amazement, while his partner stared with formidable anger, allowing nothing to catch her eye or shake her silent composure.

When we had been left alone, she came forward to peer at my face, and at first I thought she might spit in my eye. But perhaps a look at Robin, so near, caused her to reconsider.

"Hateful girl!" she hissed instead, fixing me with a look that told me she had realized our entire game. "Don't think you can continue to play me false, Marian Fitzwater. Thorn though you have been in my side since the day you were born, you shall not triumph over me. The world of court thinks you dead, do not you know? And they shall allow no dead girl to seize the manor of Denby—you have no right to it!"

"I have every right, Lady Pernelle, which birth and breeding are able to give. Sir Thomas, my regent, I dismiss you now from your duties to Denby, for I am of age and am fully prepared to take up the rule of this land for myself. If that displeases you"—I sneered, just a tad, at Lady Pernelle—"you may take up your case before the queen—although I must warn you, you may not find her to be the ally she once was. I have reason to think her loyalties may have shifted."

These words had their desired effect. Lady Pernelle, now white-faced and gasping, went into a fit of such turbulent rage that she had to be held back by Sir Thomas, or she might have attempted to strike at us both. As it was she gripped and clawed at the air and screamed out her anger in a downpour of curses, each aimed at my head. Robin and I stayed back in silence, doing our best to keep from snickering, allowing her fury to run its course.

At last she calmed enough to stand between Sir Thomas's meaty hands and pant at us, feral as a mountain cat caught in a trap.

"I shall call up every last man of Sencaster to rain like fire against your walls, believe me in this, Marian Fitzwater. I shall not rest until I see your bones burned in the pyre and your every last field salted and stoned. This land will be mine by whatever means I need to take it, and if you request a war between us, I am more than happy to oblige."

"I'm afraid that won't be possible, Mother." Stephen's voice came from behind the curtain where he had been hiding, biding his time. He now flung back the broad piece of linen and showed his face, eyeing his mother as the raptor eyes the baby chick, seeing not a young bird but his day's main meal.

"Stephen!" she gasped, barely making a sound. She struggled, I could see, to retain her composure even in the face of such great terror as she must be feeling. For her eyes showed clearly that she thought Stephen must be a phantom returned from the dead, per-haps come to claim her soul. "Stephen, how? Stephen!"

The lad himself stepped forward, as strong now as he had ever been pale and still beforehand.

"I did not die when you poisoned me, Mother, is that not apparent? I was merely sleeping beneath a mask of death for a long, still night, and when morning came I awoke again and knew what you had done to me. You, woman, are no more a mother than the harlot is a virgin, and I declare this moment that you shall never again set foot in Sencaster, not so long as I rule there." He stood before her, tall and resolute at age fifteen, as full a man as any young king taking up his own crown for the first time.

Lady Pernelle's face melted at his words, seeping into heaps of limp flesh as she tried, foolishly, to placate her child.

"But Stephen, my love, my own darling boy, how can you say such things to your mother? I who bore you, who raised you up from a weaning babe?"

But her son was in no temper to hear her, and he silenced her tongue with a flick of his hand. "Say no more of such things, woman, or I shall be forced to raise the matter of my brother, your firstborn, Hugh, the first of your children you had murdered. Do not think the eyes of heaven will look upon you with sympathy. For what you have done there is no forgiveness, no redemption, no escape."

As we watched, she turned to tears, fading before us like a shade in the mist. But even as she wept, I saw her clever eyes work from Stephen to me, retracing my duplicity far enough to see how she had been led so far wrong. Her loyal Kate was now undone, for I sat here in her place, the very viper at the breast.

STEPHEN DECLARED his own ascendance to the rule of Sencaster that day and lost little time in alerting the guards of this change in fortune. These in an instant became his men, and in the odd spin which the wheel of fortune will sometimes take, they were instructed to take as prisoner the very woman they had so long served. Lady Pernelle and Sir Thomas were bound and packed with their goods and treasures and driven in carts to the edge of Denby, where they were released to fend as they would.

To satisfy his thirst for vengeance, which knew no bounds, Stephen sent word to Queen Eleanor that as they no longer had lands to rule, Lady Pernelle and Sir Thomas Lanois were ideal candidates to sail to Germany as hostages for our dear King Richard. Not many months later we heard that she had seized on this plan and bid them farewell at the coast town of Dover, as pleased to find nobles to trade for her son as Stephen was to be rid of them.

Denby and Sencaster from that time on have been the strongest of allies in the midcountry, each hastening to the support of the other even in the dark days of King John's rule. Stephen proved an able leader, swift and firm in his decisions, although he became nearly the stuff of legend among his people. Rumors flew that he'd once died and still lived on, or perhaps had been buried alive, and this made him seem a shining phantasm in the eyes of the local laborers. But I am pleased to say that he suffered no lasting effects of body or of mind and that, once married, he and his lady lived out their days in relative harmony.

Left to ourselves, Robin and I made our new places public, passing with fanfare through every town of Denby to announce to the people the names of their newfound lord and lady. The name of Fitzwater aided us in every place, for we were met with cheers wherever we went. No one knew Robert of Locksley, but even so rumors spread that Robin Hood might reign in the manor, for he took down a hart faster than any and could still split a pole at fifty paces.

Our good fortune may have been aided as well by our forgiveness of the incoming tallage, the tax that is owed when a new lord takes a manor from an old one. Nay, I declared that as Sir Thomas had acted merely as my regent, no tallage was owed, and this gained me every support that might have otherwise been lacking.

In Thetbury I stopped to visit the Tamworths, to praise them for their care for me and to sooth John and Meg's upset and confusion. They were deeply distressed—John that he'd spoken so gruffly at times to Lady Marian Fitzwater herself, and Meg at having shared her poor house with the great lady of Denby. I did my best to reassure them, to remind John that I'd been Mary Cox when I lived with them, and as such was grateful for their every kindness. But Meg proved more difficult, and it was many hours before I was able to put her at ease and assure her that she'd cared for me as if I'd been a child of her breast.

"I can't think how you must have suffered here, Mary—my lady, I mean," Meg whispered to me. "Sleeping in rough straw, toiling away in the barn and the yard, doing field work! 'Tis a shame on our house that we made you do it, noble lady as you are."

"Nay, Meg," I said, grasping her hand in an effort to persuade her. "Do not chastise yourself. For is it not true that every mouth must find grain to eat, whether it speaks in Saxon or Norman? You took me into your home and hearth when I'd no roof to sleep beneath. You should take pride in the warmth of your heart, Meg, for you alone saved me when I was lost. You've been a mother to me, Meg, and I shall always honor you for it."

This caused her to blush and shake her head over the odd ways of the world. "Well 'tis a shock, that's for certain. Who'd have thought when you strode off together that you'd return as lord and lady? And you, a Fitzwater underneath! This much I may say, at least, my lady: You may have been a sorrowful maid when you were here, but you've nothing of sorrow about you now. It warms my heart to see you so merry."

I left the Tamworths with a stack of silver to excuse the expense they'd laid out for me, since I now proved to be no niece, and offered Matthew and Janey employment at the manor if they ever should choose it. Matthew then told me he was set to be married and would soon begin a new household in Thetbury, so we left him two oxen as our marriage gift and our every wish for joy and happiness. With Meg I sat a bit longer in tears, recalling more of our time together, while she told me I looked much as my mother once had in earlier days.

Strangely, seeing Meg put me in mind of Queen Eleanor, perhaps because they were so dissimilar. I was reminded in a glance and a blink of the night she shook me so rudely awake, bearing the sorrowful news of Hugh. What pity I feel for that Marian now, how my heart aches for her! 'Tis as though she is a foreign being, one who lives in memory only, for I feel no connection between my soul and that which lived in Warwick Castle. Nay, I feel a greatly altered being and my every fiber sighs in relief for it.

THE VERY DAY of our last encounter with Lady Pernelle, Robin and I had bade Clym travel back to Wodesley village to ask if Annie would come to us here, to work beside me as she'd always done. I knew there was now a chance she would decline, for she and Clym might choose to start some cottage life of their very own. And so when she arrived with Clym at her side, I was more grateful than I might have been and felt all the strength of the honor she did me. I quickly declared my joy at seeing her so happily settled, and she broke into a laugh and told me about Clym's heartfelt courtship and how she'd fallen so sweetly in love.

We now faced each other as wedded women, maids no more, and as such I think my love for her was more tender than it had ever been. Together we had faced many trials and much uncertainty, but we now stood surrounded by love, prepared to face a new day of our own making. Annie and Clym both settled into permanent positions at Denby Manor, and Annie, with her broom, lost no time in scurrying off to the lowest chambers, clucking bitterly at the dust she'd seen there when we last visited, six years prior.

I placed her in charge of a fleet of serving women, and from time to time I passed them working and heard her telling the entire flock some tales of Robin Hood and his band, and the bonny Maid Marian who was his love.

FOR WEEKS, Annie led the cleaning crew on a rampage of action, polishing every floor and bedpost from cellar to eaves. Late one day in midwinter, as Robin and I sat brooding over some issue of murrain disease in the northeast quarter, she dashed in at a wild clip, bearing with her two wooden carvings, ovals done with faces in relief, which she placed before me with a triumphal sound.

"What are they, Annie?"

"See for yourself, Lady Marian," she cried, pointing at the faces as if their titles were stamped right upon them.

I looked and compared and saw with a shock that what lay before me were the carved profiles of my own parents, the former Fitzwaters of Denby Manor. For a long time I stared, gauging the shape of mouth, eye, and nose and comparing it with what I knew of mine. These, then, were my long-sought parents, appearing before me when, at last, I had ceased to look for them.

"They resemble you, Marian," Robin said clearly, taking his first glance at the wooden faces. "Your parents?"

I nodded, saying nothing. But as I sat in muted thought, he took them up and placed them above the hearth mantel. "There," he said, adjusting their placement, "now we may see them every day. I suppose I ought to be thankful—your father looks like he had a fiery streak in him, just there, about the chin. He probably wouldn't have thought much of me." He looked again, then turned to shine his catching smile upon my face. "Sure they would have doted on you, though, little Miss Lucy."

I rose and came closer to look once again, feeling less certain than he. "I wish they were gazing forward instead of the profile view as they are. But I suppose this way is more accurate. In life they only saw each other; they had little time for watching over me."

Among my skirts Robin found my hand and squeezed it tight. It made me sad to speak those words, but I knew them to be true. These two had loosened a fledgling blackbird upon the world, but fate had eased their lives away before they'd had time to watch her soar.

I slipped my hand down to my own belly, where a new bird formed in its soft egg, and declared that I would not be that way— I would be here to teach this young dove and smile upon its downy head. I looked to Robin and caught his smile. Then we two turned and walked away to do what we could for the people of Denby.

Acknowledgments

THE WORLD OF Maid Marian and Robin Hood is a misty one, passed to us from mouth to ear. Oral legends and ballads tell us all we know of this mysterious outlaw and his band, so it is to the remains of the ballads that we must look. Francis James Childs' ten-volume collection of *The English and Scottish Popular Ballads* provides a great deal of grist for the mill; the University of Rochester's online Robin Hood Project also includes a nice collection of historic Robin Hood ballads. For extended reading about the Middle Ages I recommend Friedrich Heer's *The Medieval World, Europe 1100–1350*, and Bridget Ann Henisch's books *The Medieval Calendar Year* and *Fast and Feast*. Amy Kelly and Alison Weir have both written fascinating biographies of Eleanor of Aquitaine.

I would like to thank the Kitsap Regional Libraries, my parents and my brother, and my husband, Kol Medina, for his thoughtful feedback at every step. Anne-Marie McMahon, Erin Rand, and Katherine Keating have been encouraging throughout. Thanks especially to my editor, Rachel Beard Kahan, and my agent, Margret McBride, and her colleagues Donna DeGutis and Renée Vincent. If this book hadn't caught Renée's interest, it wouldn't be in your hands today.

About the Author

ELSA WATSON graduated from Carleton College with a degree in classical languages. She and her husband served with the Peace Corps in Guinea-Bissau, West Africa, for two years, where she began writing this novel in longhand, by lamplight. She now lives in her native Washington state, near Seattle, with her husband and three cats.